Devastating IN A KILT

Other Books by Anna Durand

Lachlan in a Kilt (The Ballachulish Trilogy, Book One)
Aidan in a Kilt (The Ballachulish Trilogy, Book Two)
Rory in a Kilt (The Ballachulish Trilogy, Book Three)
The American Wives Club (A Hot Brits/Hot Scots/Au Naturel Crossover)
Brit vs. Scot (A Hot Brits/Hot Scots/Au Naturel Crossover)
Dangerous in a Kilt (Hot Scots, Book One)
Wicked in a Kilt (Hot Scots, Book Two)
Scandalous in a Kilt (Hot Scots, Book Three)
The MacTaggart Brothers Trilogy (Hot Scots, Books 1-3)
Gift-Wrapped in a Kilt (Hot Scots, Book Four)
Notorious in a Kilt (Hot Scots, Book Five)
Insatiable in a Kilt (Hot Scots, Book Six)
Lethal in a Kilt (Hot Scots, Book Seven)
Irresistible in a Kilt (Hot Scots, Book Eight)
Spellbound in a Kilt (Hot Scots, Book Ten)
Relentless in a Kilt (Hot Scots, Book Eleven)
The Notorious Dr. MacT (A Hot Scots Prequel)
The British Bastard (A Hot Scots Prequel)
One Hot Chance (Hot Brits, Book One)
One Hot Roomie (Hot Brits, Book Two)
One Hot Crush (Hot Brits, Book Three)
The Dixon Brothers Trilogy (Hot Brits, Books 1-3)
One Hot Escape (Hot Brits, Book Four)
One Hot Rumor (Hot Brits, Book Five)
One Hot Christmas (Hot Brits, Book Six)
One Hot Scandal (Hot Brits, Book Seven)
Natural Passion (Au Naturel Trilogy, Book One)
Natural Impulse (Au Naturel Trilogy, Book Two)
Natural Satisfaction (Au Naturel Trilogy, Book Three)
Echo Power (Echo Power Trilogy, Book One)
Echo Dominion (Echo Power Trilogy, Book Two)
Echo Unbound (Echo Power Trilogy, Book Three)
The Mortal Falls (Undercover Elementals, Book One)
The Mortal Fires (Undercover Elementals, Book Two)
The Mortal Tempest (Undercover Elementals, Book Three)
The Janusite Trilogy (Undercover Elementals, Books 1-3)
Obsidian Hunger (Undercover Elementals, Book Four)
Unbidden Hunger (Undercover Elementals, Book Five)
The Thirteenth Fae (Undercover Elementals, Book Six)
Willpower (Psychic Crossroads, Book One)
Intuition (Psychic Crossroads, Book Two)
Kinetic (Psychic Crossroads, Book Three)
Passion Never Dies: The Complete Reborn Series

Devastating IN A KILT

Hot Scots, Book Nine

ANNA DURAND

JACOBSVILLE BOOKS · MARIETTA, OHIO

DEVASTATING IN A KILT

ISBN: 978-1-949406-52-8 (paperback)
ISBN: 978-1-949406-53-5 (ebook)
ISBN:978-1-949406-54-2 (audiobook)
Library of Congress Control Number: 2021901885

Manufactured in the United States.

Jacobsville Books
www.JacobsvilleBooks.com

Publisher's Cataloging-in-Publication Data
provided by Five Rainbows Cataloging Services

Names: Durand, Anna, author.
Title: Devastating in a kilt / Anna Durand.
Description: Marietta, OH : Jacobsville Books, 2021. | Series: Hot Scots, bk. 9.
Identifiers: LCCN 2021901885 (print) | ISBN 978-1-949406-52-8 (paperback) |
     ISBN 978-1-949406-53-5 (ebook) | ISBN 978-1-949406-54-2 (audiobook)
Subjects: LCSH: Divorced people--Fiction. | Man-woman relationships--Fiction.
     | Scots--Fiction. | Americans--Fiction. | Highlands (Scotland)--Fiction. |
     Romance fiction. | BISAC: FICTION / Romance / Contemporary. | FIC-
     TION / Romance / Romantic Comedy. | GSAFD: Love stories.
Classification: LCC PS3604.U724 D48 2021 (print) | LCC PS3604.U724 (ebook)
     | DDC 813/.6--dc23.

Prologue

Jack
Las Vegas
Two Years Ago

Alarms clang and wail, announcing that some lucky person has won a jackpot on a slot machine, but I couldn't care less about that. Everyone back home in Scotland thinks a holiday in Las Vegas, Nevada, is like hitting the jackpot without the extra money in my pocket. I'm meant to be excited by this city, but all I want to do is go home to the Highlands. Inverness seems like a sleepy hamlet compared to Las Vegas, but the little village of Loch Fairbairn, where I grew up, is a flea circus in comparison.

Of course, this is not a holiday for me. It's a business trip.

I wander past the slot machines and the roulette wheels, headed for a conference room where I will sit among a crowd of other bored professionals. Does anyone think lectures and roundtable discussions are fun? Not me, that's for certain. I stop just outside the doors to the conference room where a large sign announces, "International Alliance of Licensed Psychologists, Therapists, and Counselors: Annual Conference."

Aye, that's a mouthful to say, so I won't even try. And aye, these conferences are always as dull as the title makes them sound.

Why do mental health professionals hold their annual meeting in a city that thrives on all the things we try to talk people out of doing? Gambling, drinking to excess, indulging in illicit drugs, and engaging in generally reckless behavior.

I miss my wee apartment in Inverness.

No, what I really miss is *home*—Ballachulish and Loch Fairbairn, the villages where my family lives. But my job is eighty miles away, and somehow, I never find the time to go home.

While I stare at the sign, I rub my neck. I'd come here for the conference, but now that I am here, I can't make myself walk through the doors. Maybe I'll skip the opening remarks and the introductory discussion that doubles as a drinks party. Those things are aimed at less-experienced therapists, anyway. Not attending the opening events wouldn't be too awful, would it?

I veer away from the conference room, heading for the bar across from the casino. This hotel is enormous, and not the sort of place where I would've wanted to stay. My cousin Lachlan had insisted on paying for me to have a room in this expensive hotel—not just any room, but a suite that's too large for one person. Lachlan has plenty of money, though, and he's very generous. I would've felt like an erse if I argued about it.

Once I reach the bar, I want to order Ben Nevis or Talisker, but the hotel doesn't stock Scottish whisky. I settle for Jack Daniels and perch on a stool to sip my drink while I observe the other people here. They all look either depressed or so drunk they're almost euphoric. A large bloke sits on a stool three seats down from where I am, his bulk blocking my view of the other people who sit at the bar.

Maybe I'm depressed like all of them, though I can't pinpoint why. I have a good job and a large extended family I love. When had I last taken a lass out on a date? Cannae remember. If it's been so long I've forgotten, then it's probably been too long. The occasional poke with a willing lass hardly counts. No dinner or conversation. Poke and go, that's it.

I swallow the rest of my whisky and order another.

The large bloke slides off his stool and leaves.

And I finally get a look at the people further down the bar. My attention stalls on the closest person, a beautiful woman with blonde hair. She takes a sip from her glass, which holds some kind of amber liquid, and her lips curve into a smile of deep satisfaction as she closes her eyes. She sets her glass down, and her lids part, though they stay half-closed.

Bod an Donais, that woman is bonnie. More than bonnie. She has the most beautiful face I've ever seen, with a perfect nose and a small but enticing mouth. Her shapely figure offers curves and taut muscles, a fact I know because her dress clings to her body like she painted it on. The lass has small breasts that are no less mouthwatering because of their size and lips that I'd love to kiss.

She turns her head in my direction.

Our gazes collide, and I can't stop myself from smiling at her.

The lass smiles back, waving her fingers at me.

I want to go over there and talk to her, but I shouldn't. Should I? Approaching a stranger has never been my strong suit, but something about this woman captures my focus and refuses to let go. So I walk over to her and take a seat on the adjacent stool.

"Hello," I say, because it's the only thing I can think of.

She smiles again, and her eyes sparkle in the subdued lighting. "Hi. Want to have a drink with me? It's more fun with company."

"Love to." I hold my hand out to her. "I'm Jack MacTaggart, by the way."

"Autumn Flowerday." She takes my hand but doesn't shake it, just holding her palm against mine. "That's my name is what I mean. Some people get confused about that since my name sounds like it should be painted on a flower shop window. I'm not a florist, though."

"Your name is bonnie, just like you."

"Thank you, Jack. What a sweet thing to say. Where are you from? I love your accent."

"I was born and raised in Scotland, the Highlands. What about you?"

"Native Nevadan. Born in a tiny desert town, moved to Vegas for college and never left."

"This must be an odd place to live. It's so…loud and bright."

"Let me guess. It's your first trip to Sin City."

I shrug one shoulder. "First trip outside the UK."

She settles a hand on my arm, leaning closer. "Everybody gets overwhelmed on their first vacation in Vegas."

"Aye, it is a bit much." I hesitate to ask the question I've been wondering about since I first saw her, but I decide to go on and do it. "What is a bonnie lass like you doing in a hotel bar on a Friday evening all alone?"

"Same thing as everybody else. Trying to drink my troubles away." She picks up her glass like she's about to swallow the rest of her drink, but sets the glass down. "What about you? What's a sexy Scotsman doing here in this bar?"

"Avoiding…things." I don't want to tell her what I do for a living, which is barmy. I'm not ashamed of being a psychologist. But it isn't the sort of job that arouses the lasses.

I want this woman. Her smile, her sparkling green eyes, and her alluring body affect me in ways I've never experienced before. My cock is stiffening just from her smile and her voice. My pulse has accelerated, and all my senses seem heightened, like I've taken a drug, but I haven't. With her hand on my arm, I swear I can feel her skin on mine even with my shirt between her palm and my flesh. And she smells good, though I can't describe the scent. I want to kiss her. Touch her. Shag her.

Does she feel the same attraction? Christ, that word doesn't seem strong enough for what I feel right now. Lust is more accurate. Pure, hot lust.

I lay my hand over hers on my arm. "Autumn, you are the bonniest woman I've ever seen. I know we've just met, but I would love to kiss you."

"Yes, I'd love that too."

My pulse races even faster, and a sort of electricity sweeps over my skin. I slant closer to her, thrusting a hand into her hair. It feels so bloody soft that I long to bury my face in that hair and suck in the scent of her for hours, with those silken strands brushing my skin.

She tips her head back, leaning toward me. Her lips open a sliver, just enough to let me dive deep into her mouth.

I touch my lips to hers. Electricity sizzles through my veins and over my skin, and the softness of her mouth makes me crave more of her. When she exhales, her breath teases my lips. I slip my tongue inside and groan at the sensation of her warm, slick flesh on mine. I explore her mouth slowly so I can revel in every second of the kiss, but still, I hunger for more, for everything. I want to spend all night exploring her mouth and loving her body.

Though I break the kiss, I keep my lips almost touching hers. "Will you come to my hotel room? I want to spend the night with you. Never done anything like this before, but..."

Her lips curve into a sultry smile. "Yes, I'd love that. And I've never done anything like this before either. It feels right, doesn't it? I know that sounds crazy, but it's true."

"Aye, it does feel right." And aye, it is barmy, but I don't care. "Would you like to have a drink first? Or we could order champagne once we get to my room."

"Let's do that. And order strawberries with whipped cream too."

My mind conjures an image of this woman spread out naked on the large bed in my suite while I drop whipped cream onto her skin and lick it off.

I take her hand, leading her out of the bar. We kiss during the long ride up to the eighteenth floor in the lift. No one else is in the car, so we have no need to hold back. By the time the lift stops moving, I have my hands under her skirt, gripping her erse, while she has her leg hooked around my hip. We separate our bodies only long enough to hurry down the hall and into my suite, then we start kissing again like we want to devour each other. And we do want that. Desperately.

We're naked inside of two minutes and fucking inside of five.

Twelve days later, we're married.

Six weeks after that, she walks out the door—and our marriage is over.

Chapter One

Autumn

Never marry a man you've known for twelve days, no matter how fantastic he is in bed, and especially not if he's a MacTaggart. I learned that lesson twenty months ago when I walked away from Jack Mac-Taggart. Twenty months and three days, to be precise. I moved to Scotland for him, but when I practically begged Jack to move to America for me, he wouldn't do it. So I left. Did my heart break? Yeah, it did—more than I expected. Do I wish I'd turned right around and flown back to Scotland? Maybe. Sometimes. When I'm lying in my bed at night, alone, remembering the good times we had.

But it could never work.

Today, I'm wondering why on earth I let my friend Rika talk me into not only taking a vacation in Scotland but also agreeing to a blind date. I never wanted to come back to this country. I don't hate Scotland, but I've had this ridiculous fear that if I ever did come back, I'd bump into Jack. What are the odds of that? We'd lived in Inverness, and I'm currently sitting in a cafe in the village of Loch Fairbairn, three hours away from Inverness. Jack probably still lives there. I *hope* he still lives there.

But most of his family lives in and around Loch Fairbairn.

What kind of idiot am I? Agreeing to a blind date? *Ugh*. And Rika didn't exactly set it up. She told me about it and hyped the date like it would be a great thing for me, getting "out there" again. The person who actually arranged the whole thing is the cousin of Rika's husband, Dane. Or maybe she said he's not technically Dane's cousin, but some kind of honorary cousin? It's all very confusing. Anyway, I've never met the man, don't even know his name, yet I said yes to this setup. So yeah, I'm unbelievably stupid.

I've never been famous for my good judgment. Case in point: my whirlwind marriage to Jack.

All of this explains why I'm sitting at a table in the outdoor section of a quaint cafe in Loch Fairbairn, gazing across the quaint street that features quaint, historic buildings. After a long and expensive cab ride from the Inverness airport to this village, I hadn't seen much because it was dark. Today, on the shorter cab ride to the cafe, I had seen a sign for a solicitor, aka a lawyer, called Rory MacTaggart. My anxiety level had ratcheted up a few notches then. Rory is Jack's cousin, which I know because Jack told me stories about his family, though he never let me meet any of them.

If Rory works in this town...

No, I won't see Jack. The odds are infinitesimal. He's in Inverness, anyway.

I swallow the last gulp of my third glass of water and check the time on my phone. My blind date is thirty minutes overdue.

How long should I wait for this guy? Half an hour seems like plenty of time. Plus, I seriously need to pee after guzzling all that water. The cafe might have a restroom, but I'd rather go back to my room at the Loch Fairbairn Arms, where I'm staying. It's the only inn, hotel, motel, or bed-and-breakfast in this village.

I slap a five-pound note on the table for the waitress. Though I didn't order anything except for water, which is free, I feel like the sweet teenager deserves a tip. The pound notes they have here in Scotland look different from the ones they have in England, but I remember these funny-looking Scottish notes. I lived here with Jack, so yeah, I have a passing knowledge of the currency.

After leaving the tip, I head inside the cafe and straight to the counter. A young man who can't be more than a teenager mans the counter and smiles when I approach.

"How can I help you?" he asks.

The boy's Scottish accent reminds me of Jack. Not because the kid's voice is like my ex-husband's. Everyone who speaks with a Scots brogue reminds me of Jack. It's pathetic, but I can't help that.

"Do you have a pen and paper?" I ask. "I'd like to leave a note for the man I was supposed to meet here for lunch."

"Aye, we've got those." The boy reaches under the counter, bringing out a little pad of paper. He hands me that, plus a ballpoint pen.

I scribble my note, fold the paper in half, and give it to the boy. "If my, um, friend should show up, would you mind giving this to him? It's a blind date, so I have no idea what he looks like or what his name is."

"Aye, I'll make sure he gets it."

"Thank you."

I decide to walk back to my hotel since it's only three blocks away. That gives me a chance to admire the historic buildings and see what kind of shops the village has. Maybe tomorrow I'll explore this place more. I'd planned to rent a car once I got here, but the agency at the Inverness airport was all out. A rental agency in Ballachulish, the town half an hour from Loch Fairbairn, will deliver a car to me tomorrow. Then I can drive around and get to know this part of the Highlands. Jack hadn't wanted to show me around, always claiming he was too busy with work.

"A therapist is always on call," he would tell me.

Ten minutes later, I'm back in my room at the Loch Fairbairn Arms. I've just shut the door and kicked off my shoes, so I lean back against the door. My thoughts rewind to the note I left for my mystery man. Maybe it had been too forward, but I'd felt like giving the guy one last chance. I mean, maybe he got stuck in traffic. What, did sheep block the road? This isn't a big city with congestion. Well, he might've gotten lost. So now I've decided he's never been to this village before? Why would Rika's husband's cousin or whatever set up a date for me in this town if the guy I'm supposed to meet doesn't live nearby?

My note had said, "You get one more chance. Loch Fairbairn Arms, Room 110."

Now I'll find out if I've made another horrible judgment call.

Someone knocks on the door. It vibrates against my backside.

Has my mystery date finally shown up?

One way to find out. I push away from the door, turn around, and open it.

And I gasp, gaping at the man before me. My pulse revs into overdrive, making me feel lightheaded and a touch nauseous. I must be hallucinating. But no, I recognize that chestnut hair, those blue eyes, his muscular build, and that face—the one that can convey empathy one minute and sheer lust the next. Oh no, no, no, no, *no*.

Of course I recognize him. Like I could ever forget the face and body of my ex-husband.

Jack stares at me, not blinking, frozen in place like he's suddenly morphed into stone. "Autumn? What are you doing here?"

The shock of seeing him again still has me reeling too. "No, this can't be—You can't be—No, no, no."

"I, ah…" He shoves a hand into his hair and shakes his head. "It's been a long time. You look…bonnie. I've never seen hair that color before."

Why does my hair color unsettle him? So what if I dyed it ice blue. Colors like this are chic these days, and I think it looks good on me. "That's all you can say? You set me up for this, didn't you? Humiliating me doesn't seem like your style, but—"

"I didn't set this up. My friend Alex Thorne did." He grits his teeth and mutters something I can't quite understand, probably one of those Gaelic curses he loves. "I'm sorry. This was not my idea, and believe me, you are the last person I expected to see."

No shit. I shut my eyes, squeezing my lips together. "Ugh. This is a mess. I flew all the way to Scotland for a vacation because my friend Rika suggested it. A blind date was supposed to be fun."

"I'll go. Again, I'm sorry for this mix-up."

He turns to leave just as I open my eyes.

For some unfathomable reason, I grab his arm to stop him. "You don't have to leave. Since we're both here, maybe we should have lunch and try to bury the hatchet."

Why am I convincing him to stay? It must be the shock inspiring me to behave like a lunatic. Plus, I still really need to pee. It's hard to think when my bladder is about to explode.

"Lunch sounds good," he says. "How long are you in Scotland?"

"Two weeks." I step out of my room and shut the door. "Who knows? Maybe we'll become friends."

"Last time we saw each other, you told me I'm a shameless huckster."

"Are you going to hold that against me forever? Time to get over yourself, Jack. I might think your job is dumb, but you think the same thing about mine."

He sputters. "You quit medical school so you could become a blackjack dealer in Atlantic City. How is my profession a sham, but yours is noble? And you didn't even discuss it with me. You announced you were moving to New Jersey, with or without me."

Not quite how it went down, but if I truly plan to bury the hatchet, I shouldn't get too uppity with him. "You could have come with me. If you really loved me, you would have." I wave a hand like I don't give a hoot about anything, which is baloney. "Doesn't matter. Let's have a nice lunch and go from there. You're paying, right? I mean, you did stand me up."

"I was late. I didn't stand you up."

"Whatever. You're paying."

"Aye, fine, I'll pay."

I stop, abruptly realizing just how much I need to relieve myself. "Um, give me a minute. I need to use the bathroom."

"Am I meant to wait in the hall?"

"Yes, you are."

I hurry back into my room, do what I need to do, and then pause to glance at myself in the bathroom mirror. Does my hair look okay? Of course it does. I just fixed my hair and makeup before I went to the cafe, and all I did was sit there for half an hour. I look fine. And besides, why should I care what Jack thinks of me?

When I open the door to my room again, he's standing there with his arms crossed over his muscular chest, tapping the toe of one boot on the floor.

"Are you ready now?" he asks, sounding peeved.

"You're the one who made me wait for so damn long at the cafe. Don't get snippy because I needed to void my bladder."

"*Bod an Donais*, Autumn. Does everything need to be an argument with you?"

"Does invoking the devil's penis have to be your favorite curse?"

"I am sorry," he says, pronouncing each syllable with knife-like precision, his gaze boring into mine. "How many bloody times do I have to say it?"

"Let's just get to the cafe and try to calm down. We've both had a shock, right? So we're arguing because of adrenaline or whatever."

"That does make a kind of sense."

He moves out of the way so I can exit my room, then he lays a hand on my lower back as we leave the hotel. Jack hails a cab, the same one I'd taken earlier. Maybe this town only has one cabbie. We don't speak during the brief ride to the cafe, though he keeps glancing at me sideways. I see that because I keep glancing at him sideways too.

This is beyond weird. I'm having lunch with my ex-husband, who I haven't seen in twenty months and three days. Maybe the fact I've kept count, down to the day, means something. But I refuse to think about that.

Because it absolutely does not mean I still have feelings for Jack.

Chapter Two

Jack

Autumn leaps out of the taxi the second it stops in front of the cafe, and I rush to pay the driver and hurry after my ex-wife. She guides me to a table near the metal railing that separates the outdoor cafe from the sidewalk. We've barely sat down when a waitress approaches our table.

The lass's eyes flare wide for a second when she sees Autumn. "Oh, it's you again. Found your date, have ye?"

"Yes," Autumn says, fiddling with her napkin.

Our waitress glances shyly at me. "And it's Dr. MacTaggart, the best therapist in Scotland. You're a lucky woman."

I know I've met this lass before, but I can't remember who she is. She's not a client of mine. I would remember her name if she were. Her name tag tells me this is Deirdre, but I still can't place her.

Autumn is staring at me, her face blank.

The waitress sets down two glasses of water and hands us menus. "I'll give you a few minutes to decide what you'd like to order."

I give her a tight smile. "Thank you, Deirdre."

Autumn's blank expression transforms into a look of knowing disapproval. Her lips pucker slightly, her eyes narrow, and she crosses her arms over her chest.

That look is one I know well. Autumn gave it to me so many times during our marriage that I started to call it "The Angry Autumn Face."

Deirdre seems oblivious. She smiles at both of us and leaves.

"You know her?" Autumn asks. "She seems like a sweet girl. Must be a client of yours, hmm? She definitely has a crush on you."

"Is that my fault?" I try not to get annoyed, but I'm flashing back to every time she gave me that look when we were married. "You know I cannae discuss my clients."

"Right. Sorry." She takes a sip of her water, and her face relaxes. "If we're going to bury the hatchet, maybe you should start by explaining why you abandoned me."

"*I* abandoned *you*?" I open my menu with a snapping motion and squint at it. "You're the one who walked out on me."

"You could've come with me. I moved to Scotland for you. If you'd ever really loved me, you would've moved to America for my sake."

"Maybe if we had discussed it—" What's the point in arguing with her? Autumn believes she is always right and I am always wrong. I growl and snap my menu shut, slapping it down on the table. "I think lunch is a rubbish idea after all."

Deirdre emerges from the cafe's interior carrying a tray loaded with three bowls of what looks like tomato soup. She seems unsure about balancing that tray, biting down on her lip while she wends her way between the tables.

The waitress's activities seem to have transfixed my ex-wife.

"Autumn." Maybe I speak her name a wee bit too sharply. Can I still blame shock and adrenaline? Not sure how long those effects linger.

"What?" Autumn asks, blinking quickly and focusing on me again.

"Is that all you want to say to me?"

"You just announced you're leaving. What do you expect me to do? Beg you to stay?"

I huff. "I said lunch might be a bad idea. You're doing what you always do, looking between the lines to read things that aren't there."

"Cut the crap, Jack. You're chickening out, again. That's what *you* always do, isn't it?"

Deirdre veers around a customer who thrust his arm out as part of a sweeping gesture aimed at the woman seated across from him. Maybe he's having lunch with his ex-wife too.

"Go on," Autumn says. "Run away. Every time we had a fight, that's what you would do. Hide in your office. Hide out at one of your cousins' houses or with your brother."

"*Mhac na galla.*" I glare at her, though I don't mean to do that. Autumn has always brought out the worst in me. "That means son of a bitch, in case you forgot. It also means goodbye, Autumn."

Maybe she also brought out the best in me, sometimes, but today she's only making me angry. Or is this fear? I should know the difference, being a therapist, but I can't sort out my feelings.

I shove my chair backward, scraping it across the concrete patio.

The disaster that's about to unfold seems to happen in slow motion, but somehow, I have no time to sort out what I'm seeing and stop it.

Deirdre swerves toward me at the same instant I push my chair backward. She's trying to avoid bumping into another customer, but now I'm in the way. The tray of soup she carries teeters on her palm. Her eyes bulge, and her mouth opens, but it's too late for either of us to do anything.

The tray bumps into my head.

Deirdre tries to catch it, but the thing flies out of her reach, tipping sideways.

And the bowls of soup come crashing down—on me.

One bowl lands on my lap, upside down. Another drops onto my head like a hat, spilling soup over my entire scalp and most of my face. The third bowl splats down on the table and disgorges its contents onto the table cloth. The thick liquid cascades over the edge of the table like a waterfall and inundates my lap.

I'm covered in red. Well, at least it's cold tomato soup.

"Oh God, Jack!" Autumn cries out. She grabs both of our water glasses, hurling their ice-cold contents onto me.

Deirdre bursts into tears. "Ahm so sorry."

I glower at Autumn. Through clenched teeth, I hiss, "Why did you do that?"

"You got doused with hot soup. I didn't want you to be scalded."

Maybe I should be happy that she cares about my safety, but all I feel is an overpowering urge to smash something.

Tears stream down Deirdre's cheeks. The poor lass sobs. "It's cold to-mato soup."

Autumn's eyes bulge for a second, then she gets up and goes to Deirdre, patting her arm. "It's okay, sweetie. That was an accident. Why don't you go get cleaned up?"

I cannae speak. Or move. Or think. Is the soup splattered over my entire front side a metaphor for my relationship with my ex-wife? If it is, I have no bloody idea what the universe is trying to tell me.

Still sobbing, Deirdre scurries into the cafe's interior.

I'm sitting here like a statue, stiff and boiling mad, though drenched in cold tomato soup and ice water. The cubes stick to my shirt and pepper my lap. My breathing has become heavy, but I think that's because I'm so angry that I want to throttle someone.

Autumn. That's who I want to throttle, though the disaster isn't her fault.

Peter, the laddie who works behind the cafe counter, emerges from the interior carrying a dish towel. He holds it near my face as if he plans to clean me up with it. "Let me help you with that."

When he tries to wipe my face with the small towel, I bat his hand away. "Willnae help, will it?"

The laddie smiles sheepishly. "Suppose not."

"It's all right. Donnae worry, I can clean myself up."

Rising from my chair, I hold my arms away from my body, my fingers outstretched. I gingerly take my shirt between my thumb and forefinger, peeling it away from my body, though only by a few inches. I tip my head down to examine myself.

And I grimace. What a sodding mess I am.

"Should I get more towels?" Peter asks.

"No," Autumn says. "I'll take care of him. But thank you."

I look up at her, my head still angled down, and lift a single brow. She wants to take care of me? Since when?

"Come on," she says, waving toward the exit. "Let's go back to my hotel and get you cleaned up."

"Better walk."

She winces. "Yeah, I doubt the cab driver will want to get tomato soup all over his upholstery."

I lead the way as we exit the cafe. Other customers stare at us. Some snigger. One grins. Most of them seem dumbfounded by this turn of events. So am I. Lunch with my ex-wife turned into a disaster, but I should have seen it coming. Life with Autumn had been a disaster since the day I first brought her to Scotland.

While I hustle down the street, moving almost fast enough to qualify as running, Autumn struggles to keep up with me. When we march through the hotel lobby, the gray-haired woman behind the desk gapes at me. I am covered in red liquid that looks sort of like blood, so I can't blame her.

"Tomato soup," Autumn tells the woman as we rush past. "It's not blood. He got doused with tomato soup."

At the door to Autumn's room, I stop and wait for her to catch up.

She unlocks the door, eying me sideways like I've mutated into a monster with horns and giant fangs. But then her lips kink upward, and I know she's not frightened of me.

I follow her into the room.

"Go in the bathroom," she says, "and take your clothes off. Leave them on the floor outside the door and take a shower. I'll call the front desk to ask if they can wash your clothes for you."

For half a second, I consider asking her to help me get cleaned up. What the bloody hell is wrong with me? Yes, Autumn is still sexy, and even her blue hair appeals to me now. I haven't had a poke with anyone since Autumn, so maybe I'm feeling randy because I've been celibate for too long. It has nothing to do with Autumn.

I shake off my barmy thoughts and do what she suggested. I undress, leave my soiled clothes outside the bathroom door, and turn on the shower. But I stand there in front of the mirror for several minutes, staring at my reflection, wondering what on earth is wrong with me today. I can't stop picturing Autumn joining me in the shower, both of us lathering soap all over each other's bodies.

Bod an Donais. I want to shag my ex-wife.

<h1 style="text-align:center">Chapter Three</h1>

Autumn

Jack's mad. Okay, I get that. But why is he ticked at me? The soup debacle was an accident, and I wasn't even the one who doused him. At least he seemed a little calmer by the time we got inside my room, and he took my advice about showering. When I call the front desk, the sweet lady who saw us storm down the hall together tells me she'll have the cleaning staff launder Jack's clothes.

I've just come back from taking his tomato-soaked stuff to the front desk. Marjorie Fraser, who mans the desk, gave me extra towels for Jack. That's a good thing, because I'd managed to spill nail polish remover all over the one big towel in the bathroom. I left it in a lump on the dresser, but it's gone now, so I assume the cleaning staff took it. They made the bed too.

With towels in my arms, I approach the bathroom and raise my hand to knock. I hear the rain-like patter of the shower running. He'll need a towel once he's done, so maybe I should sneak in there to drop the towels off. I could just crack the door open and set the towels on the floor without actually going inside.

Jack's in there. Naked. Wet. Surrounded by steam while he lathers himself up and—

Oh for heaven's sake. What is wrong with me? Must be all that adrenaline still coursing through my system. Yeah, that's a good excuse for my lustful fantasy of Jack in the shower.

But he does need these towels.

I ease the door open and tiptoe inside, setting the towels down on the counter. Though I intend to turn right around and leave, my eyes have a different plan. They rotate toward the shower. I can't help seeing what I, um, see. My head decides to turn too, then my entire body swivels in that direction, giving me a perfect view of the clear glass shower stall.

A perfect view of Jack.

Warmth rushes through me, from my cheeks down to my sex.

He stands under the spray, his head tipped back, his eyes closed, facing away from the wall. Water streams down his nude body, highlighting every muscle on his chest and traveling past his hips, down his powerful thighs. The water seems to gravitate to his groin, where it beads on the hairs that nestle around his dick and trickles along the length of it. He turns around and bends his head forward, letting the water pour down his backside now, which inevitably draws my focus to his taut ass.

Slickness is gathering between my thighs. I lay a hand on my chest, trying to even out my breathing, but I can't shatter the spell that the sight of Jack naked has woven around me. He's as hot as ever, and I want to get in that shower with him.

Oh no, I do *not* want that.

Well, okay, I do. But I absolutely will not walk over there. Or get in the shower. Or fall to my knees so I can take his cock in my mouth.

Shit. What's wrong with me today?

I squeeze my eyes shut, but I can still hear the rain-like patter of the shower. The sound of rain has always made me horny. That's the only reason I want Jack right now. Well, that and his body. All drenched and sexy.

My lids open without my permission, forcing me to drink in the sight of my ex-husband, in the buff, with water sluicing down his body. The impulse is too strong, and I've never had great judgment or strong willpower.

So I kick off my shoes and walk to the shower, pulling the stall door open. The sultry heat of the water envelops me, and my nipples tighten.

Jack swerves his head to stare at me.

I step into the shower, wrap my arms around his neck, and kiss him.

He tenses up, not moving or responding to the fact I have my lips crushed to his. After a couple of seconds, his entire body relaxes, and he lashes his arms around me while forging his tongue deep inside my mouth.

Oh God, he tastes incredible, and the sensation of his tongue tangling with mine feels incredible. It's been too damn long since I experienced anything as good as this. I moan and shove my fingers into his wet hair, rubbing myself against his body, moaning again when his cock starts to harden and he groans into my mouth.

Jack pushes a hand under my shirt, trying to peel it off me.

While we keep ravishing each other's mouths, we frantically struggle to get my clothes off. I hear a ripping sound, but I don't care if he's torn my clothes. I need to be naked with him. Right now. He gets my shirt and bra off, and the steamy water dribbles down my chest, the sensation so arousing that it's almost painful. But God, it's Jack's hands that have me whimpering and struggling to get my jeans undone. He pushes my hands away and gets rid of the rest of my clothes while I nibble on his lips, his chin, his ear.

"Fuck, Autumn," he snarls.

Then he shoves me against the tile wall and grasps my thighs, lifting them, urging me to latch my legs around him. I can't think about anything, much less realize how crazy and stupid this is. With my arms around his neck, I lock my ankles behind his ass and hold on.

He thrusts into me.

And the fullness of his cock inside me makes me gasp and clutch him even tighter with my entire body. Even my inner muscles grip him, like not even one part of me can stand to let go, not until we both come so hard we see stars. His erection feels hotter and thicker than I remember, and so damn good that I can't breathe when he starts pumping in and out, the pace quickening with every thrust.

"Jack, yes."

I throw my head back against the wall, while he pounds into me, making my body bounce up and down. The heaviness that settled low in my belly when I stepped into the shower has gotten stronger, and if water weren't gushing over us, the slickness of my sex would be dribbling down my thighs and his cock. Only Jack has ever gotten me this turned on, this worked up. The tingling in my sex spreads into my belly while pressure bears down on me from the inside out, and I know any second I'll go off.

"Yes, Jack, yes!"

I don't care that I'm screaming his name. I don't give a damn who might hear us or what might happen once this is over. None of that matters, because I can't focus on anything except the way he's pummeling me with his body and pushing me closer and closer to the breaking point.

The climax slams through me so hot and hard that I can't even scream. My mouth opens, my head smacks back into the wall, and every muscle in my body clamps down on him. The pleasure intensifies with every wild spasm of my inner muscles until I can no longer breathe and black spots speckle my vision while my ears start to ring. I feel Jack's release pulsate deep inside me, but I have no mental capacity to notice anything else.

I think he shouts something, probably Gaelic, but I can't even be sure I heard that. The ringing in my ears recedes little by little. I gulp in air, and ever so slowly, I regain control of my breathing and my senses.

Jack has his head on my shoulder. He's breathing hard, and he's still holding onto my ass.

That's when I realize I still have my legs strapped around him. I wriggle free of his hold, first setting one foot down on the floor of the shower stall, then the other. Jack's body pins me to the wall, but I don't mind that so much. It feels…familiar.

He raises his head, aiming his lust-darkened gaze at me.

For a moment, we just stare at each other.

I had sex with my ex-husband. In the shower. In my hotel room. And heaven help me, I want to do it again.

He brushes a lock of hair away from my cheek.

Well, it's more like he peels it away. We're both soaked from head to toe, and my hair is plastered to my skin.

Jack drags a finger down my throat. "How long until my clothes are ready?"

"An hour, give or take."

"Good."

He sweeps me up in his arms and carries me out of the bathroom. I notice my clothes lying strewn around in the shower and just outside it as well as my drenched bra glued to the toilet tank, hanging half off it. Jack keeps hold of me with one arm while he hurls the covers off the bed. He sets me down on the mattress, my head on the pillow.

For several seconds, he simply looks at me. His gaze wanders down my body and back up to my face, and he rubs his jaw while his dick starts to swell again.

Should I say something? The only words that spring to mind are "thank you for a great fuck." No, I'm not saying that. It's idiotic, even if those words do accurately describe what happened in the shower a minute ago.

Jack climbs onto the bed straddling me. "Still need to get this out of my system."

"Huh?" My brain has gotten stuck on the shower incident, and I can't figure out what in the world he's talking about. Out of his system? If that means more sex, yeah, I need that too.

My ex-husband bends his arms to lower his face to mine, and then he kisses me. Softly. Tenderly. Like he wants to do nothing else for the next hour. I can't stop my arms from looping around his neck or my leg from hooking itself around his hip.

My voice has a mind of its own too, so when he pulls his lips away the tiniest bit, I wind up saying, "Make love to me, Jack."

And he does that. For an hour.

I fall asleep with Jack's body spooning mine.

Two and a half hours later, I wake up—alone in the bed that's still rumpled and still smells like sex and Jack. The lamp on the bedside table had been on before, but now a false twilight fills the room. The curtains are closed, and the lamp is off. I sit up and yawn, rubbing my eyes.

"Jack?" I call out. "Are you in the bathroom?"

Silence answers my question.

I flick the lamp switch, and light floods the room. Naked, I jump up and check the bathroom, but Jack isn't there. My clothes are neatly folded on the counter. They're dry too.

Maybe Jack went to get some food. We never did eat lunch.

With that hope in my mind, I get dressed and sit on the bed to wait for Jack. Ten minutes later, I call the front desk to ask Mrs. Fraser if she's seen my ex-husband.

"Yes, dearie," she says. "Dr. MacTaggart left a couple of hours ago."

"Oh. Thank you."

I hang up without saying goodbye. Then I slump against the headboard, exhaling all my silly false hopes along with the air in my lungs. Why had I wanted him to come back? We've been over for a long time. Maybe sneaking out while I was asleep is Jack's way of getting back at me for walking out on him two years ago.

But he had filed for divorce, not me.

The way he'd made love to me... It hadn't felt like revenge, or even like two people just getting it out of our systems. It had felt like something much worse.

No, I cannot still be in love with Jack MacTaggart.

Doesn't matter if I am. He abandoned me, and this time, he can't blame me for it. I'd been asleep when he skulked out like a burglar.

So I do what I usually do. I run away from the problem, canceling my vacation after thirty-six hours in Scotland. And I try to forget that afternoon ever happened.

But fate has other ideas.

Chapter Four

Jack

The day after I left Autumn asleep in her hotel room, I still can't understand why I did it. Shagging my ex-wife? That's bad enough. But making love to her for an hour and then sneaking out while she's sleeping? I've never done anything like that, not even when I had a casual encounter with a willing lass. When Autumn fell asleep, tucked up against me, I found myself gazing down at her face and wondering if I'd made a mistake by divorcing her.

No, I did not. *She* left *me*. No explanation. She barely waved goodbye when she rushed out the door.

I can't believe I ran away while she was sleeping. But I did, and no amount of self-flagellation will erase it. I'd called the hotel last night, but the bloke who was working at the front desk told me Autumn had checked out forty-five minutes earlier. Maybe I should have driven to the Inverness airport and tried to find her so I could… I don't know. Explain? Apologize? Considering the way she'd left me two years ago, I don't see any reason why I need to apologize.

But I still feel odd about the whole thing. I keep scratching my chest, though it doesn't itch—not on the outside, but under the surface, deep down where I can't reach it.

The disaster yesterday was not my fault. The blame lies squarely on the shoulders of Alex Thorne.

So naturally, I drive to his home and pound on the door.

His fiancée, my cousin Catriona, answers. "Jack? What's wrong?"

"I need to speak to Alex."

"All right." She steps aside. "Come in and—"

Before she can finish her sentence, I storm inside and straight to the closed door of Alex's study. On the way there, I notice his parents are in the kitchen, but that doesn't stop me. I throw the door open, stalking up to his desk.

Alex sits in a leather chair behind the desk.

He lifts his brows. "Jack, you look bloody awful. Did you stay awake all night shagging Autumn?"

"No." I smack my palms down on the desk. "You sodding ersehole. This is all your fault."

"Is it? Afraid I can't refute your claim unless I know what you're talking about."

"You know bloody well what I mean." I jab a finger in the air near his face. "You set me up on a blind date with my ex-wife. Don't know how you arranged it, but I'm dead certain you connived and conned until you had that noose around my neck."

Alex steeples his fingers, gazing at me with his usual disinterested expression. "Are you? How Machiavellian of me."

"Is everything all right?" Catriona asks from somewhere behind me.

"Yes, it's fine," Alex tells her. "Jack and I need to have a chat, apparently. Would you shut the door, love?"

A click tells me Cat has shut the door. Alex and I are alone.

He rocks his chair gently, his fingers still steepled. "So, Jack, what nefarious plot are you accusing me of? I admit to arranging for you and Autumn to have lunch together, but if you slept with her, that was your doing. Unless you're claiming I telepathically controlled you."

"Donnae try to wriggle out of this. How did you connive to introduce Autumn to Rika Dixon?"

Alex sighs, folding his hands on his lap. "Maybe I connived to get you and Autumn in the same room so you two could sort things once and for all. And maybe I took advantage of the fact Rika and Autumn are friends. But even the amazing Alex Thorne can't control who your ex-wife is friends with. It must've been fate."

Only Alex would call himself amazing. He was being sarcastic, but still, he can be an arrogant erse. I'd given him a free therapy session back when he'd found out he has a half-brother, but Alex had opted out of continuing as my client. He claims the only therapy he needs is the kind he gets from Catriona. I didn't ask what sort of therapy that might be since I'm fair certain I don't need to know.

Did fate intervene in my life? No, it must be a bizarre coincidence that my ex-wife became friends with Rika Dixon. Rika and Dane had lived in

New York City before they got married, and Autumn lived in Atlantic City last I heard. In a city of millions, what were the odds my ex-wife would meet Rika? And that Rika's husband would become acquainted with Alex Thorne?

Maybe it is fate, and the universe has a sick sense of humor.

Alex lifts one brow. "Did you want to castigate me for a bit longer? Or is it time for a thrashing? You've never struck me as the violent type, but your reunion with Autumn has clearly left you…discombobulated."

I have never heard anyone use that word in conversation before. Hearing Alex say it makes me want to laugh, though I can't quite manage it. Am I the one who's behaving like an arrogant erse?

"All right," I say. "Maybe you didn't use Machiavellian tactics to introduce Autumn to Rika. But you knew bloody well what you were doing when you arranged our blind date."

"Maybe I did that to repay a debt."

"Debt?" I consider that statement for a moment, and suddenly, I realize what he means. "I helped you deal with finding out you have a half-brother, so you feel indebted to me. Is that it? I helped you adjust to being with Catriona again too."

"What if that is the case? Maybe you should let me expunge the debt in my own way."

During our one and only therapy session, Alex admitted he'd never had any friends until he met my cousin Logan. Now he has a throng of MacTaggarts on his side, along with his brother and his pseudo-cousins. Aye, they thought they were biological cousins when they first met, but they soon realized they aren't blood relations. Grey Dixon, Alex's brother, is their cousin—but Alex and Grey share only the same mother, who isn't a Dixon. Still, Grey's cousins consider Alex to be their cousin too, much the way Alex calls his adoptive parents Mum and Dad when they share no blood.

Alex has started to adjust to having so many people in his life, but he'll need considerably more time to accept everything that has changed for him.

Which means I should cut him a wee bit of slack. *Bollocks.*

"Have it your way," I tell him. "Your debt is expunged. I'll deal with the aftermath on my own, though. No meddling from you or anyone."

"Meddling? Is that what I've done?" He feigns shock. "Blimey. I'd better see a doctor before the interference disease becomes terminal." He opens a desk drawer and brings out a bottle of Ben Nevis, a favorite whisky among the MacTaggarts. "Let's have a drink instead, eh?"

I slump into a chair and have a drink with Alex.

After that, I go home and try to forget about the afternoon I spent in a hotel room with my ex-wife. I refuse to remember how good it had felt to make love to her or how long I'd sat there watching her sleep before I left. None of that matters. She's gone, again, and I need to get on with my life.

So I do. For eight weeks.

Well, mostly I do that. My thoughts keep circling back to that hotel room, Autumn beneath me, the look on her face while I brought her to climax over and over. I have a full roster of clients which keeps my mind busy during the day. But at night... Two months of getting off in the dead of night while fantasizing about Autumn has left me drained in more ways than one.

On the first day of what I assume will become the ninth week of night-time torture, I'm sitting in my home reading a book about a new type of psychotherapy. The theory is rubbish, but the author has gotten on all the TV talk shows, and I figured I should read it. My clients love to ask me about trendy techniques, and I'll need ammunition to convince them not to jump on every bandwagon. It's the psychology version of fad diets.

I'm on page sixty-two when the doorbell rings.

Mhac na galla. If it's Alex again, trying to cheer me up with "maybe" and "what if" humor, I just might batter him this time. At least Alex appreciates Gaelic curses—like *mhac na galla,* which means "son of a bitch." Autumn had always disliked Gaelic.

Except when we were shagging. Then she loved it.

Why am I thinking of her while I walk to the front door? I'm an eejit, obviously, and that's why. Only an idiot would still be thinking about a woman I'll never see again.

I swing the door open.

And all the blood in my body freezes. My mouth falls open, but I can't produce anything resembling a sound, much less words.

My ex-wife eyes me up and down, adjusting her hold on the large purse that hangs over one shoulder. "Good morning, Jack. Surprise, it's me."

She shifts her weight from one foot to the other several times and adjusts her grip on the purse strap several times too.

I notice a large suitcase sitting on the porch beside her, along with two smaller ones.

Autumn compresses her lips, glancing everywhere but at my face, then she blows out a breath. "Are you going to say hello?"

"I, ah..." Shaking off the worst of my shock—literally, by shaking my head—I finally succeed in forming words. "Good morning, Autumn. Why are you here?"

"Wow, that's a cordial greeting. It's nice to see you too, Jack."

"You—I mean, I—" What am I trying to say? I have no ruddy idea. "Why are you here?"

Making me repeat myself is apparently all my brain can do right now.
She rolls her eyes. "To see you. Duh."

"But I…" Am being an erse to the woman who's standing on my porch. I move to the side. "Come in, Autumn, and have a seat."

When she reaches for her luggage, I shoo her away. Tucking the smaller bags under my arms, I heft the large suitcase off the porch floor.

She walks inside, and since we're already in the living room, she settles onto an armchair.

I stand there by the door for several seconds, unable to make my feet move. My brain finally processes the fact her hair is pink, not blue like the last time I saw her. Several seconds after that realization, I regain control of my muscles and carry her luggage inside. I set the suitcases down just inside the door, then I shut it.

"We need to talk," she says. "You'll want to sit down for this, trust me."

The only sort of conversation that requires sitting down is one that involves bad news. Does she have cancer? Christ, I hope that's not it. The thought of Autumn being sick makes me nauseous. That can't be it, can it? Maybe she wants to argue with me about why I left her in the hotel room and never even rang her to explain why.

Her tone of voice has convinced me to take her advice. I sit in the chair across the coffee table from the one she's occupying, though I stay perched on its edge.

"Do you have cancer?" I ask.

"No, Jack, that's not the problem." She drops her purse on the floor beside her chair and starts wringing her hands on her lap. "It's, um, not bad news. I think. Well, I guess it depends on how you feel about the situation. For me, this is a wonderful thing."

Good news? I slide back in my chair and slump into it, letting out the breath I hadn't meant to be holding. "Go on, I'm listening."

She stares at her lap, still wringing her hands. Her shoulders rise and fall as she takes a deep breath.

"Are you going to tell me?" I ask.

Nodding, she bites her lip and raises her head. Those beautiful eyes focus on me. "I'm pregnant, Jack."

Chapter Five

Autumn

My ex-husband stares at me for a minute, maybe two, maybe longer. I lose track of how long because I'm too busy hugging myself and fighting the urge to scratch every inch of my body. I feel a little nauseous too, and I don't think it's entirely morning sickness. How will Jack respond to my revelation? I can't decide how I want him to react, so I really can't guess what he'll say.

"Are you sure?" he asks.

"Yes, I'm sure. I did a home test, then I went to the doctor for confirmation."

"But are you sure it's mine?"

I scowl at him. "No, Jack, I slept with so many guys that I have no idea who the father might be, but I figured you've got the most money so I should hit you up for child support. Is that what you think of me?"

"No, I—" He shuts his eyes for half a second, wincing, then shoves his hands into his hair. "I'm sorry. This is a surprise, and ahmno taking it very well, am I?"

"I'm sorry too. I know you don't really think I'm angling for money." I burp. Try not to, but my body doesn't care what I want. "Do you have any crackers? Saltines, maybe?"

"Aren't you feeling well?" He jumps up. "I'll take you to the hospital."

"That's overkill, Jack. I'm nauseous and gassy, that's all. Normal pregnancy stuff." I lay a hand over my tummy. "Besides, I haven't eaten much today. Got on a plane late last night and came straight here, but the in-flight meal didn't sit well. I only ate a little of it."

"I'll make you breakfast. Eggs and toast should be all right. Shouldn't it?"

He looks and sounds so earnestly concerned that I don't want to disappoint him. Maybe eggs and toast would help more than crackers. "Sure, that sounds good. Thank you, Jack."

"Why don't you lie down on the sofa? I'll bring your food out here."

"I'm fine in this chair."

"Lie down, Autumn," he says in a stern tone and with a stubbornly determined look on his face.

Yeah, I'm well acquainted with Stubborn Jack. And with Taciturn Jack. But my favorite version of him is Sex Machine Jack. Unfortunately, I'm not going to see that part of him this morning, not after the bombshell I dropped on his head.

So I give in to Stubborn Jack and stretch out on the sofa on my side.

He exhales a big breath, his shoulders flagging, and rushes off to the kitchen.

I don't know where the kitchen is in here since I never lived in this house. We'd shared an apartment in Inverness during our brief marriage. That's where Jack had his practice back then, but he's moved home now. I wish I could've met his family before this, but Jack had never wanted me to get within fifty miles of them. His parents and his brother live in and around Loch Fairbairn, which is about three hours away from Inverness—the distance from his hometown being the sole piece of info he ever gave me about his past. He has loads of cousins too, but I've never met any of them either.

Maybe if I'd told him about my past and my family, he might've shared more with me, but I've never been good at talking about my parents and my sister. Jack might not have talked about *his* past, but he had told me lots about his family despite never wanting me to meet them.

While I lie here on the sofa waiting for Jack to bring me food, I feel so comfy that I start to get sleepy. For the entire ten-hour flight to Scotland, I'd been so anxious about seeing my ex-husband again and dropping the baby bombshell that I hadn't slept as much as I should have. Maybe I can take a teeny nap. Jack will wake me up when the food is ready.

My lids drift shut. Thoughts spiral away into the ether, and a wonderful sense of safety lulls me down into the depths of slumber.

I dream of Jack. Naked, wet, sexy Jack. We're in a big hotel bathroom inside a big shower stall with five heads spraying water over us. I'm naked too. But God, Jack with no clothes on, drenched and aroused, is the hottest thing ever. He pins me to the wall and thrusts—

"Wake up, Autumn."

The grumpy voice that speaks those words also comes with a large hand that shakes me.

I mumble something unintelligible, stretch and yawn, then pry my lids open. Blinking several times to clear my vision, I look at Jack.

"Are you all right?" he asks in that grumpy voice. "I thought you were in distress, the way you were moaning and saying 'oh God' over and over."

I talked in my sleep? Well, at least I hadn't said "please fuck me now, Jack." Sure, that's what we'd been doing in my dream, but I am so not in the mood right now. Besides, I cannot have sex with him. Our relationship is complicated enough with a baby on the way. Sex would confuse things even more, no matter how incredibly, amazingly fantastic it might be.

Might? No, it definitely would be.

Yeah, sex has never been our problem.

Now that I'm fully awake, I push up into a sitting position and swing my legs off the sofa. My feet touch down on the wood floor.

And Jack is scowling at me. While crouched inches away.

"What's your problem?" I ask. "It was a long flight, and I got sleepy. Excuse me, the pregnant woman, for taking a little nap."

"Little? You've been asleep for an hour and twenty-three minutes."

Oh shit. I slept how long? No wonder he's in panic mode. Jack doesn't do panic, though. At least, I've never seen him this way before. His usual demeanor is calm and mature. Anger isn't his forte, and he doesn't get upset very often. But panicky Jack? That's new, at least to me.

I notice a clock on the fireplace mantel, the kind that probably has hourly chimes. It tells me Jack isn't exaggerating about how long I slept.

"I'm so sorry," I say, reaching out to touch his shoulder. "Didn't mean to scare you. I didn't sleep well on the flight, and it's been kind of stressful coming here to tell you the big news. I'm not in distress, I swear it. I feel much better now, actually, though I'm still hungry."

"And the baby is all right too?"

The concern in his voice makes me want to hug him, but I don't do it. Like sex, cuddling might complicate things.

"Yes, the baby is fine." I take his hand and hold it to my belly. No one can see I'm pregnant yet, since I haven't started showing, but I think he needs to feel connected to this baby somehow. "Our child is getting bigger as we speak. In about seven months, we'll have a son or a daughter."

"How far along are you?"

"Eight weeks. My periods can be irregular, so it took me a while to realize I might be pregnant. But as soon as I found out for sure, I came to see you, Jack. I want us to raise this baby together."

The annoyance has drained out of his expression. His lips curve up the tiniest bit as he gazes at my belly, his hand still pressed into me though I've pulled my hand away. "I'm going to be a father."

"Yes, you are." I've never seen a look like that on his face before—awed and tranquil at the same time. It stabs a pang through my heart, but it feels good. "Are you, um, okay with it, then?"

"Okay?" He raises his face to me and smiles, almost beaming. "No, I'm not okay with it. I—I think I'm overjoyed."

He laughs. It's a big, joyful sound, like nothing I've ever heard from him. He sits on the sofa beside me and pulls me into his arms, hugging me gently and rubbing my back.

So this is Overjoyed Jack. I never would've guessed he could be like this.

And because I have crazy pregnancy hormones, I start to cry.

Jack pulls back, grasping my upper arms. "What's wrong?"

"Nothing. Hormones, that's all. I cried five times during the flight."

"Oh." He scoots backward to sit an arm's length from me. "We can get married, but by law, we have to give notice to the registrar at least twenty-nine days in advance. We should file our notices this afternoon."

"Married? Are you insane? I didn't come here because I wanted us to get hitched."

"We're having a child."

"This isn't the Middle Ages, Jack. People have babies without getting married." I turn toward him and try to quell my irritation, or maybe it's panic. "Considering what a disaster our marriage was, there's no way I'm going down that road again with you. We can co-parent."

"What the bloody hell does that mean? Are you running away to America again? Maybe you'll let me see the bairn in video chats."

"No, I—" A frustrated noise growls out of me. "I don't know. That's why I'm here, to figure things out and make sure our child knows both of us. I could've kept this news to myself, but you have a right to know and to be involved. But not as a couple."

"Are you moving to Scotland?"

"I haven't decided anything yet. The second I found out I was pregnant, I jumped on a plane." I rub my forehead. "Can we talk about this later? I'm getting a headache, probably because I'm starving."

He leaps up and stalks toward the kitchen, or at least the doorway he'd gone through before when he was going to make me breakfast. "I'll cook more food. Maybe this time you'll stay awake long enough to eat it."

At least he grumbled those words instead of barking them.

Will I move to Scotland so we can raise our child together? No way can I marry Jack. This will be co-parenting only. No snuggling. No kissing. No sex.

I don't care how tempting his body is. There will be no sex. None whatsoever.

Jack walks out of the kitchen holding his shirt in his hand. The dark-blue fabric seems to be soaked with a white liquid. "Need to change my shirt. Spilled milk all over it."

Oh jeez. Why did he have to take his shirt off? He has the sexiest chest I've ever seen, and my mind insists on giving me a vivid replay of our afternoon in that hotel room. I'd licked and kissed every inch of that chest.

Jack throws me an annoyed glance, then he disappears down the hallway that must lead to his bedroom.

What kind of bed does he have? A king-size one, for sure. Plenty big enough to fit both of us and leave room to play naughty games. Jack always loved role-playing sex. So did I. My favorite was when he put on a kilt and played the medieval Highlander who kidnapped me to his castle. He would whisper dirty Gaelic to me, and I would fondle his—

Cut that out. No sex with Jack, remember?

I blame the pregnancy hormones. They're making me crazy. That's all it is.

Sure, hormones. *So what was your excuse eight weeks ago, huh?*

Groaning, I flop back against the sofa. I'll be fine as long as Jack doesn't take off any more of his clothes in front of me.

Because the universe hates me, he saunters out of his bedroom wearing only boxer shorts. He's carrying a shirt and a pair of jeans.

What in the world? Who cooks in boxers?

At the end of the hall, he stops and stares at me. "*Bod an Donais.* I forgot you were here."

"You forgot?" I say. "Come on, you saw me two minutes ago, sitting right here."

"Ah, sorry." He tugs his clothes on, cursing under his breath while he stumbles twice and struggles to get dressed. "Donnae know what I was thinking."

"It's called shock. Shouldn't a psychologist know that?"

Fully clothed now, he flashes me a scowl and stomps into the kitchen.

Well, at least he's not half-naked anymore.

Chapter Six

Jack

I have gone completely insane. Haven't I? No, it's only shock, like Autumn said. The fact that she had needed to tell me it's shock should've clued me in, but then, I'd been in shock for pity's sake. And of course, she'd felt the need to imply I'm an idiot and a rubbish therapist because I should have recognized my own condition. *Mhac na galla.* She's right about that. Then again, most people don't realize what kind of state they're in until someone else points it out to them.

But why did my ex-wife have to be the one to say it?

She's pregnant. We're having a bairn.

Bloody fucking hell.

I fling the refrigerator door open and start grabbing items, though I have no conscious idea what I'm doing.

How will Autumn and I raise a bairn together? We can't stop arguing, never could. Well, except when we're having a poke. Autumn stops harassing me then, and the only words she speaks are filthy ones. She shouts my name too. And she makes a wide variety of noises. Every sound that comes out of her mouth during sex makes me need to fuck her even harder.

But the rest of the time, I fight a nearly overpowering urge to strap duct tape over her mouth.

I rest my hands on the island and gaze down at the food items I've amassed. Lorne sausage, broccoli, a half-eaten haggis, eggs, scones my cousin Kirsty made for me, several kinds of cheese, whipping cream, gravy that looks like it has mold growing on it, and a solitary kiwi. What the bloody hell do I think I'll be making with these ingredients? Cheese kiwi haggis with whipped cream on top?

Another curse grumbles out of me.

Seven months from today, or thereabouts, I'll have a child. A son or daughter. I scratch my head, still staring at the bizarre assortment of food on the island. Autumn wants us to "co-parent," but I have no idea what I want. I will be there for my child, that's all I know for certain. What does co-parenting mean? She lives in America, but I live here. How can we work out the logistics when we can't say a civil word to each other?

I keep the eggs and sausage out but throw everything else back into the fridge. Then I grab a loaf of bread and start cooking.

Ten minutes later, I walk into the living room carrying a tray of food.

Autumn is sitting there on the sofa, exactly like she was when I left the room, but now she's studying her hands. She has them clasped on her lap.

I clear my throat. "I made you something to eat."

Her head pops up, and she blinks several times quickly. "Oh. Thanks."

"You'll feel better after you eat." I set the tray on her lap. "Drink the milk and the orange juice. You need all the nutrition you can get, what with a bairn growing inside you."

She picks up the fork and starts to eat.

I sink into a chair and watch her daintily consuming the meal I made for her. I used to love cooking for Autumn, and I especially loved feeding her while we were naked. Aye, for a short while after sex, we got on like a normal married couple. Raising a child together will put even more strain on our already fractured relationship. The one thing I'm sure of is that I don't want my son or daughter to have two parents who can't stand each other.

There's only one solution, but Autumn will resist the idea. She'll probably whack me over the head with a lamp when I suggest it.

I wait until she's done eating, then I raise the issue. "For the sake of the baby, we need to find a way to coexist without arguments and recriminations."

"Yeah, I know."

"We need couples therapy."

Her mouth crimps into a flat line, and she narrows her gaze on me.

Aye, that look has always been her favorite. I saw it more than any other expression during the entirety of our brief marriage.

"Oh no," she says, "you don't get to go Stubborn Jack on me and issue commands."

Stubborn Jack? She says that like it's my name.

"Have I issued any commands?" I cross my arms over my chest. "Well, have I?"

"Not as such. But you just told me we need couples therapy."

"It was a statement of fact, not an order."

"Fact?" She puckers her lips, scooting forward until only her rump rests on the sofa cushion. "Psychology has nothing to do with facts or reality. It's nothing but a way to make people feel like they're failures."

"No, it's a technique for healing damaged relationships."

"How many people have you cured?"

I huff. "Psychology isn't about curing anyone. It's about helping—"

"Oh please, Jack." She flicks her gaze up to the ceiling, shaking her head. "We never could have a reasonable discussion about your job, or anything, because you always have to start prattling on and on about 'the process' and all that garbage."

"Maybe we could have a civil conversation if you would stop calling my life's work garbage."

Autumn studies me for a moment, or maybe it's closer to a thousand years. Then she sighs and says, "Who would be giving us this therapy you claim we need?"

"I would."

Her face goes blank. She blinks once, slowly.

And she bursts out laughing.

What on earth is she laughing about? Therapy isn't humorous. Well, not usually.

She laughs so hard her eyes water, and she holds her belly like her guffaws are straining her abdominal muscles. When she finally stops laughing, she wipes her eyes and looks at me. "Thank you. I really needed that."

"What did you need?"

"A really good laugh."

"I haven't told a joke." Did I growl those words? I can't be sure, and I don't think I care. This entire day so far feels like an art-house film, a bizarre and confusing mishmash of…everything.

"Oh, you just told me a whopper," she says. "Or do you seriously think you can be my therapist and yours too? I mean, it must be a conflict of interest or an ethical violation or something for a psychologist to treat his ex-wife. And self-administered therapy sounds unethical too. Not to mention being a terrible idea."

She's right, of course, and I am a sodding eejit.

"*Gòrach pìos de cac,*" I hiss.

Autumn lifts her brows. "What did you say? Don't remember that Gaelic phrase."

"It means I'm a stupid piece of shit."

"No, you aren't." She moves to sit on the coffee table in front of my chair, resting a hand on my knee. "You're a lot of things, but never a stupid piece of shit."

Why is she touching me? Comforting me? It makes no sense, but I can't help liking the way it feels to have her hand on my knee. Autumn has the most beautiful eyes. They're like emeralds lit from behind by the light of heaven. Oh bollocks, what is wrong with me? I should not be thinking of poetic ways to describe how bonnie she is, much less remembering the last time we made love. But aye, that memory barrels through my mind while I gaze into her luminous eyes.

"I want our child to be happy," I say. "You and I can't get along, and that is going to affect our bairn."

"We have months to figure this out." She squeezes my knee. "Besides, we did get along in the beginning. Those twelve days in Vegas were the best days of my life."

Mine too, but I can't make myself tell her that.

I fidget in my chair, but I can't get comfortable. "Our six-week marriage was a disaster."

"Because we made it that way. If we created the problem, we can fix it." She pulls her hand away and rubs her eyes. "We need to figure out how to co-parent in peace. For our child."

"Aye." I grimace when she stretches, raising her arms above her head, because the movement lifts her bonnie breasts. My *slat* jerks, the way it always has whenever Autumn stretches like that. But I tear my gaze away from her bosom and ask, "What exactly do you mean by 'co-parenting'?"

"We raise the child together. Duh."

"Together? As a couple? You said you don't want that."

"No, I meant together, but separately. You live in your house, I live in mine, and we both raise our kid. We have months to work out the logistics, but our relationship needs a serious makeover."

"If we won't be living together, why do you keep talking about 'our' relationship?"

She rolls her eyes at me. "Honestly, Jack, you're a psychologist. You ought to know there are different kinds of relationships, not just the romantic type."

Of course I know that, but I'm still in shock. Aye, that's my excuse and I'm sticking to it.

"We can't co-parent," I say, trying not to wince, although that term is starting to annoy me, "unless we both live in Loch Fairbairn. America is too bloody far away."

"Naturally, you assume I'll be the one to move. You could go to America, you know."

"My practice is here. My family is here. You moved to Scotland when we got married, so I don't see any reason why you can't live here. I want our child to grow up where I did, the way I did."

"The way you did? What does that mean?"

"In Scotland, that's what it means."

She slaps her hands on her thighs. "Of course. You make all the decisions, and I'm supposed to sit here like a good little concubine and do whatever my master dictates."

"Aye, that's right." I leap out of my chair and grab her hand, tugging to make her stand, though she does not move. "Let's go. We need to file our notices today, and you'll need to fill out a declaration of immigration status."

"What are you talking about?"

"Getting married. I told you earlier, there are rules and procedures—"

Autumn flies off the table and smacks me in the chest with her fist. "You're back to the marriage thing? I already said no to that dumb idea, and I told you I'm not here because I want to get back together with you. Considering how much we argue, marriage is the last thing we should be talking about."

"I counsel married couples all the time, and I see what divorce does to the children. Ahmno raising my bairn that way, shuttled back and forth between parents."

"You should've thought of that before you fucked me in a hotel room without using a condom."

My mouth opens, and a scathing retort wants to come out of it, but I clamp my teeth together and fight the impulse. Arguing is exactly what we don't need to do right now. I take a few slow breaths to calm myself. "We're both too on edge right now to have a proper discussion. We each need to be alone for a while, so we can come to terms with what's happened. Only then do we have a chance of working this out."

"Okay. You're right. Time alone sounds good."

She walks past me, heading for the door.

I seize her arm. "Where are you going?"

"To a hotel."

"But Inverness is three hours away."

She gives me a look that says I'm an eejit and an erse. "Why would I go that far? There's a hotel right here in Loch Fairbairn."

Everything inside me freezes, including my muscles. I can't even blink. She intends to stay here, in my hometown, at the one and only hotel in this village.

"No," I snap, almost shouting the word as I slap my hand on the door to stop her from opening it. "Ye cannae leave this house."

"Excuse me?" She plants her hands on her hips and lifts her chin. "I will go wherever I want. Now move your hand. Please."

Though she said "please," it didn't sound like a request.

"You need to stay here," I tell her. "I have family in the village, and friends too. Practically everyone in Loch Fairbairn knows me. If they see you, they'll think—Donnae know. But there will be gossip, and we will both get tangled up in the MacTaggart grapevine."

"So what? They can gossip about how your ex-wife came for a visit. Big whoop."

"It is a 'big whoop,' Autumn. This is my home. Ahmno having the entire village know that—Well, thinking that you and I—"

"What? That we're getting chummy? Or that we're screwing each other's brains out?"

Bloody hell, why did she have to say that? My mind forces me to relive that afternoon at the Loch Fairbairn Arms like a movie playing out in my head. A pornographic film.

Somehow, I marshal enough willpower and wits to sound reasonably calm. "Stay in this house, please. I need time to figure out how to tell my family you're here and explain why."

"It's nobody's damn business. And why do you care so much what your family thinks?"

"Because they *are* my family. You don't understand what the MacTaggart clan is like."

She still has her hand on the doorknob, but now she's twisting it left and right, over and over, in tiny movements. "I don't understand your family because you never let me meet any of them. For the entire six weeks we lived together in Inverness, you would never introduce me to anybody. Your cousins kept calling, wanting to meet your wife. Your brother stopped by our apartment, but you slammed the door in his face. Oh, and let's not forget that I was forbidden to answer the phone in case it was one of your relatives."

"I know. I'm sorry."

Autumn relaxes slightly, but she keeps her hand on the doorknob. "That's a start, but you can't hide me from your family forever. We're having a baby, not hooking up one more time for the hell of it."

"Will you stay here? For now?"

Her shoulders wilt, and she lets go of the knob. "Fine, okay."

"Thank you."

"But I need some fresh air, after being stuck in a cramped airliner for hours and hours, not to mention the long and very expensive cab ride to get here." She waves toward the sliding glass doors that access the backyard. "I'll go out there."

"No, ye cannae," I snap. "Someone might see you."

She flaps her arms. "So now I can't even go outside? What on earth is wrong with you, Jack?"

I scratch behind my ear, though I have no clue how that's going to help. "Please, just stay inside the house until I figure out how to break the news to my family."

"Now I'm your hostage?"

"Donnae be ridiculous. You are not a hostage. I'm asking you to do this for me as a favor."

She bows her head for a few seconds, then throws it back and moans. "Fine, I'll hide in your house like a fugitive from justice." She looks at me, her gaze sharp and clear. "But not for long. You'd better sort out your shit quick, or I'm out the door for good."

"Aye, not for long."

How will I sort this mess I've made for myself? I have no idea. Somehow, I will fix things. Somehow.

"I have a spare room," I say. "Let me show you."

Chapter Seven

Autumn

I follow Jack down the hallway, past a closed door as well as the bathroom, which I can see because that door is open. He's left the bedroom doors open too, so I get a glimpse of where he sleeps as he hustles me into the spare room. Jack's bed is either bigger than I remembered, or he's bought a new one in the last two years. Sometimes I still can't believe it's been that long since we went our separate ways. It feels like yesterday when we were living in a cozy apartment in Inverness.

Cozy? Sure, except when we were arguing. So yeah, most of the time it wasn't cozy at all.

Still, we had a lot of good times, even some that didn't involve sex.

Jack stops in the middle of the room. "This is where guests stay. We'll have to share the bathroom, but you'll have this room all to yourself. The door locks too, if you want an extra layer of privacy."

Does he think I don't trust him? I can't decide if I do or not, but I get a little queasy when I realize he might not trust me. No, that's just morning sickness. It's afternoon right now, but pregnancy nausea can happen anytime day or night. I'm not queasy because I want Jack to trust me, to like me, to…love me.

No, it's definitely not that.

"Thank you," I say, though I don't see why I should be grateful when he's basically holding me hostage. I'm going along with this for the sake of our baby, but if Jack doesn't stop acting like a crazy person pretty soon… What will I do? He's the father of my child. Am I going to run away again, raising our baby on my own and hiding the father's identity? Jeez, then I really would be a fugitive—from my own husband.

Ex-husband. *Duh, Autumn, you're not married to him anymore.*

Jack gestures toward the closet. "You'll find extra pillows and blankets in there. I'll get your luggage for you."

He hurries away before I can speak.

I perch on the bed's edge and survey my surroundings. Flower-print wallpaper. Pale wood floor. A big picture window that overlooks the garden and its flowering bushes, including one that sits right outside the window. I bounce a little, testing the mattress. It feels cushy, with just the right amount of springiness. A flower-print comforter covers the bed, and the decorative pillows laid out at the head of the bed have similar flower patterns on them. I also notice two regular bed pillows hidden behind the decorative ones. The pillowcases have flowers on them too. Oh, and there are flowers in a vase on the bedside table. Artificial flowers, I think.

Why does Jack, a manly Scot, have a room filled with feminine stuff? Maybe he has a girlfriend, and that's the real reason he doesn't want me to leave the house.

I get slightly queasy again when I think about Jack having someone else in his life.

No, I don't. It's those damn hormones making me nauseous and sentimental.

Jack returns carrying my bags and sets them on the floor just inside the doorway. "I'll let you rest. If you need anything, I'll be in my office."

"You don't need to leave the house to get some space from me. I'll shut the door and stay in here, like a good little hostage."

His lips warp into an expression that looks like he wants to scowl and smile at the same time. "I'm not leaving the house. My office is at the end of the hall."

"Oh, you mean in that secret room with the closed door."

"It's not a secret. But that's where I'll be."

"Don't worry." I pat the comforter. "I'll stay right here, though I might start digging an escape tunnel with my nail file."

He makes that scowl-smile expression again, then he leaves.

I pad over to the doorway and turn my biggest suitcase onto its side. I've just unzipped it when I hear footsteps clomping down the hall. Then I see Jack's feet beside me.

So I crane my neck to look up at him. "If you're here to chain me to the bed, the answer is no."

Honestly, though, I would probably go right along with the chains idea provided we're both naked.

No, no, no, I'm not having sex with him. No way.

His mouth warps into that scowl-smile yet again. "You're mocking me, aren't you?"

"A little bit. Did you have another command for me?"

Jack glances out the window, scrunching up his entire face for about three seconds, then he returns his attention to me. "Do not answer the phone, please. And don't open the door either. In fact, it would be best if you stayed away from the windows too."

"What? Come on, Jack, that really will be like prison."

He twists his mouth left, then right, then left again. Finally, he sighs. "You can look out the windows on the back of the house."

"Gee, thanks. Should I wear a hood with two eyeholes cut out of it so no one will recognize me?"

"Now you're being ridiculous. Do as I ask, please."

Well, since he said please... "All right. I'll be the invisible woman."

He nods once and walks away.

Jack must be beyond stressed out to behave like this. Commanding me to stay here, inside, until he works up the nerve to introduce me to his family... Yeah, he definitely needs some serious therapy.

He can't do that for himself, but maybe I can help. Surreptitiously. Without him realizing it.

Sure, piece of cake. I'll trick my ex into secret therapy. Because I'm suddenly a licensed psychologist with years of experience. Well, maybe I'm not. But I did live with an experienced therapist for the better part of two months. Jack loved to spout all that psychobabble stuff. Of course, I shouldn't use the official terminology, or he might catch on to my nefarious plan.

I put my stuff away in the dresser and closet, and I lie down on the bed to start plotting.

After ten minutes or so, I fall asleep. I'm guessing about when that happened because I wasn't staring at a clock the whole time, though there is a cute wind-up clock on the bedside table. When I wake up about twenty minutes later, I feel even more refreshed than I had when I slept for over an hour this morning. Must be jet lag.

But now I'm hungry again.

Deciding not to bother my grumpy and half-insane ex-husband, I amble out to the living room. Jack's office door is shut. I start to turn left toward the kitchen.

Someone knocks on the front door.

I should ignore it, right? I mean, this is Jack's house. I'm a guest, sort of. Guest-slash-hostage. And he told me not to open the door.

After a few seconds of silence, that someone outside knocks again with more conviction.

Jack told me not to answer the phone or go outside or look out any windows other than the ones at the back of the house. He never said I shouldn't speak to anyone *through* the door.

I chew on my lip for a second, then I pad over to the front door. There's no peephole, so I have no idea who might be out there.

"Hello?" I say, loud enough for the mystery visitor to hear but, hopefully, not loud enough for Jack to hear. "May I help you?"

Silence. Then the mystery person clears their throat. "Is this still Jack MacTaggart's house?"

The speaker has a Scottish accent and sounds male.

"Uh, yes," I say.

"Is Jack home right now?"

"Yeah, but he's busy working."

The man clears his throat again. "May I come in? I'm Jack's brother, Callum."

His brother? A weird kind of excitement zings through me. I've never seen any of Jack's relatives except in pictures. I desperately want to open the door and get a look at his brother, but I promised not to do that. Damn.

How will I explain that to his brother without actually explaining it?

"Um, sorry, but…" A great excuse would be awesome right now, but I can't think of anything—except for a truly awful lie. "I have chicken pox. You can't come in."

"I've been vaccinated, and I had chicken pox when I was a laddie. So has Jack."

"Well, I wouldn't want to risk it."

Callum says nothing for several seconds. When he speaks again, he sounds highly amused. "May I at least know to whom I am speaking?"

Jack never said I shouldn't tell anyone my name.

"Autumn Flowerday," I tell Callum.

He chuckles. "Ah, you must be the mysterious ex-wife. It's a pleasure to finally meet you, even if I cannae see your face. What a lovely voice you have."

"Thank you. Your voice is nice too."

"We were beginning to wonder if you really existed, or if you were only a figment of Jack's imagination."

Yeah, I can understand why his family might think that.

"I'm real," I say. "But you should probably go. Jack doesn't want to see anyone right now. He's got, you know, spots all over his face."

Only after I say that do I remember Callum said he and Jack both had chicken pox as children. Well, he might've caught a different strain or whatever from me and my imaginary illness.

"Ah, of course," Callum says, still sounding amused. "May I at least have a look at you through the window?"

"No." Did I shout that? Not quite, but almost. "Sorry, I just don't want anyone to see me all spotted and poxy."

"Come on, lass, just a wee peek."

Footsteps pound behind me.

"What the bloody hell are you doing?" Jack demands as he comes up beside me. He grabs my arm and drags me away from the door. In a softer voice that sounds no less angry, he hisses, "I told you to stay away from the door."

"No, you said not to open the door, go outside, look out the windows, or answer the phone."

He squints his eyes and flattens his lips into a hard line.

"Jack, is that you?" Callum hollers. "I hope you're not seriously ill."

My ex-husband blusters a breath out through his nostrils.

I shake his hand off my arm.

"What did you tell my brother?" he asks.

"That we have chicken pox. You caught it from me." I throw my arms up. "What did you expect me to say? Gee, sorry, I can't open the door because your brother is holding me hostage?"

I spoke as softly as Jack had, so Callum couldn't have heard it.

Jack leans in until his face is inches from mine. "Donnae be talking to anyone through the door, any door. Or through the windows. Understand?"

"Kind of late for that command. I already spoke to Callum. He knows I'm here."

"But he doesn't know who you are."

I bite my lip and hunch my shoulders.

Jack shuts his eyes briefly, and his hard expression disintegrates. "*Bod an Donais*, Autumn. Do you have any idea what you've unleashed?"

I can't help laughing just a little. "Unleashed? You make it sound like I opened Pandora's box."

"Might as well have. Now that Callum knows you're here, everyone will know. The news will spread like wildfire until every MacTaggart in creation has heard that you're in my house."

"So what? I don't get why you're freaked out by the idea of your family knowing I exist." I point toward the door. "Did you know your brother thought I was a figment of your imagination?"

Jack's mouth kicks up at one corner, the tiniest bit. "Callum was having you on."

"But he was serious when he said he has no idea what I look like. Right? You never showed anyone a picture of me."

He stares at me for a moment, then sighs and runs a hand over his eyes. "No, I never showed anyone pictures of you."

"Can I come in now?" Callum asks.

"No," Jack shouts over his shoulder, toward the door. "Away and boil your head, ye *fanaidh bàlaichean*."

"All right, all right. I can tell you need some alone time with Autumn. I'm sure your 'chicken pox' will last for days and keep the neighbors awake all night."

Oh yeah, when Callum said "chicken pox," he meant sex. His tone made that clear.

Jack snarls another Gaelic curse at the door.

His brother chuckles, then I hear footsteps receding.

"That was very rude," I say. "Your brother wanted to see you."

"Aye, until he heard your voice. Then he wanted to see you."

Jack stomps over to the picture window, which is hidden behind curtains, and peeks out. His body had been as stiff as concrete when he stormed into the living room, but now he exhales a big sigh and relaxes.

I walk up beside him, laying a hand on his arm. "Would it be so awful if your family met me? Nobody will know I'm pregnant. I haven't started showing yet."

He covers his eyes with his hand. "Please, Autumn, I need to figure out how to tell them."

"You just said Callum will tell everyone. Problem solved."

"No. The problems have just begun."

I slide my hand up to his shoulder and give it a light squeeze. "What's the real reason you're panicking about this?"

He lowers his hand, straightens, and turns away. "I have work to do."

Jack takes two steps.

"If you work from home," I say, "doesn't that mean your patients will be coming here?"

He freezes, hissing something under his breath that's probably another Gaelic curse.

"Should I hide under my bed while you're talking to your patients?" I ask.

Jack turns his head to look at me. "They're clients, not patients. But you know that already."

"I forgot. Pardon me for not having perfect recall."

He bores his gaze into me, and a muscle ticks in his jaw. "I'll reschedule my appointments for this week."

The second he lifts his foot to take a step, I ask, "What does *fanaidh bàlaichean* mean?"

"It's the Gaelic version of fannybaws, which means the other person is a bloody annoying erse."

With that, he stalks back into his office and slams the door.

I flop onto the chair he had sat in earlier, turn on the TV, and watch UK television shows.

Chapter Eight

Jack

I drop into the chair behind my desk and rotate it toward the window so I can glare at the bushes rather than my wife. Ex-wife. Christ, what's wrong with me? If anyone finds out I'm holding my ex-wife hostage in my home, I will lose my license to practice therapy. Callum knows Autumn is here, but he can't have guessed I won't let her leave the house. She told him we both have chicken pox.

Bloody hell. No one will believe that lie.

After calling my clients to reschedule our appointments, I go back to staring out the window. I told everyone I can't see them this week because I have chicken pox. Might as well perpetuate the ridiculous cover story Autumn created. Since my brother knows she's here, I have no doubt the rumor will spread through the entire village of Loch Fairbairn and probably to Balla-chulish too. I have family in both places. I have family everywhere. Cannae escape them if I wanted to, and even if I tried, they would hunt me down like a pack of wolves.

They only do it because they care. I understand that, but knowing why doesn't help me at all right now.

What am I going to do with Autumn? I have no idea how long it takes for a pregnancy to show. We might have weeks or months. Maybe I should ask Autumn about that, but I know if I see her again, I might snarl at her or make an even more unreasonable demand.

Or shag her.

Aye, maybe that's the answer. A good poke ought to ease my stress. A good, hard, hot poke.

Bod an Donais, ye dafty, that's not the solution.

Work is the only appropriate distraction, but I've rescheduled all my appointments. I have nothing left to do but sit here and picture Autumn naked. Her creamy skin. Those bonnie breasts. Her strong thighs. When we shag, she loves to grip me with those thighs and—

"*Mhac na galla*," I snarl.

I have nothing else to distract me if I'm not going to fantasize about Autumn. Nothing. My entire life is work. I spend time with my family too, but I can't do that now either. Not until I can explain what on earth I'm doing with my ex-wife. Since I don't have a clue, I can't explain it to anyone else.

But I need a distraction.

Playing games on my computer keeps me occupied for ten minutes, then I can't stand to do that anymore. I try crossword puzzles, but though I normally love doing those, I can't concentrate on deciphering the clues. For another half an hour, I struggle to read a psychology journal. That doesn't work either.

Someone knocks on my office door.

"Jack," Autumn says, "is it okay if I take a shower? There aren't any windows or telephones in the bathroom."

"Fine, aye, have a shower."

"Thank you."

Why is she so polite? I'm treating her like my prisoner.

Since she's going into the bathroom, I wait a few minutes and then leave my office. My mouth is dry, so I need to get a drink. But I can hear the water running in the shower, and my mind conjures a memory of that afternoon at the Loch Fairbairn Arms when Autumn had stepped into the shower with me.

Wet clothes. Wet hair. Deep, hot, penetrating kisses.

My *slat* twitches. Aye, my cock is ordering me to go into the bathroom and get my end away with the last woman on earth I should ever shag.

I mean to head for the kitchen to get a drink and maybe a piece, but my body seems to have a mind of its own. My feet drag me to the bathroom door.

The sound of water running like a warm rain in the shower makes blood rush to my groin, hardening my cock into a flaming erection that strains my trousers. I should walk away. And I definitely shouldn't listen to her softly humming a song I don't recognize, because hearing her voice triggers a resurgence of *that* memory.

Undressing her in the shower. Thrusting into her slick heat. Water sluicing over us while we both come.

Autumn stops humming, and a new sound starts up. It sounds like a mechanical hum.

What the…

She gasps, then begins to pant in an ever-quickening rhythm.

My *slat* throbs because, aye, that sound is familiar. I know what she's doing. My ex-wife is wanking off in the shower.

Autumn lets out a strangled cry. The mechanical hum ceases, and the shower shuts off.

I can't move a muscle. When I didn't want to move, my body overruled me. Now that I need to move my bloody erse, I can't convince even one muscle to work.

The door swings open.

Autumn's eyes go wide. "Jack? What are you doing?"

"I—Well—" What in the name of heaven can I say? She's wearing nothing but a towel.

Her gaze flicks down to my groin, and her lips curl up at the corners. "Guess the sound of running water makes you horny too. How come you never told me that? All those times we made love during a rainstorm, and I said how much I loved—"

"Never mind. I'm having a piece if you want one."

Before she can respond, I hurry to the kitchen.

I'm bent over, peering into the fridge, when Autumn strolls into the room.

She comes up alongside me, lays a hand on my back, and leans over to see what's inside the refrigerator. "Mm, I'm in the mood for something decadent."

My erection had gone away, but the sultry tone of her voice threatens to bring on another one.

"I don't have desserts," I say. "Only healthy food."

"Since when are you a health nut?" She rubs her hand over my back in slow circles. "I remember how you loved to get one of those cans of whipped cream and spray it all over my body. Then you would—"

"Enough, Autumn. Donnae need a reminder of things I'd rather forget."

"Oh, I see." She straightens and puckers her lips. "It's okay for you to hold me hostage, but I can't reminisce about those twelve days in Vegas when you acted like a real human being."

"I'm always a real human being."

"Not with me, you weren't. Not after you brought me home to Scotland, anyway."

She might have a valid point, but I can't think about that right now. Autumn isn't wearing a towel anymore, but her billowing dress is semi-translucent, giving me glimpses of those luscious curves.

"I'm not hungry anymore," I say, then I grab a bottle of water and slam the refrigerator door. "Eat anything you like."

Before she can speak, I whirl around and stalk out of the kitchen. I hesitate in the living room. Though I want to run outside and as far away from her as possible—aye, I'm that sort of coward—I realize I can't do that. Someone would see me. My brother or one of my army of relatives will hear I've left the house and hunt me down for an interrogation. I still don't have a bleeding clue how to explain my new, ah, living situation.

Muttering a Gaelic curse under my breath, I hurry into my office and shut the door.

What will I do now? I've canceled all my appointments.

I'm sitting in my chair, elbows on the desktop and head in my hands, when *she* knocks on the door again.

"Jack? Are you okay?"

"Fine, aye. Go away."

"That's not a very nice thing to say to your pregnant ex-wife."

I lift my head, my gaze aimed at the door. She sounded sarcastic when she told me that, but I am behaving like a *bod ceann*. Something about Autumn has always turned me into a bampot. I went completely off my head in Las Vegas, but at least we'd been getting along then. She's right about one thing. I turned into a different sort of bampot when I brought her to Scotland.

"May I come in?" she asks.

A sigh groans out of me. "Yes, all right."

The door opens, and Autumn sashays into the room. She settles onto the chair across the desk from me and glances around like she's looking for something. "Where's the couch? I thought therapists always had one of those."

"That's a cliché. I prefer chairs." I point toward a pair of high-backed, upholstered chairs positioned at either side of the window seat. "Therapy sessions take place over there."

"Oh, I get it. More psycho-manipulation, huh? Create a cozy little space by the window so your patients will feel less icky about sharing super-personal stuff."

"Everything you just said is an insult to my career and my skills."

"Once that stick wedged itself up your ass, you never wanted to yank it out, did you?"

"If you plan on insulting me all afternoon—"

"No, Jack, I don't plan on doing that." She arches her back, shoving a hand behind it to massage her muscles. "Could we talk in the living room? This chair is making my back hurt. And my ass. And, well, basically every part of me."

"We could sit over there." I wave toward the two chairs by the window.

"Those don't look any more comfortable."

Now she's insulting my furniture. What sin did I commit that warrants this kind of torture? My irritating ex-wife will be in my life forever, thanks to the bairn growing in her belly.

If she weren't so sexy, maybe I could deal with the situation in a more mature fashion.

"All right," I say, rising. "Let's talk in the living room."

She gets up and follows me out there, where I reclaim the chair I'd sat in earlier and she takes a seat on the sofa, propping her feet on the coffee table.

Autumn leans back, resting her head on the sofa, and sighs. Her lips curve up the slightest bit. "Much better."

I brace my ankle on the opposite knee and drum my fingers on my chair's arm. "What did you want to talk about?"

"Us. How we're going to co-parent."

I grunt.

She warps her mouth into a strange expression of annoyance. "Grunting is not a response."

"You don't want to hear my solution."

"How do you know unless you tell me?" She lifts her head to squint at me. "Are you still stuck on the silly idea we have to get married?"

"It's not silly. My family is very traditional."

"Uh-huh." She sits up straighter, her gaze nailed to mine. "Have you forgotten you told me all about your family? Wouldn't let me meet them, wouldn't even let them see me or speak to me on the phone, but you told me lots about them. Like how Erica was two months pregnant when she married Lachlan. Rory slept with Emery the night they met, then he convinced her to sign on for a marriage of convenience designed to last only one year. And what about Iain? He was a professor who slept with a student and got her pregnant, though he didn't know about that until thirteen years later."

I can't help staring at her. Maybe I vaguely recall talking about my family, but I can't believe I said all of that. I have only one excuse for it.

Autumn turns me into a stark-raving bampot.

"What my cousins have done is irrelevant," I say. "Ma and Da are very traditional. They won't understand how I could marry a woman I met in Las Vegas, then divorce her less than two months later after she walked out on me. And they really won't understand the two of us having sex in the Loch Fairbairn Arms, then going our separate ways. And as for the bairn..."

"You are so full of shit, Jack. What's the real reason you don't want anyone to know we're having a baby?"

My mouth opens. I can't speak, though. Can't think.

Autumn smirks. "Yeah, that's what I thought."

"I haven't said anything."

"Your silence told me everything I need to know."

Groaning, I sink back in my chair.

"Okay," she says, raising her hands in a conciliatory gesture, "on to a different question. Will you at least try to answer this one?"

"Yes." Promising to try doesn't mean I *will* answer.

She sets her hands on her knees and looks straight at me again. "Did you ever love me?"

Magairlean. That means bollocks.

Chapter Nine

Jack stares at me, seeming not to move a single muscle in his body, not even to blink. Is he breathing? Of course he is. Even Jack isn't so uptight that he stops breathing when I ask him a simple question. Why is it so hard for him to answer? Either he loved me or he didn't. A yes or no is all that's required, but he keeps staring at me like I've asked whether he wants to jump into a vat of boiling acid.

"What?" he finally says.

"Did you ever love me, that's what I asked."

Jack's mouth opens, but no sound comes out of it. He snaps his jaw shut, and his stunned expression evaporates. Now he's clenching his jaw. "The one who walked out with no explanation gets to answer that question first."

How did I not anticipate that response? Jack thinks I won't answer, and maybe he's right. I'm not sure what I can say. Did I love him? I thought so at the time, but now… Jeez, I have no idea. The way he's behaving today has me so confused I can't understand anything, not even my own feelings. But I shouldn't blame him for my confusion. I did show up at his house with no warning and drop a giant bombshell on him.

We can't go on arguing and sniping at each other. Our lives have changed. We need to find a way to compromise.

Jack shakes his head, twisting his lips into an irritated slant. "You expect me to answer questions that you won't answer. Nothing's changed."

My first impulse is to deny I have any culpability. But I can't do that. More is at stake here than my pride or his.

"Okay, fine," I say. "You want my answer? I don't know, Jack. Our relationship was a whirlwind, and I never had the chance to figure out anything. Did I love you? In Vegas, I was sure I'd fallen head over heels. That's all I can tell you."

He exhales a long breath, slumping in his chair. "I don't know either. For those twelve days, I thought I was... I don't know. In love, I suppose."

I can't help feeling a little wounded by that statement. In love, he supposed? My answer wasn't any less vague, so I shouldn't be upset. But I can't help it. I am hurt by it.

"Guess it doesn't matter how we feel about each other," I say. "We need to get along for the sake of our child, period."

Jack scrunches his lips, an expression I remember well. It means he's kind of annoyed, and he thinks I'm being unreasonable. "We can't get along unless you explain why you ran away the first time."

"The first time? You're the one who ran the second time."

"Deflection won't work, Autumn. I'm a therapist, remember? So tell me why you left me."

I'd known I would have to explain myself eventually. I was kind of hoping it wouldn't be right here, right now. Can I still use jet lag as an excuse to wriggle out of this conversation? I've slept a lot today, so no, I guess I can't reasonably use that excuse.

Damn.

I think back to that day not quite two years ago when I'd walked out, and everything I'd felt at that moment comes rushing back, constricting my throat. I'm not crying, not yet, but the pricking of tears that might flow stings in my eyes. How can I still be this emotional about something that happened so long ago? Two years isn't that long ago, but sometimes it feels like yesterday. Other times, it feels like forever.

Taking a shaky breath doesn't help. It's hormones, nothing more.

You're so full of shit, woman.

I can't look at Jack when I speak, so I look at my hands. "Those twelve days in Vegas were amazing. You were so passionate and fun and exciting to be with. I fell for that guy, the one who swept me off my feet and made me feel like nothing else existed in the world but the two of us. I'd never slept with a guy five minutes after meeting him until I met you."

My eyes want me to glance at him, but I won't do it.

"Aye," he says, "those were good days."

Good? For me, it had been like the best dream ever, except I wasn't sleeping. It had been real.

I have to keep talking, to explain the best I can. "When you suggested we should get married, and do it right then, I didn't hesitate. Even when you wanted to take me home to Scotland with you, I was so excited." I rub my palms up and down my thighs because they've gotten clammy all of a sudden. "But once we got here, everything changed. You changed. I wanted to meet your family, but you wouldn't let me. At least you didn't hold me hostage. But it felt like you were ashamed of me, ashamed that you'd married a gauche American you'd known for less than two weeks. That hurt me, Jack, a lot."

"That's why you left," he says in a flat voice. "Because I didn't rush to introduce you to my family."

"No. Well, yes, but that's only part of it." I hug myself, but the chill shivering through me has nothing to do with the air temperature. "You shut the door on me, Jack. Having a conversation with you was like talking to a computer that speaks only Gaelic. Every time I tried to have a serious talk, you would run away to your office or your family. Now you're complaining because I don't want to talk about the most painful time of my life. Can't you see how hypocritical that is? I had no one to run to for comfort. No one."

"You have family. Never wanted to talk about them, only mentioned your parents and your sister once, but you do have them."

"I can't go to them. It's...complicated."

He sighs. "I'm not the only one who doesn't like to talk. You still haven't explained—"

"Yeah, I know. I'm getting to that." How can I explain something even I don't understand? The longer I'd been with Jack, the more miserable I felt. Why? I still can't figure that out. "I wish I had an easy answer for you, but I don't. I felt like you had abandoned me, and it became painfully obvious you wished you hadn't married me."

"I never said that."

A smart retort wants to burst out of me, but I won't be the bitchy ex-wife. Not anymore.

"On that last day," I tell him, "I asked if you loved me, if you still wanted me around. You didn't say anything."

"You gave me an ultimatum. Or have you conveniently forgotten? You said I had to trot you out in public, in front of my family, or you would leave."

"I asked to meet them, that's all. Why was that impossible for you to do?"

He stays silent for several seconds until I can't stand it any longer and have to look at him. His expression is stony, like he doesn't care about anything I've said.

"You were ashamed of me," I say. "Since you wouldn't say anything, I had to assume that was the problem. I told you I needed to get away from Scotland for a while. I begged you to come with me to America, but you did worse than say no. You said nothing." I slump against the sofa, struggling not to cry. I hate tears. I hate feeling this way again, but I have no choice. I can't run away anymore. "So I left. But you're the one who filed for divorce so fast I got whiplash. I mean, it only took a few days."

"Why wait? I wanted closure. And it took a week, not a few days."

"But jeez, you sent me a text message the day after I flew back to America saying our marriage was over."

"I didn't use the word divorce, did I? You assumed that's what it meant. We were still married until a week after you abandoned our marriage." His expression turns hard, more than stony, more like a steel-reinforced shell has clapped down over his face. "So if you fucked someone else during that time, you're an adulteress as well as a coward."

"Adulteress? Do you seriously think I was sleeping with other guys the second I got home?"

He shrugs one shoulder. "Donnae know what you did. Considering how quickly you gave up and went home, I assumed you wanted someone who would shag you incessantly. You did keep telling me I wasn't giving you everything you needed."

"Why did you assume that meant sex?" I slide forward like I'm going to get up, but I freeze perched on the sofa's edge. Even my body seems to be confused. "For heaven's sake, Jack, is that what you think of me? All I care about is sex?"

"You complained I wasn't as exciting once I brought you home with me."

I want to make him believe I never cheated on him and he meant more to me than sex. But why do I feel the need? If he wants to think the worst of me, he can go for it—as long as his opinions don't affect our child. Arguing won't help anything. My need to convince him of the truth does not mean I'm still in love with him. I don't even know if I ever was.

Liar, a tiny and very annoying voice in my head whispers.

Shut up, I tell it.

No, I don't love him anymore. No way. That little voice is full of crap.

My back has started to ache. I get up and stretch, then pace the width of the room in front of Jack. "How did you get a divorce in a week? That seems ridiculously fast."

"My cousin Rory, who's a solicitor, helped me get a divorce in Guam. I had to be in residence there for seven days, but then it was over."

"I don't understand. You live in Scotland. Why file for divorce in Guam?"

He knifes a hand through his hair, his focus on the floor. "In Scotland, there needs to be a one-year separation before the parties can start divorce proceedings. But you're a US resident, and Guam is a US territory, so it was easier to dissolve the marriage there. Don't you remember the papers I sent you? They explained everything."

"Yeah, but I had no idea divorce would come through so fast." I turn around, starting another circuit across the room. "What was the rush? Couldn't wait to get rid of me, huh?"

He raises his face to me, but it reveals nothing. "*You* got rid of *me*. I sped up the paperwork, that's all."

Since I don't know what to say to that, I don't bother trying to respond.

I want to ask him something, though it's not my place to butt my nose into his personal affairs. But I need to know, and maybe the truth will help us make peace.

Yeah, I won't hold my breath for that.

Still, I can't stop myself from asking. I'm standing six feet from his chair, facing him, when I finally give in to the impulse. He's watching me with an unreadable expression, like he had done while I was pacing, except then his eyes had tracked my every movement. Now, his gaze is glued to mine.

I start to feel itchy all over, which is so stupid.

Clearing my throat, I ask, "How many women have you been with since we, um, went our separate ways?"

He raises a single brow. "Donnae see how that's any of your concern."

"We need to be honest with each other, Jack." I feel the urge to remind him he's the therapist in the room and should already know that. But I realized about thirty seconds after I walked into this house that he's beyond stressed out. So I won't chastise him for not behaving like a psychologist. "Maybe it isn't strictly my business, but I'd appreciate a forthright answer."

Jack says nothing for several seconds, though he keeps watching me. Then he shifts his gaze to the wall. "None."

It feels like time stops for a long moment, like the entire world has ceased to exist except for this little bubble inside this house. None? No, that can't be right. He's a passionate, virile man.

His response has me so stunned that I blurt out, "You mean you didn't sleep with anybody until after the divorce came through, right?"

Though he keeps staring at the wall, he shakes his head slowly. "I haven't been with anyone but you since the night we met."

My brain, or maybe it's my heart, insists that has to mean something. But I know better than to indulge in the fantasy that Jack had pined for me for twenty months.

He swerves his attention to me, his face a stoic mask. "How many men have you shagged since you abandoned our marriage?"

"None. I've only been with you since the night we met."

Does he believe me? I have no idea. His impenetrable stoicism tells me nothing. Maybe it does mean something that neither of us has slept with anyone else, but talking about that seems like a bad idea right now. I got one honest response from him. That's enough for today.

A word he used twice resurfaces in my mind. Abandoned, that was the word. Twice he said I abandoned our marriage. Does he mean I abandoned him? I guess I had, kind of. The fact he used that word twice must mean something, but I'm too jet-lagged and shell-shocked to figure it out right now.

Jack heaves his body out of the chair. "I'll be in my office."

"Doing what?"

"Paperwork."

He heads down the hall, disappearing through his secret door.

I swear I hear a lock click. Does he seriously need to lock the door to keep me away? He must be either furious or emotionally raw. Not sure which option is worse.

He's scared, that's for sure. But he won't tell me why.

And yeah, I'm scared too. Terrified, actually. If Jack and I can't reach some kind of détente, I don't know what will happen. The only certainty is that I will do whatever is necessary to protect my baby.

Chapter Ten

Jack

I've resorted to hiding in my office like a bleeding coward. No wonder Autumn walked out on me after six weeks of marriage. I need to get a grip, but I can't seem to find anything to grab onto, which means I won't be getting a grip anytime soon. The "paperwork" I'd claimed I'd be working on doesn't exist. All my client notes are up to date, all my bills are paid, and I haven't got a ruddy thing to do right now except sit here and think about Autumn and the bairn on the way.

After ten minutes of that, I feel like I'm going insane.

That's when I decide to alphabetize the books on the shelves behind my desk. That keeps me busy for a while, but mostly because I have trouble figuring out how to alphabetize all the books that have multiple authors as well as editors. Calli, the wife of my cousin Aidan, is a librarian. She could help me with this, but I can't ring her. She'll want to come over here to show me how to catalog or classify or whatever the hell it is she does to organize books. Since I'm currently holding my ex-wife hostage, I can't let anyone inside the house.

I get on my computer and search for instructions on how to arrange books the librarian way. It's so bloody confusing and complicated that I get a headache after a few minutes of trying to sort out the instructions. Aye, this was a brilliant idea. Calli has a master's degree in library science. My PhD is in psychology, so I'm completely unqualified for the job.

A phone rings elsewhere in the house.

The one in the kitchen. It has to be.

"*Mhac na galla*," I hiss, and I rush out there to stop Autumn from answering. I told her not to, but she did speak to my brother through the front door, so I'm not sure I can trust her not to pick up the phone.

I've raced to the kitchen doorway when I realize she's not in there.

"Ahem," Autumn says from somewhere behind my back. "Looking for me? I wasn't going to grab the phone, you know. I said I wouldn't, and I keep my word."

Except when she vowed to love, honor, and cherish me forever. I should've made her vow to obey me instead of the modern version of the vows.

The phone rings one more time, then goes to the answering machine.

I finally turn my entire body toward Autumn.

She's sitting in my chair. Well, the one I'd sat in earlier at any rate.

"This is Dr. Jack MacTaggart," my recorded voice announces via the answering machine. "I'm away right now, but leave a message so I can get back to you. If this is a client emergency, please ring my mobile."

A beep follows.

"Now you're away, are you?" Callum says, his tone more sarcastic than earlier when he'd knocked on the door. "Would that be 'away' as in getting your end away? Or away with the fairies?"

That sodding ersehole. What is he doing?

I spin around, intending to run to the phone and grab it before Callum says anything else, but I trip and nearly fall down. While I curse under my breath and struggle to get my footing, my brother keeps talking.

"Autumn, if you're listening, donnae mind my brother. Jack is uptight, and that makes him go off his head over things like having a poke with his ex-wife." Callum pauses, then sighs. "Donnae worry, Jack. I didn't tell anyone she's there. Though I really think you should tell Ma and Da. They've wanted to meet Autumn since the day you announced you'd married an American lass. What's the state secret, eh? Does she have a beard? Or three legs?"

I snatch up the phone. "Haud yer wheesht, ye bleeding *tolla-thon*."

"You're calling me an ersehole? You're the one who's got your ex-wife locked up like a prisoner. She must be very bonnie if you're keeping her as your private sex slave."

"Stop talking, Callum. And donnae tell anyone I answered the phone because I willnae be doing that ever again."

He chuckles. "You'll never answer your phone again? All those clients of yours will be frothing at the mouth after a few days of that. Or have you shipped them all off to an asylum? Jack MacTaggart's Private Clinic for the Unwanted."

"You are not funny. If you tell anyone Autumn is here—"

"I know, I know. You'll sick Logan on me, right? After all, Dr. Jack Mac-Taggart never gets angry, and he certainly never shouts or assaults anyone."

He thinks I'll have our cousin, the former MI-6 agent, batter him in my stead.

Bollocks. How did I come to this point? I know exactly how. I had sex with my ex-wife in a hotel room, multiple times, and didn't even think about using protection.

Now I'm stuck with her forever.

Is that a bad thing? I can't decide. But when I think, for only a second or two, about Autumn leaving, I feel...odd. Almost queasy. Does that mean I still have feelings for her?

No, that's rot.

"Goodbye, Callum," I say and hang up the phone.

My brother won't tell anyone about Autumn. He might be an enormous pain in the erse, but he never betrays a confidence.

I turn around and see Autumn still sitting in that chair. "Never mind my brother. The *cacan* thinks he's helping."

"What's a *cacan?*"

"The word is Gaelic for 'wee shit,' which is what Callum's acting like."

Her lips tighten and curve up a touch. "I like him. He's funny."

"Annoying as hell is more like it."

She watches me for a moment while I resist the urge to scratch myself everywhere. "Callum is a firefighter, right?"

"He used to be. Had an accident six months ago and quit his job."

"What does he do now?"

I can't stop my fingers from scratching my neck. "Nothing interesting."

"Oh come on, Jack. Give me a little info. If I can't meet your family, you could at least satisfy my curiosity."

"Callum is—"

I'm saved from needing to explain because the phone starts ringing again. Autumn gives me a peeved look as I spin around but freeze when I realize I can't answer the phone. Not even if it's Callum. Especially not if it isn't him. How can I explain to anyone what I'm doing? Hiding my ex-wife? They'll think I've gone insane.

Which I probably have done.

My recorded greeting plays, followed by the beep.

"Hello, Jack, you sneaky sod. I've heard a rumor your ex-wife is on the premises. I suppose you're too busy shagging her to answer the phone, aren't you?"

Alex Thorne, that monumental *tolla-thon*, sounds too smug and pleased with the situation, like it's a bloody great joke.

"I understand if you and Autumn need time to get…reacquainted," Alex says, and he makes getting reacquainted sound like the worst sort of debauchery. "I'll leave you to it, then. But you should know that Lachlan happened to drive past your house right when Autumn walked inside, so the grapevine is positively sizzling with the news. Don't do anything I wouldn't do. What am I saying? You know I'll do almost anything, so I should amend that statement to say 'don't get in too much trouble.' Cheers, Jack."

Thankfully, he hangs up.

I turn back to Autumn.

She's standing now, and watching me with her gaze narrowed and her lips puckered, not to mention her arms crossed over her chest.

And that posture pushes her breasts up, which inexorably drags my focus to them.

"Who was that?" she asks.

"Alex Thorne."

"Would that be the same Alex Thorne who set up our blind date?"

I stifle a growl. "No, I have ten mates called Alex Thorne. What do you think?"

She rolls her eyes and huffs.

"What are you wanting me to say or do?" I demand. "Should I have picked up the call and told Alex to piss off? Or would you rather I invited him over for a tea party?"

"Neither. Both. I don't know." She rubs her forehead, her entire posture sagging. "I'm sorry."

"It's all right. And I'm sorry too." I glance at the clock on the microwave. "It's time for dinner. Why don't you relax on the sofa while I make us some food?"

"Okay." She lays a hand over her belly. "Nothing too fancy. Don't think my tummy would like that."

"Are you all right? Should I take you to a doctor?"

"No, I'm fine, I swear. Just wiped out and stressed out. So please stop threatening to drag me to a hospital."

I can't stop myself from walking to her and clasping her upper arms, then rubbing them gently. "Rest. I'll bring you some plain food."

"Thank you, Jack."

Making dinner takes my mind off the problems at hand, or rather, the problem at hand. But the distraction only works for so long since I can't keep cooking all night and all day tomorrow, certainly not for the rest of eternity, though it would be brilliant if I could. As Autumn pointed out, I am a therapist. I should know how to deal with the situation.

After a good night's sleep, I'll be better equipped to figure out…everything. Well, at least one thing. Or half of one thing.

We eat in the living room with Autumn on the sofa while I take the chair. I turn on the television, and we watch a ridiculous comedy show while we finish our meal. After that, I drop the dishes off in the kitchen and come back to the living room to watch murder mystery shows for the rest of the evening. Neither of us speaks. I let Autumn have control of the TV remote, and I don't comment on her choice of entertainment. I don't even say anything when the psychologist in one episode spouts utter rubbish. When it turns out the bloke shagged five of his clients and murdered two of them, I decide it doesn't matter that he spewed all that rubbish after all.

At ten p.m., just as the mantel clock chimes the hour, we've both had enough. Since Autumn has been yawning off and on for an hour, I announce, "It's time for bed."

"Uh-huh," she says while yawning. "Thanks for watching TV with me. It's nice to have company."

I escort her down the hall to the spare bedroom. "Do you need anything? More blankets, more pillows, more—"

"Breathe, Jack. I'm fine, the baby's fine, and we will figure all of this out, eventually. Tonight, we both need to sleep."

"Aye, we do." I lean in like I'm going to kiss her, then freeze inches from her face when I suddenly realize I'm not meant to be kissing her anymore, not even to say good night. We're divorced. I straighten and clear my throat. "Good night, Autumn. Sleep well."

Her eyes are wider than usual, and she seems to have stopped blinking. "Good night, Jack."

I watch her go into her room. She gives me a small, sweet smile just as she shuts the door.

And I go to bed.

What might happen next, I have no idea. Whatever comes, I can't deny one inescapable truth. My ex-wife will be in my life permanently, but I can't decide if that's good, bad, or…something else.

Chapter Eleven

Autumn

The sun shines through the window, glowing through my lids while I let my mind slowly rise to the surface of wakefulness. When I flutter my lids open and yawn, I glance at the clock on the table. I've slept until ten fifteen. Wow, I was more exhausted than I realized. Since I fell asleep the second my head hit the pillow last night, that means I've slept for about twelve hours.

I feel fantastic this morning, despite the stress of everything that's happened between me and Jack. I feel oddly horny too. Pregnancy hasn't affected me like this until now. Until yesterday. Until I saw Jack. Damn, that man is still hot.

But sex is a horrible idea. I'll stick to getting off in the shower with my vibrator standing in for Jack. Not there's any comparison. I remember in vivid detail what sex with him is like. During our twelve-day courtship in Vegas, he'd been so passionate, so adventurous, so…incredible. It had been more than hot sex, though. He'd made me laugh so hard my eyes watered and told me all about his family, including his many cousins and the Americans some of them had married. He'd joked that he should marry me since I'm American.

I had assumed he was joking, at least. Two days later, I realized he was serious. We were naked in bed, having just enjoyed amazing sex, when Jack sat up and smiled at me like I was the sun and he hadn't seen my light in months.

"You're wonderful," he said. "Bonnie and sweet and fiery, full of wild energy, and clever too. I've told you several times I need to go home soon, but tonight I realized I cannae leave without you, Autumn."

"I don't want you to leave either, Jack."

He picked up my hand, fluttering his lips over my knuckles. "Marry me, Autumn. Tonight. This city has chapels that are open twenty-four hours. Let's get dressed and go to the nearest one. I need to be married to you, *mo gaoloch*."

I couldn't do anything except gape at him. "Are you serious?"

"Aye." He straddled my body, bending his arms so he could kiss me. "Cannae live without you, *gràidh*."

Warmth had blossomed in my chest, the sweetest warmth I'd ever experienced, and it brought with it a kind of euphoria that swept through me with intoxicating power. "Yes, Jack, let's get married. I can't live without you either."

Half an hour later, we stood face to face inside a chapel decorated like a casino. Statues of Elvis flanked the altar while the King's ballad "Love Me Tender" played through loudspeakers. The officiant dressed like Elvis from the fifties, but thankfully, he didn't imitate the singer's voice. I love Elvis, but come on, who wants to hear the wedding spiel in that voice? It's too weird.

Our witnesses were two Elvis impersonators.

So yeah, our marriage began in a totally traditional way.

Maybe that was why it had ended. Sure, I can blame the Elvis impersonators, right? That makes complete sense. No, it wasn't how we met or how we got married that doomed us. Jack had changed once we arrived in Scotland, and I still have no idea why.

I get up and get dressed, then head for the bathroom.

Jack is just walking out of the bathroom, and he stops inches away from running into me. "Autumn. You're awake. I mean, good morning."

"Good morning to you too, Jack." The fact he's wearing a towel that seems to be held up only by his hand does not alleviate my horniness problem. Damn, he looks good all damp and half-naked. But there will be no reprisal of our steamy shower two months ago. "Did you sleep okay?"

"Yes. What about you?"

"Great. I feel fabulous this morning." I wish he'd shaved, but no, he hasn't done that yet. He's got sexy stubble, and combined with his bare chest, that makes me so turned on it's getting ridiculous.

"Were you wanting a shower? I can get dressed in my room."

"No, I'm good. Had a shower yesterday." I wave toward the other end of the hall. "I'll go make breakfast. You've been cooking for me, so now it's my turn."

"You don't need to do that."

"I don't mind, really. I love cooking, remember?"

"Aye. But you're pregnant."

"Which doesn't mean I'm incapacitated." I feel my lips tightening into a smile. Can't help it. He's being adorably silly. "You told me all sorts of stories about how your cousins acted when their wives' got pregnant. They wouldn't let those girls so much as lift a feather. You made lots of sarcastic comments about that, but now you're doing the same thing."

"I—No, it's different."

Stifling a laugh makes me splutter, though only a little. "Different how, exactly?"

He screws up his mouth, but it takes a few seconds before he manages to speak. "Donnae know. It just is."

"That's one convincing argument you've come up with."

Jack eyes my hair, his mouth crimped. "First, it was blue. Now, it's pink. What's next? Lime green?"

"Yeah, maybe I'll go green just to annoy you."

His gaze gravitates to my chest, where my low-cut top reveals a portion of my breasts. The nipples are jutting, in part because it's a little chilly here in the hallway, but also because he looks so damn sexy. His mouth slides into a slow, sensual smile.

I throw my hands up. "Oh no, Jack, not again. We've done the whole inappropriate-sex thing already, and it did not work out well."

The sex was amazing, but the consequences hadn't been. Not that I regret this baby. I could never feel that way.

Jack tosses his towel over his shoulder. It falls into a lump on the floor.

And I get my first good look at his equipment since that afternoon in the hotel. It's not fair for him to be so gorgeous and skilled in bed. Maybe I'm shallow since I fall for it every time he shows off that body.

But not today. No sex until we've worked through our issues.

I mean no sex, period. Ever.

He grabs his clothes off the sink counter and pushes past me.

Does he rub his dick against me on purpose? I think he does. *You rat, Jack.*

He pauses to whisper in my ear, "The bathroom is yours. Do whatever you like, but you don't need a vibrator. I'll make you feel better than any mechanical device can."

With that, he walks away.

I go into the bathroom, but only because I need to pee. Getting dressed in my bedroom, with the door locked, seems like the prudent approach. The bathroom has no lock on the door, and I can't risk Jack sneaking into the shower with me.

Not that I want a shower. I had one yesterday and still feel plenty clean.

A memory of Jack in the hotel shower flares in my mind.

I tell that memory to go jump in a lake. Or a loch. That's what Scots call a lake, right? It's been a while since I needed to think about the Scottish versions of words.

No more lusting for Jack. None. Zero. I'm over it.

But I do change my mind about the shower, strictly to wash the temporary pink color out of my blonde hair. Unnatural shades seem to make Jack uneasy, and I'm trying to be cooperative.

I'm in the kitchen making breakfast when Jack saunters into the room. He's wearing jeans and a T-shirt that clings to his body, highlighting every muscle. Has he dressed that way on purpose? To make me lustful? Not that I need any help in that department. Jack has always been the Achilles heel of my willpower.

He stops on the other side of the island from me. "Pancakes? Shouldn't you eat something healthier?"

Great. Now he wants to tell me how to eat.

"For your information," I say, "these are whole wheat pancakes with blueberries. And besides, I see an awful lot of unhealthy foods in your fridge."

"You're pregnant. I'm not."

I point my spatula at him. "The man who's holding me hostage shouldn't be so hypocritical about food."

"You are not a hostage." He punches a hand through his hair and avoids looking at me. "If you want to go outside, we can eat breakfast on the patio. It overlooks the garden."

"That sounds lovely. Thank you." I flip a pancake while Jack watches my movements like it's the most fascinating thing he's ever seen. "Do I get phone privileges yet? Or front-door privileges?"

He flattens his lips, but they seem to be trying to kick up at the corners anyway. "If you need to make a call, you can use the phone. I would prefer you didn't answer calls until I decide how to tell my family about you and the baby."

"Sure, I get that. I won't go out the front door, but I'd like to be outside sometimes, even when you're not with me. Okay?"

"Aye." His brows knit together. "Why are you being so amenable today? I'm a hostage-taker."

"No, you're stressed, that's all. I am too. We need to cut each other, and ourselves, a little slack."

"That makes sense." He comes around to my side of the island. "Let me do the rest of the pancakes. You can start on whatever else you planned to cook."

"I saw some Lorne sausage in there. Thought it would go nicely with the pancakes."

"Aye, that does sound good."

We collaborate on the rest of the meal, whipping up some panfried potatoes too, and I set the table while Jack finishes up with the food. The house doesn't have a formal dining room, so instead, there's a table in the kitchen by the window. Jack had suggested we could eat outside, but a few minutes later, I decide eating in the kitchen is fine with me. It will make Jack feel better. He must've guessed I'm placating him, but he doesn't say anything about it. I'm doing what I said, cutting him some slack. I'll go outside later, if the weather's nice, but we're having our breakfast here.

Though we eat in silence, he finishes before I do—and he asks me a question I hadn't expected. Maybe I should've expected it, but for some reason, I never imagined Jack might ask me this.

"Do you think I'll be a good father?" he asks.

"Of course you will."

"How can you think that? I haven't treated you very well."

I swallow my last bite of food and set my fork down. "Jack, you're a good person. The fact we didn't work as a couple doesn't mean we can't be good parents. Isn't that what you'd tell your patients?"

"Clients." He leans back in his chair and gazes out the window, his expression pensive. "Yes, that's what I would tell any of my clients. It's different when I'm the one dealing with a surprise bairn."

"And a surprise visit from your ex-wife."

"That too."

"I understand if you need to hide out in your office again. But I think I'll go outside and enjoy the garden."

He nods, his focus still on the view outside the window. "Maybe I'll join you later."

"That would be nice."

We clear the table and wash the dishes, then Jack retreats into his office with the door closed. I don't blame him for needing alone time. I could use a bit of that too. The fact he wants to join me outside later shouldn't make me feel excited, but it does. No, not excited. It's more like…I'm anticipating the chance to talk to him more.

Yeah, that's all.

Chapter Twelve

Jack

Yes, I'm hiding in my office again. Unlike yesterday, this morning I manage to read several journals that I'd been meaning to read for months. Nothing like a surprise visit from my ex-wife and a surprise baby announcement to knock a man off-kilter. At least I'm not holding Autumn hostage anymore. She volunteered to ignore both visitors who knock on the door and every nosy *bod ceann* who rings the house phone.

Autumn is bonnie. And I'm still attracted to her. That doesn't mean I love her or that I've missed her.

Will I be a good father? Autumn assured me I will. But she would say that, wouldn't she? Telling me I'll be rubbish for sure wouldn't be the intelligent thing to do, and Autumn is very clever.

Once I've finished off my entire backlog of journals, I find Autumn in the living room and suggest we go out into the backyard. She was outside earlier, which I know because I might've peeked out my office window to see her. When I suggest going out into the garden together, she grins and leaps off the sofa like I've invited her to tour the village and meet all my relatives and friends. I know I should introduce her to my family, at least my brother and my parents, but I can't face them yet. How will I explain why I married a woman I'd known for twelve days, then brought her home but refused to let anyone see even a photograph of her, then she left me six weeks later and we got divorced? I suppose it would be much easier now if I had told them everything two years ago.

Autumn and I walk out the back door into the yard. A stone wall surrounds the space, and the half of it that contains the garden has flower-covered trellises. A few bushes fill out the floral display, but there's also a birdbath and a sundial.

"It's beautiful," Autumn says. "So many flowers and—Oh! Is that a birdbath?"

"Aye, it is."

"You have a gorgeous garden, Jack. Never knew you were into flowers."

"The garden came with the house."

She clasps her hands under her chin, smiling with the sweetest look of excitement and happiness. "Thank you for letting me come out here." She inhales deeply, her eyes shutting for a moment. "It smells heavenly out here. Mind if I explore the garden?"

"Go on. I'll keep you company."

While she wanders among the flowers and I walk beside her, we talk about inconsequential things like whether those are roses or carnations on that bush in the corner. I haven't got a bloody clue, and I tell her that.

"How can you not know?" she asks. "It's your garden."

"I told you it came with the house. I pay someone to keep it in good condition."

"Oh, I see. How long have you lived here?"

"Eighteen months."

She pauses in front of a bush that has flowers I do recognize—irises, my mother's favorite. "So you moved back to your hometown a few months after, um…"

"You abandoned me? Aye, that's right." Why do I keep saying she abandoned me? I used that word more than once yesterday, but I have no idea why. She left me rather suddenly, but I never felt abandoned. That would mean I'd loved her.

"I'm sorry, Jack," Autumn says. "I shouldn't have left like that. It was selfish and stupid, and I've regretted it ever since."

"But you don't regret leaving me. Only how you did it."

"I don't know." She rubs her arms. "Everything happened so fast…"

"Are you cold?" I ask. "Maybe we should go back inside."

"No, I'm fine."

I study her and the way she's still whisking her palms up and down. "But you're rubbing your arms like you're cold."

She glances down as if she hadn't realized she'd been doing that. Her hands go still on her arms, then she shoves them into the pockets of her trousers. "I think it's a nervous gesture. I do that sometimes when I'm not cold, so it must be something like that."

"That would make sense. Neither of us likes talking about what happened back then."

"Why don't we not talk about it for a while, then? You know, like a moratorium on discussing the past. Just until we get comfortable with each other again."

"Sounds like a reasonable plan." Unlike every idea I've concocted since the moment she knocked on my door yesterday. "We could take a drive through the Highlands if you'd like. I can show you my favorite places."

Her eyes light up like I haven't seen since those days in Las Vegas. "Are you serious? You'll give me the grand tour? I wanted you to show me everything, but you were always too busy."

"No, I told you I was too busy. I could've taken the time, but I didn't. I'm sorry, Autumn."

I gaze into her eyes, and suddenly, I remember exactly how it felt to be with her when things were good. Laughter. Dancing. Teasing. And oh aye, lots of sex. I want to kiss her, need to kiss her, but I know I shouldn't do it. The memory of our last kiss, eight weeks ago in the Loch Fairbairn Arms, rushes through me complete with every sensation I'd experienced then. And I can't stop myself. I take her face in my hands and mold my lips to hers.

She stiffens.

Bod an Donais, the feel of her lips, it drives me mad. I've kissed other women, though no one except her since the day we met. I shouldn't feel this way from touching her lips, but my pulse accelerates, and my skin becomes so sensitized that I swear I can feel the air on my flesh. The scent of her, I can't get enough of it, sweet and feminine and intoxicating.

A breath rushes out of her nostrils, and even that makes me hungry for her. Her body relaxes as she lays her palms on my chest and leans into me. Her mouth relaxes too, and she moans softly.

I wrap my arms around her and thrust my tongue between her lips. The first taste of her makes my cock jerk. Her body feels warm and right in my arms, like I should've been doing this every day for the past twenty months, like our bodies were made for each other and no one else will ever do. I slide a hand down to her erse, cupping it.

She pulls away, stumbling backward one step. "This is a bad idea."

"Aye, it is." I move closer, settling my hands on her hips. "But those are the ideas that feel the best."

"Please don't seduce me. Not sure I could say no right now."

"We both want it. What's the harm?"

She laughs, but it sounds more nervous than cheerful. "Do I really need to remind you of all the ways our relationship went sideways? We had fantastic sex, but everything else was painful and devastating."

I freeze, gawping at her for a long moment. Painful and devastating? That's what she thinks of our marriage. Things had gotten tense, maybe even painful, but only at the end. Or am I fooling myself? Maybe I did treat her so horribly that she can't bear to sleep with me again.

Aye, that makes sense—if we both pretend that afternoon in the Loch Fairbairn Arms never happened. She wants me as much as I want her, and I see no reason why we shouldn't enjoy each other's bodies while we work out everything else.

I fold my arms over my chest. "We had a poke two months ago. If sex is such an awful idea, why did you beg me to make love to you over and over and over?"

"You're exaggerating. I only begged the one time."

"Aye. You said, 'Please, Jack, make love to me over and over and over, please.' That's what you wanted, so I gave it to you."

Her lips pucker, but with a teasing slant at the corners. "Oh-ho, I seem to remember a certain Scot pleading with me to ride him like a Highland lassie breaking a wild stallion."

I had said that? Maybe I sort of remember speaking words similar to those, but not exactly like that. I might've said something about…a bucking stallion. But I'm fair positive I did not beg her to fuck me.

Besides, we hadn't done it like that. We made love for hours. It had been tender and passionate, desperate even, but not wild. Las Vegas had been another story.

"Maybe I said that," I tell her, "but we didn't do anything wild. I think you're confusing Loch Fairbairn with Las Vegas."

"Yeah, I remember Vegas." She smiles in the sexy way she always does when she talks about shagging. "We did lots of crazy things back then. My favorite time was that night when we sneaked down to the casino at two a.m. and had sex up against a slot machine. You claimed you could make me come before the wheel stopped spinning, but I dared you to prove it. So you fed the machine some coins and pulled the lever, and we screwed each other's brains out while the wheels spun. You did make me come before the machine stopped."

"But we didn't hit a jackpot."

"Uh-uh. We hit the big O jackpot."

Orgasms, she means. I hadn't understood that the first time I ever heard her refer to climaxing as an O. We'd been in my suite in Las Vegas, naked and about to have sex for the first time, when she'd told me, "I know this is going to be amazing, and I can't wait to have you inside me. I desperately need a good hard O."

I'd asked what that meant, but she'd shown me instead of explaining. After giving me a bloody fantastic blow job, she'd smiled and said, "That's an O, Jack."

Here in the present, I tell her, "You said sex is a bad idea, but you're reminding me of our time in Las Vegas, when we shagged so often I had to buy a second box of condoms."

She grins. "Remember the night we met, when we got all the way up to your suite before we realized neither of us had any condoms? You ran downstairs barefoot to buy a box in the gift shop, and by the time you got back to the room, you had to lie on the bed to recover from all the running. You had taken the elevator to the lobby but ran the rest of the way."

"Aye, you drove me barmy with lust. I couldn't wait, and it only took me five minutes to get what we needed." I lower my arms and sigh. "All right, we won't have sex. If that's what you really want."

"Yes, please. I think that's the best way to go. Sex will confuse things."

She might have a point, and I will do my best not to seduce her, but I can't stop my body from wanting her.

Once she has explored the entire garden, we go back inside the house. Autumn wants to "veg out in front of the TV," so I tell her I'll do the same. Loafing isn't my strong suit, but I do feel a bit on edge and television shows might numb my brain for a while. I let her choose what we watch. Autumn turns on a documentary series about aliens and other bizarre nonsense. Still, I find myself getting engrossed in the ridiculous stories about ancient astronauts, a term I'd never heard before but learn means creatures from other planets supposedly visited Earth thousands of years ago.

After the third episode of the series, I have to ask her a question. "I don't remember you watching these programs while we were married. Is it a new obsession?"

"It's not an obsession, it's an interest. I've been watching these shows for years, but I figured you wouldn't like them, so I didn't let on that I love this stuff."

"Why would you do that to please me? I never asked you to change yourself for me."

"No, but I wanted our marriage to work. And you did call our wedding venue 'the most crackbrained sort of rubbish,' so I played it safe."

Had I said that? I must have done. Autumn might have faults, but she's no liar. In my defense, we got married in a place called The Chapel of the Eternal King Where Love, Peace, and Rock Live Forever. Aye, that was a mouthful. It had been the closest wedding venue within walking distance from the hotel. The chapel also featured crystal busts of Elvis and the Dalai Lama.

"I didn't mean to make you feel that way," I tell Autumn. "That chapel was barmy, though."

"Yeah, but it was a memorable wedding." She pulls her mobile out of her pocket, taps the screen several times, then aims it toward me. "This is my favorite picture of us."

The image shows me and Autumn standing at the altar of the chapel with an Elvis lookalike officiating. We're kissing because the officiant just announced we're husband and wife. We have our arms wrapped around each other.

Aye, that had been the best night of my life. Is she showing me that picture to make me sentimental? I doubt that, but seeing the image does make me feel…something. Maybe I should think about why that night was the best in my entire life.

"I like that picture too," I say, my throat suddenly thick.

She tucks her mobile back into her pocket. "What should we watch now? You can pick since I'll probably make you suffer through more 'barmy' stuff."

"You choose. I don't mind watching those programs."

Her lips kink upward, making her cheeks dimple. "Are you admitting—kinda, sorta, grudgingly—that you like my kooky shows?"

"Aye. 'Kinda, sorta, grudgingly.' That's the best I can offer at the moment."

"I'll take it." She grabs the remote control. "I think we're making progress. Don't you?"

"Yes, though I'm not sure what we're progressing toward."

"Friendship." She punches buttons on the remote until another episode of the outer space show starts playing. "That's a good thing. Wouldn't you say?"

"It's a very good thing indeed."

Chapter Thirteen

I wake up the next morning feeling more refreshed than yesterday and more hopeful for the future—for our future. Jack and I have made great progress toward becoming friends, which seems like a good thing considering we're stuck with each other forever, thanks to our impending parenthood. Maybe we haven't delved into those prickly issues from the past, like why he changed after we moved in together in Scotland and why I ran away from him. I'm not going to play the blame game, but we need to work through those issues together.

Jack gets that. I know he does. But sometimes he goes into Stubborn Jack mode and won't come out of it unless I kick him in the shin. Figuratively. I'm not going to actually kick him. Well, probably not. I suppose it depends on how deeply he digs his heels in.

Yeah, he's a mule. A big, sexy, Scottish mule.

I walk out of my room carrying an armful of clothes, heading for the bathroom so I can take a shower. The door to Jack's room is open, and I can see he's not in there. His office door is shut. I can't resist peeking into the living room and kitchen to see if he's there, but he isn't. Jack must be in his office.

My curiosity gets the better of me, a chronic disease I don't even try to cure, and I press my ear to the closed door.

Rhythmic breathing noises originate from inside the office.

Is he doing relaxation exercises? That seems unlikely since I haven't known Jack to go for that sort of thing. Given the rhythm and the sharpness of those exhalations, I can think of only one other thing he might be doing.

But I decide to be polite and knock on the door. "Jack? Are you in there?"

"Aye."

"Just wanted to say good morning."

"You can come in, Autumn. It's not locked."

I open the door and take a few steps, then stop dead when I see what he's doing. Not jerking off like I'd assumed. But what I see still sends a hot tingle racing over my skin.

Jack stands between his desk and the window—completely naked. He's holding hand weights, big ones, and doing curls with them. He exhales every time he lifts the weights. His biceps flex with every repetition, but I can't stop my focus from wandering over his entire body, not just his arms. Has he gotten more muscular since the last time we had sex? That was only eight weeks ago, so I kind of doubt that.

My attention lands on his dick and stalls there.

Admiring that part of him, I get warm and tingly in the last place I want to feel that way. If I don't stop staring at my ex-husband's naked body and all those flexing muscles, my tingling will become slick heat between my thighs.

I'm still clutching my lump of clothes, but I hug it tighter as I rip my gaze away from his manly parts and focus on his face. "You exercise in the nude? In front of a big window?"

"That's right." He sets down his weights and grabs a small towel, patting it on his skin to soak up the sweat that glistens on his body. "After spending a week at a nudist resort, I thought I'd try nude exercising. Decided I like working out this way. It's…freeing."

"Uh-huh." I barely heard whatever he just said, what with my brain insisting I need to rake my gaze over every inch of his sweaty, sexy body one more time. After a few seconds, his statement finally penetrates my mind. I blink quickly, meeting his gaze. "You went to a nudist resort?"

"Yes, I did." He tosses the towel onto his desk, and his mouth tightens. "You don't need to look quite so shocked, do you? I fucked you in a casino. The fact I tried naturism shouldn't stun you."

"Naturism?"

"That's what some nudists like to call it."

"Oh." I try so hard not to stare at his dick, but my eyes refuse to obey me. While I'm focused on that part of his body, I say, "When we were married, I told you I went to a nude beach back in college, and you told me you were shocked and you would never do anything as crazy as that."

"I also said I admired your lack of shame." He strides up to me and takes the clothes I'm holding. "Let me carry these for you. I assume you're having a shower."

"Yeah. Thanks." While I follow my naked ex-husband to the bathroom, I ask, "What made you change your mind about nudism?"

"Alex Thorne. He and my cousin Catriona had their wedding at the Au Naturel Naturist Resort in Oregon. Guests weren't required to go nude, but I gave it a go."

"Jack MacTaggart attended a wedding at a nudist resort. You've got many facets, don't you?"

"So do you." He steps inside the bathroom to set my clothes on the counter, then exits. "Enjoy your shower, *gràidh*."

"Thanks."

He called me "darling" in Gaelic. Huh. He's used other Gaelic phrases lately, but most are gibberish to me.

I watch Jack's naked backside as he heads back into his office. Holy heaven, I'd love to have sex with him again. More than love to. I crave it like he's a big box of candy and I haven't had sugar in years, a fact I blame on these crazy hormones coursing through my veins. Well, it's not like he can knock me up again. Why shouldn't I enjoy getting horizontal with my ex?

Because it's a bad, bad, bad idea, you moron.

Right. Sex would complicate the hell out of…everything.

So instead, I grab my vibrator and get in the shower to give myself the happy ending I'd much rather receive from Jack. Okay, yes, I fantasize about him while I'm doing that. Fantasies are much safer than the real thing.

I've just opened the bathroom door when Jack walks out of his office.

He freezes. "Oh. There you are."

"Yep. Here I are."

At least he's wearing clothes now, though honestly, his sweatpants and T-shirt do nothing to alleviate my lust.

"I was going to make breakfast," he says. "After that, I thought we should have an informal session."

"Do you mean therapy?"

"Yes. I can't be my ex-wife's therapist, or my own, but we can talk about those things that usually make us start arguing." He shuts his office door. "I have ideas for how to prevent that."

"A cure for arguments? You must have psychology superpowers to pull that off."

"I've never tried it before. But we need to do something, or else we'll wind up as bickering parents who turn our bairn into a bampot."

"We aren't so awful that our kid will go nuts."

"I was exaggerating for effect."

"Maybe you shouldn't do that when we're still struggling with becoming friends."

He sighs. "Fair point. Sorry."

"It's okay. Now, let's make breakfast. I'm starving."

Collaborating on a meal with Jack has always been one of my favorite things to do with him. We hadn't done that in Vegas, but here in Scotland, we'd often cooked together in that cute apartment in Inverness. Okay, maybe "cute" isn't the right way to describe it. Jack's cousin Evan had lent him his swanky apartment that had a view of the River Ness. Evan hadn't needed the place anymore after he married Keely, the older American woman he'd wooed and won. Since Evan is a billionaire, he kept the Inverness apartment for whenever he and Keely visit the corporate headquarters of his company, Evanescent Security Technologies Limited, and they also lend it out to friends and family.

For six weeks, I'd shared those luxury digs with Jack.

I like this house better. It feels like a home rather than a model house that real estate agents might show off to their clients.

Jack has calmed down a lot since I first showed up on his doorstep and seems way more relaxed this morning, but he still doesn't seem quite ready to joke around much. I suppose that's to be expected, considering the shock I gave him on the day I arrived.

We eat breakfast on the patio that overlooks the backyard and flower garden. I wonder if all of Scotland is as beautiful as this, but I imagine it's like any country, with various regions that have their own landscapes and mini-climates. Honestly, I don't know much about Scotland. Jack wouldn't let me leave Inverness. Yesterday, he offered to take me on a tour of the Highlands once things settle down a bit. I believe he means that, and I can't wait for our grand tour.

During breakfast, he catches me up on the goings-on in his ever-expanding family, including the Brits who aren't related to him but who have become good friends. Alex Thorne is family now, since he married Jack's cousin Catriona a couple of months ago. She's pregnant too, and Evan and Keely had a baby recently. Logan MacTaggart married an older American widow who happens to be best friends with Evan's wife, but Logan and Serena don't have plans for babies since she already has a teenage son. Logan is the ex-spy, but he hadn't been close to his cousins until last year.

I love listening to Jack relate the story of how Logan and Alex met and eventually became best friends, and how Alex and Cat reunited after eleven years apart, though it took them nine more months to realize they still loved each other. For years, she called him all sorts of names including the British

Bastard, and apparently, she still likes to tease him with those insults. Jack met Alex when Catriona asked him to give the Brit a "mental tuneup," as Jack phrases it. After that, the two men became good friends. So when Alex heard about me, the "sneaky sod"—Jack's words, not mine—finagled a surprise reunion for us with that blind-date craziness.

Based on the phone message Alex left on Jack's machine yesterday, I figure the Brit hasn't quite finished his meddling plans yet.

I still can't wrap my head around the fact that Jack stayed at a nudist resort for a week and likes to work out in the nude.

After breakfast, Jack insists on washing the dishes on his own. I decide against arguing since we have made a lot of progress toward getting along, and I don't want to spoil that. I head into the living room.

Five minutes later, I hear a car pull up. The engine shuts off.

A visitor? Maybe it's Callum again. I really, really want to get a glimpse of him. I've seen pictures, but an up-close view would be even better. I know I shouldn't peek through the curtains. I know that, I swear. And I don't mean to walk over to the big picture window. Honestly, I don't. My feet have their own ideas, and so do my fingers, because two of them sneak between the curtains and part them a sliver, just enough that I can take a quick gander.

The visitor is not Callum.

My quick gander becomes an extended viewing as I try to figure out who the man and woman standing on the front porch might be. I've never seen them in Jack's family photos. They're young, probably in their twenties, though I've never been great at guessing ages. They're whispering to each other and seem excited—to see Jack, I assume—but I can't make out their words.

If I skulk over to the door and press my ear to it…

No, I absolutely should not do that.

My feet carry me over there anyway. Since I'm here, I might as well try to hear what they're saying. I mean, they might be plotting how to break into the house. I should check it out strictly so I know whether to scream at Jack to call the cops. Right? That makes sense.

Yeah, I'm hopeless. And nosy. I should work on my bad habits—later.

I plaster my left ear to the door and plug the right one with my finger. Now, I can make out what those two are saying.

"You're the one who wanted to come here right away," the man says. He sounds British. "Now you suddenly think it's a bad idea?"

"No, but you're the one who insisted we should wait until tomorrow," the woman says, and she's clearly American. "You claimed you were too 'knackered' to do it today."

"I said I was exhausted, not knackered."

"But you meant knackered. That's the British way to say it."

"Well, we're here now. Should I knock or not?"

"Of course you should knock, Grey baby."

Grey? I guess that's the man's name, but I've never heard Jack mention anyone called Grey, not even earlier when he told me all about Logan and Alex and the great meddling campaign.

"All right, Jess," Grey says. "But don't blame me if Jack doesn't answer the door."

I pull my head away, anticipating a knock.

Half a second later, a fist raps on the door several times.

Jack bolts out of the kitchen and straight to me. In a rough whisper, he demands, "What the bloody hell are you doing?"

"Standing here," I say, whispering too. "There are two people out there called Grey and Jess."

Jack stops blinking, his gaze nailed to mine. "What? How do you know? I thought we agreed you wouldn't open the door."

"Yes, and I stuck to that. But you never asked me not to peek out between the curtains or glue my ear to the door to eavesdrop."

He compresses his lips but then exhales a big, blustery sigh. "Never mind. Would you at least wait in the kitchen while I talk to Grey and Jessica?"

"Sure."

I trot into the kitchen and stay out of sight of the doorway, though I'm right next to the threshold, so I should be able to hear their conversation. Unless Jack goes outside and shuts the door. Or he whispers to them. I swear I have never been an eavesdropper before, but Jack's weird aversion to letting anyone see or speak to me has turned me into a snoop.

Jack opens the door. I know because I can hear the click when he unlocks it and see the spray of sunlight that streams through the partially open door.

"What are you two doing here?" Jack asks, sounding only halfway grumpy. "Aren't you meant to be on your honeymoon?"

"No, we postponed that," Grey says. "Logan and Alex told us your ex-wife has come to town, and she's living with you."

"Autumn is staying with me. We are not living together."

I'm impressed by how calm he manages to sound when I know he must be on edge again.

"Grey and I wanted to check on you," Jessica says. "Logan and Alex told us you haven't been answering your phone or the door. They thought maybe you guys killed each other."

"Or you're too busy shagging to notice anything else," Grey says. "You helped me and Jess with our problems, and we're grateful to you. If there's anything we can do to to help you and Autumn—"

"We don't need help."

"All right. I'm glad to hear that, but everyone would love to meet Autumn."

Yes, and Autumn would love to meet them. But Jack won't let her.

Jack groans, and I can picture him making his Resigned Jack face. "I will introduce her to everyone, eventually. Right now, we have some, ah, things to work out between us. Alone."

"Sure, we get that," Jessica says. "If you're really okay…"

"I am. We both are."

"We'll see you later, then. We're staying at Dùndubhan, but you can call us on our cells if you need anything."

"Thank you."

"Cheers, Jack," Grey says, then I hear footsteps receding and the click of Jack shutting the door.

I emerge from the kitchen. "Dùndubhan? That's the castle, right? You mentioned your cousin Rory owns it."

"Aye, but it's mostly a museum now. Rory and his wife live in Loch Fairbairn. His sister Jamie and her husband run the museum."

"Right, I remember now."

His brows hike up. "You remember? Didnae think I told you about that."

"You told me lots of stuff. I wasn't allowed to meet any of your family, but everything you told me about them is indelibly etched in my memory."

"Soon, I promise. You'll meet them soon."

"I'm looking forward to it. What should we do now? TV gets boring after a day or two."

He clears his throat and straightens his shirt. "It's time for our informal therapy session."

Did I hear a thump? That must've been the other shoe dropping.

Chapter Fourteen

Jack

As we walk into my office, I wave for Autumn to sit in the chair in front of my desk. I drop onto the chair behind it. But she does not sit where I indicated she should. No, the bloody-minded woman has to amble over to the window seat and stretch out on it with her back against the frame.

"You're meant to sit there," I say, pointing at the chair across the desk from me.

"I'm comfy here, thanks."

"But that's not how I do sessions."

"This is an informal discussion, right?" She clasps her hands on her lap and crosses her ankles. "That means we don't have to do things the official way."

"How am I supposed to talk to you when you're halfway across the room?"

"We're talking now, aren't we? So my way works." She pats the bench. "You could always join me over here."

"Maybe I'll sit in the chair by the window."

"No, Jack. Sit on the bench with me."

"There's no room. You're sprawled over the entire bench like a Roman empress."

She rolls her eyes. "Grumpy Jack has returned. Try pulling that steel rod out of your spine just for today."

"Donnae have a steel rod in my back. I'm known as the easygoing Mac-Taggart, the one who's always calm and reasonable."

She snorts because she's clearly trying to stifle a laugh. "Guess none of your relatives have ever lived with you, huh?"

"I'm only 'Grumpy Jack' when I'm talking to you."

"Let's figure out why that is." She wriggles around until she's gotten into a cross-legged sitting position, then she pats the bench again. "Come on, Jack. I won't bite unless you beg and plead because you're so desperate for me to do that to you."

I wish she hadn't said that in a sultry voice. Blood will rush into my cock any second if she speaks that way again. To avoid a bigger problem, I give in and go to the bench, sitting on the opposite side. I keep one foot on the floor and brace the other ankle on my knee.

"Tell me about your family," I say.

"No, we're starting with you."

"I've told you about my family. You're the one who needs to open up and share."

"Open up and share? You're the king of doing the exact opposite of that." She holds up a hand when I open my mouth, about to speak. "Yes, I know everything about your relatives. But I don't know *you*, Jack, not really. Please answer one question for me. That's not too much to ask, is it?"

No, it shouldn't be. But I have a suspicion about what she wants to ask, and I don't have a ruddy clue how to answer. The therapist in me knows I should tell her what she wants to know. But I'm not sure I can.

"All right," I tell her. "Ask your question."

"Why did you turn into a different person once we got married and came to Scotland?"

"You've got it backwards. I was a different person in Las Vegas."

"But you said all your relatives think you're level-headed and affable, not grumpy and closed off."

I don't recall saying that, but I suppose she's paraphrasing and interpolating.

Autumn sighs, and her shoulders slump. "I never knew that version of you, so I guess that's why I can't reconcile the man I met and married in Vegas with the way you were after that, or the way you are now."

The last thing I want to do is explain to Autumn why I behaved the way I did in Las Vegas. I don't think I can explain it, anyway. But she wants to know, and if we're going to get on at least well enough to raise a child who doesn't turn out to be a neurotic mess, then I need to try.

"I've never had much luck with the lasses," I say. "I've had girlfriends, but nothing serious. Eventually, I gave up on serious dating and settled for the occasional poke with a willing lass."

"What does that have to do with Vegas?"

"By the time I flew to America for that psychology conference, I had essentially decided I would never marry or have children. It wasn't in the cards for me."

Autumn watches me, but I can't decipher her expression.

Cannae believe I'm telling her this. But now that I've started, the words keep flowing. "When I saw you… I don't know. Something woke up inside me. I knew I needed to shag you, but it felt like more than that. Those twelve days with you were the best time of my life. I became something I never imagined I could be—uninhibited, free, happy."

She blinks slowly, her eyes wide. "You weren't happy until then?"

"Well, ah…" Why had I said that? It's ridiculous. "Of course I was happy when I was a wee laddie. And once I grew up, I enjoyed my life. But with you, I was…happier."

"Oh. I get it, I think." She bites her upper lip, releasing it slowly while she studies me like she can't decide if I'll snarl at her. "If you liked the person you became in Vegas, why did you change once you brought me home with you?"

"I didn't mean to. But I suddenly realized what I'd done, marrying a woman I'd just met, and I knew I'd made a mistake."

Her lips tighten, but I can tell she's not angry. Her bottom lip quivers a wee bit, evidence that she's hurt by what I said.

"I don't mean that the way it sounds," I say.

"Marrying me was a mistake. Kind of hard to misinterpret that." Her voice quivers a wee bit too.

She wasn't happy being married to me. Why should what I said fash her?

I'm about to speak when the phone on my desk rings. I can't help glancing toward it.

Autumn sighs. "You want to answer the phone, don't you?"

"That's my mobile. I have to answer in case it's an emergency."

"Uh-huh. Whatever." She swings her legs off the bench and gets up. "You always have work as your escape plan."

The mobile rings again.

I don't have time to respond to what she said. Rushing to my desk, I pick up the call. "Dr. MacTaggart."

"Jack, it's Effie McKellar. I'm sorry to disturb you, but I need to chat to you about your former client, Hamish Clacher."

Autumn has just reached the door.

"One moment." I cover the phone with my hand and say in a hushed voice, "It's urgent. Cannae put it off."

I have no idea if it is urgent, but as Autumn said, I use work as my escape plan. And I need to get away from our conversation for a while, at least until I can decide how to explain aspects of my behavior that I don't understand.

Autumn shakes her head, the movement so slight I almost don't notice it, then she walks out the door and shuts it.

Bod an Donais. I don't have time right now to chase after my ex-wife and apologize for whatever I've done. I remove my hand from the phone.

"What did you need to tell me about Hamish?" I ask Effie.

"I've had to refer him to another psychologist, a colleague I know well who has dealt with obsessional issues a fair bit."

"Hamish's issues are nothing new, but I don't know why you're telling me about the referral. I'm not involved in Hamish's treatment anymore."

"Aye, but..." She hesitates for so long I wonder if we've been disconnected. "I don't feel I'm making progress with him, which is the reason for the referral. But I received a call from Roy Murray, the psychologist I referred Hamish to, and he's concerned about Hamish's recent behavior."

"I don't mean to sound grumpy, but this isn't my concern anymore." Autumn would love this, wouldn't she? I'm getting grumpy with everyone these days, not just her.

"No, um, Hamish's behavior might affect you," Effie says. "That's why I've rung you, Jack. He seems to have reverted to his obsession with you."

"Me? I haven't seen him in almost a year. The non-harassment order expired, and I didn't try to have it extended."

"I'm hoping it won't go that far this time. Roy is working with Hamish to stop anything like what happened last time."

"Why didn't Dr. Murray call me directly?"

She hesitates again. "He thought it might be easier to hear coming from me, since we're friends."

"I see. Well, you've told me. Thank you, Effie."

"Hamish might be sliding backward and may get worse than he was before."

"But Hamish has never been violent, if that's what worries you."

"Just be careful, Jack, that's all I'm saying. I'll let you know if there are any developments you need to be made aware of."

"Thank you, Effie."

I hang up and march out into the hall, glancing left and right. Autumn doesn't seem to be in her bedroom or the living room. When I enter the kitchen, she isn't there either. I did tell her she could go outside if she stayed in the backyard.

So I look for her out there.

Autumn is lying on the grass on her back, gazing up at the sky and the puffy clouds moving across the blue background. Her lips have curled up a touch. She looks...happy.

I halt near her feet.

She smiles. "Lie down, Jack. The grass is much nicer than that window seat, and the sun feels wonderful on your skin."

Why does she keep speaking in that sultry tone? If she doesn't want me to shag her, she shouldn't talk that way.

"I'm fine standing," I say. "That call was from a colleague. She needed to discuss something to do with a former client of mine."

"Uh-huh." She skims her palm over the grass beside her. "Please lie down with me, Jack."

"Why?"

"Because I'm asking nicely."

What lying on the grass has to do with anything, I haven't got a clue. But it seems important to her for some reason, so I do what she wants. I lie down beside her.

"Happy?" I ask.

"Yes. Thank you." She smiles up at the sky. "Do you ever look at the clouds and imagine what their shapes look like? You know, that one is a moose or whatever."

"A moose? I don't see any clouds like that."

"It was an example."

Watching her face while she watches the clouds is more enjoyable than staring at the sky. She looks peaceful, and I wonder why she suddenly feels that way.

"You were annoyed when I took that call," I say, "but now you're happy."

"Relaxation will do that to a person." She closes her eyes and takes a deep breath, releasing it little by little. "I started doing yoga last year, and it's really helped me feel more centered. You should try it."

"I don't think so. That's a woman's thing."

She eyes me sideways. "My first yoga teacher was a man."

"Did you shag him? Is that why yoga is so relaxing for you? If that's how it works, I might give it a go after all."

"Ha-ha. I already told you I haven't slept with anyone but you since the night we met."

"Aye, you did say that." And I still wonder why neither of us has been with anyone else. The obvious answer is that we still have feelings for each other, but I don't know if that's true. Or if I want it to be true. "You keep saying I changed, but you did too. Once we were married, you pulled away from me."

"Because you pulled away from me first."

"Let's not play the 'you did it first' game."

"Okay, you're right." She shuts her eyes for a moment, then sighs and turns her face toward me. "You were ashamed of me, weren't you? That's why you withdrew emotionally."

"You keep saying I was ashamed I'd married you, but that's not what happened."

"What, then?"

I rub my eyes, trying to figure out how to explain. "I was confused, I suppose. Couldnae understand how I could do something so rash. Everyone thinks I'm calm and rational, not the sort who does things on a whim. But that's not the only reason for my confusion. I had…work problems too."

"What kind of work problems?"

"You know I can't discuss that."

Autumn sits up, twisting her torso to gaze down at me. "You can tell me in general, without revealing anything confidential. Can't you? We need to work through this, Jack, not hide behind jobs and family."

"Says the woman who won't tell me about her family."

"Yeah, you're right." She faces forward, folding her arms over her knees. "I'll tell you everything you want to know. Right now."

Chapter Fifteen

Autumn

Though I just told Jack I'll explain about my family, I can't seem to make the words come out of my mouth. I sit here hugging my knees and staring at the grass, but my brain refuses to help me form coherent thoughts. My pulse has sped up, and I feel a little nauseous too. Why have I always felt so weird about talking to Jack about my family? I guess I've worried he won't understand, or he'll think I'm a shiftless idiot.

But Jack isn't a jerk. Even when we argue, he's never mean.

Okay, time to spill my guts to my ex-husband.

"I think maybe the real problem," I say, "is that you would never introduce me to your family, but you told me tons of stories about them. I feel like I know the MacTaggarts, and they're such wonderful people. So I've been afraid to talk about my family because they're nothing like yours. I'm a disappointment to everyone, even myself."

"You are not a disappointment."

"As a wife, I was."

Jack settles a hand on my back, a comforting gesture I remember from when we lived together. "I'm sorry if I've made you feel that way, but I was only disappointed when you walked out with no explanation."

And I believe him, I realize. Have I been transferring my fears onto him? That way I don't need to deal with any of it because it's all his fault. But it isn't.

"I'm sorry too," I say. "Guess I've always assumed I'll be a disappointment to you because I have been to my family. It's time I tell you about them."

"Aye, it is." He rubs his palm over my back in gentle circles. "Take your time."

God, he's so nice. I love the way he touches me, whether it's comforting or sexual.

I suck in a breath and blow it out, then I start talking. "My father was a major in the US Army, though he'd gotten out before I was born. Since then, he's worked for a private military contractor as a kind of operations manager. My mom is a cardiothoracic surgeon, and my sister runs a charity for sick children with her husband. Oh, she also used to be a member of the US Marine Corps. My mom served in the army too."

"Are your parents still married?"

"Yes. They're the perfect power couple."

Jack stops rubbing my back, moving his hand to cover mine. "I understand your family is impressive on paper. But what have they done to make you feel unworthy of love?"

I've never phrased it like that. Unworthy of love. But now that Jack has said it, I know he's right. That is how I feel. "My parents expected me either to join the military or become a doctor. I didn't want to be a soldier, but I didn't really want to go to medical school either."

"But you did do that."

"Eventually." I get up, needing to move even if it's only to pace in front of Jack. "I always put pressure on myself to be as good as they are, as brave and selfless and dedicated to their jobs. But I failed. Not academically. I did fine with that, but I failed to live up to their expectations. So I announced I wasn't going to college. Instead, I found a job working at a dude ranch."

"Your parents didn't approve, I gather."

"No. They ordered me to go to college—for my own good, as Dad put it." I rub the back of my neck. "For five years, I only spoke to my parents during the holidays. I would talk to my sister, Michelle, on the phone a few times a month, but I couldn't face Mom and Dad. Dennis and Brenda Flowerday could not understand why their shiftless daughter refused to follow in their footsteps like Michelle had done."

"Autumn, you're not shiftless." Jack stays on the ground, sitting there watching me pace. "You went to university at some point since you were in medical school when we met."

"Yeah, after five years of bouncing from one dead-end job to another, I gave in and went to college. Mom and Dad were thrilled." I stop beside a bush that has pretty lavender flowers. It smells nice too, and I take several breaths to appreciate the scent. "I was bound to disappoint them, though. That's the only thing I'm good at."

"Why do you feel that way?"

He's in psychologist mode now, isn't he? I need to talk to Jack, not Dr. MacTaggart. Well, maybe I need both.

"Because it's true," I say. "Got through college, but med school was too much for me. I don't want to be a doctor. No idea what I do want. My parents haven't spoken to me since I dropped out of med school. Michelle and I still talk sometimes, but we're not close. I've never kept a job for more than a year, usually closer to six months. Nothing I try ever seems to fit. I'm a failure and a disappointment to everyone."

"You think I see you that way too."

"Don't you?"

With a long groan, he heaves his body off the ground and walks over to me. He stops right in front of me, halting my pacing, and grasps my upper arms. "No, Autumn, I have never thought of you as a failure or a disappointment. Never. Not even when you left me."

"But you hate me because of what I did."

He shakes his head slowly. "I have never hated you. I was angry, yes, but not because I think you're a terrible person."

"Why, then?"

Jack scrubs a hand over his mouth. "I was angry because you hurt me. I wanted you to stay."

I have no idea what to say to that. I'd assumed he was sick of me, since he wouldn't let me meet anyone and he didn't want to talk to me or have fun with me. I assumed he didn't want me anymore, as a wife or a lover. But he *did* want me? The revelation has me reeling.

"Guess it's true," I say. "You always hurt the one you, uh, care about."

The one you love, that's the saying. Why couldn't I say that? Because I still don't know if I love him now or if I ever loved him. Maybe I just can't admit the truth to myself.

"Aye," Jack says. "It is true. But I don't want us to be like that anymore."

"Neither do I."

"There's only one solution." He lowers his hands and squares his shoulders. "It's time I introduce you to my family."

For a few seconds, all I can do is gape at him. Did he actually say he wants me to meet his family? I didn't hallucinate that, did I?

"Do you want to meet them or not?" he asks, sounding a touch grumpy.

"Yes, of course I do. I'm stunned, that's all. I mean, for as long as I've known you, this has never been an option."

Jack rolls his gaze toward the sky and sighs. "Let's not turn this into a major event, and please, let's not argue in front of my family."

"You're the one who's getting grouchy. I'm psyched."

"We're already arguing. Maybe it's not a good idea after all."

"Oh no, you do not get to nix the idea thirty seconds after suggesting it." I grab his shirt in both hands and tug him closer. "You said you would introduce me. No backpedaling now. Besides, you are the one who's getting annoyed, not me."

"I know." He slips an arm around my waist, pulling me even snugger against his body. "Let me apologize."

Oh, I remember what "apologize" means to Jack. He wants to have sex. Yeah, that sounds fabulous, and I'd love to get naked with him. But sex will only confuse things. Right? Or maybe it would help by, you know, relaxing us both.

Sure, because that always worked before.

"No sex," I declare, trying to sound resolute when all I want to do is drag him down onto the grass and unzip his pants.

"You want me."

Duh. Of course I want him. He's hot and amazing at sex.

I manage to convince my mouth to say the right thing instead of the wrong, but incredibly hot, thing. "No, Jack. I won't sleep with you, but I would love to meet your family."

He backs away a few steps. "I'll call my parents."

Jack marches into the house while I'm still standing there dumbfounded. Jack is the most confusing man I've ever known. He can go from calm and rational to hot and steamy in one second flat. It's like being a passenger in a car that's racing down an icy road and suddenly the driver yanks the steering wheel, making the whole car spin across the ice.

Did I mention there are no seat belts in my imaginary car?

I trudge across the lawn and into the kitchen.

Jack is hunched over the island, one hand braced on it, the other cradling the phone to his ear. He keeps nodding, and occasionally he grunts like he's agreeing with whatever the other person has said. He glances up at me, frowns, and returns his gaze to the countertop.

I lean my hip against the island to watch him from across the counter.

"Aye," he says, almost groaning the word. He listens for a few seconds, then screws up his mouth. "Didn't I just say that? Yes, Ma, we'll be there."

He hangs up, plants both hands on the counter, and looks at me.

"We'll be where?" I ask.

"At my parents' house for lunch."

"When?"

His gaze flits to the clock on the microwave. "We need to leave right now."

"Now?" I jerk away from the island and fling my hands up to pat my hair. "I need time to get ready. Jeez, is that grass in my hair?"

"Yes, it is."

"Why are you so calm? I can't keep up with your whirlwind moods." I glance down at my clothes and see green marks on my jeans. "Oh no, I have grass stains. I need time to change and—Oh God, I stink, don't I? I need to take a shower too and—"

Suddenly, Jack is behind me with his body plastered to mine and his hands on my hips. He slides his palms down to my thighs, pushing his fingertips between my legs. My pulse had already kicked into high gear, but the feel of his hands on me has pushed it into overdrive.

"What are you doing?" I ask, my voice breathy.

"You need to calm down, *mo leannan*. I'm helping you with that."

"How? I don't—"

Jack pushes his entire hand between my thighs, cupping me intimately. "Be quiet and I'll show you."

God, I love it when he speaks in that rough, sexy voice. My panic can't overwhelm the desire that's firing up inside me. Jack has always known how to get me hot with barely a touch. His big hand on my mound is making me tingly and wet so fast that I'm having trouble catching my breath.

He unzips my jeans and slips his palm inside my panties, pushing it down, down, down so slowly that I can't breathe at all anymore.

"Jack, please, you have to stop."

"Shh. Let me relax you."

He pushes his hand between my folds.

A series of knocks rattles the front door.

Jack hisses a Gaelic curse under his breath and stomps out of the kitchen.

I stand frozen for several seconds, my body on fire, my thoughts a whirling mess.

"Where are ye hiding the lass, Jack?" Callum hollers louder than seems necessary since he's talking to his brother. I recognize his voice, though I can't see him.

"Callum, ye *cacan*," Jack says, "what are you doing here?"

I rouse from my lust-induced trance, zip up my pants, and hurry into the living room.

Jack holds the door halfway open, blocking it with his body, while Callum leans to the side to peer into the house.

"Told Ma and Da I'd make sure you two arrived safely," Callum says, his brows shooting up when he sees me. His mouth slides into a wicked smirk. "There she is. No wonder you've been hiding the lass. She's bonnie, very bonnie."

I come up beside Jack, though his arm bars me from getting too close to his brother. Jack has one hand firmly planted on the jamb and the other on the door.

"Nice to see you, Callum," I say, offering him my hand by pushing my arm under Jack's. "I'm Autumn Flowerday."

"Callum MacTaggart," he says, shaking my hand. "Ma and Da are excited to meet you. My brother seems to have been holding you prisoner like a princess in a tower until today. I wonder what changed his mind."

He glances at Jack and waggles his eyebrows.

Jack scowls.

I lay a hand on Jack's, the one that's planted on the jamb. "Isn't it nice of Callum to pick us up? Just let me get changed, and we can go. I'm excited to finally meet everyone."

"Everyone?" Callum says. He grins and gives Jack a playful slug in the gut. "The version I heard from Ma was that no other MacTaggarts are allowed to 'shove their ruddy noses' into this until Jack gives the go-ahead. He made Ma swear it on the bible."

"No, I did not," Jack says, his tone getting grumpier by the second. "I asked her not to tell any other family members yet."

I can't help smiling. Callum seems like lots of fun, and I can't wait to find out what Jack's parents are like. "I'll change. Back in a sec."

As I race down the hall, I hear Callum shout, "You two have time for a quick shag first. Jack looks like he needs it."

The last thing I hear is Jack snarling in Gaelic.

Chapter Sixteen

Jack

"Away and chew a brush, Callum," I growl. "We'll see you at Ma and Da's house." I don't expect my brother will leave, though I start praying that an angel will grab him by the throat and drag him away. I love my brother, but he clearly thinks the situation is hilarious and a perfect opportunity to harass me.

I can't blame him. Everyone knows I'm the calm brother, though I can't claim to have the inner calmness or fortitude of my cousin Iain. He's made it an art form. Still, I do not get angry. Snarling at my brother? No, I don't do that either. But I have been holding Autumn hostage, and I keep trying to seduce her, so maybe I have snapped.

Callum is still smirking at me.

"Away," I growl, waving my hand in a gesture meant to chase him off.

It doesn't work.

My brother shakes his head but maintains his snarky expression. "I was a firefighter, Jack. Takes more than a surly psychologist to intimidate me. Besides, I promised Ma and Da I would drive you and Autumn to the party."

"Party?" Everything inside me goes cold, and I can't move a muscle, not even the ones in my eyelids. "I said immediate family only. That means you, Ma, and Da."

Callum snorts. "Did you honestly think Ma wouldn't invite anyone else? Besides, you told her 'immediate family' without the 'only the three of us' qualification. Letting our mother interpret the term immediate family is dangerous, you know that."

Aye, I do know. But I could've sworn I told her... Ah, bollocks. I didn't say "only the three of you."

My brother chuckles and slaps my arm. "Cheer up, Jack. I doubt Ma could wrangle the whole clan in less than an hour."

"Only half of Scotland will be coming, then. What a relief."

"You used to love family gatherings."

That was before Alex the interfering ersehole had tricked me into a blind date with my ex-wife and before she turned up on my doorstep with life-changing news. I haven't had time to fully adjust to the idea of having a bairn. And what am I going to tell my family about why Autumn is here?

I take a deep, calming breath and tell Callum, "Please wait in the car. I need to talk to Autumn alone before we leave."

"Ready for that quick shag, are ye?" He slaps my arm again. "Have at it, mate."

Callum heads for his car, where it's parked at the curb. My car is parked in the garage. Callum's Land Rover is ancient, but it's bigger than my vehicle, so I guess we should take his.

I shut the door just as Autumn walks out of the hallway. My cock twitches.

She's wearing sky-blue leggings, what Alex calls "pseudo-trousers" because they're so tight they seem more like undergarments than clothing. Autumn's shapely legs look even better in those leggings, and the long, loose-fitting shirt she's wearing makes her curves even more enticing, not to mention that the fabric is thin enough I can glimpse the outline of her white bra when the sun shining through the windows streams over her.

Christ, she's bonnie. My brother might be an irritating erse, but he's right about one thing. I do need to have a poke with Autumn. Even her canvas shoes with flowers on them make me want to tear those leggings off, shove her against the wall, and fuck her.

"Are you okay?" she asks when she reaches me. "You look like you're in shock again, the way you were on the day I showed up here."

"No, I—" *Need to fuck you so hard the house will shake.* I don't say that, of course. I might be slightly off my head this week, but I'm not that far gone. "I'm surprised you want to wear skintight leggings, that's all."

"Why?"

"You're pregnant. Isn't it uncomfortable?"

She smiles sweetly. "I'm not even showing yet, Jack. Now, I might vomit all over you in the car, but tight pants don't bother me yet."

"Are you ill? Maybe we should call off the—"

"No way, Jack." She wags a finger in my face. "You promised to introduce me to your family. Don't backpedal now. There's nothing wrong with me except normal pregnancy stuff. No excuses, we're going to your parents' house."

She peers around me. "Why is Callum sitting out there in what looks like the oldest, dumpiest Land Rover in the world?"

"He insists on driving us to Ma and Da's house. And he bought that Land Rover off our cousin Iain, who finally upgraded to a modern, rust-free vehicle after he married Rae."

"Why doesn't Callum get a nice car?"

"He likes the Rover. Donnae ask me why."

She tilts her head side to side, her gaze glued to the Land Rover. "Well, it is kind of cute in a dilapidated way."

"Willnae be saying that after a ride in that rust heap."

I glance down at my clothes, wondering if I should change into something else. Autumn looks bonnie and well-dressed, but I'm wearing old jeans and an old T-shirt. Maybe I belong in a rust heap like Callum's Rover.

"Give me a minute to change," I say and take off for the bedroom without even bothering to close the front door.

"I'll wait for you in the car—with Callum."

By the time I race out the door, slamming it shut, and climb inside Callum's death trap of a car, I'm breathing so hard I'm almost hyperventilating.

Autumn sits in the front passenger seat, laughing at something Callum must've said right before I clambered into the backseat and slammed the door.

My brother smirks at me over his shoulder. "In a hurry, are ye, Jack? Cannae wait to introduce the folks to your girl?"

"She is not my girl. She's my ex-wife."

Fortunately, he starts up the car and navigates down the street which means he can't smirk at me anymore.

Callum and Autumn chat to each other for the entire drive to Ma and Da's house. It's only a five-mile trip, but it seems to take forever. I don't like the way Callum keeps smiling at Autumn, or the way she keeps smiling at him. I've become a jealous *bod ceann*, haven't I? She's not my wife anymore, and we're not even dating, but I can't stand to see her having a good time with my brother.

We turn down the gravel driveway that leads to my parents' cottage on the outskirts of Loch Fairbairn. My brother and my ex-wife continue their incessant chatting. Maybe I feel a wee bit left out, but I can't think of anything to say to either of them. They're having a good time while I'm brooding in the backseat. Callum has no trouble getting on with Autumn while I can't seem to hold a civil conversation with her for more than a few minutes on a good day.

The way she smiles and laughs at his jokes gives me a strange pain in my chest.

"Here we are," Callum announces as the Rover rattles to a halt in front of the house. "Welcome to the place of Jack's birth."

"I was born in the hospital," I say, "not in this house."

"But you grew up here. I'm sure Autumn doesn't care about the little details."

My ex-wife turns her head to grin at me over the back of her seat. "I finally get to meet your parents. This is so exciting."

I try not to grimace. Whether I succeed or not, I have no idea. Autumn has already faced the front again, so she won't see it even if I am grimacing. Exciting? No, it's more like standing in front of a firing squad. I don't see any other cars, and that gives me hope that only my parents are waiting for us.

My slender thread of hope lasts about thirty seconds, until we all get out of the car.

That's when the front door of the house swings open, and the horde descends.

"Horde" might be an exaggeration. Six people pour out the door and swarm us, and the introductions begin whether I like it or not. No one looks at me. They're all gawping at my ex-wife.

My mother throws her arms around Autumn. "I'm so happy to meet you, dearie. You're even more beautiful than I imagined." She takes possession of Autumn's hands, clasping them to her chest. "I'm Greer MacTaggart, and the bald man behind me is Alistair, my husband. You've already met our son Callum."

Ma smiles with her lips sealed and winks at me.

I have no bloody clue what that means except that my mother is thoroughly pleased with herself.

Autumn is still grinning. "It's wonderful to meet you, Mrs. MacTaggart. And you too, Mr. MacTaggart."

"Oh tosh," Ma says, making a dismissive hand gesture. "You're family, so ye donnae need to be formal. Call us Ma and Da."

"We're not married," I announce so loudly everyone in the entire village probably heard it. "Autumn and I are divorced."

Alex Thorne pushes through the crowd to reach us, looking smugly pleased like usual. "You might be divorced, but you are living together at the moment."

"Living together?" Ma says, and now she's grinning just like Autumn. "Oh aye, definitely call us Ma and Da, lassie."

Alex offers his hand to Autumn. "Since Jack seems unlikely to introduce us, let me do it for him. I'm Alex Thorne, and that gorgeous brunette over there is my wife, Catriona, who also happens to be Jack's cousin."

Cat emerges from the crowd to give Autumn a quick hug, then she hooks her arm around Alex's. "It's a pleasure to meet you, Autumn. I've heard so much about you, but not enough."

Autumn keeps grinning even when two more people she's never met or seen before approach to introduce themselves.

"Logan MacTaggart," my cousin says. "About time we got a look at the mysterious ex-wife. This is Serena, my wife."

Serena hugs Autumn. "Welcome to the family. Most of the MacTaggarts married Americans, and I hear you're from across the pond too. You'll fit right in, and you're just in time for the monthly meeting of the American Wives Club."

"Autumn can't be a member," I say, pushing past my relatives to stand beside her. "We aren't married anymore. Autumn is my ex-wife. Ex. Can any of you get that fact through your thick heads?"

"Jack's a little nervous about letting me out of the house," Autumn says. "He thinks you guys will all be mad at him for never introducing me to any of you until today."

"Mad?" Ma says. Then she drags Autumn into a bear hug. "How could Jack ever think we'd be angry? Having a daughter is a blessing."

I open my mouth to state once again that Autumn is not my wife, but I don't get the chance. Ma puts an arm around her shoulders and leads her into the house. Everyone else piles in after them, except for Alex. He waits until everyone has gone inside, then he stops me on the porch.

"How are you, Jack? Grey told me what happened when he and Jessica knocked on your door."

Of course he did. Alex is his brother, after all.

"I need to apologize to Grey and Jessica," I tell Alex. "I need to apologize to everyone, but especially Autumn."

"You seem less…anxious today."

"No, I haven't shagged Autumn."

Alex feigns being offended. "Did I suggest you have? I would never be so gauche."

"Like hell you wouldn't."

He claps a hand on my shoulder. "Let's go inside and face the army. Or rather, the contingent the army sent to reconnoiter before the salvo begins."

Aye, the rest of the MacTaggarts won't wait much longer to meet Autumn.

I exhale a long sigh and follow Alex into the house.

Chapter Seventeen

Jack's parents don't have a separate dining room, and the table in the kitchen isn't quite big enough for all of us, so we gather around a picnic table in the backyard. Greer tells me she and Alistair have lived in this lovely cottage since before Callum, their younger son, was born. She and Alistair both grew up on farms outside the village, but Jack and Callum spent their childhoods in this house. Jack's parents love living in Loch Fairbairn, and I can see why. It's a beautiful, picturesque village—the bits and pieces I've seen of it. Plus, tons of MacTaggarts live in and around the village, so they can easily visit their family just by walking through town.

Maybe they should rename this village MacTaggartville.

I sit beside Jack at the picnic table with Alex on the other side of me. His wife, Catriona, is next to him. Logan, Serena, Callum, and Greer occupy the bench across from us while Alistair sits at the head of the table. This is a real family gathering, the kind I've never experienced before. My parents didn't go in for stuff like this. I love just listening to these wonderful people ribbing each other and telling funny stories.

Alex tells me about the nudist resort where he and Cat held their wedding and turned it into a week-long event. Alex's half-brother, Grey Dixon, finally won the love of his best friend, Jessica, during that week.

When I ask Alex if he engaged in some of that famous MacTaggart-style meddling, he smiles mischievously and says, "I may have sort of...given Grey a push in the right direction. Honestly, it didn't take much interference from anyone. Grey had been in love with Jessica for eight years, and she felt the same way, though she was in denial about it."

"Jack told me about the American Wives Club. Did they conspire with you to meddle in your brother's love life?"

"No, I did that all on my own. I'm a member of the club now, you know."

"You're an American wife?" I say with a laugh.

"They've expanded the club to include the American wives of Brits who have become friends with the MacTaggarts too. That means the wives of the Dixons have become members of the British Branch of the American Wives Club." He smiles again with a touch of smugness this time. "But I was named the Original British Branch Husband with Grey as the Second British Branch Husband. Since then, they've inducted the rest of the Dixon boys into the fold too. When Richard Hunter and Maddie Solberg get married in a few months, they'll both join the British Branch too."

"Wow, this is getting awfully complicated."

"Yes, it does seem a bit like we're forming our own country, doesn't it?"

There's a question I'm dying to ask Alex, but I don't want to offend him. He's strange, sure, but I like him. Though I haven't spent more than half an hour with him so far, I get the feeling he's not easily offended.

So I ask, "Why did you trick me and Jack into going on a blind date?"

"It wasn't a trick. The American Wives Club served as my inspiration."

"But why did you do it? You haven't known Jack for very long."

"No, but he counseled me during a bizarre period in my life. I returned the favor in my own way."

"I assume by 'bizarre period,' you mean when your parents and that Australian guy kidnapped you and Catriona. Jack told me about that."

Alex lifts one brow. "I thought you and Jack couldn't hold a civil conversation. That's the story he told me. Now I hear you're gossiping about me."

"We still have, um, issues to deal with. But we're getting better at talking to each other without it turning into an argument."

"Glad to hear it. Love lost and regained can be a beautiful thing."

For a second, I think he's being sarcastic. Then I realize he means that. I know the story about Catriona dumping Alex and cursing his name for eleven years, followed by their reunion last year. Now they're happily married and about to have a baby. Jack and I weren't apart for eleven years, but we did screw up our marriage and go our separate ways, twice, only to be brought back together by a baby.

Not quite the epic love story of Alex and Catriona. But Jack and I haven't finished our story yet.

We won't end up with a fairy-tale love like theirs. It's not in the cards for us.

"Jack also counseled my brother, Grey," Alex says. "He's the best psychologist on earth, though sometimes he doesn't seem to know how to repair *his* relationships."

"He gets along fine with his family."

"I meant his relationship with you. The plural construction was strictly for effect."

Alex Thorne is very, very strange for sure. The more I talk to him, though, the more I understand why he and Jack have become close. I can't quite put my finger on the exact reason. It's more of an intuition that these two were meant to become friends.

Once lunch is over, we mill around in the yard chatting and laughing. I wind up having conversations with everyone, though not all at once. Greer and Alistair are such sweet, endearing people. No wonder Jack turned out well with parents like them. I run into a problem, though, when Greer asks me a seemingly innocuous question.

"Were you and Jack in touch after your blind date?"

"Uh, well…" I glance at Jack, who's talking to Alex and Logan, and give him a look I hope conveys the fact I need him to get his ass over here right now. But I have to downplay the urgency a bit so nobody will think anything's up. When Jack starts heading this way, I pretend to be fascinated with the stone path we're standing on, the one that leads to the rear gate. "These are such pretty stones. I've never seen any like this."

Greer and Alistair look at me like they can't figure out what the heck I'm babbling about.

I can't figure it out either.

Luckily, Jack reaches us, stopping beside me. "So, what have you and Autumn been talking about, Ma?"

Greer aims a motherly smile at me. "I think I embarrassed your lass, Jack."

"In what way?"

"By asking if you stayed in touch after your blind date."

"Ah, well…" Jack scratches his jaw. "We were both busy and didn't have time to blether."

"You invited her to come for a visit, aye?"

I know Greer isn't trying to be nosy. She's asking normal questions that any normal couple would know the answers to, but Jack and I aren't normal. We're not a couple either.

"Autumn is visiting," Jack says. "That's true."

"For how long? We'd love to spend more time with her."

"Well, it's, ah, complicated."

Oh jeez, I thought Jack would do better at sidestepping these questions than I would. Nope, he's fumbling too.

Alistair slips an arm around his wife. "So, when will ye be getting married again?"

Jack's jaw drops. Seriously. It falls open so far I think I can see his tonsils.

"We're not thinking about that right now," I say, amazed by my sudden ability to speak coherently in the face of awkward questions. "Just getting reacquainted, that's all."

The message Alex had left on Jack's answering machine replays in my mind. He'd made getting reacquainted sound filthy, like Jack and I are jumping each other's bones day and night. I'd love to do that. God, would I love to. But I won't. Nope. Not going to happen.

Jack shoves his hands in his pants pockets. "Aye, we're getting re—getting to know each other again."

I wonder if my use of the R-word made him flash back to Alex's message too.

Greer lays a hand on her chest and smiles with her cheeks dimpled. "Oh, that's wonderful. Cannae wait to spend more time with you, Autumn. You're so bonnie, sweet, and clever. Just the kind of woman Jack needs."

"We're not getting back together," I say, trying to sound calm. "Jack and I want to become friends, that's all."

Right now, I'm glad we agreed to keep the baby news to ourselves for a while. If Jack's mom knew about that, she'd assume we're reconciling. Greer is so kind, and I don't want to disappoint her. Can Jack and I ever be a couple again? I don't know.

"The best marriages start with friendship," Alistair says. "That's how it was with me and Greer."

"Autumn and I were already married," Jack says. "Didnae work out. Friends is all we can be."

"You never did tell us about that, Jack," Alistair says. "Why did ye marry a woman you'd known for two weeks? And why did ye never let us meet her until today?"

"It was twelve days, not two weeks," Jack replies, and I hear the tension sneaking back into his voice. "The rest is our business and no one else's."

"But why—"

Jack grabs my hand. "Autumn is tired. I'm taking her home."

He drags me around the side of the house to the driveway while his parents gape at us. Everyone else has stopped talking too, and their gazes follow us as we flee like criminals escaping from the cops. In the driveway, Jack stops. His mouth is crimped, his shoulders are bunched up, and his gaze darts this way and that like he's searching for something.

"Bollocks," he hisses. "We came in Callum's car."

"Guess you'll have to hot-wire it, huh? I mean, we are criminals guilty of felony fibbing who are escaping from your sweet parents."

Jack scowls at me. "You are not helping."

"No, I'm not. Because I have no frigging idea why we're running away."

"So we don't have to—It's because we—" He throws his hands up and growls. "You know we cannae answer their questions without explaining about the you-know-what."

"Now our baby is a you-know-what? Maybe we should just tell them."

"It's too early, you said. We should wait. That was your idea."

"Yeah, I know. Maybe I was wrong." I move in front of him, laying my palms on his chest. "How else are we going to explain why I'm living in your house? Your parents think we're a couple again, and I don't want to lead them on."

"Because you'll never come back to me."

I gaze into his eyes, unable to speak or move. Does he want us to be a couple again? I've assumed he doesn't want that based on his anger about the way I left him two years ago. But his tone of voice when he spoke those words a few seconds ago makes me wonder. He sounded like…he wants to be with me as more than a friend or a baby daddy.

A deliberate throat-clearing shatters the moment.

Behind Jack, I see Callum standing a few yards away.

"Sorry to interrupt," he says, "but you two came in my car. You'll need the keys."

Jack turns around to face Callum. "How will you get home?"

"Alex and Cat can give me a ride. I'll pick up my car in the morning." He tosses Jack the keys. "I think you and Autumn need a wee break from the family."

Callum heads off in the direction of the backyard.

He's limping. I hadn't noticed that before, but then, I hadn't seen him walking until we arrived at Greer and Alistair's house earlier. Once we got here, there had been too many people around for me to notice if Callum had been walking awkwardly.

Jack and I climb into his brother's car. He insists on driving.

While he steers the Rover down the streets of Loch Fairbairn, I ask, "Why is Callum limping? I know it's none of my business, but I'm curious."

"I told you he was injured six months ago, when he was still a firefighter."

"Right. Does he have a lingering injury?"

"Aye, but Dr. Buchanan, the family GP, thinks Callum should've recovered fully by now, and his physical trauma has healed which means it's psychological. I offered to refer Callum to a good therapist who could help him work through it, but he won't go."

"Your brother doesn't trust your professional judgment?"

"He's bloody-minded, that's all. It's a MacTaggart family trait."

"No kidding." I gaze out at the quaint shops whizzing past us. "You never did tell me what Callum does for a living these days."

"He works for our cousin Aidan, who owns a construction company. Callum is a carpenter. He used to do that as a hobby, but Aidan suggested he should try it as a profession now that he's not a firefighter anymore."

"It's good to have a backup plan. I've never had an actual plan, so I couldn't have a backup."

We lapse into silence for the rest of the ride home. Once we're inside Jack's house, he announces he needs to take care of paperwork in his office. Yeah, right. He needs to hunker down for a while until he recovers from our visit with his family. At least I've met some of them, finally. Jack volunteered to introduce me to them, so I decide to cut him some slack for the rest of the day. He can hide in his office if that makes him feel better.

I take a nap. Maybe some sleep will clear my mind and help me figure out what to do about everything.

Chapter Eighteen

Jack

Istay in my office until dinnertime, then I crawl out of my cocoon and look for Autumn. She isn't in her bedroom or the bathroom which I can tell because the doors are open, and she's not in the living room either. The kitchen is also empty. I peer out the kitchen window into the backyard.

There she is, relaxing on a patio chair. Her eyes are closed, and her lips are curved into a faint smile.

Bod an Donais, that woman is bonnie.

I knock on the window. When she looks at me, I wave for her to come inside.

Autumn walks into the house a moment later. "What's up?"

"What would you like to have for dinner?"

"Could we go out to eat?"

I can't help grimacing. "The only restaurant in town is the cafe."

"You mean the one where we had our ill-fated blind date. No pizza delivery?"

"The cafe does deliver, but they don't have pizza."

"Great. Let's order in. Whatever they've got is good with me."

She always was easy to please when it came to restaurants—and easy to please in bed too. I try not to think about seducing Autumn while we wait for our food order to arrive, or while we're eating our meal, or while we wash the dishes, and especially while we watch television together. I let Autumn choose what we watch, and she picks a series about single women in New York City who love to blether and love to shag. The sex scenes make my cock ache. I keep glancing at Autumn, admiring her lovely breasts and her lips, wondering how long I can wait before I'll need to shag her again or risk going insane.

It's a bad idea. She's right about that.

But my cock thinks it's a bloody fantastic idea.

When we finally say good night and retreat into our respective rooms, I have an erection that throbs like it's demanding I go into the other bedroom and fuck my ex-wife. Rubbing one off doesn't help. I start thinking about Autumn again immediately after I come, and within ten minutes, I'm hard again.

All right, I was thinking about her *while* I rubbed one off. That's the problem. I cannae stop fantasizing about her. I swear her breasts have gotten larger, but I imagine that's common during pregnancy. Still, the sight of her tits, even concealed under her shirt, makes me want to suck on her nipples until she starts writhing and moaning.

I'll never get any sleep if I cannae stop thinking about her.

Which means I need a drink.

Crawling out of bed, I walk into the hallway.

Autumn almost runs into me. "Oh, Jack. What are you doing?"

Going to my office to get drunk. That's the truth, but I won't admit it to her.

The nightie she's wearing barely covers her erse. The neckline dips low enough that I can see the entire side slopes of her breasts, and the slender straps leave her shoulders exposed. The sight of her bare legs makes me imagine having them wrapped around me while I thrust into her wet heat.

"Are you okay, Jack?"

I've been standing here like a coma patient someone propped upright with a metal pole. She must think I'm off my head.

"Need the bog," I say. "Ah, the bathroom."

"I remember what 'bog' means." Her attention flicks down to my groin. She jerks her gaze back to my face, her eyes a touch wider than before. "Better say good night."

She starts to walk away, but I catch her arm.

What am I doing? I should not shag my ex-wife. But being in the same house with her, seeing her in that scrap of a nightgown… All of it is driving me over the edge. That's the only excuse I have for saying, "Donnae go yet."

"We shouldn't do what you're thinking of doing."

"Aye, we should." I back her up to the wall, pressing my entire body against hers. Christ, she feels perfect, soft and warm, and she smells perfect too. "You want it as much as I do. Can ye tell me honestly that's not true?"

"Of course it's true. We've always had incredible sex, but we'll only be more confused later if we give in to our desires now."

Part of my mind knows she's right. The rest of it can't think, not anymore, and that part of my brain wants only one thing—to push inside her body and make us both come.

"Tell me to stop," I say, sliding a finger underneath the slender strap of her nightie, pushing it off her shoulder.

She shuts her eyes, her lips parted. "Oh God, it's been too long."

I drag my lips down her throat to her shoulder, where I plant an open-mouth kiss on her skin.

"Jack, we shouldn't, but…" She moans when I tug the satin fabric away from her breast. "I want you so much."

That's not a no, is it? She hasn't told me to stop, so I cup her breast in my hand and seal my mouth around the tip. When she moans again, I scrape my tongue over the peak, then suck on it.

Her hands grasp my head, holding it to her chest.

I massage her breast and keep suckling it.

Suddenly, she shoves my head away. "We can't do this. I'm sorry. We'll both regret it later if we do this now."

No, I won't regret it. Well, maybe I will. But I don't care.

Autumn lays a hand on my cheek, her lips curling upward a touch. "Please don't be mad. I do want this, want you, but… I don't know. It's got to be wrong somehow, right?"

I'd like to believe her use of "wrong" and "right" in the same sentence, separated by only one word, represents a Freudian slip of some sort. She admitted she wants me. For a moment, she desperately wanted me to take her.

She kisses my cheek and sashays into her bedroom, shutting the door.

The woman I crave more than any other lass on earth told me yes, then no. What am I meant to make of that? The woman is going to drive me barking mad.

I go into my office and get out an opened bottle of Ben Nevis. Single-malt Scotch whisky, that's what I need. How much will it take to dull the lust? I pour two fingers into a glass and down it in two swallows. The warmth rushes through me, followed by the faintest sensation of relaxation. I drop onto my chair behind the desk and pour three fingers this time, forcing myself to sip and enjoy the flavor of the whisky rather than mainlining it. The tension eases out of me little by little, and I lean my head back against the chair.

Closing my eyes, I try to empty my thoughts.

A memory flares in my mind. Autumn. In that nightie. Her breast in my hand and my mouth. Her skin is soft as silk, and it smells like powder and woman. The feel of her fingers in my hair, her hands clutching me to her...

"*Mhac na galla*," I mutter, then I down the rest of my whisky in one gulp.

It burns down my throat, but I need the burn to rouse me from my fantasy of Autumn. It's no fantasy, though. I had her pressed up against me, her nipple in my mouth. If she hadn't pushed me away, I could've had her, full stop. *I do want this*, she'd said, *want you*.

With a groan, I pour another finger of whisky. I don't drink it, though. Getting drunk isn't the way to convince Autumn sex is not a bad idea. Maybe I need to show her I care about giving her pleasure, not just getting my *slat* inside her so I can *caith*. Yes, I want to fuck her and come inside that beautiful body, but I need her to enjoy it too.

More than enjoy it. I need her to crave me as much as I crave her.

She wants us to be friends first, but I can't focus on repairing our relationship when I have fifty-seven erections a day.

I pick up my glass and swirl the amber liquid inside it.

An idea sparks to life in my mind, one that will show Autumn I'm not a selfish *tolla-thon*, at least not when it comes to sex.

Setting down the glass, I march out of the office and straight to the closed door to Autumn's room. I don't see any light leaking out under the door, so it must be dark in there. Maybe she's asleep.

Not for long.

I turn the knob slowly, careful not to make any noise, and ease the door inward just enough that I can slip inside the room. The glow of the moon shines through the window, casting its milky light on the womanly shape in the bed. She's lying on her back, her head turned to the side, the covers concealing her up to her hips. One strap of her nightie has fallen off her shoulder, and her hair sprays across the pillow.

Tiptoeing closer, I hesitate at the foot of the bed.

She stirs, moaning softly, but seems to be asleep.

I move closer, peeling the covers away from her body inch by inch, careful not to disturb her. Then I hesitate again, suddenly wondering if my plan makes me a selfish erse after all. No, this is for her, not for me. It's a gift.

Or maybe I'm a bloody stupid *bod ceann*.

Either way, I'm doing this.

I crawl onto the bed, position my head above her hips, and gently slide the satin fabric up to her belly. The scent of her envelops me—the scent of her cream. Is she dreaming about sex? If she is, I hope she's dreaming about me shagging her, not some other bloke.

Time to give her what she needs.

Chapter Nineteen

Autumn

I'm dreaming about Jack, about the two of us getting it on like horny teenagers, when an odd sensation rouses me from my steamy fantasy. Though I'm not asleep anymore, I haven't reached full wakefulness, lingering in that blissful reverie between dreams and reality. That sensation, it's like a feather fluttering over my skin, starting on my thigh and moving higher until it reaches my hip. Whatever it is, this feels so good.

Something damp flicks over my skin.

A tongue? Whose tongue? I must still be dreaming. Don't care. I want this delicious, teasing sensation to go on and on. I'm wet from my dream of Jack, so maybe this imaginary feather-tongue feeling will make me come. I'd love that.

Two hands push my thighs apart.

Okay, that's not imaginary. Is it? Oh who cares. I love the way those lips—yeah, not feathers, I realize—move over my skin and that tongue leaves a warm, damp trail that cools once the warmth of that mouth moves further down. Fingers glide up my inner thighs, then back down, only to glide up again.

A hard body lies between my legs.

"Jack?" I mumble, still too sleepy to understand what's going on.

"Shh," he says, and then his stubbly chin grazes my inner thigh as he licks and kisses the hollow of my hip. "Relax and let it happen."

Let what happen?

He nuzzles my mound, then dips his head to push his mouth between my folds.

Oh God, he's going to do this. Now. While I'm fuzzy-headed from sleep. Who cares? That dream got me so hot that I need an orgasm desperately.

So I spread my legs wider and grasp the slats in the headboard.

His tongue darts out once, twice, three times, like he's sampling the taste of my flesh before he devours me. Groaning deeply, he latches his mouth onto my hard nub and suckles it.

"Jack," I moan, gripping the slats harder.

Licking, suckling, groaning and almost growling, he consumes me with his mouth while he massages my folds. I'm tingling down there, burning for release, gripping the slats hard enough it hurts, but I don't care. My breathing turns harsher and sharper, like rough gasps, until I can't catch my breath. He slides a finger inside me, pumping it while he releases my clit and rasps his tongue over my inner folds.

"Oh God, yes," I cry out, writhing and panting.

With two fingers, he thrusts into me in a measured rhythm as he draws my clit into his mouth and nips it.

My entire body freezes, trapped in that exquisitely rapturous moment right before climax. Can't breathe, can't speak, can't do anything except wait to plummet off that cliff. His tongue pushes me over the edge, and suddenly, I'm in free-fall, tumbling and tumbling and tumbling, reveling in the exhilarating release as my body pulsates like it's trying to grip his fingers but can't do it. I need *him* inside me, not just his fingers.

As the climax fades, it leaves behind a lingering warmth and tingling, the aftermath of intense pleasure.

Jack kisses my tummy, slides off the bed, and walks out the door, closing it behind him.

What on earth? He sneaked into my bed strictly to give me an orgasm? I can't understand why he would do that. He got nothing out of the encounter.

For a moment, I consider chasing after him to demand he explain. But I decide against that. Why complain when he gave me the release I've needed ever since I saw him again a few days ago? It would be rude or something. Plus, that orgasm has left me feeling so relaxed and satisfied that all I want to do is go back to sleep.

And that's what I do.

I wake up in the morning feeling as good as I had last night after Jack's little visit. After ten minutes of lounging in bed, reminiscing about how my ex-husband skulked into my room in the dark, I finally make myself get up. Jack's bedroom door is still closed when I go into the bathroom. I take a nice long shower, smiling every time I remember last night and wishing Jack would skulk into the shower with me.

He doesn't. I get clean all alone.

Jack is in the kitchen making breakfast when I emerge from the bathroom. While he whips up a meal, he's whistling and dancing.

I stop on the threshold, watching him, stunned by his behavior. Jack dancing? Jack whistling? He doesn't do that. During our time in Vegas, he did lots of things I'm sure no one who knows him would believe he'd ever do, stuff like belting out love songs off-key and doing bad ballroom-dance moves. I didn't care that we both sucked at singing and dancing. It was fun and romantic. We had such a great time back then.

Post-Vegas, things weren't so much fun. And he still hasn't explained why, not fully.

Jack notices me and grins. "Good morning, *gràidh*."

Then he rushes over to me, pulls me into his arms, and twirls us over and over while we dance a circuit around the island. We halt by the stove, but Jack keeps dancing with me, though we stay in one spot this time.

And he's still smiling, his eyes sparkling.

It's cloudy outside, but I swear the sun still makes his eyes glitter with good humor. Fantastic humor, actually. I haven't seen him like this since Vegas.

"What's gotten into you this morning?" I ask while giggling because he just dipped me.

"I'm in a good mood," he says. "Donnae ruin it. Just enjoy the moment."

Jack is telling me to "enjoy the moment." When I left my room, did I stumble through a portal into another dimension? This must be a parallel-universe version of my ex-husband.

But I take his advice. I enjoy the moment.

Until I can't stand the suspense anymore and have to ask, "Why are you so happy? I would've thought sneaking into my bed last night would've made you grumpy today."

"Why?"

"Because you gave me an incredible climax and then left. You didn't get your happy ending."

He stops dancing, though he keeps his arm around me and his hand in mine. The joy on his face mutates into something almost melancholy. "I don't know if there will be a happy ending, but I want to make the most of every day with you."

My throat goes thick. I gaze into his eyes but can't figure out what he's feeling right now. I know he won't tell me if I ask. That's Jack. He counsels other people through their problems, but he won't talk to me, not really. I know I hurt him when I walked out on our marriage, but I want to make it right with him. I need to do that.

"I meant 'happy ending' as in having an orgasm," I say. "You scurried away right after giving me one of those. I wanted you to stay, Jack. I wanted us to have sex."

"So did I, but you said we shouldn't do that."

"Oral sex is okay, but you won't make love to me because that would go against what I said." I lay my hands on his chest, gazing into his eyes again. "That doesn't make a lot of sense."

"It did last night, after two glasses of whisky."

"Oh, now I get it." I tap a finger on his lips. "Which kind of booze gave you that epiphany? The American kind spelled with an E before the Y? Or the Scottish version without the E?"

"Ben Nevis. The Scottish brand without the E."

"You should've invited me to have a drink with you."

His brows hike up. "You're pregnant. That means no alcohol."

"I could've had apple juice. And I would've loved to share a drink with you, Jack, even a nonalcoholic one." I lean in to place a soft kiss on his lips. "I'd love to share anything with you, if you'll let me in."

"You're inside the house right now."

"Don't get snarky on me. You know what I mean."

He stares at me, impassive, for several seconds. Then he pulls away. "I need to finish making breakfast before it all gets burned and cold."

I stop myself right before I point out nothing can be burned and cold at the same time. My suggestion that I'd share anything with him if only he'd let me in seems to have upset him, though I'm not sure why. Yesterday, he suggested "informal therapy" for us. Today, he doesn't want to talk to me. I hate that I ruined his good mood, but I had to do it.

At least we've got several months to deal with our issues.

What if that's not long enough?

After breakfast, while we're still sitting at the kitchen table, Jack clears his throat and announces, "Let's go for a walk around the village."

"Huh?" I swerve my attention away from the window and straight to Jack. "What did you say?"

"I said let's go for a walk in the village."

"Are you serious? The hostage is allowed to explore the area?"

"You are not a hostage. I took you to my parents' house, didn't I?"

"Sure, but you dragged me away before I was ready to leave."

He slouches in his chair, twisting his mouth into that scowl-smile expression I've seen before when he can't figure out what to say. "Ma was asking questions. I was afraid you might accidentally tell her about the bairn."

"Not sure how I would've accidentally spilled the beans, but it's interesting you used the word 'afraid' to describe your behavior."

"Donnae be analyzing me, Autumn. I'm the psychologist, not you."

I fold my arms over my chest, leaning back in my chair, though I'm not slouching like he is. "We talked about this already. You can't analyze yourself, which leaves me to handle the therapizing of you."

"Therapizing is not a word."

"As of three seconds ago, it is. I'll scribble it into that big dictionary you keep on the shelf behind your desk."

"You would deface the *Oxford English Dictionary*?" He looks genuinely horrified at the prospect.

"Why do you have a British dictionary, anyway? You're Scottish."

His scowl-smile returns, and he makes a derisive noise. "At least I'm not using Webster's dictionary. Bloody stupid ersehole, that Webster bloke."

"Don't diss an American icon. And it's called Merriam-Webster's now, has been for ages. Noah Webster codified the American way of spelling things which, if you ask me, makes a lot more sense than the British way." I slant forward, arms still folded. "Don't even get me started on the Scottish way of spelling and talking."

"I should get Alex over here to explain to you why UK English is the real version."

"Sure, invite him over. I'd love to see him and Cat again."

"Ahmno arguing about language with you." Jack smacks his elbows down on the table and rests his forehead in his raised palms. "Do ye want to go for a walk or not?"

"Yes, I do. Right now." I push up out of my chair. "Let's go."

"The dishes—"

"Can wait until later." I move around to his side of the table and grasp his arm, tugging gently. "Get off your 'erse,' Jack. You said you'd show me the village, and I'll keep pestering you until you do what you promised."

"Aye, I know." He groans out a sigh, then gets up. "Donnae expect excitement. Loch Fairbairn is a sleepy wee village."

"Just show it to me. Now."

We exit the house a few minutes later, and Jack practically jogs down the sidewalk which forces me to hustle too.

"Slow down," I say. "What happened to worrying about my delicate condition? You know, how you think I'm not supposed to lift a pillow or walk farther than from the bedroom to the kitchen."

He slows his pace to something approaching normal. "Sorry."

"What's up with you? First, you're dancing and whistling, then you turn back into Stoic Jack."

"Please stop making up bloody stupid names for me. I'm Jack, that's all. It's not necessary to add adjectives in front of my name."

"Yeah, it is."

He flashes me a frown as he stops us in front of a big house that has a sign identifying it as a historic landmark. "Here's your first tourist destination. Alpin Lithgow built this house for his bride in 1783, one week after he founded the village of Loch Fairbairn."

"How does a person found a village? Did he, like, stab a Scottish flag into the ground or what?"

"There was a settlement here long before that, but Lithgow gave it a name and everyone agreed when he said it was now a village, not just a settlement." Jack stuffs his hands into his pants pockets. "That's how he did it."

His story doesn't explain everything, not to my satisfaction, but I decide he's edgy enough without me pestering him for more details.

Jack seizes my hand, all but dragging me down the sidewalk.

Well, at least he's dragging me at a fast walk instead of a sprint.

He veers across the street with me in tow.

A car horn blares.

Jack gestures wildly with his free arm and shouts something in Gaelic, and the driver of the car that honked gives him the finger.

"Donnae be driving so fast in town," Jack hollers at the man behind the wheel. "Everybody knows you don't look where you're going, Ranulf. Too busy gawping at the lasses."

The man in the car—Ranulf, apparently—thrusts his head out the window. "Outta the way, MacTaggart, or you'll be needing a real doctor, Mr. PhD."

Jack and I hop onto the sidewalk.

Ranulf floors it, tires squealing as he rockets away.

I resist when Jack tries to drag me down this side of the street. "I'm not moving another inch until you stop acting like a lunatic."

"Me? Ranulf is the lunatic. He drives like a bat out of bleeding hell, and everyone knows you've got to watch out for that eejit's car coming down the road."

"I believe you, but that doesn't explain your behavior. You've been dragging me along like an unwanted suitcase."

Maybe that comparison doesn't make total sense, but I don't care.

He rubs his forehead. "I know. I'm sorry."

"Tell me what's wrong, Jack. Please."

"Not sure."

"Which is code for 'I donnae want to tell ye.' That's not good enough anymore."

He screws up his mouth, but it seems like he's trying not to smile instead of trying not to scowl. "Why are you suddenly making fun of the way I talk? You never used to do that."

"Everything is different now. We're not married anymore, and I'm not afraid to tell you the truth anymore."

"Aren't you?"

"No." Facing him, I take both his hands in mine and look him straight in the eye. "I've told you about my family. That was the big thing I was afraid to say, but there is more stuff. I want to tell you everything, Jack."

"Here on the street?"

"We're on the sidewalk, but that's beside the point." I thread our fingers, inching closer. "You like to talk about Vegas like you weren't in control for those twelve days, but you were. And if you ask me, which I seriously doubt you ever would, you were more yourself in Vegas than you are when you're at home in Scotland."

His brows squish together. "That makes no sense."

"You weren't drunk the entire time or high on drugs. You chose to be that person, the uninhibited, sexy, adventurous man who made me feel like I could do anything as long as I was with him. With you, Jack."

"What you mean is you were disappointed when I brought you home and you saw who I really am."

Holy heaven, he's stubborn. The pigheaded man can't admit I saw something in him that nobody else ever has, as far as I can tell. Cracking his shell might take longer than I could ever have imagined.

We have seven months.

"I know this is hard for you," I say, "opening up and being honest with yourself, not to mention me. But I will not bring our baby into the world with two bickering parents."

"What do you want me to do?"

"I need total honesty from you, and I'll give you the same. Our marriage was a disaster, and that's down to both of us. It's time to rip open all those old wounds."

He winces.

I don't like saying these things to him, but if I want honesty from him, I have to give it first. "I get that you're embarrassed by the way you acted in Vegas, but I wish I could convince you there was nothing wrong with anything you did back then."

He makes a derisive noise. "I almost got arrested."

"Yeah, but you didn't. And watching you dance in a fountain, just to make me smile, was the most amazing thing anyone has ever done for me."

"I did that only because you were fashed when I told you I needed to go home soon."

"Not fashed. Sad. I didn't want to lose you, but I wound up doing that anyway."

He curls his fingers to clasp my hand, and his voice grows hushed. "I didn't want to lose you either."

Peripherally, I notice several people have stopped to watch us.

"Uh, maybe we should start walking," I say, though I don't want to move, don't want to look away from him because he's never gazed at me with so much longing before. "People are staring at us."

He glances around like he's just remembered we're on a public street.

The people watching us seem very interested, though they're too far away to hear what we're saying. Neither of us has spoken in a raised voice.

Jack releases my hands and turns to start walking, but he hesitates, glancing back at me. When he speaks, his voice is soft, almost tender. "You think I didn't love you, but you have no idea how I feel."

He ambles down the sidewalk.

I stand there paralyzed, totally confused by his conflicting tenses. He said I think he "didn't" love me, past tense, but he also said I have no idea how he "feels," present tense. Yeah, my stupid heart wants to interpret that to mean he did love me and he still loves me. But I won't let myself get false hope for us.

So I hurry after him.

Chapter Twenty

Jack

At least I'm not dragging Autumn around like "an unwanted suitcase," as she phrased it. We walk side by side, though not holding hands, while I show her Loch Fairbairn. Honestly, there's not much to the village. A few shops, a handful of professional offices, the cafe, and the village square. I quicken our pace when we pass by the cafe, and of course, Autumn notices.

She smiles and laughs. "Slow down, Jack. The cafe is not the scene of a vicious crime. I kind of doubt the cops will arrest you for arguing with your ex-wife in public."

I decide she's right and I am being an eejit, so I slow down to a normal walking pace. "Sorry. I don't like to think about how I behaved that day, during our ill-fated blind date."

Autumn halts, tugging my arm to make sure I stop too. "I know I called it that the other day, but our blind date was not ill-fated. It was a mess, for sure, with you getting covered in soup. Believe it nor not, that wasn't the worst date I've ever had."

"How could it not be? I acted like a *bod ceann*." I suddenly realize I might not have ever explained that phrase to her. "Which means I'm a dickhead."

Her laughter is gentle and affectionate. "No, you're not a dickhead. Pig-headed? Absolutely. Confusing? Sometimes. But never a *bod ceann*." She raises her hand to silence me when I open my mouth to speak. "Yes, you kinda sorta held me hostage for a day or so, but I get why you reacted that way. It's all right, Jack. Stop beating yourself up."

"Maybe I'm not a *bod ceann*"—I am for certain, though she's too kind to tell me so—"but I have made you feel unwelcome. I ruined our blind date, and I haven't behaved well since."

"We both ruined our blind date, but it wasn't ill-fated. Two stubborn, scared people can't have a good experience when their friends set them up like that. We hadn't seen each other in almost two years."

"Aye, but I was the one who sneaked out while you were sleeping."

"You mean at the hotel. After we made love for an hour."

Why does she need to mention that? It doesn't matter how long we shagged. Does it? Maybe I'm in denial about what our hour-long encounter meant.

"Yes," I say, "I'm talking about that afternoon. I know you think I got up and left as soon as you fell asleep, but that's not what happened."

"I woke up, and you were gone. That's what happened."

"But I didn't leave straight away." I study the concrete paving stones under my feet while a strange itch creeps over my skin. "I sat there watching you sleep for eighteen minutes, then I left."

"You did what?"

I force myself to look at her. "I had, ah, some, well, trouble making myself leave that room."

She stares at me, her mouth open, for several seconds. Then her lips curve into a sweet smile. "That's wonderful, Jack."

Wonderful? I just confessed to abandoning her without saying a word or leaving her a note. How is that a good thing?

Autumn touches my cheek, still smiling sweetly. "You didn't want to leave me. That's important."

"How? I did leave you. Crept away like a bloody criminal."

"But you had to work hard to convince yourself to skulk away. That means you don't hate me."

She thought I hated her? The daft woman couldn't possibly have believed that.

I hadn't given her any cause to think I don't hate her. I've blamed her for the breakup of our marriage, when I know I was culpable too. The fact I had to force myself to walk out of that hotel room suggests I have feelings for her. Suggests? No, it's bloody obvious to everyone but me, I'm fair certain of that. Why else would Alex trick us into a blind date? I'd talked to him about Autumn before that, though I hadn't said much. Is Alex Thorne, the British Bastard, intuitive enough to sense how I feel about my ex-wife even when I don't? Catriona had to virtually whack him over the head to make him see he loved her. I suppose he learned from that experience.

As for my feelings for Autumn…

Gazing into her luminous green eyes, I get a pain in my chest. Aye, even I'm not thick-headed enough to ignore the signs. I do have feelings for her. What sort, exactly, I'm not sure yet. But I don't want her to leave me again.

Christ, am I having a breakthrough moment? I tell my clients that sort of bollocks can happen, but I never imagined I would experience it.

"Of course I don't hate you," I say, my voice hushed, though I didn't intend to speak that way. "I wanted our marriage to work. Losing you was the most devastating thing that's ever happened to me."

She rubs her thumb over my cheek, her sweet smile softening and her gaze full of emotion.

Why am I telling her this? She'll think I'm an eejit and an erse.

But I can't stop the words from coming out. "I know I changed once we were married, and I know you think it's because I was ashamed of you. That's rubbish. I was ashamed of myself, of the way I talked you into marrying me and moving to Scotland for me. I never asked what you wanted because I wanted you, full stop. It was selfish and cruel."

"No, Jack, you have never been cruel to me. Never." She takes my face in both her hands. "I wanted the same thing, for us to be together, and I didn't care if we lived in Scotland or Antarctica."

I notice movement out of the corners of my eyes and swivel my gaze left and right to see what's going on. The crowd has grown. A smattering of onlookers has become a true audience, though I doubt they can hear what we're saying to each other. They can see our expressions and body language, I'm sure. Right now, we must look like a couple having an emotional and intimate conversation that involves intense but conflicted feelings.

That's what we *are* doing. But has the crowd figured that out yet?

"Jack, are you listening to me?" Autumn asks.

"No, sorry." I nod toward one part of the crowd. "Haven't you noticed the audience?"

She glances around, and her eyes widen for a moment. "Oh. Maybe we should continue this discussion later. In private. Wouldn't want anyone to get the wrong idea."

By "the wrong idea," I assume she means those people might think we're reconciling and will be remarried next week. Of course, we can't get married that quickly, according to the law.

Not that I want to marry her again.

I turn and gesture for Autumn to start walking. "Let's finish our tour of the village."

"Sure."

A trio of figures separates from the crowd and approaches us.

My three cousins—Isla, Kirsty, and Elspeth, the self-proclaimed Witches of Ballachulish—grin and chatter softly in Gaelic to each other. The barmy lasses are talking about whether Autumn and I are properly aligned in the zodiac and whether we need a "chakra adjustment." Autumn seems confused, though she must've understood at least two of the words my cousins said—zodiac and chakra.

Isla smiles in her beatific way, though I have no idea why she looks so happy about seeing me with my ex-wife. Isla turns her gaze to Autumn, then to me, and she sighs with deep contentment. "It's wonderful to see you two getting along. We heard about the incident at the cafe, and I feared my sweet cousin would never speak to his wife again."

"She's my ex-wife," I pronounce, and I might have sounded less than pleased.

"Chill out, Jack," Autumn says. "Don't get grumpy again. Be polite, hey? Introduce me to your cousins."

Autumn sounds pleasant, not grumpy like I apparently did. *Mhac na galla*, why did my cousins have to see us having an intense conversation? Maybe they won't tell anyone else. Maybe I should ask them to keep it to themselves. Aye, and maybe I can get everyone who's been watching us to sign nondisclosure agreements.

I clear my throat and introduce my cousins. "This is Isla, Kirsty, and Elspeth. They're Logan's sisters."

"The Witches of Ballachulish?" Autumn says, excitement in her voice and on her face. "Jack told me all about you guys. I met Logan yesterday, and I'm so happy to meet more of Jack's family. Ballachulish is a village nearby, right? Do you three live there?"

"Not all of us," Isla says. "We grew up there, just like some of our other cousins. I've stayed in Ballachulish, but Kirsty lives in Loch Fairbairn, and Elspeth moved to Fort William last year. That's just down the road from Ballachulish."

"I'd love to see all those towns. Love to see everything in Scotland."

"Didnae Jack show you the sights when you were married?"

"No. He, um, was so busy with work that he didn't have time."

Is Autumn making excuses for me? Why would she want to do that?

"Oh, aye," Kirsty says. "Jack is a lot like Rory in that respect. They both work too hard. Well, Rory used to until he met Emery and she sorted him out."

Elspeth grins at me, then Autumn. "Maybe you can sort Jack out. The MacTaggart men have a habit of not dealing with their underlying issues until the right woman gives them a kick in the erse. I hear British men are the same way. Cat says Alex is for sure, and Rika Dixon told me—"

"Autumn and I have to go," I say. "She wants to see the village. All of it, not just this one section of pavement."

Christ, I'm sounding grumpy again. I should call Logan and tell him to rein in his sisters before they drive me barking mad.

"We could go with you," Kirsty says.

Isla gives me a sympathetic smile. "We have shopping to do, don't we? Besides, Jack and Autumn need time alone to get reacquainted."

At least Isla didn't make that word sound filthy, the way Alex had done.

The Witches of Ballachulish wish us "blessed be" and wander away.

My ex-wife gives me an annoyed look. "I wanted to talk to them. Get the scoop on you and your family from your family. I'd also love to ask them if they really have magical powers."

"I can tell you the answer to that question." I lean toward her. "No, they bloody do not have magical powers."

"Are you sure? You can be kind of closed-minded about stuff like that."

"Not being fascinated with so-called documentaries about ancient astronauts does not mean I'm closed-minded."

She pats my cheek. "You should hang out with the Witches of Ballachulish more often. Maybe they can open your mind and widen your horizons."

"I donnae need sorting out, not from you or anyone."

"Bullshit, Jack. You need tons of sorting, washing, and ironing out."

Now she's comparing me to laundry? I have no idea how to respond to that, so I gesture one more time for her to start walking. This time, no one interrupts us. The crowd dissipates, and we pass only the occasional bystanders as I show her the rest of the village. Since there isn't much to it, our walk doesn't take long. I love this village, but it's not a bustling metropolis. Will Autumn be happy here? She's lived in Atlantic City ever since she walked out on me.

Or has she? I never bothered to ask where she'd been living.

Autumn grabs my arm, forcing me to stop.

"What is it?" I ask.

"The sign on that office we just passed. 'Rory MacTaggart, solicitor,' it says. He's one of your cousins, right? I saw that sign last time I was in Scotland."

"Aye. Rory is Cat's older brother, the second oldest in their family."

"Right. Lachlan is the oldest, then it goes Rory, Fiona, Catriona, Aidan, and Jamie. All of them except for Fiona are married."

Why is she reciting a branch of the family tree to me? I know that already. They're my cousins, after all.

Then I realize something and ask, "Why have you memorized the birth order of my cousins?"

"Because you told me about them back in Vegas. I loved hearing all your stories about your family, including every cousin. I have a really good memory, so that information is stuck in my brain forever."

"Do you have a photographic memory? Logan does, but he's the only person I know who has that."

"Not sure. I remember things, that's all I know." She hunches her shoulders, averting her gaze to the street. "At least, I remember the things you tell me. Not so much with other people."

For a moment, I can't think or speak. She holds on to every scrap of information I tell her about my family. Because *I* told her those things. She listened to every minute of my blethering.

"Rory's not in his office today," I announce, strictly to change the subject. "He's semi-retired now and only in his office on Mondays and Thursdays."

"He's semi-retired because he married Emery and now they have twin babies. He wants to spend plenty of time with his wife and kids."

"Aye, that's right." I hesitate, then ask the question I thought of earlier. "Where have you lived since we got divorced? I assumed it was Atlantic City."

"Partially. I quit being a blackjack dealer two months after I started the job. It was too stressful, and I didn't really like working in a casino. So I went back to Nevada."

"What did you do after that?"

"Various temp jobs, nothing special."

She's still staring at the street with her shoulders hunched.

I touch her arm. "If you're worried I'll be disappointed in you, don't. I've never been ashamed of you and never will be."

Her gaze veers back to me, her eyes large and shimmering. "You mean that, don't you?"

"Yes. And I don't want to hear any more about what a disappointment you are, because you're not." I clasp her hand. "Let's go to the cafe and order dessert."

"You mean let's return to the scene of the crime."

"No, I mean let's have a piece at the cafe."

She smiles. "I'd love that."

And I love seeing her smile.

Chapter Twenty-One

Autumn

I thought 'have a piece' meant eating a sandwich," I say as we walk into the Cafe of Doom side by side. Jack has relaxed somewhat, but encountering his three cousins knocked him off-kilter even more than he had been before they showed up. We had a real conversation, an important one, right before that, so I'm feeling pretty darn good right now.

Jack doesn't hate me. That's what I call progress.

He'd told me that when I left, it devastated him. I still don't know what to think or say about that. The end of our marriage devastated me too. But I was the one who left, so it's up to me to fix things and make sure we can at least be friends. Our child deserves that much.

We've just sat down at one of the outdoor tables when a waitress approaches us. It's Deirdre, the girl who spilled soup all over Jack last time we were here. She halts several feet away, her eyes going wide.

"Don't worry," I say to her. "We're only ordering dessert. And we won't be sniping at each other the entire time either."

The girl relaxes, her eyes no longer bulging. She gives us menus. "Would ye like me to wait while ye decide what to order, or should I come back in a few minutes?"

"You can wait," I say. "I already know what I want. But I don't know how to pronounce it, so I'll point instead."

I jab a finger at the item on the menu labeled "*cranachan.*" What that is, I'm not entirely sure. The description on the menu calls it "a popular

Scottish dessert made with toasted oats, raspberries, cream, and Ben Nevis single-malt Scotch whisky." Sounds yummy. But only if I can order an alcohol-free version.

Jack raises his brows at me. "Do you even know what *cranachan* is?"

"Sure. The menu told me."

He seems skeptical, like he thinks I'll be shocked by what the dessert contains. "It has whisky in it, you know."

"I was going to ask for a whisky-free version." I glance at Deirdre. "Can I do that?"

"Of course," Deirdre says.

Jack gives our waitress a polite smile. "We'll both have *cranachan*. Thank you, Deirdre."

The waitress blushes like she did the last time Jack and I came to this cafe, then she bustles off to get our treats.

"You do know that girl has a big crush on you," I say. "She blushes every time she sees you."

"How would you know that? You've seen the lass twice."

"And both times she blushed and gazed at you dreamily. Face it, she's crushing on you."

Jack rolls his eyes, contorting one side of his mouth. "You are imagining things. The lass does not feel that way about me. I donnae even know the girl."

"But *she* knows *you*." I lean forward and lower my voice. "I bet you've got a fan club of darling wee lassies who think you're the hottest thing since Tabasco sauce."

"I don't know what you're on about, but it's rubbish."

"No, what you're full of is rubbish. If you don't understand what I said, you can't know if it's stupid or not."

"Aye, I can. The idea that I have a fan club or even that Deirdre thinks I'm 'hot' is complete bollocks."

"But you are hot, Jack. I'll testify to that fact in court."

"There's no court for certifying lust."

Deirdre comes back with our desserts, each one housed in a tall glass that's filled up with layers of cream, raspberries, and oats. God, that looks good. I want to eat the whole dang thing right now. Deirdre gives us two spoons and bats her eyelashes at Jack.

"There you are, Dr. MacTaggart," she says, almost cooing the words. "I hope you and your friend will enjoy the *cranachan*."

She smiles shyly, then walks away.

I pick up my spoon. "Told you. That girl has a serious crush on the dreamy Dr. MacTaggart."

"Bollocks." He stabs his spoon into his dessert, pulling out a huge lump of it. "You're hallucinating, Autumn."

Jack shoves the giant spoonful into his mouth.

I take a dainty spoonful of my treat and slide it between my lips. Mm, it's so good. I moan because it not only tastes delicious, but it also makes me feel good too. There's no whisky in it to get me tipsy, so I must feel this way for the simple reason that I love a decadent dessert.

And maybe also because I now know Jack doesn't hate me.

We enjoy our treats while talking about where Jack wants to take me on our road trip around the Highlands. He thinks we should wait a few days for that, but not too long. He has to get back to work soon. When I suggest we could do day trips instead of one long road trip, he agrees that might be a better idea. That way neither of us will get too exhausted. I love sightseeing, but long car rides aren't my favorite thing.

Jack knows this, but I didn't know he knew until he says, "Donnae want you getting motion sickness. You're prone to it anyway, but now that you're pregnant, it might be more likely."

I don't think I ever told Jack I get car sick. He must've noticed without even asking. I get a funny warmth in my chest when I realize that.

After our snack, we head back the way we came, toward Jack's house. No crowds gather to watch us this time, and we don't say much during the trek. I admire the scenery more on the way home since I'm not being dragged down the streets of Loch Fairbairn by a stubborn man who's determined to avoid dealing with his issues at any cost. At least we did have a brief talk. That's a start.

Why did I think of Jack's house as home? I'm a guest there, not a room-mate or…anything else.

Once we get back to Jack's house, he brings out a road map and shows me the places he'd like to take me to on our day trips. It all sounds great, and I can't wait to explore Scotland. I also can't wait to get out of town with him, even if it's only for a day at a time, because I have a feeling he'll relax more when we're away from his hometown. Despite introducing me to some of his relatives, he still seems anxious about it.

Maybe he worries I'll accidentally blurt out the details of our time in Vegas and all the wild things we did together. I would never divulge those secrets, but he must worry I will.

Wondering is a kind of torture, so I decide to ask him.

"Are you afraid I'll tell everyone how you behaved in Vegas?" I ask. "Is that why you don't like me to spend time with your family?"

"No." He scrunches up his face. "Maybe. Ahmno sure."

"That's a super helpful answer. Thanks."

"What do you want me to say? Yes, I'm uncomfortable with the idea of anyone knowing about all the out-of-character things I did back then. But I haven't got a clue if that's why I'm acting like such a dafty now."

"I would never tell anyone personal stuff about you, not unless you say it's okay. You know that, don't you?"

"Aye." He folds up the map. "Let's not talk about that anymore. I should make lunch, anyway."

I watch Jack hustle into the kitchen, deciding I should let him make lunch alone this time. He seems like he needs time away from me. At least he's not hiding in his office with the door closed.

Since I have nothing else to do, I watch TV. Wow, does that get boring after days of doing not much else. I'm thinking about either going into the kitchen to help Jack with lunch or going out into the garden for fresh air when someone knocks on the front door. Should I answer? Jack hasn't said it's all right for me to do that, but he has introduced me to some of his relatives. Does that mean it's okay for me to open the front door?

I play it safe and shout, "Jack! Someone's at the door."

"Yes, and I'm feeling very unwelcome at the moment," the person outside hollers.

That sounds like Alex Thorne.

I'm about to shout that information to Jack when he trots out of the kitchen and straight to the door, swinging it open.

Alex leans against the jamb, arms crossed. "Ah, so this isn't a closed ecosystem after all. Are invasive species allowed inside?"

Jack gives him an exasperated look. "What do you want?"

"To warn you." Alex smirks. "The American Wives Club has a new mission, and it's you. Well, you and Autumn."

I hurry to the doorway, halting beside Jack. "The American Wives Club? You told me about them, and so did Jack. He calls them 'bonnie bampots' who interfere in things that aren't any of their business."

"That's right," Alex says. "And they have plans for you two."

Jack groans, his shoulders sagging. "What are they plotting now?"

"Not sure about the specifics. But you should expect a call from Emery. And do try not to snarl at her, Jack."

"Donnae snarl at anyone."

I try to suppress my laugh, but it bubbles out anyway.

"Autumn seems to have a different opinion," Alex says. "I've been on the receiving end of your snarling, so I can corroborate her story."

"She hasn't said anything," Jack tells Alex.

"Oh, her laughter tells me everything I need to know." Alex pushes away from the jamb. "Well, I've warned you. Cheers, Jack. Cheers, Autumn."

Alex walks away.

Jack shuts the door, leans against it, and sighs. "We're doomed."

"Come on, the American Wives Club can't be that bad. I thought you liked them."

"I do, individually. But when they get together, the meddling starts. Then their husbands get roped into it, and soon every MacTaggart winds up interfering in the lives of whoever their targets are at the time."

"We're their targets." I hold my hands over my belly without meaning to do it, holding them where our baby is growing inside me. "Maybe we should just tell everybody I'm pregnant. Then they'll understand we're not getting back together. I'm here strictly so we can figure out how to co-parent our baby."

"You said we shouldn't tell anyone yet. It's too early."

"I know, but that was before the meddling started. I don't want you to turn all grumpy again because the ladies in the American Wives Club have decided to play matchmaker."

Jack steps away from the door, scrubbing a hand through his hair. "No, let's wait to share the baby news. I know that's what you want, and you're right about the reasons for waiting. If those bloody women want to butt their wee noses into our business, we will ignore them."

"Okay," I say slowly because I'm not convinced that will work. "What if they show up at our door like Alex, Callum, and Grey and Jessica did?"

"I'll tell them to sod off."

"That's a friendly response. I'm sure the grapevine will quiet down right away after you growl that at them."

He bows his head, grasping it in both hands, and makes the most pitiful moany noise I've ever heard. "We really are doomed."

I peel his hands away from his head and kiss the top of it. "Relax, Jack. I'm sure it won't be as bad as you think. I mean, how much trouble can your family cause?"

Jack raises his head to look at me, his mouth twisting into a sardonic little smile. "You don't know the MacTaggarts."

That's true, but I still can't believe their meddling will be as big a headache as he makes it out to be. We don't have to cooperate with their meddling. Besides, we already got set up on a blind date, and we're already living in the same house. What more can anybody else do?

In the kitchen, the phone rings.

Jack groans. "That's Emery, I'm sure."

"Emery is the wife of your cousin Rory, the solicitor."

He nods. "I'd better answer, or the pair of them will show up on our doorstep."

"I'd love to meet them."

"Not today. Please."

While the phone rings for the third time, Jack hurries away to answer. I probably shouldn't follow him, but I can't fight the impulse that urges me to do just that. I'm standing in the kitchen doorway when Jack picks up the phone. He says hello, then listens intently while maintaining a slight grimace the whole time.

"Aye, Lachlan, I've already been warned," Jack says. "Alex stopped by a few minutes ago. Don't suppose I could convince you, Aidan, and Rory to lock up your wives for the next year or so, just until they give up the idea of meddling in my life."

He listens again, though his grimace has softened.

I move closer to lean against the island a few feet from him.

Though he glances at me, his expression doesn't change. "Those women are a public health hazard." He stays silent for a few seconds, then rolls his eyes. "Why? Because they interfere in the lives of people who don't want their so-called help. And no, Autumn doesn't want their help either."

Now he's speaking for me? Oh hell no.

I snatch the phone from his grasp. "Hi, Lachlan, this is Autumn Flowerday. Jack's ex-wife, the one he claims to speak for even though he does not speak for me."

"Hello, Autumn," Lachlan says. "It's a pleasure to meet you, even if it is over the phone."

"Yes, it's wonderful to meet you too. Over the phone." I aim a pointed glance at Jack. "I'm sure we'll meet in person very soon."

Jack swings his gaze up toward the ceiling, shaking his head like he can't believe how presumptuous I am. Well, he's afraid to let me speak to his relatives, which means I have to shove him out of his comfort zone. It'll be good for him. Right?

"Emery will be ringing you," Lachlan says. "She has a special invitation for you and Jack, but I promised Rory I wouldn't spoil it for her by telling you myself. You'll like Emery. She's clever and sweet but with the right amount of fire to keep Rory from reverting to his old persona as the Ogre of Loch Fairbairn."

"Sounds like there's a great story in that statement." Jack had told me some of it, but I sense there's a lot more.

"Aye, but Emery should tell it to you." Lachlan pauses as a woman's voice says something in the background of the call, but I can't understand the words. "My wife needs help with putting up new curtains, so I have to go now. Erica can't wait to meet you."

"I'm sure it will be soon. Goodbye, Lachlan."

The second I hang up the phone, Jack speaks. "You thought it was rude when I wouldn't let you answer the door, but it's all right to steal the phone from me and chat to my cousin."

"Yes, that's right. Would you have let me talk to Lachlan if I'd asked first?"

Jack flattens his lips. "No."

"That's what I thought. If you want more privacy, I can get a room at the Loch Fairbairn Arms."

"No." His eyes flare wide for a heartbeat, then he turns his head away and squirms. "Sorry. I only meant that you don't need to do that."

"I know I don't need to, but maybe I should. Having me around twenty-four seven is making you a little crazy."

He still won't look at me, and his squirming has turned into scratching his arms. "If you'd rather stay somewhere else, I understand. But I, ah, would prefer it if you, ah, stayed here."

"You want me to stick around? I thought you let me stay in your house only because you didn't want your family to know I'm here. In Scotland, I mean."

"No, I—"

The phone rings again.

Jack curses in Gaelic, though I have no idea what's he saying. His tone tells me it's something sweary.

"Let me answer this time," I say. "Promise not to divulge any secret information."

He sighs and nods.

I pick up the phone. "Jack MacTaggart's house. How may I help you?"

Jack shakes his head again, but his lips twitch upward.

"You must be Autumn," a woman with an American accent says. "I'm Emery, Rory's wife."

"Emery, it's so nice to hear from you. I was just talking to Lachlan on the phone a minute ago, and he said you might call."

"Yeah, Rory insisted he had to let Lachlan know about my idea so he could warn Jack."

"Oh, he's been warned twice over. Alex stopped by the house."

"Good, then maybe he won't get grumpy about it the way most MacTaggart men do when we ladies poke our noses into their lives."

"I wouldn't count on that," I tell Emery. "Jack has been kind of grumpy today. We ran into Logan's three sisters earlier, and for some reason, Jack didn't want me to talk to them."

Jack sharpens his gaze on me, clearly hoping to cow me into shutting up.

Like that would ever work.

I haven't divulged secret info, which means he has no reason to be annoyed.

"Have you ever slept in a castle?" Emery asks.

"Can't say I have."

"Then you absolutely must spend the night at Dùndubhan. It's the castle Rory and I own, though it's now a museum. But the museum is closed for a week while Jamie and Gavin, who run the place, go on a trip to England to visit the Dixons and the Hunters."

"Jamie and Gavin?" I sift through my memories of everything Jack ever told me about his family, which I'm sure he's regretting having done right about now. "Jamie is Lachlan's sister, and Gavin is the brother of Aidan's wife. Right?"

"Yep." Emery hesitates. "Jack told you about the family?"

"Uh-huh." I show superior self-control by not blabbing that he told me that stuff while we were naked in bed in a Las Vegas hotel-slash-casino. "I know all about the MacTaggarts, but not the Dixons or Hunters. I do know Rika Dixon, but she hasn't dished all the dirt to me."

"I'm sure she will soon. I bet you and Jack will be invited to the wedding when Richard Hunter and Maddie Solberg tie the knot."

"Perfect. I'd love to meet all those Brits, and to catch up with Rika."

"She'll be happy to see you, I'm sure." Emery lowers her voice, almost whispering. "Now, about that invitation to spend the night at Dùndubhan. Sleeping in a medieval castle is super romantic, and there are several rooms to choose from plus various bathrooms. I recommend the ground-floor bathroom if you want lots of space to have a steamy good time."

"Jack and I aren't—" I almost said we're not sleeping together, but that would be divulging something private. I amend my statement. "Jack and I are still getting reacquainted. Not sure we're prepared to share a room."

When I glance at Jack, he seems stunned. Or maybe scared. Possibly annoyed. Sometimes it's hard to tell the difference with him.

"You can take separate rooms," Emery says, though she sounds a touch confused. "I'm sure a night in a sexy old castle will help you two reconnect. What do you say?"

"We'll do it."

"Yay! How about tomorrow night?"

"Sounds good."

Emery and I say goodbye, and I hang up the phone.

Jack is still giving me that narrowed-eyes look, but now he's drumming the fingers of one hand on the island. "What did you and Emery conspire about?"

"Our wedding. It'll be on Saturday. That's okay, right?"

His expression goes blank, and he doesn't move a single muscle.

I slap his arm. "Just kidding. I thought a joke might loosen you up, but I was wrong. Sorry."

Jack bows his head for a moment, then blows out a breath and meets my gaze. "Don't apologize. I'm the one being a *tolla-thon*. What did Emery want?"

"For us to spend the night at Dùndubhan. Tomorrow."

Chapter Twenty-Two

Jack

*D*ùndubhan? You can't be serious." I stop drumming my fingers on the island, though my palm still rests on it. I don't want to look at Autumn because I've been behaving like a selfish *tolla-thon*, but Autumn needs to understand what's really going on. "If we go to Dùndubhan, it won't be a quiet getaway for the two of us. My family will turn up there, mark my words. Not all at once, most likely. But they will find flimsy excuses to traipse into the castle while we're there and do whatever meddling rubbish they think will make us fall in love all over again."

"All over again? That implies you loved me at some point."

Bloody hell. I didn't mean to phrase it like that, and I did not mean to imply anything of the sort.

Did I love her? I can't say for sure. I have been experiencing…odd feelings ever since she turned up on my doorstep. And aye, I'm probably in denial about most everything where Autumn is concerned.

"We can't stay at Dùndubhan," I say. "It's a setup."

"So what if it is? I've never slept in a castle, and I want to do it. You can stay home if you're determined to be a grouch about it."

"Autumn—"

"It's only for one night, and Emery says there are lots of bedrooms. You don't need to sleep anywhere near me if the idea of sharing a bed bothers you so much." One corner of her mouth slants upward. "Though you don't have a problem with sneaking into my bed late at night."

I'd loved doing that. Maybe I should consider why, but analyzing myself is a bad idea. Autumn was right about me not "therapizing" myself. Should I let her be my therapist? She's not licensed for it, but that doesn't matter since it's informal therapy. Letting my ex-wife poke around in my head sounds dangerous. Then again, maybe I need to push myself out of this rut I've gotten into, the one I'd escaped from for twelve days in Las Vegas. I want to be that man again, the one who cut all the strings holding him back and had the best bloody time of his life.

Because of Autumn.

Ever since she arrived a few days ago, she's been understanding and patient. She wants to stay at Dùndubhan. After the way I've behaved this week, the least I can do is give her one thing she wants.

"All right," I say. "We can stay at Dùndubhan."

She rushes at me, throwing her arms around my neck. "Thank you, Jack. Thank you, thank you, thank you."

I slide my arms around her. "If I'd said no, would you have gone on your own?"

"Yes, but it wouldn't have been as much fun." She kisses my cheek. "I'm glad you're coming with me. Have you stayed at the castle before?"

"Aye, once. When Catriona brought Alex home with her, I gave Alex a free therapy session in the sitting room at Dùndubhan, and then I stayed on to offer moral support until after he proposed to Cat on the green."

"On the green?"

"It means the field behind the castle, outside the walls."

"Walls?" Autumn gapes at me like she's never heard of a wall before. "You mean, like the kind that keeps barbarians from invading?"

"Aye. Though I doubt the walls will keep my family from invading."

"You need to stop assuming the worst." She tickles the back of my neck with her fingertips. "Is this castle out in the boonies?"

"I suppose it is. The driveway is quite long, and trees surround it. Rory and Emery own a hundred acres around the castle."

"Wow." She smiles. "That means we can make all the noise we want."

"Ah, yes. I suppose it does." I palm her erse in one hand. "What happened to 'we shouldn't have sex'?"

"Changed my mind. It's your fault."

"What is my fault?"

"That I changed my mind. Ever since you skulked into my room and gave me a fabulous orgasm, I haven't been able to stop thinking about sex."

Neither have I. No other woman on earth could make me as randy as Autumn does. But being alone in a castle with her? With all those rooms? All those places where I can shag her? Aye, a night at Dùndubhan might turn me back into the man I was in Las Vegas.

Didn't I want that to happen a few minutes ago? Here's my chance.

I slide my palm up her side until I can close my hand around her breast. "I cannae stop thinking about sex either."

"We don't have to wait until tomorrow night to get it on."

"But if we wait, it'll be more exciting."

She raises onto her toes and kisses me.

Her lips feel dry but soft, and I can't stop myself from wrapping my arms around her body and pushing my tongue between her lips. She moans softly when I glide my tongue around hers and crush her body to mine. *Bod an Donais*, I love the way her breasts mound against my chest with their hard peaks rubbing on me. I've always loved the feel of her body against me, under me, on top of me, anything as long as we're in full contact. Naked is better, but I crave the anticipation almost more than I crave her hot, slick body around my cock.

I explore her mouth slowly, letting myself revel in the sensations of our tongues clashing and sliding, licking and thrusting. When she moans again, I groan into her mouth, resisting my every impulse to hoist her onto the island and yank her trousers down so I can shag her.

Tomorrow night. I'll have her tomorrow night.

She wraps her leg around mine.

Christ, I need to be inside her. But sometimes giving up the chance to satisfy a need, delaying it until later, makes it even more satisfying when the need is finally quenched.

So I grasp her shoulders and peel her luscious body away from mine. "When we're at Dùndubhan, ahm going to fuck ye even better, for even longer, than ah did in Las Vegas. Mah cock willnae have it any other way."

"Oh yes, that sounds so damn good." She nips my chin. "And I can't wait for our night of mind-blowing sex in a medieval castle."

"Neither can I."

Her lips stretch into a sexy closed-mouth smile.

"What?" I ask. "You look like you've just thought of something wonderful."

"I have." Without touching any part of my body, she hops up on her toes and leans in to whisper in my ear, "Emery told me there's a big bathroom on the ground floor that's perfect for a steamy good time."

"Aye, there is. It has an enormous tub, a shower with multiple heads, and a drain in the floor to handle as much splashing as you want."

"Fantastic. I'm already thinking of what I want to do with you, and to you, in that bathroom."

I turn my head just enough to graze her ear with my mouth. "Ahm doing the same thing for you."

"Mm, I'm wet already."

And my cock is getting hard. But since we aren't having a poke today, I need to change the subject.

"Need to finish making lunch," I say. "Let's do it together. Anything you want to eat."

She takes a step backward and rubs her palms together. "Ooh, so many options to choose from."

"Take your time. I'm needing the bog."

I do need to relieve myself. I'm not going to the bathroom just to have a wank. Refusing to take matters into my own hands is part of the anticipation effect.

By the time I return to the kitchen, Autumn has more ingredients laid out on the island beside the ones I'd already gathered. I can't figure out what she plans for us to make.

When I ask, she spreads her arms wide and says, "I have no idea. What do you think?"

I survey the items she's brought out. "We could have clapshot if we get out the turnips too."

"Clapshot? That sounds like a venereal disease."

"Very funny. No, it's mashed potatoes and turnips with butter and chives mixed in. And I've got some Scotch pies in the freezer that Ma made for me." I pick up a potato and roll it in my hand. "She thinks I don't eat well enough."

"Is she right?"

Setting the potato down, I shrug. "Lately, I've been eating soup from a tin or ordering from the cafe. Only when you came did I start making food myself again."

"Oh, you definitely need to do that more often. Why haven't you eaten the whatever-it-was pies your mom made for you?"

I shrug again.

Autumn rolls her shoulders back, standing up straight. "Well, we are going to have ourselves a good lunch, starting with those whatsit pies."

"Scotch pies."

"Uh, what's in one of those? If it's full of sheep intestines or whatever…"

I can't help chuckling. "No, *mo leannan*, it's not filled with haggis. Ma makes the pies with beef or chicken. The traditional way is with minced mutton, but Ma doesn't like that. Scotch pie is a lot like pot pie."

"Okay, that does sound pretty good. Let's make that clapshot stuff too, though I think that dish needs a more appetizing name."

After lunch, we go outside to sit on lawn chairs and enjoy the garden view. It's cloudy, as it often is in Scotland, but the warm temperature makes it pleasant to sit outdoors. I can't help looking at Autumn instead of the garden, loving the way her lips curl up a wee bit and her eyes drift half-closed like she might fall asleep.

I love watching her sleep, but I don't think she's that tired yet.

After a while, she turns slightly toward me. "Maybe we could stay longer than one night at Dùndubhan."

"Why?"

"For fun. We can still do our day trips, but go back to the castle in the evening."

"Don't you like my house?"

"Yes, of course I do. It's adorable."

I shouldn't care if she likes my house, but for some reason, I feel relieved to hear that she does. Aye, I'm definitely off my head, but I like the way it feels.

"What do you say?" she asks.

The sweetly hopeful look on her face makes it impossible for me to say no. Maybe a holiday at Rory's castle will be good for us.

"Let's do that," I say. "Let's stay on past tomorrow night. Dundubhan is a beautiful place, especially the way Rory and Emery have fixed it up. Let me ring them to make sure it's all right."

"Thank you, Jack."

I get up, then bend down to touch my lips to hers. "You're welcome, *mo leannan*."

"What does that mean? You keep calling me *mo leannan*."

"Better call Rory right away."

Yes, I ignored her question.

I hurry into the house to use the landline phone to make the call. Though I could've used my mobile that I had in my pocket, I needed to escape before Autumn asked me again what *mo leannan* means. It's Gaelic for "my sweetheart," but I have no idea why I've started calling her that.

I might be in denial about that.

Sometimes I wish I weren't a psychologist. My training makes it bloody difficult to be properly in denial about anything.

When I ring Rory and Emery's number, she answers.

"Hello, Jack," she says. "Did Autumn tell you the plan?"

"Aye, but she'd like to stay at Dùndubhan for more than one night, if that's acceptable to you and Rory."

"Sure, it's cool."

"Don't you want to ask your husband?"

Emery snorts. "I know what my husband thinks before he does."

"Did Kirsty teach you how to read minds?" Not that I believe for one second Kirsty has psychic powers.

"No, Jack, a wife doesn't need ESP to know what her husband thinks. Isn't Autumn like that?"

I glance out the window where I can see Autumn reclining on her chair. "No, I don't think either of us knows what the other's thinking."

Could that be a clue to why our marriage failed?

No, that's bollocks.

"Hmm," Emery says. "Well, anyway, you guys are welcome to stay for the rest of the week. We have tour groups on the weekend and other events planned after that."

"We'll be gone before then. Thank you, Emery."

"Have fun, Jack. The fridge is full, so feel free to eat everything and use the whipped cream however you like."

After we say goodbye, I go outside to tell Autumn the good news. She throws herself at me again, her entire body pasted to mine, and showers kisses on my face. Why she's so excited about staying at Dùndubhan, I can't explain. It's a castle, not a free trip to the moon.

But she is excited, and that makes me feel...good.

Chapter Twenty-Three

Autumn

For the rest of the day, Jack retreats into his office to "take care of paperwork," which I interpret as "to avoid you, Autumn." He needs a little alone time, I get that. It's been a whirlwind this week, and neither of us has gotten a chance to come to terms with the situation. We're starting to do that now, but adjusting takes time.

While Jack hides out, I prefer to do my adjusting a different way. I'd like to talk to his cousins, the Witches of Ballachulish. Not sure why, but I really want to do that. First, I have to call Emery to find out how to contact the sisters, and she gives me Kirsty's number.

"You'll love them," Emery says. "Those girls are so sweet and so much fun."

After thanking Emery for her help, I call Kirsty. She's thrilled that I want to hang out with her, and she suggests Isla and Elspeth should come too. Kirsty offers to call them to arrange everything. We'll meet at Kirsty's house in half an hour.

With my plans in place, I knock on the office door and announce, "I'm going out, Jack. Be back for dinner."

Then I turn around, about to walk away.

Jack tears the door open. "Where are you going?"

At least he doesn't sound testy or grumpy or anything in the annoyed-Scot oeuvre.

I glance at him over my shoulder. "I'm going to Kirsty's house to hang out with her, and Isla and Elspeth too."

"Why on earth do you want to do that? They're Logan's sisters, not mine."

"Am I only allowed to visit your immediate family? Come on, Jack. I'm sick of staring at the TV, and socializing is a lot more stimulating than being a couch potato."

He scratches his cheek, his expression faintly pinched. "I suppose it is. I haven't given you much in the way of entertainment."

I kiss his cheek. "See you at dinnertime. Don't stay holed up in your office for too long. Go see Alex or Logan or any of those big, sexy men in your family."

"You think Alex and Logan are sexy?"

"Duh. They're gorgeous, and I like men." I kiss his cheek again. "Don't worry, I'm not interested in sleeping with anyone but you."

I didn't intend to say those words, but they came out anyway. My mouth insists on speaking the truths I try to avoid. Jack and I both admitted to each other that we haven't been with anyone else since the night we met. All I know for sure is that I love being with Jack, even when he's grumpy, and even when he holds me hostage.

I haven't wanted any other man since the moment I laid eyes on Jack.

"Glad to hear it," he says. "I don't want to sleep with anyone but you either."

A glowy sensation sprouts in my chest, spreading outward until it encompasses my heart. I don't care what that means, not right now. All I need to know is that he means it.

"Take my car," he says. "The keys are in the kitchen, hanging on a hook by the light switch."

"You're so sweet to offer, but I'd rather walk. Kirsty doesn't live that far away."

"But you're pregnant."

I smile and lay a hand on his cheek. "You showed me the entire village this morning, and we walked the whole way."

"Aye, so you need to rest now, not go for a marathon walk."

Stubborn Jack has returned, but I know he also genuinely worries about me and the baby. So I give in. "Okay, I'll take the car. Happy?"

"Yes."

Jack goes back into his office with the door closed, but I hope he'll take my advice and spend time with at least one of his friends who are also relatives.

Does he have friends who aren't related to him by birth or marriage? Well, I suppose Grey and Jessica Dixon count as non-family pals. Though Grey is Alex's half-brother, so maybe he's family in some complicated way.

I grab the keys and rush out to the car, more excited than I should be about meeting up with the Witches of Ballachulish. It takes maybe two minutes to get to Kirsty's house, and I'm not speeding, so it's genuinely not far to get there. I could've walked, for sure. But my ex-husband has gotten paranoid about the welfare of our baby—and me.

Kirsty opens the door before I even reach the last step on her porch. She grins at me. "Autumn, I'm so glad you're here. Come inside, please."

"Thank you for having me." I follow her into the house, taking in the lacy curtains and flower-print sofa, not to mention the zodiac poster on the wall and the deck of tarot cards on the coffee table. "You have a lovely house, Kirsty."

"You're sweet to say so, but I didn't decorate it. The house came furnished, though I added a few personal touches. It's a rental, so I don't want to change too much."

She gestures for me to sit on the sofa, and we both settle onto it.

I glance at the tarot cards. "Are you into reading the cards and stuff like that?"

"Oh, aye. But Isla is the one who's an expert at tarot readings. I dabble in it, but my gift is more…esoteric."

"Your gift?"

She nods, then taps her temple. "I have *da-shealladh*, the gift of the two sights."

"Two sights?"

"Aye. The ability to see this world and the spirit dimension. It's commonly called second sight or psychic ability."

"I see." I've never met anyone who believes they have extrasensory perception until today. "Logan doesn't seem like the type who accepts that supernatural abilities exist, and Jack sure isn't. But I prefer to keep an open mind."

"And that's all I ever ask of anyone. You're right about Logan. My brother refuses to believe it's even possible, but I'm sure one day he will accept it." She taps her temple again. "I've seen it."

"I'd love to have that ability, so I could peek inside Jack's mind."

"You two are having trouble adjusting to the idea of a baby on the way, aren't you?"

I freeze, and a wave of cold washes through me. "Why did you mention a baby?"

"Because you're up the duff. I knew that the day after you and Jack had your blind date." She smiles, the expression sweetly sympathetic. "I know what it's like to be with a man who's afraid to open up to you and doesn't understand your ways. Jack is a good man, though, and he'll come around."

Do I look pregnant? I'm not showing yet, so I don't see how I could look like there's a baby growing inside me. Jack would never have told Kirsty about the pregnancy, and I doubt he told Alex or Logan either.

Kirsty leans toward me to pat my knee. "It's all right, Autumn. No one else knows. I sensed it with my *da-shealladh*."

"What else did you see?"

"I don't want to say too much and risk influencing you one way or the other. But rest assured, your bairn will be healthy and happy, and so will you and Jack."

The doorbell rings, and Kirsty jumps up to let her sisters into the house. Isla and Elspeth sit in the two armchairs that flank the coffee table while Kirsty returns to her end of the sofa.

The four of us chat for a while, but I mostly listen. These wonderful women tell me all sorts of stories about the MacTaggarts, some that Jack had told me and others I haven't heard before. I laugh so much my sides hurt. The MacTaggarts are a wild bunch, for sure, but they also love each other fiercely and would do anything to help a family member.

Kirsty and her sisters are fun and smart and loyal to their family and friends. I love that about them.

Isla offers to give me a tarot reading.

"Not sure about that," I say. "What if it shows I'm doomed?"

Yeah, I'm only half kidding. I have no idea what will happen between me and Jack, except that we'll have lots of sex tomorrow night.

"Tosh," Isla says. "Kirsty sensed good things ahead for you. But maybe you'd prefer a palm reading. Kirsty learned how to do that in America, when we all flew to Oregon for Alex and Cat's wedding."

"It was at a nudist resort, right? Jack told me."

"Aye. Kirsty was the only MacTaggart who didn't go nude at all. She's shy about that."

"I am not shy," Kirsty says, fake scowling at her sister. "Not everyone has to embrace nudism the way you did."

"Even Jack joined in."

"Logan too," Elspeth says. "It was strange to see my brother naked, though. I averted my eyes. And so did you, Isla, so donnae act like you fully embraced the naturist lifestyle."

"I have my limits, Elspeth. Everyone does." Isla glances at Kirsty. "But our sister wouldn't even give it a wee go. She stayed fully clothed the entire time."

Kirsty sighs and slumps against the sofa.

We talk for a while longer, though not about nudism. Eventually, Isla and Elspeth leave, and both hug me and kiss my cheek when they say goodbye.

I'm about to leave too, but Kirsty lays a hand on my arm.

"Donnae leave just yet," she says. "I'd like to read your palm if that's all right."

"Sure. That might be interesting."

We return to the sofa, but this time Kirsty sits closer to me so she can cradle my hand in hers and run her fingers over the back of it while studying my skin.

Then she turns my hand over. "Palmistry is an ancient and personal art. I learned about it from Damian Petrescu, the concierge at the Au Naturel Naturist Resort. He has gypsy heritage, so he also offers palm and tarot readings to guests."

"That's cool."

Kirsty glides her fingertip over the lines on my palm, tracing and retracing them. "I'm not an expert at this yet, but I can tell you've struggled to find your place in the world and you're constantly searching for it. But more than that, I see you have a good heart and a deep, spiritual connection."

"To what?"

"Not what. Who." She sandwiches my hand between her palms. "You have a deep connection to Jack and vice versa. I don't know what happened to split you two apart, but it was more than Alex's meddling that drew you back to each other."

"Yeah, it's the fact I got knocked up." I tried for a breezy tone, but it came out with a slight edge to it. Weird.

"Even before that, you were drawn to each other." She starts tracing the lines on my palm again, her focus riveted to the task. "Passion pulls you back to each other. Twice, the power of your sensual connection has revitalized your bond. And it will happen again, don't worry about that."

Okay, I'm guessing she means when we were set up on that blind date and when I knocked on Jack's door the other day. I didn't feel revitalized either time. Well, maybe a little.

"What do you mean it will happen again?" I ask. "I'm already here with Jack. We're not a couple, but—"

"Listen carefully," Kirsty says, pinning her earnest gaze to mine. "When it happens, don't panic. You have the power to bring back what is lost."

"Can't you be a bit more specific?" Not that I'm buying into this hooey. Kirsty is sincere, I can see that. She's not conning me, but there's no way she could foresee the future.

She releases my hand. "You're wanting to get back to Jack. I've taken up enough of your time and enjoyed every minute of it."

"Me too. You and your sisters are terrific."

"You are too. Never forget that."

I bite my lip, wanting to ask a question that's not really my business.

"Go on and ask," Kirsty says.

No, she couldn't have read my mind. She saw me biting my lip and figured out I wanted to ask her something. Right?

"I'm just curious," I say. "What do you do for a living?"

Kirsty's lips form a gentle smile. "I own a metaphysical shop here in Loch Fairbairn. That means I sell items related to Wicca and alternative spirituality. Herbs, incense, spell kits, candles, crystals, even clothing."

"I'll have to visit your shop sometime. It sounds amazing."

She escorts me to the door and swings it open.

As I cross the threshold, she touches my arm to stop me. "You'll believe soon enough. When the moon is high and the clock strikes six, four words will change everything."

"Uh, thank you, Kirsty."

What on earth can I say to that? No idea. She honestly believes in second sight, and I would never want to insult this woman who has become a friend in the space of two hours. I feel like I've known Kirsty and her sisters forever, but maybe that's because of the stories Jack told me.

On the drive home, I hear Kirsty's voice in my head repeating her prediction, over and over.

When the moon is high and the clock strikes six, four words will change everything.

It's got to be bollocks, as Jack would say. But a part of me wonders if maybe, just maybe, something magical will happen at Dùndubhan.

Chapter Twenty-Four

Jack

Autumn comes home at five o'clock, which seems early for dinner-time. I don't mind, though. I might have spent the last several hours slumped in my office chair, sipping whisky and thinking about her. Maybe I also picked up my mobile and started to dial her number, then hung up before it even rang at her end. Christ, now I sound like Alex. Maybe this, might that. Is being an evasive erse contagious?

I rush into the living room the second I hear a car door shut outside and yank the door open just as she reaches the porch steps.

Autumn kisses my cheek when she walks past me. "Hey, Jack, miss me?"

"Well, I…" Yes is the answer, but I won't say that. She'll think I'm a dafty if I do. But then again, she did ask the question. "I'm glad you're home."

That's all I can make myself admit to right now.

"You're so sweet," she says, pinching my cheek.

Autumn seems happier than when she left earlier this afternoon, and she has a kind of spiritual glow about her. Spiritual glow? What rubbish. I'm going soft in the head, that's for dead certain. The fact was proved beyond any doubt when I had raced to the door a moment ago and felt excited at the prospect of seeing her.

I shut the door and rest my hand on it, staring down at my own feet, suddenly having no clue what to do with my feet or my hands or my voice. I'm relieved she's come back. So relieved in fact that I feel like a teenage laddie having his first serious crush on a lassie.

"Everything okay?" she asks.

"Aye, fine."

She sets her purse on the table by the door and wanders over to the sofa, flopping down onto it. "Come sit with me, Jack."

I head for the armchair, but she shakes her head and points to the empty space beside her on the sofa. She wants me to sit next to her. I'm not sure that's wise considering all my barmy thoughts.

But I do it anyway. I settle onto the sofa beside her, though I keep an arm's length between us.

"How was your visit with Logan's sisters?" I ask.

"Good. I like them a lot." She wriggles until she's facing halfway toward me. "Kirsty has psychic powers, you know."

"I know she thinks she does."

"Don't you ever feel like believing in something you can't explain or prove? Sticking to the scientific facts gets awfully boring."

Naturally, Autumn would want to believe in that nonsense. She watches so-called documentaries about aliens and crop circles and all manner of bollocks. I treat it as a charming quirk rather than a sign of a mental imbalance. My therapist side knows that sometimes people need to believe in things that can't be proved to exist. It gives them comfort. I do believe in certain things that aren't scientifically explainable, but not in witchcraft.

I don't believe Kirsty can see the future. She's a kind and clever woman, but even intelligent people can latch onto silly ideas.

Autumn wriggles closer to me, her knee brushing against me. "She said something about us, but I don't think I should tell you yet. Might influence your decision-making."

"The only decision it might influence is whether I go back to holding you hostage to keep you from listening to my barmy cousins."

"If you try that again, I'll lock *you* in *your* room and see how you like being the hostage for a change."

"Maybe I'd enjoy that. Letting you have your way with me." Aye, being a hostage could be very enjoyable if it means we're naked and she's doing erotic things to me. "Maybe we can try that tomorrow night at Rory's castle."

She licks her lips and smiles with just enough sensuality to make my groin tighten. "You can count on it, provided I can find something to restrain you with."

"You have scarves. I saw them lying on the dresser."

"Ooh, that's perfect." She lifts her brows. "Isn't it Emery's castle too? She is Rory's wife after all."

"True, but he bought the castle well before he met her. We all got used to calling it Rory's castle."

"I get it." She hesitates, gnawing on her lip. "I think it's time we talked about the past, really talked about it. I don't want to wait until two weeks before our kid is born to have The Talk."

Mhac na galla. I was hoping she'd forget about that.

"All right," I say. "What do you want to know?"

"Tell me what you were feeling on the day I left."

"Which time?"

She leans closer, her nose almost touching mine. "I left you once. You left me the second time."

"Oh. Aye." So it's *that* talk. The Why Is Jack a Bleeding Ersehole conversation. I stifle a groan. That's the wrong attitude to have when starting a discussion like this. As a therapist, I know that. But it's different when I'm the one on the couch, so to speak. Well, literally in this case. "What was I feeling? All right, I'll do my best to explain it. I knew you'd been unhappy, but I had no idea how unhappy until that day."

Twenty months ago

I woke up feeling a wee bit off, though I couldn't explain why. It was a cloudy morning, but that's typical for Scotland, so I couldn't blame the weather. Since Autumn and I hadn't argued yesterday, I couldn't blame that either. Aye, we argued sometimes, mostly about whether I would ever introduce her to my family. But yesterday, she'd been quieter than usual and had kept to herself all day. Maybe I should've talked to her, asked what was fashing her. I didn't.

What if she said she wanted to leave me?

No, she wouldn't do that. We could work through our problems if she'd talk to me.

A shower didn't make me feel any better, and when I walked out into the living room, Autumn was lying on the sofa, on her side, watching TV. She had her hands clasped under her cheek, and she wore a dressing gown over her favorite nightie.

Still in her sleeping clothes? Autumn always dressed when she woke up and fixed her hair too. Today, her hair looked like she hadn't brushed it yet.

"Good morning," I said.

Autumn glanced at me, moving only her eyes. "Morning."

She sounded tired, or maybe depressed. That wasn't like her at all.

I approached the sofa and knelt in front of her. "Are you all right, *gràidh*? Feeling unwell?"

She shrugged one shoulder.

"Please tell me what's wrong," I said, brushing hair away from her eyes. "Whatever it is, I can help. If you're ill, I can take you to the doctor. If it's not physical, I can still help. I'm trained for that, you know."

Though I tried to make that last bit sound lighthearted, I knew I failed. My chest had started to ache in a way I'd never experienced before, my palms felt clammy, and my mouth had gone dry.

"Not sick," she said. "Just tired. So damn tired."

I kissed her forehead. "Tell me, *gràidh*. Whatever it is, you can tell me."

She looked straight at me, not blinking, her gaze locked onto mine like she was searching for something in my eyes. She stared at me like that for so long that I started to feel even more anxious than I had when I woke up this morning.

Finally, she veered her focus away from me and sighed. "Maybe later."

I didn't want to walk away from her without finding out what the problem was, but I needed to eat breakfast and drive to my office to meet with my first client of the day. Autumn did eat the breakfast I made for both of us, but she still wouldn't speak to me. Twice, I caught her watching me while I was focused on my food. Both times, she jerked her gaze away the instant she realized I'd seen her watching me.

What on earth was fashing her?

Somehow, I got through the day. I gave my clients the advice and encouragement they needed and put on a good show of being my normal self. I wasn't anything close to that, though. I felt like I'd stepped into that old television show, *The Twilight Zone*, and I was now living in a mirror-image version of my own life.

I should've done more to repair our relationship. *Fuck work*. I needed to be with my wife and convince her to tell me what was wrong.

On my way home, I picked up a pizza from our favorite restaurant plus the garlic cheese breadsticks Autumn loved. Would food cheer her up? I hoped so because I had no other ideas about how to make her feel better.

Never could I have guessed what awaited me at home.

I walked through the door to our apartment carrying the pizza box balanced on one hand and a plastic bag in the other hand. Kicking the door shut after me, I hurried into the living room, heading for the open kitchen.

Autumn wasn't there.

Setting the food down on the kitchen table, I trotted into the hallway—and froze halfway there.

My wife had just stepped out of the bedroom. She carried two small suitcases, setting them down alongside the two larger ones that already sat on the floor. Autumn wore a long coat over her sweater and jeans, and boots covered her feet.

A chill shivered over my skin.

I hurried to her, halting an arm's length away. "What's happening, *gràidh*? You look like you're going somewhere."

She clamped her lips between her teeth. The start of tears shimmered in her eyes. "I am going somewhere, Jack."

"Why? Where?" I swallowed hard, but the thickness in my throat wouldn't go away. "Has something happened?"

"I—I can't do this anymore." She sniffled, though her tears stayed trapped in her eyes. "This isn't working, and I can't—We aren't—" She swiped at her eyes and sucked in a breath. "I'm going home, Jack."

"You are home. This is where we live."

"No, it's where you live. I'm not a part of your life, not really. This isn't anybody's fault, it's just the way it is." She met my gaze, her bottom lip quivering. "I tried, we both did, but it wasn't enough. I'm going back to America."

"That's bollocks. We've been married for six weeks. Ye cannae give up so soon."

"Do you love me?"

Her question stopped me. How could she ask that when she was packed and ready to walk out the door?

Autumn grabbed my shirt with both hands, tugging me closer. "Come with me, Jack, please. Let's go back to Vegas where things were good."

Everything I wanted to say, needed to say, got stuck somewhere between my brain and mouth, and I couldn't make the words come out. *I'll do better. Give me another chance. Please don't leave. Let me show you I can be the kind of husband you need. Yes, let's go to America, anywhere to be with you.*

I never said any of that. Instead, I asked, "What about medical school? Rory and Lachlan pulled a lot of strings to get you transferred to the University of Edinburgh, but you quit before you started there. What will you do in America?"

She straightened and lifted her chin, and though her eyes still glistened faintly, she squared her shoulders. "I got a job in Atlantic City."

"When? How?"

"A jobs website, that's how. Yesterday, I got online and found a new career as a blackjack dealer."

"Have you ever done that sort of work before?"

"No. It's a new casino that's only been open for six months, so they're willing to give me on-the-job training to speed up the hiring process instead of me having to go to dealer school first."

Dealer school? I'd never heard of such a thing.

She was leaving me to become a blackjack dealer. What the fuck was that about? She hated living with me so much she'd take any sleazy job to escape?

"If you really want me to stay," she said, "you can prove it by introducing me to your family."

"Are you giving me an ultimatum?"

"Yes, I am."

"I don't respond to threats. An ultimatum is a manipulation tactic."

"Fine." She sniffled again, but then cleared her throat. "You give me no choice. I'm leaving."

"Ye cannae go," I said, surprised by the edge of anger sharpening my voice. I felt a maelstrom of conflicting emotions, but I couldn't understand any of them. "Ye donnae have any money. How are you paying for your airline ticket? Where will you live?"

"I used our credit card to buy the plane ticket." She puckered her lips, but I thought I saw a slight quiver in them. "Don't worry, Jack, I'll pay you back. It's all your money, anyway, right? I was the broke, unemployed American slut you seduced in Vegas."

Never had I called her that. Didn't think it either. Autumn was beautiful, sweet, clever, passionate, and so many other wonderful things.

Yet she was leaving me.

"I'm a therapist, Autumn," I said. "Give me a chance to help you work through your issues."

"You specialize in couples therapy. I'm one person."

"But I treat individuals too. You know that."

She shook her head slowly. "Therapy is bullshit, Jack. Anyone who falls for it is a fool, and the people like you who practice it are nothing but shameless hucksters."

Was that how she honestly felt about my job? A sensation came over me, like I was falling through the floor into a deep, dark abyss that went on forever.

I grasped her shoulders, intending to beg her to stay. But the words that came out sounded nothing like that. "Fine, run back to America. Don't expect me to give you alimony."

Why did I say that? Who gave a damn about money? I wanted her to stay, but she wanted to go.

The only woman I'd ever loved couldn't wait to abandon me.

Later, I would realize my anger at that moment stemmed from fear and pain. Understanding would come too late, though.

Autumn shook my hands off. "Goodbye, Jack."

Someone rang the doorbell.

I watched numbly as she opened the door and asked a taxi driver to help carry her luggage out to his vehicle. He took the two large suitcases. She picked up the smaller ones and marched toward the door. On the threshold, she paused to glance back at me over her shoulder.

Was it my imagination or did her lips tremble? Were those tears trickling down her cheeks?

Just as she turned away, I opened my mouth to speak. Not one bloody word came out.

She pulled the door shut behind her.

My wife was gone.

I stared out the living-room window, watching her get into the taxi, watching the car drive away.

Run after her, you fucking eejit.

But my feet wouldn't move.

I dealt with my wife leaving me the way so many of my clients did. I pretended I didn't give a shit. Maybe I'm still pretending.

No, not anymore.

Autumn had listened while I told her my side of how we ended things. She didn't speak or make any irritated faces. She just listened.

I told her everything—except for the parts about how I'd wanted to beg her to stay and how she was the only woman I'd ever loved. I glossed over the intensity of my emotions on that day too. Someday soon, I'd need to tell her all of that, but not today. I can't handle it right now.

A bad excuse, I know.

"That's what you wanted to know," I say. "Isn't it?"

"Some of it, yeah." Autumn studies me for a moment. "But I'm not dumb. I know you're leaving out a lot of the emotional side of things. You're not good at that stuff, not when it's your feelings on the line. Helping other people is one thing, but dealing with your own issues is hard for you, I get that. Dealing with me is hard for you too."

Why is she being so understanding? It doesn't make sense.

"I don't have a good excuse for my behavior," I tell her. "My feelings for you have always been powerful, but I've let my emotions take control. That's not healthy. I'm a ruddy psychologist, I ought to know that. There needs to be a balance between emotion and rationality."

"Sure, but you seem to swing back and forth between all emotion and all cool rationality. At least with me, you do." She turns fully toward me, sitting cross-legged. "I'd like to see how you are with your family when you're not stressed out."

"Not sure that will be possible anytime soon."

"Maybe our stay at Rory's castle will help you relax."

"Don't know, but I suppose it can't hurt."

"Glad you feel that way."

I suddenly remember what she told me a moment ago. "Why did you say you have no doubts I'm a great therapist? When you left me, you said I'm a shameless huckster. And the other day, you told me therapy only makes people feel like failures."

She rubs her forehead, hiding her face. Then she aims her gaze straight at me. "I said those things because I was hurt and scared. I'm sorry, Jack, it was a stupid thing to do. But you were so angry when I said I was leaving, and I thought you didn't give a damn if I walked out. And the other day, I was terrified of telling you about myself and my family."

"I gave a damn, Autumn."

"Yeah, I know that now." She leans in to kiss me, her lips touching mine for only a second. "Enough soul-baring. Let's go out to eat."

"That means the cafe."

"Fine with me." She grins and pokes my belly. "Come on, we both need to get out of the house more. It'll be fun."

"All right." I'll do anything to make sure she keeps smiling. No more *tolla-thon* behavior. We need to get along for the sake of our child, and maybe for each other too. "I'll need to change clothes."

She hops off the sofa, still grinning. "Thank you for being honest and open with me, Jack. I feel like a weight's been lifted. Not the whole weight, but a big chunk of it."

I feel that way too, but I'm not deluding myself that we've solved all our problems in ten minutes. We *can* solve them, though. I'm starting to believe that. Even if she never loves me the way I love her, at least we won't raise a neurotic child.

And aye, she's still the only woman I've ever loved.

Chapter Twenty-Five

Our dinner at the cafe is lovely. Jack shares more stories about his family, stuff about events that happened since we split up. He also tells me about the Dixons and the Hunters. One day, I'll get to meet all of them. But for now, I'm happy to be spending time with Jack and getting to know his family.

Jack seems way more relaxed tonight. I'm glad I suggested eating out because I think that's been the catalyst for him chilling out. I'd love to think it has something to do with me, and how he feels about me, but that's probably wishful thinking. Seeing him this way, sharing his stories while smiling and laughing, I remember how good things were in Vegas. I want that side of him to come back, but I love every side of him—even when he confines me to the house.

I love him? That's what I just thought, essentially. If I love every side of him then… I love *him*.

After dinner, we go home and relax in front of the TV for a while. I let Jack pick what we watch, and he chooses a romantic comedy movie. Seriously. Jack picks that. He suggests we sit on the sofa together to watch it too. I expect him to sit on the opposite end of the sofa from where I am, but he voluntarily sits beside me. He even slips an arm around my shoulders.

We're cuddling. Me and Jack. Cuddling.

This is the biggest progress we've made since we got married.

After the movie, Jack kisses me good night at the door to my bedroom. It's a sweet kiss, and afterward, we go into our separate rooms. Maybe tomorrow night, at the castle, we'll finally share a bed. Feels like forever since we've done that.

I still want to know what he was feeling, really feeling, on the day I walked out the door. Men aren't good at expressing that kind of pain, though. From what he has told me, I can tell I hurt Jack deeply. Never meant to. Never wanted to. But I let my fears get in the way and mess everything up. I still don't know he felt about me back then or how he feels today, but I can wait for those answers.

When morning comes, I feel better than I have in ages thanks to a good night's sleep and the intimacy Jack and I shared yesterday. I feel closer to him now, but I don't know if we'll ever truly be a couple again. Still, we're not arguing. That's a big step up from the way we've behaved before this week.

I find Jack in his office—with the door open. He's sitting at his desk, leaning forward while he studies a folder full of papers.

"Good morning," I say, leaning against the jamb. "So, I'm allowed to see inside your inner sanctum, huh? Guess I'm not the evil ex-wife anymore."

He closes the folder and leans back in his chair. "You were never evil. This morning, I decided not to lock you out of my office anymore because it was a daft thing to do. But I still can't tell you about my clients."

"I know." Walking over to his desk, I perch my butt on its edge opposite where he's sitting. "Tonight's the big night."

"Best to temper your expectations. There won't be any magic spells woven around us or whatever nonsense Kirsty told you."

"Maybe you should open your mind, expand your horizons a bit, and consider the possibility that some kind of magic could exist." I lean over to ruffle his hair, which earns me a grudging smile, though he rolls his eyes too. "Magic doesn't have to mean spells and premonitions. You and I made some hot magic back in Vegas."

"Aye, we did." He folds his hands over his belly and rocks his chair gently. "I ate breakfast earlier. Just oatmeal. If you're wanting more than that, I can make it for you."

"No, I'm not that hungry. But I appreciate the offer." I glance at the window seat, then look at Jack. "Let's go sit over there, hey? I've got some stuff I need to tell you."

We amble over to the window bench and sit facing each other with our backs against the wide sill.

"This might sound dumb," I say, "but I dreamed about us last night, about you, and when I woke up this morning, I knew what I needed to tell you."

"It doesn't sound dumb. Dreams can be helpful that way. It's the subconscious mind's attempt to work through issues that you don't acknowledge when you're awake."

"Could you not talk like a psychologist right now? Just be my ex-husband? My friend?"

"Yes, I can do that." He crosses his ankle over the other knee and keeps his gaze on mine. "Sorry. I sometimes forget to leave my job out of personal conversations."

"I wasn't chastising you. Being a psychologist is part of who you are, and I'd never want you to feel like you need to hide that part of yourself from me." I squirm, suddenly uncomfortable though I know it's only nerves. I'm about to tell him things I've had trouble explaining even to myself. "That day, when I left, I begged you to come with me. But you wouldn't do it. Before that, I'd tried to get you to let me meet your family, but you wouldn't do that either. I didn't know what else to do, and I got scared that the rest of my life would be like that. Shut away so none of your family would ever see me. I wanted you to come with me, and after I left, I kept hoping you'd show up on my doorstep and say you wanted to be with me no matter where we lived. I had this stupid story in my head of you doing that, like in a fairy tale or a romance movie."

"Life isn't as simple as that."

"I know." Nausea is rising in my stomach, thanks to anxiety mixed with morning sickness. I need to keep going, even if I wind up vomiting all over Jack's pretty window bench. "You were the first serious relationship I ever had. So yeah, I panicked and ran away. Living with you was difficult, but leaving you was the worst pain I'd ever experienced. I'm glad Alex meddled and tricked us into a blind date. Otherwise, I know I would've spent the rest of my life wondering if you and I could've worked things out." I take a deep breath and ask the big question. "Can we? Work things out, I mean."

He scrubs a hand over his face, exhaling a breath that deflates his shoulders. "I don't know the answer, Autumn, to that question or a thousand others. You turned up a few days ago, pregnant, and now you want me to have the solution to our problems."

Jack doesn't sound annoyed, thankfully. He's calm today.

Oh boy, here comes the hardest part.

I pull my knees up to my chest, wrapping my arms around them. "I did love you, Jack. In Vegas, and after we came to Scotland. I loved you so much."

No, that's not the absolute hardest thing I need to say. The worst part is coming any second when I know he'll ask…

"Are you saying you don't love me now?"

I swallow, but the lump in my throat won't go away. "No. I'm saying… I still love you, Jack. Never stopped loving you. But I'm terrified things will go sideways again. The most important thing I need to do is take care of this baby."

He gazes out the window, seeming unaffected, but his Adam's apple jumps like he's swallowing hard.

With my shoulders hunched, I turn my gaze away from him, afraid of what his response might be.

"I will be a part of this baby's life," he says, "no matter what happens between us. You're the mother of my child. That's all that matters right now."

I look at him, but the best I can do is give him a tight, lopsided smile. God, I want to believe everything will work out. I want it so badly.

He hasn't responded to the other thing I said. The part about loving him.

"Enough emotional upheaval for one morning," he announces as he stands up and stretches. "Let's go on our first day trip. I'll show you Ballachulish, and if we have time, Fort William."

I can't help grinning as I jump up and throw my arms around him. My feet are dangling above the floor. "Thank you, Jack, that sounds amazing."

He groans. "It's a wee drive around this corner of the Highlands. I'm not buying all of Scotland for you."

"Feels like that to me." I keep my arms looped around his neck, though my feet touch down. "You're showing me your country. It's a big deal for me."

"Aye." He clasps his hands at the small of my back. "Don't get too excited, though. Ballachulish isn't Las Vegas."

"No, but it's a part of you."

That's what matters most to me, seeing his homeland through his eyes. Getting to know Jack at last. Coming to understand him. And maybe one day he'll say the words I want him to say more than anything.

I can wait for that. As long as it takes.

Chapter Twenty-Six

Jack

Autumn loves me. I should've said something in response to that, shouldn't I? But I couldn't think of anything. Well, I thought of something, but I couldn't manage to say it. I made her miserable when we were married, so I have no right to tell her…anything. I realized yesterday I've never stopped loving her, but if I tell her that, she'll want things I don't think I'm capable of giving her.

I fucked up our marriage. What if I do that again?

Why, then, did I agree to spending the night at Dùndubhan and having sex while we're there? I know what's happening to me. Any therapist with half a brain would understand it. I'm afraid of losing her again, and I'm on the verge of sabotaging our newfound intimacy to protect myself.

No more of that rubbish, ye cacan.

Aye, no more. I won't give in to the fear.

Taking Autumn on a tour of Ballachulish is how I prove she matters to me because this is what she's wanted from the start. We drive through Fort William, though I would like to show her the sights there too. First, I need to introduce her to the village where my cousins grew up and where some of them still live. Lachlan and Erica have a farm in North Ballachulish, but we're not visiting relatives today. This is Autumn's chance to see more of the parts of the Highlands where I spent my childhood.

All right, it's also my chance to show her where I came from and what these places mean to me.

I can't believe I refused to bring her here when we were married. My parents loved her at first sight, just the way I did, and she seems more comfortable here than she ever did in Inverness. I'd lived there solely because a colleague offered me a position at his practice. But I'd hated that job, hated being away from my true home, hated the assembly line of clients and the need to care about assiduously counting every minute so it could be charged to the clients.

Of course, my colleagues called them patients.

This is more than my mental reminiscences. I'm telling all of it to Autumn while we drive over the Ballachulish Bridge.

"What's wrong with calling them patients?" she asks. "I remember you always called them clients, but I don't understand why the distinction matters."

"Because they're not in an institution. They're average people who need some advice."

"You genuinely care about your clients, don't you? That's why what you call them is so important."

"Of course I care. I'd be a bastard if I didn't."

I glance at her sideways and see she's gazing out the window at the loch and the bridge and the mountains in the distance. Her lips have curved into a soft smile, like she loves this place as much as I do. Why did I never give her the chance to see it until now?

Because I'm an idiot, that's why. It's much easier to be comforting and supportive to strangers than to my wife. Except she's not my wife anymore.

"What did you mean," she says, "when you told me you had 'work problems' to deal with around the same time that I left you?"

"I can't tell you. Client information is confidential."

"Not asking for your client's phone number and medical history, Jack. I just want to know what had you so distracted that you let me walk away because of it."

How can I explain without explaining? I won't reveal personal details of my client's problems, but maybe I can tell her in general what was going on.

"One of my clients," I say, "became obsessed with me. I was trying to help him, but he seemed to think that meant I was his best friend. Not long after you left, I got a non-harassment order against him, then I found a colleague who was willing to take him on as a client. Effie McKellar is one of the best therapists in Scotland, so I knew she could handle him."

"Did this guy threaten you?"

"No, he wanted to be mates. Kept inviting me to dinner and showing up at my apartment with gifts, things like that. He's not dangerous, just confused and lonely."

"But he's not your problem anymore. Your colleague takes care of him now."

"Well, she did." I grip the steering wheel tighter. "But I heard from Effie this week, and she had to hand this bloke over to another therapist because he'd become problematic for her too. She thinks he might get worse instead of better."

"Are you worried about this guy? That he might come to find you?"

"No, I can't see that happening. Let's get back to enjoying our road trip, all right?"

"Sure."

Would I have let Autumn leave me if I hadn't been distracted by Hamish's nonsense? I don't know, and there's no point in thinking about that. The past can't be undone. I've wished I'd chased after her every day since she left me, but all I can do is find a way to make it up to her in the future.

Not in the future. Today.

I drive through some of the back roads to let Autumn get a better idea of what this area is like for the locals and not only the tourists. She loves everything we see on our journey, and I love watching her see it all.

This morning, she told me she's glad Alex meddled in our lives. Right now, I'm glad too. But I will never tell Alex that.

We take a detour from the route I had in mind so Autumn can see the Highland Titles Nature Reserve. Since she grew up in Nevada, the lush landscapes of the Highlands are a treat for her, and she loves it when I suggest we take a walk through the reserve to get a close-up look at the wildlife, trees, and flowers. We brought lunch with us—nothing special, just sandwiches—and eat it while sitting beside a lochan. A red deer trots by, which makes Autumn so happy I swear she glows. Or maybe that's the pregnancy hormones. Either way, she looks bonnier than ever.

"One question," she says after finishing her sandwich. "What's a lochan?"

"A small lake. You could call it a mini-loch."

"I should've guessed. Lochan, loch. It's obvious once you think about it."

"Or once I tell you. It's dead obvious then, isn't it?"

She bumps her shoulder into mine. "I like it when you tease me."

"And I like teasing you. So it works out well, aye?"

"Uh-huh." She steals a potato crisp from my bag, chewing it before she speaks again. "What should we do next?"

"Have you ever been on a steam train?"

"No, I haven't."

"Then let's take the Jacobite steam train from Fort William to Mallaig and back. My parents took me and Callum on the train when we were laddies, but I don't know if it will seem as impressive and exciting now that I'm older and taller."

She slants toward me, her lips near my ear. "You are definitely impressive and exciting, Dr. MacTaggart."

Hearing her call me doctor makes my cock twitch. She spoke those words in a sultry tone, so maybe that's why I'm getting aroused, not because she called me doctor.

It might be both.

"Why would you say that?" I ask. "The only excitement I've given you was when I ordered you to stay indoors and not answer the phone."

"Have you forgotten about the other night? When you sneaked into my bed?"

That was exciting, for sure. I'd loved making her come, but I'm looking forward to our night at Dùndubhan so much that the anticipation is almost killing me.

Only Autumn has ever affected me this way.

She leans into me, slipping an arm around my waist, and nuzzles my neck.

I abandon my lunch and sling an arm around her to pull that sexy body even snugger against me, loving the feel of her breasts crushed against me and the scent of her. The second she lifts her head, surprise on her face, I claim her mouth. The kiss is deep and hot, and it sends blood rushing into my cock, obliterating my thoughts, not that I mind losing the ability to think. Her tongue feels velvety, warm, and slick, and I want to keep kissing her for the rest of the day and then tomorrow and every day after that.

When we finally give up each other's lips, her cheeks are pink and my *slat* is rock hard. As much as I want to shag her right here on the banks of a secluded lochan, I won't do it. Tonight, we'll make love. Until then, I owe her everything I refused to give her when we were married.

So we hike back to the car and drive to Fort William to take a trip on the Jacobite steam train. Autumn loves it, of course. But I can't focus on the majestic mountains or the shimmering lochs or the sound of the steam engine chugging along. My world telescopes down to her and only her. All I need to nourish me is the look on her face while she admires the scenery and asks me questions like "what mountain is that" or "how far are we from Ballachulish."

I think she loves this land as much as I do.

After our day trip, we go home to pack for our night at Dùndubhan. Autumn walks into my room while I'm finishing my packing. She comes up behind me, wrapping her arms around my midsection from behind, and whispers to me.

"Bring your kilt."

"Why?" I ask. "We're not having Highland games."

"Oh, there will be plenty of Highland games, just not the kind you mean." She curls her tongue around my earlobe. "Bring the kilt, Jack. You'll be glad you did."

Then she leaves.

I don't know what she's up to, but I can't wait to find out.

And I pack the kilt.

Chapter Twenty-Seven

The journey to Dùndubhan takes a while, but I don't mind. The landscape is gorgeous here, with all those shimmering lochs and green mountains. The sun came out today like the universe wanted to give us the best weather possible for our first-ever road trip together. Jack has been so relaxed and happy today that I've started to believe we *can* make this work, make *us* work.

Will our child have two happily married parents? God, I hope so. I want Jack as more than a co-parent. I want him, period.

The ride to the castle gives me time to reflect on my relationship with Jack, and I can't help reminiscing about those twelve magical days in Vegas and especially the night we got married.

I lay on my back on the huge, round bed in Jack's suite, which he kept calling "our" suite, enjoying the delicious afterglow of sex with my insatiable Scot. Jack had skills, high-level ones, when it came to turning me on and making me come like I never had in my life before I met him. He was more than a great lay, though. Jack made me laugh too, and I loved every last story he'd told me about his family. I loved his sense of humor but also his intelligence, his sweetness, his smile, and so many other little things about him.

Soon, he would go home. I got an ache in the pit of my stomach every time I thought about that.

Jack rolled onto his side, slinging an arm over my belly. "What should we do now? Have another poke?"

I giggled every time he used that phrase, like I was a sixteen-year-old virgin who'd just heard her boyfriend say the F-word for the first time. "Have a poke" was silly and kind of cute, but weird too. Scots had a language all their own, I'd learned. Jack was teaching me about it with every word he said.

Rolling onto my side to face him, I skimmed my fingertips up and down his chest. "I'll do anything you want, and I do mean anything. Have a poke, shag, or even things that don't involve sex. I love being with you, Jack, so I'm up for anything."

He danced his fingertips up my arm, then slid them down to my hand, threading his fingers with mine. "I have a radical idea."

"You? Nah, that's not possible." I closed my fingers around his hand. "You are the guy who talked me into sex behind a slot machine, though."

He had seduced me into doing all kinds of wild things. I'd always been a bit of a free spirit, but not to the extent I was now. Jack MacTaggart brought out a wildness in me I'd never known I possessed, and I loved it.

"This idea I've got," he said, "might be the most radical one yet."

"Why don't you just tell me? I'm dying to know what the Wild Scot has in mind."

"No one back home would ever call me wild. You inspire me to cross every line and suck every crumb of marrow out of life." He lifted our joined hands to kiss the back of mine. "I love the way I feel when I'm with you, and I never want it to end."

"Neither do I. You're amazing, and I don't want you to go home."

His expression turned serious as he stared at our hands like he was searching for the meaning of life in the way our fingers melded. "There is another option. To stay together."

"Like what?"

Jack cleared his throat and looked me straight in the eye. "We could get married."

For a moment, I could do nothing except gape at him. Married? I'd known him for not quite two weeks. Wasn't getting hitched kind of a big thing to do on the spur of the moment? Sure, I loved being with him and I wanted more time with him, but marriage...

That was huge.

But if he went home, I'd miss him so much it would hurt. I knew that, though I couldn't say how I knew. Maybe I sensed it because of the way my stomach hurt every time I thought about him leaving.

It was crazy. I couldn't marry a man I'd met twelve days ago. Sure, I felt closer to him than I ever had with the guys I'd dated before Jack. Could I do something this crazy?

"Where would we live?" I asked. "Once we're married."

My voice had a slight hitch in it when I spoke the word married, almost like a giggle, but not quite.

"I'd love to take you home to Scotland with me," he said, holding my palm to his chest. "Please, Autumn, I don't want to leave you. And you said you don't have any real ties here, so..."

Though I hadn't told him about my parents, I had mentioned that I was alone here in Nevada. Most of my friends had moved away over the years, and so had my family. What did I have to tie me here?

Nothing.

But I had one large, sexy something to lure me to another country.

Jack sighed and flopped onto his back, though he still held my palm to his chest. "It's too much to ask. I shouldn't have—"

"Yes." The word flew out of my mouth before my brain even registered it. Was I insane? Possibly. But it felt too good to fight it. A giddiness overtook me, making me lightheaded, and I knew I didn't want to take back that one word. "Yes, Jack, I'd love to marry you."

He went stone-still, his face blank, his gaze aimed at the ceiling—the gold-colored ceiling that had gaudy images of cherubs painted on it.

Yeah, that was Vegas.

Jack's mouth split into a wide grin, and he laughed so loud it echoed off the walls of the huge suite.

Some people might say anything you do in Vegas stays there, but my Sin City mistake followed me to Scotland and Atlantic City after that. No, it wasn't a mistake. That's the wrong word. My wild adventure stuck with me even after I left Jack and scurried back to America with my tail between my legs. The memory of those days with him in Vegas kept me warm on more nights than I cared to count.

I knew I would never forget him.

Our wedding was, naturally, a Sin City extravaganza. Jack called the concierge, who told us where the closest get-hitched-quick chapel was, which turned out to be The Chapel of the Eternal King Where Love, Peace, and Rock Live Forever. I barely remember the ceremony now. We said our vows, but all we really had to do was say "I will" several times after the officiant recited the vows for us. We never actually said we would love, honor, and cherish each other until death parted us. It wasn't death that did us in, though.

It was fear and pride and shame.

But on that night, in a glitzy little chapel, we meant those vows. I know we did.

My reminiscing is over for now, and I'm gazing out the car window at the scenery that whizzes past. That's how our courtship and marriage had been too—a blur. No, not quite that quick. I do remember every moment of those days in Vegas even though nearly two years have gone by, remember it like it was yesterday.

I miss the Jack I knew then, but I love the way he is now too. Glimmers of the wild Scot who had swept me off my feet show occasionally through the calm-psychologist exterior. I know he genuinely is calm and kind, it's not an act. But I'm sure he's also been hiding that wild side I know so well, afraid he'll shock everyone if he lets it show.

But I think he's wrong. His extended family includes the shameless Alex Thorne, Logan the strange ex-spy, and Rory the Steely Solicitor who tried to strip naked on the Loch Fairbairn town square just to show his wife how much he loved her. Alex stripped naked on the lawn at Dùndubhan when he proposed to Cat. Nobody shuns them for their wild behavior.

I get it, though. Stepping out of your comfort zone takes guts.

Jack has the guts for it, I know. He needs a little more time to realize that. One day, I know he'll stop hiding half of himself and let go.

And I can't wait for that day.

Jack insisted on driving for the whole trip to Dùndubhan because he knows the way to the castle and he told me it's kind of complicated to get there. He's not exaggerating. I lose track of how many times we turn down this narrow side road or that overgrown gravel road. Finally, we turn onto a two-track that leads into a deep forest, and we keep going down that path until we come to a metal gate that hangs open like it's waiting for us.

I guess it is. Rory and Emery must have made the place ready for us.

When will I get to meet those two? They sound like fun. Well, all the MacTaggarts seem like fun. That family is a far cry from mine. Is it any wonder I've never fit in with my own family? Now I'll have a new one with Jack and our baby, not to mention the rest of the MacTaggarts.

I lose track of my thoughts as I absorb the stunning sight before us. Holy heaven, nothing Jack said about this place could've prepared me for the reality of it.

He had told me it was a castle, but I don't think I fully grasped the meaning of that word until this moment as we drive through the metal gate and break out of the trees into the open area around the medieval fortress. It's massive. The boxy structure fills most of the huge clearing inside which it sits, while a high wall fashioned from grayish-brown stone surrounds the castle compound. I see the top of a large building that sports two square turrets and a chimney, plus windows. The windows are unevenly spaced on the exterior, making it hard to tell how many floors the structure has. A gravel driveway leads us closer and closer to the fortress.

The Scottish flag, with its white X on a blue background, flies from the summit of the tallest turret.

As we drive through the entrance—two massive wooden gates, which hang open—and into the castle compound, I glimpse more buildings. They're much smaller, but one of them is connected to the main building by a covered walkway. I also see a walled garden with a cottage attached to one side of the wall.

Tonight I'll be sleeping in an honest-to-goodness medieval castle.

Jack parks near a section of the main building that juts out. While I'm still gaping up at the turrets, Jack hurries around to my side and opens the car door for me.

"Welcome to Dùndubhan, my lady," he says, offering me his hand. "Afraid I don't have a golden carpet laid out for you, but I have another option."

I take his hand, letting him help me out of the car. "Option for what?"

"Carrying my lady to her quarters."

"Oh no, you don't need to—"

He sweeps me up in his brawny arms. "Yes, I do need to."

What can I say? No one has ever carried me over a threshold, not even Jack—until now. He kicks the car door shut and strides toward the doorway set into the jutting section of the castle with all the purpose and self-assurance of a medieval knight. God, that's hot. I want to rip his clothes off the second we enter the castle, but I can't. He doesn't set me down. Somehow, he manages to open the door while still cradling me in his arms, and then he kicks it shut like he did with the car door.

Oh yeah, he's beyond hot.

And I can't help myself. I start unbuttoning his shirt while he strides through the castle. I see a stairwell just inside the doorway, and Jack marches toward it.

"Wait," I say. "Don't I get a tour or something? What are all these rooms?"

"Tour later. Shag now."

He almost sounds like a caveman when he speaks those words, like he's suddenly forgotten three-fourths of the English language in his zeal to get me naked.

"Hold up, Jack," I say. "I'm hungry. Since I'm pregnant, for the sake of the baby, I shouldn't put off eating."

"All right. We'll eat first." He veers away from the stairs toward a doorway that seems to lead to the castle's interior, and we emerge into a hallway. "Cannae have our bairn or his mother starving."

"Thank you."

After we eat, I know we'll have one steamy night. Jack will feed another, deeper hunger I'm feeling now more than ever, a hunger for his body.

Chapter Twenty-Eight

Jack

I'm standing in our bedroom on the third floor, which is the fourth level of the house, including the ground floor. This is the room Rory and Emery shared before they moved into a smaller house near Loch Fairbairn. Though the castle is a museum, only the ground floor and first floor are a part of the displays. The second and third floors are bedrooms for guests, mostly members of my family and our mates.

This bedroom is the most spacious and the nicest since it was redecorated by Emery. It also has the largest bed. For those reasons, I chose this room for me and Autumn. When I carried her in here—yes, I insisted on doing that, despite her claim it was unnecessary—Autumn's eyes grew large and her mouth fell open. The second I set her down, she started exploring, wandering into every corner, opening the closet and the dresser drawers, and finally dropping onto the bed on her back with her arms and legs spread.

Aye, she's adorable. And sexy. And I need to make love to her tonight.

Now, I'm gazing out the window into the night. There's no moon because it's already set, and only the stars interrupt the darkness. I'm wearing the kilt, of course, because Autumn wanted me to wear it—and nothing else. So aye, as my cousin Aidan would say, I'm swinging free under the plaid.

While I watch a thin cloud pass over the stars, I link my hands behind my back.

A faint click tells me Autumn has returned.

"Don't turn around," she says. "Stay just like that."

"What are you plotting, *mo chridhe*?"

"Something you'll like, promise."

I listen to the whisper of her feet padding across the floor, imagining what sort of erotic surprises she has in store for me tonight. Our afternoon in the Loch Fairbairn Arms had been incredible, but I suspect we'll have an even better time tonight. I know she's close behind me when I smell the light, flowery scent of her body lotion.

Christ, smelling that has always made me want to fuck her.

"May I turn around yet?" I ask.

"No."

She's never given me orders before. I wouldn't have thought I'd like that, but I do. The mystery of what she's doing back there makes my blood heat up and my skin tighten.

"Do you trust me?" she asks, her voice so close I can feel her breaths tickling my earlobe.

"Aye."

"I mean do you really trust me, all the way."

"Didn't I just say aye? Yes, Autumn, I trust you."

"Good. I trust you too, and that's all we need tonight." She drags her tongue down my neck. "You, me, trust, and a kilt."

My blood has done more than heat up. It's on fire, burning the hottest in my cock. The sensual whisper of her voice does that to me.

But what does a kilt have to do with shagging her?

She splays her palms on my back, moving them up and down, swirling them over my skin, her touch light and all the more arousing for the delicacy of it. *Bod an Donais*, I want her. Need her. But she keeps moving her hands, now running them down my back from the base of my neck to the base of my spine, her fingers dancing over my vertebrae.

I'm about to shift my hands so I can touch her, but I don't get the chance.

Autumn slides something silky around my left wrist, knotting it snugly, then she does the same with my right wrist.

"What are you doing?" I ask.

"Binding your wrists with a scarf."

"I figured that out. But why?"

She skates her hands around my sides, then glides them up to cover my pectoral muscles. "You're my hostage now, Jack."

"Is this payback for when I wouldn't let you leave the house?"

"No, it's foreplay. Duh."

Even the word duh sounds erotic when she speaks it in that soft, throaty voice.

"Autumn, I—" A gasp bursts out of me when she pinches my nipples and flicks her thumbs over them. "This isn't what I thought—I mean, it's not the way you usually are when we're about to have sex."

"Things have changed. We're closer now than we ever were before, and it's thanks to more than the baby." She drags her palms down to my waist where a leather belt holds the kilt in place. "I feel free now, with you. Free to try anything, feel anything, touch you in all the ways I was afraid to before. I'm not scared anymore, Jack. That's the gift you've given me, and I plan to return it in kind."

"But… Ah, fuck," I groan, because she's rubbing her body against me, her naked breasts rubbing on my back and the hairs on her mound scraping over my erse. "Why did you tie my wrists?"

"For fun. You're at my mercy now, hmm? You said you'd like that if we were naked."

"I know. And I do like it, but, ah…"

"What? You can say anything. I won't get upset." She pushes one finger inside the waist of my kilt, under the leather belt. "I can't wait to take this off and get you naked, but I've got plans for you first."

"What plans?"

"No more questions, or I'll make you watch me creating my own happy ending without you."

"Go on. I'll make you come over and over anyway, so one self-made orgasm won't matter."

"Oh, you'll still be tied up, maybe your feet too, so you won't even be able to make yourself come."

Every word she says makes my cock harder, my breathing heavier, my pulse faster. Autumn has always been adventurous in the bedroom, but not like this.

And I love it.

"No more questions, Jack. Save that for later."

"May I speak at all?"

"Sure, but only if it's dirty." She moves in front of me. "God, you're the sexiest man in the world. I love your chest, and all those hard muscles, and the hairs that form a trail down to your kilt."

"I love your tits, *mo chridhe*. They're indescribably bonnie, and they taste like sweets. I want to suck on them for hours while I rub my *slat* in all that succulent cream I can smell already."

"You talk dirty like nobody's business. Does anyone else know that about you? Like those willing lasses you screwed?"

"No. Only you ever heard me talk that way."

She captures her bottom lip with her teeth, letting it slide free little by little. "That's the hottest thing you've ever said."

"Hotter than 'your clit tastes like honey'?"

"Oh God, Jack. Hearing you say that makes me need to do this right now."

"Do what?"

She kneels in front of me and shoves her head under my kilt.

I stop breathing. In the muted lighting, all I can see is the lump of her head under the plaid, though I feel every breath that escapes her lips, whispering over my shaft, warm and moist and exciting.

Her lips touch the head of my erection, and I jerk, gasping again. But when she rubs her cheek on my *slat* and grasps the base, I lose the ability to breathe. My entire body freezes. I know what she means to do, and I want it like I've never wanted anything before. She drags her tongue up my length, millimeter by millimeter, her breaths teasing my skin, then she drags her tongue back down to the crown.

And she flicks her tongue across it.

"Fuck," I growl, trying to move my hands to cradle her head, but I can't do that. I'm bound by her scarf. All I can do is lean my hip against the windowsill and hope that's enough to keep me standing.

She swirls her tongue over my crown while slowly pumping me with her hand.

A strangled sound rushes out of me, and pressure builds in my cock while she laps up the moisture beading on the head. *Bod an Donais*, her tongue. She coils it around me again and again, taking her time, and the only quick movements she makes are the flicks of her tongue over my crown. I'm breathing so hard I might be hyperventilating. A sensation like electricity spreads down my spine, rushing closer and closer to my groin, and I know I'm on the edge, about to come any second.

She pulls her head out from under my kilt, and her mouth forms the most sensual, ravenous smile I've ever seen. "Not yet, Jack. I want to play with you more."

"Donnae know if I'll survive that. Might pass out from lack of oxygen."

"That's okay. I'll wake you up again." She rises inch by inch, swaying her hips and running her palms up my torso from the waistband of my kilt to my throat. There, she spreads her fingers as she presses her body against mine. "You have no idea how badly I've wanted to do something like this to you, or for how long I've wanted it."

"What's different tonight?" Other than my iron-hard, throbbing cock, that is. Even Autumn has never gotten me this turned on before.

"Everything is different," she says, gliding her hands up my throat and around to my nape. "We're different. No more secrets between us, right? We trust each other. That's what makes tonight special."

She takes two steps backward.

"What are you doing now?" I ask, though I'm fair certain she's about to torture me with that body.

And I don't care.

"Just getting a good look at you before I get rid of that kilt," she says. Her gaze travels over me from head to toe while she drags her tongue over her lips, then she sashays up to me and slips her arms around my waist. "Time to set you free."

She's already done that several times over, starting on the night we met. Why hadn't I realized that until tonight? Even tied up, I feel free— because I'm with her.

Autumn unfastens my belt and tosses it away. My kilt slumps onto the floor. She finds the scarf that's wrapped around my wrists and unties it, tossing that away too, and as it lands on the bedside table, she spreads her hands over my chest. "There. You're liberated."

More than she could ever know.

I pick her up and carry her to the bed. Earlier, I'd pulled the covers back, knowing we would be making love tonight. Though I want to do everything with her—wild, uninhibited things—for now, all I need is to love her body for as long as she'll let me.

She smiles, the soft and sexy way, when I lay her down on the bed.

I straddle her body, gazing into her eyes, and the best kind of pressure weighs down on my chest. No secrets, she said a moment ago. But I do have a secret from her, one I need to tell her now before I lose my nerve.

The shimmering depths of her green eyes draw me in, but I won't let myself sink into them just yet. Not until I've told her.

I bend my arms to get closer to her face, our gazes aligned and only inches apart. "I love you."

Her soft smile tightens into the sweetest expression of happiness. "I love you too. But you already knew that."

"Aye, you told me yesterday. I'm sorry I didn't say it back until now."

"Doesn't matter when you said it, only that you did."

The pressure in my chest evaporates, replaced by a sensation I can't describe, like I'm flying and grounded at the same time, part of me soaring because she said those words and another part of me unable to leave the ground unless she's with me. I love her more than those words can convey, and there are other things I need to tell her too, but not tonight.

"I still have a few secrets," I say, "and I'll tell you everything another time."

"Secrets about what?"

"How I feel. For tonight, though, I don't want to talk, not even if it's dirty."

"Okay. No words. We don't need them, anyway. The way you touch me and kiss me and look at me tells me everything I need to know."

I kiss her, taking my time exploring her mouth, memorizing every sensation as our tongues glide over each other and our breaths tease each other's skin. Somehow, she tastes even better tonight, feels even better, and I never want this kiss to end.

But I have to end it. How else can I worship her body the way she deserves?

I kiss a trail across her cheek to her ear, nibbling the lobe before I move down her throat using my lips and tongue to tease her. She arches her neck, exhaling a breath that's almost a moan. I cup her cheek in one hand, then drag my palm down her throat while I move my lips over her collarbone, and lower to her breast. With my hand covering the other breast, I pull her nipple into my mouth and scrape my tongue across it over and over until she starts to writhe under me.

She pushes a hand into my hair, curling her fingers to wrap the strands around them.

The scent of her skin, it's like nothing I can describe, but I can't get enough of that scent or the flavor of her skin. I lick my way down her belly, diving my tongue into her navel, and run my hand down her side while my mouth reaches her mound. Nuzzling the hairs there, I pull in a deep breath through my nostrils, relishing the scent of her cream that's already strong enough to intoxicate me. She's aroused and ready for me, which makes my cock throb again, but I won't rush this to satisfy my *slat*.

She spreads her legs for me, her fingernails grazing my scalp.

I seal my mouth over her taut nub. The flesh is slick and hot, the taste of her so powerful it's almost like a drug. I've always gotten this way with her, and I've always lost my mind when I'm inside her. I don't want to wait one more second, but I will wait for as long as I can stand it.

For her. This is all for her.

"Mo chridhe," I murmur as I look up at her without removing my head from between her thighs. "Autumn, *mo leannan, mo chridhe*, I love you."

I close my mouth around her clitoris again, but I keep my gaze bound to hers while I lick and suckle it. Her eyes are half-closed, her lips are parted, and she massages my scalp with her fingertips in time with the movements of my tongue. I swipe it up and down, side to side, while she thrashes and cries out my name even when her breathing turns rough and shallow.

When I slide a finger down her folds, she throws her head back and lets out a long, guttural moan.

I tear my mouth away from her clit, rising onto my hands and knees. "Donnae worry, ahmno leaving ye hanging for long."

Her breasts jiggle every time she sucks in a labored breath, and her chest is dappled with a rosy shade of pink, just like her cheeks. I allow myself the space of three breaths to admire the sensual beauty of her body.

Then I plant my hands at either side of her head and plunge inside that beautiful body. Once I'm in as far as I can go, I pause to let myself enjoy this. The sensation of her slick heat around my cock feels so good I'm almost lightheaded, and I don't even care how ridiculous that sounds. It's been too long since I had her smooth flesh wrapped around me. Eight weeks at most, but it feels like a lifetime.

She grasps my wrists and murmurs, "Please, Jack, please."

I know exactly what she's begging me to do, and I want it as much as she does. So I pull my hips back and thrust into her again, trying to go slow but knowing I can't keep that up for long. I've craved her for two months, but since she turned up on my doorstep I've hungered for her more than ever, so much that it was almost painful having to hold back. Now, here in a medieval castle in the middle of nowhere, I have her at last.

And it's bloody incredible.

She's unbelievably wet, and her cream coats my cock with every measured thrust. I roll my hips, groaning because her channel is so hot and velvety around me, even better than I remember. She bends her knees to frame my hips with her thighs, but when she tightens her inner muscles around me, I suck in a sharp breath.

"Fuck, Autumn," I gasp.

"Yes, Jack, don't stop."

I can't speak or think anymore, because the way her body molds to my cock and her tits bounce every time I push inside her steals all my brainpower—and my willpower. Cannae stop myself. I thrust harder, deeper, faster, while she hooks her ankles behind my erse and grips my wrists tightly, crying out and arching her back. Her nails dig into my skin, but I donnae give a shit about that.

She comes so hard it tears a harsher, wilder cry out of her, and her body pulsates around me like it never wants to let go of my *slat*.

I cannae hold back either. My every muscle goes rigid, and the only part of me that can move is my hips. I keep punching into her until I come while buried deep inside her, my body bowing inward with the final thrust. A hoarse shout erupts from me. A series of electrifying shocks fires through my cock, and I spend everything inside her.

By the time it's over, I'm breathing so hard I can't speak or move, frozen in the final thrust.

Autumn looks slightly dazed, her smile so relaxed it's almost silly.

Christ, I feel like a senseless moron too. We've always had incredible sex, but this was different.

I pull out of her body and fall onto the mattress beside her.

For a few minutes, we both just lie here catching our breath. My heart is pounding, every beat thundering in my ears.

Autumn recovers first. Laying a palm on her chest, over her heart, she grins again in that silly but adorable way. "Wow, Jack, that was…the best sex we've ever had."

I rub my eyes with the heels of my hands. "Aye, it was. I think saying we love each other made it more intense."

"Definitely." She flips onto her side, sprawled half on top of me with her cheek on my chest. "I'm so happy you said it. That you love me."

"Had to tell you how I feel. You're one hell of a woman, *mo leannan*." I comb my fingers through her damp hair, and even the scent of her sweat makes me want her—again. "For the record, I've loved you since the night we met."

She lifts her head to aim the loveliest little smile at me. "I loved you that first night too, but I didn't think I'd ever hear you admit to that. Love at first sight isn't calm or rational."

"No, but it felt wonderful. I think that's why I acted like such an erse when I brought you home to Scotland. Couldn't reconcile the way I felt about you, the things I did in Las Vegas, with the way I am at home."

"You don't need to explain it. Just feel it, Jack. Just feel it."

For the first time since our wedding night, I let myself revel in every last beautiful thing this woman makes me feel.

And I'm not ashamed of it anymore.

Chapter Twenty-Nine

Autumn

I rest my cheek on Jack's chest again, listening to his heartbeat as it slows gradually. We've never had sex like this before. It was emotional, intense, hotter than hot, and so many other things I can't describe. He let me bind his wrists. He trusts me that much, more than I'd ever realized until tonight. Part of me had assumed Jack would say no when I asked if he trusted me all the way, but he didn't even hesitate before saying yes.

God, I love him.

"You need to know something," he says, gliding his hand down my back and up again, over and over, in a slow rhythm. "I was never ashamed of you. I couldn't accept my own behavior, and I assumed everyone would be horrified if they found out I'd acted like a sex-crazed eejit in Las Vegas. It was hard enough when my family found out I'd married a woman I barely knew."

"The MacTaggarts I've met don't seem judgmental at all."

"No, but I was ashamed of myself." He groans miserably. "What I'd done to you, talking you into marrying me and moving to Scotland, refusing to let you meet my family. I didn't even tell them myself that I'd gotten married. Evan found out when he stopped by my apartment a few days after I brought you home. I wouldn't let him inside, but he saw the wedding ring on my finger."

"Ohhh, so that's how the news made it into the MacTaggart grapevine."

"Evan told Rory, who did some legal digging. Everyone knew I'd been in Las Vegas, so finding the marriage license wasn't difficult for someone as clever and well-connected as Rory."

Well, at least I now understand how the news got out. I'm also starting to understand why Jack panicked back then and why he did again it this week. He's spent years, maybe his whole life, cultivating the kind of persona that a psychologist needs, calm and rational, unflappable, reassuring. But with me, in Vegas, he cut loose for the first time and discovered his wild side.

"Listen, Jack, I need to say a few things."

He stops rubbing my back. "All right."

"Relax, it's nothing bad." I fold my hands on his chest and rest my chin on them. "You don't need to pretend with me. I don't care if you stay Therapist Jack around other people, but with me, you can show every side of yourself. Passionate Jack, Grumpy Jack, Stoic Jack, Hot Fuck Jack, anything. I'm in this for the long haul, so you don't need to worry about me walking out again. You're stuck with me."

"No one else I'd rather be stuck with."

I glance at the scarf lying on the bedside table. "Want to have some more fun?"

"Aye. What did you have in mind this time?"

"Proving that I trust you the way you trusted me earlier." I crawl across the bed to the table and snag the scarf, then crawl back to him. Sitting back on my heels, I offer him the scarf. "Blindfold me, Jack."

"What?"

He sounds surprised, but the look on his face tells me it's the kind of surprise brought on by sexual excitement. He likes the idea.

The way his dick is getting bigger confirms it.

Jack sits up and takes the scarf. "Do you have another one of these?"

"I've got several."

"Find another one. I want you to blindfold me too."

I can't help grinning. Jack loves to play, and I love that about him. Refusing to have sex with him all week was a dumb idea, but I won't give in to regret. Everything that happened needed to happen exactly the way it did.

He slaps my ass. "Get another scarf, *mo chridhe*."

While I slide off the bed, I ask, "What does that phrase mean? And what was that other thing you said when we were in the middle of screwing each other?"

"I prefer to think of it as loving the fuck out of each other," he says with a smirk. "*Mo chridhe* means 'my heart.' And *mo leannan* means 'my sweetheart.' Both are Gaelic."

"I'm your heart?" I say as I open my bag and get out another scarf.

"Aye, you are my sweetheart and my heart. The best part of me is you, Autumn."

Who knew Jack would turn out to be a romantic? A die-hard one at that. I still have plenty to learn about him, and I want to spend the rest of our lives uncovering every last facet of the man I love.

I climb onto the bed and hand him the other scarf.

"Lie down," he says. "On your back, love."

Even if I'd wanted to resist him, which I never have, I wouldn't have been able to with the way he's speaking to me in a rumbly, sexy voice that makes my tummy flutter. So I lie down, head on the pillow and scarf in hand. "You're the best part of me too, Jack. We fit together like puzzle pieces."

"Aye, we do." He sits on his haunches between my feet. "Tie the scarf over your eyes, *mo leannan*."

He raises his scarf and begins to fold it until it's the right width for a blindfold, then he ties it around his head.

I do the same with my scarf. Some light leaks through the fabric, but I can't see Jack. He can't see me anymore either. Not seeing each other makes it even more exciting, and I'm already breathing harder—not to mention getting wet and tingly.

The mattress shifts as Jack moves around.

My pulse accelerates.

His hands settle onto my knees, but I suspect he had to feel around for them before he finally hit the right spots. He skates his palms up my thighs, and I instinctively open my legs for him.

"I can smell ye," he says. "It's intoxicating."

"This is so hot, isn't it? Not seeing you, not knowing where you are or what you might do."

"Aye, it's hot all right."

He slides his hands over my belly and up to my breasts, fondling them like he's mapping my tits. He finds one nipple and rubs his thumb over it.

A tiny electric shock shoots through me, from my nipple straight down to my core.

I stretch out one hand, searching for his cock. I find his chest first and run my palm down his skin until I reach his hip, then I move my hand lower and more to the right.

My fingers bump into a long, hard, thick object that's bobbing below him.

Eureka. I close my hand around his erection.

Jack blusters out a ragged breath.

I pump him with my hand, brushing his balls with every swipe.

He groans so deeply it resonates in his chest. "Ahm wanting to fuck ye, lass. But if ye keep doing that... Ah..."

"So do it, Jack. Fuck me."

"More orders?" He pushes my hand away from his dick. "You have no idea how it affects me every time you get bossy."

"Better show me, then."

He slides his hands under my thighs and hoists them up, though he keeps his hands under them.

I'd assumed he wanted to put my legs over his shoulders, but no, he's not doing that. Blindfolded, I can't even guess about what he's got in mind. Not that it matters. I love everything he does to me, and the thrill of not seeing anything gets me more turned on than ever before. He slides his hands up to my knees and tugs me closer until my ass is pushed up against his knees and slightly elevated.

"Whatever you're doing," I say, suddenly struggling to catch my breath, "keep going because I love it."

Jack plunges into me with one long, leisurely motion, filling me up in the most delicious way, his cock buried to the hilt. With every thrust, he pushes deep inside me in a way I've never experienced before. No one has ever gotten me into a position like this, and maybe that's why it feels so damn good. It's new and exciting. I grasp the headboard slats, helpless to keep from moaning and gasping, too caught up in the moment to do anything else. Being blindfolded forces me to focus on sensations, and I swear my senses are heightened to the point I could hear a pin drop outside the door.

Suddenly, he shoves his arms under my body and hoists me up onto his lap. He never stops thrusting, not even when he falls backward onto the mattress with me on top of him and takes hold of my hips, urging me to move with him. Jack doesn't need to tell me what to do, though. The second he'd toppled over, I'd known what he wanted. So I splay my palms on his chest and ride him, rocking my hips, listening to every sound he makes and learning exactly how to get him worked up when we can't see each other. He loves it when I pinch his nipples, which I can tell because he hisses in a breath when I do that.

He walks his fingers up my inner thighs until he finds my clit, then he massages it until I'm panting and crooking my nails into his chest. I must be clawing his skin, but he doesn't seem to mind.

The climax builds inside me little by little, like a pot rising to a full boil. I move faster, grip his shoulders, rotate my hips, anything to get me to the boiling point faster—and take Jack there with me.

He shouts something in Gaelic, rubbing me harder.

Every muscle in my body tenses in anticipation, but somehow I keep moving, keep pushing us both higher and higher toward—

A cry explodes out of me as my body clinches him so many times and so hard that I can't keep track. I grip his shoulders until my nails are digging into him for sure this time, and just when I think I'm done, he goes off. He lets out a hoarse shout, bucking into me, and the feel of him coming apart inside me sends another jolt of pleasure through my body.

I fall onto Jack, incapable of staying upright or moving off him. His cock is still inside me, but I don't care. For a few minutes, we both lie there, limbs entangled. That orgasm stole my breath away for sure. I'm positive it had the same effect on him since his chest is heaving beneath me.

At last, Jack removes my blindfold. He tosses the scarf away and then gets rid of his blindfold too.

Now I can see we're sprawled across the width of the bed, near the foot.

He combs his fingers through my hair gently. "That was bloody incredible, even better than the first time."

"Which one? The first time tonight, or the first time ever?"

"Both." He slings his other arm around me. "I'm glad we came here to Dùndubhan. There's something deeply erotic about shagging my ex-wife in a medieval castle."

"I agree. Maybe we should move in here, if this is what castle sex is like."

"We can visit anytime we want." He kisses the top of my head. "But our cottage in Loch Fairbairn is a better place to raise a child."

"Absolutely." I raise my head to look at him. "You just called it 'our' cottage."

"Did I?" He sits up, keeping me in his arms, and rearranges us so we're lying on the bed the right way, then he pulls the covers over us. "Let's talk about that in the morning. Right now, we both need sleep."

"I'm not sleepy," I say as a big yawn overtakes me.

"Aye, that's a convincing statement. Sleep, *mo chridhe.* Everything else can wait until tomorrow."

I love it when he calls me his heart. And for tonight, I'm going to do what he said and sleep. My mind sinks into slumber oh-so-slowly, and one thought whispers through my dreams all night.

He loves me.

Chapter Thirty

Jack

I'm standing at the window again this morning, though I'm not wearing a kilt this time. I don't have any clothes on. Why bother? As soon as Autumn wakes up, I plan to make love to her again. Last night changed everything, though it wasn't only the sex that did that. I know we still have things to work through. The prospect doesn't fash me anymore. I look forward to everything with her, even the parts that require me to open up and share like I tell all my clients to do.

Aye, it's not enjoyable being on the other side of therapy. But for Autumn, I'll do anything.

The sun has just started to rise, though only its glow is visible on the horizon. I lean against the window frame to enjoy the oncoming sunrise, but my gaze keeps drifting back to Autumn lying asleep in the bed. She's sprawled over it on her stomach, her cheek on the pillow and a soft smile on her lips. What is she dreaming about? I can ask her when she wakes up.

She stretches and moans with pleasure, her eyes still closed.

"Good morning, *mo leannan.*"

Her lids flutter, and she rolls onto her back, rubbing her eyes before she stretches her arms above her head and moans again. She aims her green eyes at me. "Good morning, Dr. Sex Machine."

I chuckle. "Donnae think I've ever been called that before, not even by you."

"Yeah, I just thought of it." She stretches again, getting her whole body into it this time, and smiles at me. "I feel fantastic."

"So do I. Should we have a poke before breakfast?"

"Yes, please."

Autumn shimmies to the bed's edge, slides her legs off it, and yawns while stretching yet again. The movement makes her breasts lift. She exhales a long breath as she rakes her gaze over me, licking her lips. "You should become a nudist, Jack. A body like yours shouldn't be covered in clothes."

"I'll become a nudist if you will too."

"Maybe we could do it part-time. Not sure Scotland is a great climate for that lifestyle." She hops off the bed and walks over to me, slipping her arms around my waist. "But we could go nude inside the house."

"Let's be naked all day, here in the castle."

She grins. "Count me in."

I clasp my hands behind her back and tug her closer. "First, I need to confess."

"Uh-oh."

"No, it's not bad. Well, sort of, I suppose." The worry on her face makes me want to kiss it away, but I need to use words this time, not sex, to tell her how I feel. "I'm still worried you'll leave me again. I know you don't want to, and you wouldn't mean to, but you haven't worked through all your issues yet. Neither have I. And that's why I worry about it."

"Last night you said you trust me."

"I do trust you. That sounds contradictory, I know, but human emotions are messy and confusing." I shut my eyes for a moment while I try to figure out how to phrase my words. "I'm a therapist, *gràidh*. I know people don't get over their fears in five minutes. A breakthrough isn't a cure. We both need to do a lot more talking and sharing."

One side of her mouth kicks up. "You make 'sharing' sound like a root canal."

"Dealing with your fears isn't a painless process, but it's not a dental procedure either."

She chews on her lip. "I know we have work to do. But for today, can we just be happy?"

"Aye, we can do that."

"Maybe we should have breakfast before we run wild through the castle in the nude."

I slide a hand up to fondle her breast. "But I was hoping to shag you up against this window first."

"Pre-breakfast sex? Oh yeah, I'm in."

She presses her open mouth to my chest, flicking her tongue over my skin.

Movement down on the green catches my eye, and I glance out the window.

"Oh bloody hell," I groan.

Autumn lifts her head. "What's wrong?"

I nod toward the window. "The MacTaggart clan is gathering outside for a castle siege."

"Are you serious? They're outside?"

"Have a look."

She cranes her neck to gaze down at the green.

Eight people are already down there, but from this distance, I can't tell who they are. I see a blonde woman, so that must be Emery. Rory will be with her, but I don't know who else they've brought. I also have no idea what the bloody hell they're doing here. What happened to having the castle to ourselves?

Autumn bounces on her tiptoes. "I get to meet more MacTaggarts. This is great."

I sag against the window frame while I watch more people walking, trotting, and skipping onto the green. Well, one person skips. I think it's… Catriona? No, she's not silly like that. But I'm sure that's Alex with her—I can tell by the way he walks—so it must be Cat skipping along beside him.

Alex makes her so happy she prances around like a silly wee lassie? I know they're enjoying life these days, but I hadn't realized quite how happy she is.

I wonder if Autumn will ever skip with joy for me.

The woman in question taps my lips with one finger. "Don't get grumpy. I'm sure they're only stopping by to say hello or…something."

"It's the 'or something' that worries me. You have no conception of the lengths my family will go to if they think one of us needs 'help.' It can turn into a right mess."

"Have you ever been on the giving end of their help?"

"Giving end?" I glance down at the green and stifle a groan because I see another group of MacTaggarts arriving. "I don't know what you mean by that."

"Have you ever participated in the meddling?"

"No."

Autumn steps back, tipping her head to the side, her gaze trained on me. "Really. Because Logan's sisters told me how you were instrumental in helping Alex and Cat work through their issues. And you did the same with Grey and Jessica."

"I offered them each a therapy session. That's a legitimate use of my skills and experience, not meddling."

She shakes her head, though she's smiling. "Face it, Jack. You meddle too. So maybe you should let your family do their thing and get it over with."

Maybe I am being a bit of a hypocrite, but I have never engaged in the level of meddling the rest of the family has instigated. Besides, this is *my* life they're interfering in. Aye, it was fine when they interfered with some-one else's life.

Bod an Donais. I *am* a hypocrite.

"You don't even know what they're planning to do," Autumn says. "Why not find out before you turn into a fire-breathing dragon and incinerate them?"

"Aye, fine," I say with a sigh. What's the point in fighting the inevita-ble? "Let's get dressed and head downstairs. Looks like they're all coming inside whether we like it or not."

She slaps my arm. "That's the spirit."

Naturally, she's being sarcastic. I deserve it.

We reach the last flight of stairs just as the door to the outside opens. By the time we get down into the vestibule, several people have entered the house. I see Alex, Cat, Rory, Emery, and Callum.

My brother is in on the meddling? He'll get an earful about that next time I have him alone, the sodding scunner.

Through the open door, I notice a small crowd gathered in the courtyard.

"Only two dozen people?" I say to Alex. "Couldn't drum up the entire clan this morning, eh?"

"It's not two dozen," Alex says, coming up to lay a hand on my shoulder. "It's only twelve people besides this smaller contingent."

He waves a hand to indicate the others who have come inside the house.

Cat shuts the door.

My brother smirks at me. "We're here for you, Jack. Whatever you need, we can provide it." He rolls his eyes toward Autumn. "I'm here to help in any way necessary."

"I don't know what you're implying," I say, "but I'm developing a strong urge to punch you."

Alex squeezes my shoulder. "Calm down, Jack. This is a mission of mer-cy, not an invasion. Well, it might be a small invasion of a sort. Or perhaps it's a moderate one. Whatever the case, we're here to force-feed you whatever help Cat and Emery decide you need."

Moderate invasion? Force-feed? Aye, now I want to punch Alex. Hard.

Autumn sidles up to me, hooking her arm around mine. "Take it easy, Jack. I'm sure Alex is kidding."

"Maybe, but Callum isn't." I suddenly notice my brother is using a cane. "Have you re-injured that knee again?"

He shrugs. "A wee bit. Can't have any fun without pain, aye?"

"The physical therapist said not to push it."

"Months ago he said that. I'm fine, Jack. Go back to scowling at your girl." He tips his head to the side, puckering his lips like he's thinking hard. His attention is focused on Autumn. "But if Jack is too grumpy for you, lass, I'll gladly fill in for him."

I grit my teeth.

Callum holds up one hand. "Only in a platonic way. I'm more fun at parties, though not as much fun as Alex or Aidan. Nick Hunter is the most fun, but he's not around right now."

"Thank you for the offer, Callum," Autumn says with a smile. "But Jack is the only man I need."

"Well, I'm on standby if you change your mind. I'm a dead brilliant dance partner."

I squint at him. "Why would she need a dance partner?"

My brother grins and wags his eyebrows.

Yes, Callum is just like Aidan and Nick. They're all a bunch of annoying erses.

Alex, who still has his hand on my shoulder, says, "Maybe we should share our plan with Jack and Autumn. Emery, why don't you do the honors? It was your idea, after all."

Emery squeezes past Callum and Rory to get to us. She offers her hand to my ex-wife. "Hi Autumn, we haven't officially met yet, though we talked on the phone yesterday. I'm Emery, and that big hunk of Scottish hotness behind me is Rory, my husband and Jack's cousin."

"Oh, I know all about you guys," Autumn says while shaking Emery's hand. "Jack told me all kinds of stories."

Emery raises her brows, her gaze darting to me. "Did he now. Guess we'll need to share some Jack stories with you, then."

I huff. "There aren't any 'Jack stories' for you to tell. I'm boring. Just ask Callum."

"Boring?" Emery says, shaking her head. "Oh no, sweetie, you are not dull. I mean, you're the guy who gave Alex Thorne a good head-shrinking and got his noggin screwed on straight. That was a treacherous mission."

"Was it ever," Cat chimes in. She pats her husband's cheek. "Alex's head was…askew. Now it's facing the right way."

Alex pulls his hand away from my shoulder at last, but only so he can grab his wife and drag her into him. "Careful, Catnip. I might think you're trying to seduce me with your erotic wordplay."

"There's nothing erotic about your head being askew." She wriggles against him. "Sex with you is so much better now that you're not a flaming ersehole anymore."

I might be snarling when I say, "Would you two lay off it? Donnae need to hear about your sexual proclivities."

Autumn cuddles up to me, rubbing her cheek on my arm. "Aw, it's okay, Jack. I'll tell you all about my sexual proclivities if that'll make you feel better."

"May I eavesdrop on that conversation?" Callum asks.

I throw him a scowl. "No, you *bod ceann*, you may not."

Callum grins. "I think Jack needs a cracking shag, Autumn."

"Yes, he does," she agrees.

Alex clears his throat. "Shall we head into the dining room? Mrs. Brody has whipped up a breakfast feast for us, and we can explain our plans to Jack and Autumn while we eat."

"What about the others outside?" I ask.

"They've already had breakfast."

Alex leads the advance troops into the hallway and down to the dining room. The rest of the army will lay siege to Dùndubhan later. I wind up sitting with Autumn on one side of me and Alex on the other. Rory takes the head of the table while his wife occupies the chair at the other end. Cat and Callum sit opposite us.

Once we've all got food on our plates, I ask the inevitable question, though I dread hearing the answer. "What sort of event do you lot have planned? If it's Highland games, I'm not in the mood."

Alex gives me his patented devious smile. "No, it's not the games this time. We need something different for you and Autumn."

"Such as?"

"A ceilidh, of course."

I smack my fork down on my plate and sink back in my chair. A ceilidh? That means dancing. Which I despise.

Alex aims that smile at me again. "Don't worry. There will be plenty of booze on hand."

Well, at least there's that.

Chapter Thirty-One

Autumn

Jack is flustered, for sure, by the invasion of the well-meaning Mac-Taggarts. I know Jack isn't angry at them. He's frustrated that they seem ready and willing to stick their noses into our relationship, and he clearly hates the idea of a ceilidh, whatever that is.

My ex-husband shoves a huge mouthful of food into his mouth, managing to look miserable even while he's chewing.

"What's a ceilidh?" I ask.

Alex smiles and winks at me. "A raucous do with dancing and music."

"He means a party," Catriona says. "A do is a party, and so is a ceilidh. But a Scottish do is much more fun than the British version."

Alex clutches a hand over his heart. "Catriona, my love, my darling, you wound me grievously."

"Like hell I do." She grabs his face and plants a big smacker on him. "Finish your breakfast, *mo leannan*. You need the energy to fuel all the rubbish that comes out of your mouth twenty-four hours a day."

I love these people. Every MacTaggart I've met, and I'm counting Alex as one too, is cheerful and funny and full of life. I want whatever they're on. Is it whisky? Wild Highlands weed? No, I think it's the way they are naturally. Why shouldn't they be happy? They belong to a large extended family that loves and supports its members no matter what.

For the rest of breakfast, everyone discusses the preparations for the ceilidh. No one mentions when it will be until I finally raise my hand.

"You have a question, Autumn?" Rory asks.

"Uh, yeah. When is this big dance party?"

"Tonight."

Jack chokes on the sip of water he's just taken and starts coughing. When he manages to speak, he sounds a little hoarse. "Tonight? That's not possible. Ye cannae arrange a ceilidh that fast."

"Of course we can," Alex says. "We're nosy, bossy arses, aren't we? Nothing is beyond our reach."

Rory rolls his eyes at Alex but speaks to me. "He means we have the connections and the money to make it happen. When our wives get an idea in their heads, it's best to humor them."

"Hey!" Cat and Emery say at the same time.

Callum chuckles. "If you lot want to sleep in your own beds tonight, best apologize to the bonnie lasses."

The conversation moves on from there, and soon it seems like the whole party is organized, though it's clear everyone had started working on it before they showed up at Dùndubhan. Jack is more relaxed after breakfast. I think he finally gave in and decided to let his family do whatever they want. Surrender can be liberating.

Surrendering to Jack last night was, for sure.

I get why he worries I'll leave him again, but I won't do that. It's up to me to prove it to him. Still, I can't help feeling disheartened by the fact he claims to trust me but thinks I might walk out on him again.

After the dishes have been cleared away and put in the dishwasher, we all head outside onto "the green" which turns out to be a big lawn. The green occupies a large clearing behind the castle, and it's where they like to hold the MacTaggart Highland games. I'd love to see those, but a ceilidh sounds like fun too. I'm no great shakes at dancing, but I'm pumped to learn all the traditional moves.

Jack, not so much.

"I know the dances," he tells me as we cross the garden, heading for the door in the back wall that leads to the green. "I don't like dancing. That's the problem."

"But maybe you could loosen up a teeny bit and give it a try? For me?"

The others have just exited the garden, and I can see the green beyond it.

Jack takes hold of my upper arms, halting us halfway to the door. He moves in front of me, looking straight into my eyes. "I will do anything for you, *mo chridhe.*"

My throat goes dry, and I bite my lip. He'll do anything for me. Nobody has ever said that before. Nobody. I'm positive he means it because he wouldn't lie to me.

"I know, Jack. Thank you."

He starts to turn away, to head for the door.

I grab his arm. When he glances back at me, I say, "I'll do anything for you too."

Jack lays his hand over mine on his arm. "I know."

"But you still think I'll leave you."

He looks away for a moment, then turns his face to me. "I told you earlier, I believe you don't want to run away, but I also know you still have unresolved issues. I want to help you with that, but it's a slow process."

"I'm ready to do whatever it takes to show you I'm in this for the long haul."

Jack pulls me in for a hug. "Donnae worry, *gràidh*. I love you, and if you should run away again, I'll be running after you this time. I'm not letting you go again without a fight."

He wants to chase after me? I'd prayed he would do that when I walked out two years ago, but he hadn't. Our reunion has changed things between us, and I believe he means it when he says he won't let me leave without fighting for me, for us.

I won't run away. Never again.

Jack kisses my forehead and leads me out onto the green.

A bunch more MacTaggarts are out here. They've gathered stacks of folding chairs as well as folding tables, boxes full of plates and glasses, more boxes stuffed with decorations, and crates of drinks. That includes booze, yes, but also nonalcoholic options like soda pop and sparkling water.

I meet Jack's cousins and their wives including Lachlan and Erica, Aidan and Calli, and Iain and Rae. I don't get to meet Evan the billionaire and his wife, Keely, because they're in America right now where Evan's company has offices. Jamie and her American husband, Gavin, who's Calli's brother, introduce themselves too. They all welcome me like I've been a part of the family for years. No one mentions the fact that Jack and I are divorced. I'm sure they all know about the blind-date debacle, but they're too polite to mention it.

Though I haven't met a billionaire yet, I do find out several MacTaggarts are multimillionaires. Lachlan, Rory, and Iain fall into that category, which I know only because Jack had told me about them back when we were married.

I also meet two teenagers. Chase is the son of Logan's wife, Serena, and he's Logan's stepson. The sixteen-year-old seems to have a crush on the other teenager on the premises—Malina, the fifteen-year-old daughter of Iain and Rae.

Jack confirms my assessment when he whispers in my ear, "They're sweet on each other. Everyone knows it, but they're both too shy to admit it."

Their teen crush is adorable, but I don't get a chance to think about that. Preparations for the ceilidh are in full swing. We're having a massive confab on the green. With so many people here, it could've turned into a hopelessly out-of-control mess, but Rory and Emery keep things orderly, and everyone respects their commands. The discussion is lively but manageable.

Lachlan is conversing with Rory about the logistics of holding a ceilidh on the green when Iain hollers, "Hold on."

Everyone falls silent.

"What is it, Iain?" Rory asks.

Iain raises his cell phone. "I checked the weather forecast. Rain is expected this evening, so an outdoor ceilidh might not be the best idea."

Rory whispers something to Emery, then he nods crisply and speaks to the crowd. "The ceilidh is moving into the great hall. Start grabbing chairs, boxes, tables, whatever you can carry."

Without any argument or delay, every MacTaggart and every spouse of a MacTaggart does exactly what Rory said. I intend to pitch in too, but when I reach for a box of decorations, Jack rushes over to stop me.

"You can't do that," he says. "You might…strain something."

I know he's worried about the baby but doesn't want to say so out loud, since nobody else knows I'm pregnant, but he's being overprotective again. "Take it easy, Jack. I'm not an invalid, and this box isn't heavy, anyway. I won't 'strain' anything, unless you strain my patience by acting like I'm incapable of lifting a cardboard box full of ribbons and streamers."

"But you're—" He crimps his mouth like he's working very hard to avoid speaking the word pregnant in front of his family. "You're in a delicate condition."

Yeah, that won't tip anyone off at all. Delicate condition? He makes it sound like I have a horrible disease.

"Why is Autumn in a delicate condition?" a male voice asks from behind Jack.

Since we're both crouching near the box I'd wanted to pick up, I can see the man who has approached us.

Logan lifts his brows. "Well, Jack, what's wrong with Autumn?"

Aidan, who's standing several yards away, clearly heard Logan's question. He veers his attention to the three of us. "Something's wrong with Autumn?"

More MacTaggarts look at us, and several trot over to check out what's the matter with me.

"Is she ill?" Lachlan asks. "Maybe we should ring Dr. Buchanan."

"She looks fine to me," Iain says. "But maybe she's feeling the stress of this whole ceilidh nonsense."

"A ceilidh isn't nonsense," Aidan proclaims. "Besides, Alex told us Autumn loves a party."

Iain smiles in the patient way Jack describes as his Buddha smile. "Alex said he didn't think she would mind one. He never said she'd love it."

Jack leaps to his feet. "Would you lot quit your havering? You're turning into blue-haired busybodies."

"Is Autumn all right, then?" Rory asks.

Maybe I am getting a teeny bit nauseous, but there's nothing wrong with me. It's morning sickness. Listening to all these people bickering over whether I'm sick will make me even queasier if they don't cut that out.

Emery, who's standing beside her husband, glances down at my belly. Her mouth slides into a knowing smile.

And I suddenly realize I'm holding my hand over my belly in a protective gesture.

"Quiet!" Emery shouts, loud enough that her voice echoes off the walls of the castle compound.

Everyone shuts up.

Rory stares at his wife.

"The only thing wrong with Autumn," Emery says, "is that you guys are arguing about what's wrong with her. She's fine. Give her some space, okay?"

The men who had gathered around me and Jack mutter "aye" and shuffle back to their wives.

Emery winks at me, then escorts her husband back into the crowd.

God bless that woman.

Jack picks up the box that had started the commotion. "Please let me carry these boxes. You can help with the logistics, all right?" He holds up a hand when I open my mouth. "I know you're not an invalid, but I can't stop myself from worrying about you and the bairn."

I study him for a moment, and a realization hits me. He's not just being overprotective. He honestly worries that something might happen to the baby—and me. I wish I could do something to make him feel less anxious.

All I can do right now is hug him. So I snatch the box from him, setting it on the ground, and wrap my arms around him.

He stiffens. "Ah, everyone is watching us. Again."

"Better hug me back, then, huh? Don't want anybody to think we're having problems."

"I suppose not," he says carefully.

Jack slips his arms around me and shoves his face into my hair.

Cheers break out. Several people whistle, and I'm pretty sure it's the men, not the ladies, doing that. The women are beaming at us.

Alex smiles at me, then spreads his arms wide and announces, "Reconciliation is at hand. Tonight's ceilidh will be a celebration of Jack and Autumn's reunion."

Jack groans against my neck. "One of these days, I'm going to murder Alex Thorne."

I rub his back and kiss his cheek. "Wait until tomorrow, huh? I'm looking forward to the party tonight, but I won't get to dance with you if you're in jail."

"Fine, I'll hold off on battering Alex until tomorrow. But I'm only dancing with you, no one else."

"Thank you, honey."

He lifts his head to look at me. "Honey?"

"I said that, didn't I? Well, there's nothing wrong with me calling you honey. We both said the L-word, after all."

"Aye, we did." His entire demeanor relaxes, and he smiles tenderly. "I have been calling you *mo leannan* and *mo chridhe*. It's only right that you come up with a pet name for me too."

"Sorry I don't have fancy Gaelic things to call you. The best Americans can do is 'honey' or 'sweetie' or maybe 'sugar pie.' But I'll see if I can think of something else later."

"Donnae care what ye call me, lass, as long as you're happy."

"I am."

Jack carries the box toward the garden door, and I follow.

No, I could never walk away from him again.

Chapter Thirty-Two

Jack

The ceilidh is in full swing by the time Autumn and I enter the great hall hand in hand. MacTaggarts and mates of MacTaggarts have already begun the dancing, and laughter and chatter fill the air, though not at a deafening volume. Thank heaven for that. Sometimes our family parties get so raucous that I need two aspirins when it's all over, though not entirely because of the noise. Aye, whisky is a staple at our celebrations.

I've never been a fan of big parties, and this do has turned into quite a gathering. I'd expected to see my cousins and their families here, but Grey and Jessica Dixon have turned up as well. I also see Domhnall Sterling, who is clearly my cousin Fiona's date for the evening. I knew they had become a couple, once Domhnall stopped trying to destroy Grey and get Jessica back, but I hadn't thought I'd see them at a MacTaggart event. Yet here they are, dancing The Gay Gordons.

Every MacTaggart man in attendance is wearing a kilt, and so are Alex and Grey. I've got mine on too, but that's because Autumn asked me to wear it. I hadn't known my male relatives planned to dress this way. I also wear a suit jacket over a white shirt, but that's not to match my family members. Aidan is wearing a T-shirt that says "kiss my kilt" and features an image of a puckered mouth, while Alex is wearing a ridiculous billowing white shirt that looks like something out of the Middle Ages.

Autumn is grinning while she watches the dance in progress. "This is wonderful. I've never done this kind of dancing. My skills are limited to foot-shuffling and hip-grinding, but this stuff looks like so much fun."

There's a band set up on a dais in the far corner. One gent does drum rolls while another plays a jaunty tune on his accordion. The rest of the band members tap their toes and wait for their turn—in an upcoming number, I assume. The instruments include a tin whistle, an acoustic guitar, and a chanter.

When I explain that to Autumn, she asks, "What's a chanter? Never heard of that instrument."

"It's the tube-like part of bagpipes, and it's what a piper uses to create a tune."

"Oh. Cool." She turns her head left and right, watching the ongoing dance. "Can we give this one a try? I know you hate dancing, but it looks like fun. Please, Jack, please. You said you would, for me."

She's holding her hands clasped under her chin while looking at me with the most adorable expression of fake pleading.

How can I say no to that?

"All right," I tell her, leading her toward the dance floor. "We'll join in The Gay Gordons."

"The whats?"

"Gay Gordons. It's a traditional march that originated during the First World War, and eventually, the music inspired a dance too." We stop at the edge of the dance floor. "It's a round-the-room dance, which means—"

"Everybody goes around the room in a big circle. Yeah, I figured that out based on the fact I can see everybody moving that way."

She keeps grinning while I instruct her on how to join in the dance. I stretch my right arm behind her, at her shoulder level, and she takes hold of my hand with her right one. Then she reaches across my waist with her left hand to take hold of mine. When everyone sees that we want to join in, they pause and make a space for us in the circle. Once we're in position, the dance resumes.

I give Autumn instructions as we go, speaking only loud enough to make sure she hears me. While the march plays, we follow the routine I know better than I wish I did. It's like second nature, though I don't enjoy dancing. "Forward, two, three, four. Reverse, two, three, four."

As we go round and round, hand in hand, I find myself relaxing into the rhythm of the music and the steps. Autumn keeps smiling, and I swear her eyes sparkle with joy. I get more into the movements and the song the longer we dance, infected by her enthusiasm. She's bonnier than ever tonight, only in part because of her bonnie dress and the way it accentuates her figure, though not overly much. Just enough to make me want to hold her in my arms all night long.

Whether we're dancing, shagging, or sleeping.

After the Gay Gordons, we do the Canadian Barn Dance and the High-land Schottische. Autumn loves all of it, and I love how happy she is tonight. I want to keep making her happy, but I know I must have hurt her when I said I worry she'll run away from me again. Why had I told her that? I trust her, but I think she'll leave me. No wonder she's confused.

We take a break after the third dance. Autumn says she needs to sit down, so I escort her to one of the tables set up along the periphery of the dance floor. I bring her food from the buffet and a glass of sparkling, lemon-flavored water. Then the American Wives Club joins her at the table, leaving nowhere for me to sit. I don't mind. She wants to get to know everyone, so I leave her with the other American lasses and wander off on my own.

I find Alex leaning against the wall, alone. When I lean against it beside him, he glances at me with his usual slightly sarcastic smile.

"Has your woman banished you?" he asks. "Cat told me to 'bugger off' so she can have a 'good blether' with her sisters. But I see Autumn has been commandeered by the lovely Americans."

"Aye, she's having a blether with them."

"Don't you love knowing your ex-wife is chatting to a bunch of nosy women? She's probably telling them all about what you did last night."

"You don't know what we did last night. Autumn wouldn't tell them, anyway."

Alex catches sight of his wife across the room, so he smiles and blows her a kiss. She does the same thing. "It's worth all the female rubbish to have a good woman in your life."

"Yes, it is. But I never thought I'd see the day you turned lovey-dovey."

"Ah, but it can happen to anyone." He points toward where my cousins, the Three Macs, are laughing and joking with each other. "Just look at Rory. I hear he was known as the Ogre of Loch Fairbairn before he met Emery. She's a miracle worker, isn't she?"

"That's for dead certain. I tried to talk Rory into a therapy session, but he scowled at me and called it 'the most ridiculous load of stinking bollocks on earth.' Of course, I didn't take offense."

Alex glances at me sideways. "You never do—unless Autumn is involved."

I can't argue with that.

"Why are you so bent out of shape these days?" Alex asks. "You two are in love, everyone can see it. Why not marry the girl?"

"It's complicated."

"So am I, but that didn't stop you from discussing me—with me."

He's right, of course. Maybe I should tell him a little of what's happened. No one understands the challenges of reuniting after a messy break-up better than Alex Thorne.

"I told Autumn I trust her," I say, "but then I said I'm afraid she'll leave me again. I think she's confused and hurt by that, but I don't know how to explain what I mean. It makes sense in my head, but the words that come out of my mouth sound like rot."

"The eternal dilemma," Alex says with a sigh. "Mankind struggles to explain to womankind the things that our male brains think make perfect sense."

"What are you saying? I'm doomed?"

"No." He turns partway toward me, still leaning against the wall. "I'm saying have a stiff drink, take Autumn somewhere private, and spill your ruddy guts to her."

I feel queasy even hearing him say those words. Spilling my ruddy guts means telling Autumn every last confusing, humiliating thought I've had concerning us.

"Have you spilled your guts to Cat?" I ask.

"Of course. She wouldn't have let me get away with not doing that." He smiles with a touch of smugness. "Though I doubt Autumn will be as creative, or as devious, in how she convinces you to confess as Cat was with me."

"Probably not." Maybe it would involve a scarf, though. I think I'd like that. Might not mind ripping my insides open to expose everything to her if we're naked and playing a sex game. "Thank you for the advice, Alex. I know what I need to do now."

His smirk deepens. "Maybe I should start advertising myself as a therapist. Apparently, I'm a genius at it."

"Donnae get up yourself again, Alex. I was just starting to view you as a human being."

"Well, I can't have that, can I? It will ruin my mystique."

"You're not qualified to be a therapist, anyway."

He shrugs. "I'm sure I could whip up some credentials. With the internet and a laser printer, anything is possible."

I know he's joking. Or maybe I hope he's joking. With Alex, it can be hard to tell.

The band has switched to a waltz that I know well, so I find Autumn, determined to wrench her away from the American Wives Club for a stroll around the floor. Those lasses are laughing when I get to the table, laughing so hard in fact that some of them are wiping at their eyes.

I hold my hand out to Autumn. "May I have this dance, *mo leannan?*"

She smiles and settles her hand in mine. "Nobody else I'd rather dance with."

The rest of the women at the table say "aw" or "ooh" or make some other silly noise.

"What is this dance?" she asks. "The music sounds like a waltz."

"It's the Pride of Erin Waltz."

"You'll have to teach me the steps, but I'd love to waltz with you."

"This is a simple dance to learn. You won't have any trouble." I lead her onto the floor where couples are already waltzing and clasp her hand. "Back to back, then turn around. Good. Now just follow me. One step back, one step forward, one step back, and turn." I raise my left hand so she can walk under it, then hold both her hands again. "One step forward, one step back, one step forward, and…" I place one palm on her back and clasp her right hand in my left. "Your left hand goes on my shoulder. Now we waltz."

I can't be sure I'm giving her the exactly correct instructions since I haven't done this dance in ages, but it doesn't matter. She's smiling sweetly at me, and I can't help smiling at her too. This feels right, the two of us together, trying to do a waltz and having a good time at the ceilidh. Why had I refused to let her meet my family? The reasons had seemed vital and proper two years ago, but now I realize what a bloody stupid erse I'd been.

We spin around the floor at a leisurely pace, a bit slower than most of the other couples who are enjoying the waltz. Everyone else could disappear, and I wouldn't stop dancing with Autumn. Not even if aliens landed on the green and started shooting their death rays at us.

Bod an Donais. I need to stop watching that alien astronauts rubbish with her.

Once the song ends, I lead Autumn out of the great hall. She doesn't complain or even ask where I'm taking her. The lass has no reason to trust me, but she does. And it's time I tell her why I've acted like such a bampot since she came back into my life. Well, explain as best I can. Alex was right. I need to confess, even if I end up with my guts torn out and tossed onto a bonfire.

So I guide Autumn through the foyer and out into the courtyard, heading for the garden. Once we're inside the garden walls, I take her to the concrete bench near the arbor and wave for her to sit down. I settle onto the bench beside her.

The stars glitter above us, but the only light comes from the windows inside the house and the solar-powered "fairy orbs," as Emery calls them, that line the path through the garden. The meager, milky lighting makes Autumn's face seem even more angelic than usual.

"It's beautiful out here, and kind of romantic," she says. "But why are we in the garden in the semi-dark?"

"Because I need to talk to you. Alone."

She rubs her arms. "Okay. I'm listening."

"Are you cold?" I take my jacket off and drape it around her shoulders. "I didn't think it would be chilly out here. We could go back inside."

"I'm not cold right now, but thank you for lending me your jacket." She sniffs the fabric. "Mm, it smells like you."

After she's done wearing the jacket, it will smell like her. I may never wash it again.

Clearing my throat, I rub my hands up and down my thighs, which makes the kilt slide up a few inches.

She glances at my legs and smiles with her lips closed. "Showing some skin. I like it. Those black socks cover your calves, and I've been dreaming about your thighs while we were dancing."

Dreaming about my thighs? She's seen them before. Many times. Like last night and this morning.

"I need to explain," I say. "About my behavior. I've been a *bod ceann*, and I need you to understand why. Or give you some idea of why. It's, ah, complicated."

She rests a hand on my thigh, just above my knee, her skin touching mine. "Whatever you want to tell me, I'm listening. And I won't get upset, you have my word."

"But you have every right to be angry. I cannae understand why you've been excusing my behavior."

"Not excusing. Forgiving."

I shove a hand through my hair, then can't figure out why I did that, so I set my palms on the bench and grip the edge. Since I can't look at her while I speak, I focus on the ground. "When you left me, I think I went through all the stages of grief in five minutes. When the door shut behind you, I stood there like a bloody statue staring at the place where you'd been a second earlier. Then I told myself it wasn't true, you hadn't abandoned me, you'd come back in a few minutes and say you'd just stepped out to get a newspaper. That lasted about ten seconds. Then I got angry, cursing under my breath and snarling every horrible insult I could think of at you, but you weren't there to hear it. I even punched my fist through the wall."

"You did what?" She sidles closer until her shoulder is almost touching mine. "Jack, I had no idea."

"I know. You think I calmly went on with my life and never thought about you again."

"That's not what I've ever thought. But I didn't think you were...grief-stricken."

Swallowing hard, I risk glancing sideways at her. "Were you?"

"Grief-stricken? Of course I was. I begged you to go with me, and when you didn't, I kept watching for your car to come roaring up behind the taxi, or for you to find me in the airport and throw me over your shoulder to haul me back home."

"You wanted me to act like a raging ersehole? That's bollocks."

"No, it's true. For weeks afterward, I had this fantasy of you showing up at my apartment in a kilt so you could carry me away to Scotland." She sighs and squeezes my thigh. "But I interrupted. Please finish what you needed to say."

"After I punched the wall," I tell her, "I slumped to the floor and cried."

"You…cried? Because of me?" She sounds almost breathless, shock evident in her tone.

"Aye. Then I squeezed my eyes shut and begged God or the angels or whoever might've been listening to send you back to me. It didn't work. So I sat there for an hour, slumped against the wall, feeling numb and alone."

"But if you went through all the stages of grief, that means you came to accept that I was gone."

"No, I never did. Kept thinking I should find you and bring you home, but you hadn't cared enough to stay and work through our problems. Why would anything be different if you came back to me?" I set my elbows on my knees and plant my face in my raised hands. "It's my fault you left. I know that. The truth is, I don't worry you'll leave again because of your fears. I worry I'll drive you away like I did before."

Only while I was telling her all of that did I realize the truth. Aye, she left because of me. I haven't changed, have I? No signs to the contrary. That means she will have no choice but to walk away from me again. This time, I don't know if I'll survive it.

She wraps her arms around me. "No, Jack, you didn't drive me away. We both made mistakes, and we're both to blame. But now we're talking, really talking, and that's why everything will be different this time. I believe that. I know it's true."

The conviction in her voice almost makes me believe it too.

"Put your arms around me, Jack."

I never can resist her, so I turn toward her and do what she said. We hold each other for a long time, it feels like, but it's probably a minute or two. I haven't held her like this for longer than I can remember. Did we ever do this before? Maybe not. We shagged, we argued, we split up. This time it is different, like she said. I wish we hadn't both been so bloody-minded and foolish the first time around, but we won't repeat those mistakes.

"Let's go inside," I say. "Everyone will wonder where we went."

"Emery and the other American girls did mention there would be some kind of surprise after the dancing."

"Surprise? Bloody hell."

"Don't be a grump about it."

I take her advice and do not act like an ogre. We walk back into the great hall hand in hand to find the dancing has already ended. But the ceilidh is not over yet. They've moved one of the round tables into the center of the room, though there's nothing on it except the table cloth.

"Guess it's surprise time," Autumn murmurs.

Rory, Iain, and Alex stand behind the table while everyone else waits at the periphery of what had been the dance floor.

No one is speaking. The great hall has fallen into a deep silence.

Alex raises his arms high and shouts so loudly his voice echoes off the walls and ceiling. "Bring in the surprise!"

Chapter Thirty-Three

Autumn

The second Alex hollers that command, Lachlan and Callum carry an enormous platter into the great hall and set it down on the table where Alex, Rory, and Iain wait. The silver platter has a big silver lid covering it.

Alex lifts the lid.

The platter holds a large, six-layer cake. Is that a wedding cake? Who's getting married? Not me and Jack. Not yet, anyway. It's way too soon for us to be planning a wedding, but I doubt Jack's meddling family and friends care about "too soon." They want us to be as happy as they are, and I know they mean well.

Did Alex arrange this surprise? Jack told me Alex hated it when the MacTaggarts interfered in his relationship with Cat, but now he's doing the same thing to Jack and me.

I don't mind, but Jack might go ballistic.

"What's that for?" Jack asks calmly, nodding toward the huge cake. "Is it Lachlan and Erica's anniversary?"

Alex chuckles. "Guess again."

"There are so many married couples in this room that it must be someone's anniversary. Or is it your birthday, Alex?"

"Do you see any candles on the cake? No, it's not my birthday. Only Cat knows when that is, and she will never tell."

"Henry and Imogen must know your birthday."

I know Henry and Imogen are Alex's adoptive parents. Logan's sisters mentioned them during our "feminine blethering bollocks," as Jack called it.

"Stop guessing," Alex tells Jack. "You're bloody awful at it."

"Then tell me what the sodding hell you're up to now, ye *cacan*."

Okay, Jack isn't quite ballistic—yet—but he is starting to fume.

Iain slaps a hand on Alex's shoulder. "Let's just tell them, before the calm and rational therapist turns into a large, green ogre."

Emery claps. "Yay! The Incredible Hulk. But it would be sexier if Jack turned into Superman."

Rory throws his wife a long-suffering, but affectionate, look. "Please, Em, no more comic-book references tonight. All right?"

She gives him the thumbs-up sign and blows him a kiss.

"Back to the surprise," Alex says. "The cake is for you and Autumn, to celebrate your reunion and shag-a-thon and the fact you've finally released Autumn from her lovely little prison. Ah, sorry. Her bedroom."

Alex is smirking, naturally.

Jack steps closer to the table, eying the cake with a touch of suspicion. "That's all the surprise is for? Celebrating our reunion? We're not getting married, if that's your Machiavellian secret plan."

"I'm Machiavelli again?" Alex says with a chuckle. "If you're that suspicious of a cake, I can't imagine how you'd react to an engagement do."

"Engagement?" Jack's eyes fly wide for a heartbeat. Then he fists his hands and hisses through his gritted teeth, "I knew you were plotting something. *Falbh a ghabhail do ghnùis airson cac.*"

"Allow me to translate," Rory says. "He just snarled 'away and take your face for a shit.' I've never heard Jack curse like that before. Seems you've worked your magic again, Alex. Getting MacTaggarts up to high doh is your specialty."

"Thank you, Rory," Alex replies with a perfect deadpan expression and a matching tone in his voice.

"What's 'high doh'?" I ask.

Alex smiles. "It means I get them so riled up they can't see straight."

Jack looks like he's about ready to throw himself at Alex. As much as I'd love a good tussle involving sexy men rolling around the floor, I don't think it's a good idea right now. Although they might rip their shirts off so they can wrestle more easily, and then they'll get sweaty… No, it's still not a good idea.

I snuggle up to Jack, my arms around his waist. "Cake sounds yummy. Why don't we enjoy our surprise tonight, and you can pummel Alex in the morning?"

He slips an arm around me. "Whatever you want, *mo leannan*."

"Go on," I tell Alex. "Finish your presentation."

Jack almost smiles. "You should've seen the spectacle he made of his wedding."

Alex smiles like a true Machiavellian. "Wait until you see what I have in mind for yours."

"You will not be getting anywhere near our wedding until we walk up the aisle."

Well, at least Jack is now ribbing Alex instead of threatening to rip his ribs out of his chest to wear them as a hat.

Alex clucks his tongue. "The groom doesn't walk down the aisle with the bride. She shuffles up to the altar with her father."

I get a sharp pang in my chest when Alex mentions my father.

Jack hugs me a little tighter to his side. "Let's eat the ruddy cake."

Alex slices the cake while Rory and Iain hand out pieces on paper plates. Jack and I get the first, and biggest, slices. The cake is delicious—caramel, I think, with buttery caramel icing too—but after ten minutes of reunion festivities, I whisper in Jack's ear that we should sneak off to our bedroom upstairs.

He nods his agreement and rushes over to grab two more slices of cake, both stuffed onto one plate, while I wait by the doorway. Alex waylays Jack when he's halfway to the door. They have a brief conversation during which Alex glances furtively at me, and it ends with Jack patting Alex's arm.

Then Jack and I scurry away.

Once we're ensconced in our room, I ask Jack what he and Alex were discussing.

"You," he says while he's getting undressed. "Alex noticed you were anxious when he mentioned your father. I didn't think you'd mind if I told him you aren't close to your Da. Alex understands that since his parents are con artists."

"My dad isn't a criminal. He's disappointed in me, that's all." I bite my lip. "Did anyone else notice my reaction?"

"No. Alex is very perceptive, and he almost has a sixth sense about people who have strained relationships with their families."

"Oh, so you do believe in second sight."

He tosses his kilt onto the chair beside the bed. "No, I do not believe in that rubbish. I said Alex *almost* has a sixth sense. But it's only that he recognizes the signs because he knows what it's like not to be close with your parents."

"Uh-huh." I poke him in the side as he's climbing onto the bed. "I think you pooh-pooh the supernatural because you're afraid Kirsty might actually have psychic abilities."

"Can we stop talking and shag?"

"Yes. I will allow you to wriggle out of admitting you don't think Kirsty's a kook."

"Never said she was. Kirsty is a lovely, clever woman, not a kook."

At least he kind of admitted his cousin might have genuine ESP. I don't believe one hundred percent, but I'm open to the possibilities.

The second night in the castle with Jack is just as hot as the first. I swear he gets more passionate and adventurous every day, like he's loosening up and letting himself become the man he was in Vegas. I love Jack no matter which version of himself he lets the world see, but I never want him to hide his true self out of fear or shame.

I don't want either of us to do that anymore.

Morning is hot too—because we have sex, but also because we take advantage of the big bathroom on the ground floor. Emery was right about that. Jack and I make use of the spacious tub and the multi-head shower, not to mention the two sinks and the tile walls.

We manage to get clean too.

Mrs. Brody, the housekeeper who works part-time at the castle and part-time at Rory and Emery's house, left us a nice breakfast. After eating, we set out on another day trip around the Highlands. This time, we drive around strictly to appreciate the scenery—the green fields overflowing with wildflowers, the stunning mountains unlike any I've seen in America, and the deep, dark lochs. I've seen mountains and lakes back home, having taken solo road trips, but there's nothing like the craggy green mountains of Scotland.

I finally get why Jack doesn't want to live anywhere else.

After a long day of exploring—and, okay, having sex in the car—we return to Dùndubhan. Mrs. Brody has stopped by to make us dinner, but I ask if she minds if I cook for Jack instead. I don't want to offend her since she drove all the way out here for that purpose, but Mrs. Brody smiles at my suggestion.

"Donnae worry, lovey," she says while touching my arm. "I'm not easily offended. Couldnae have worked for Rory during his ogre days if I had thin skin. I'll stay to clean up the dishes after you're done. Rory wanted me to give the office a good dusting, anyway. Oh, and he'll be in the office tomorrow, but the dear boy promised not to bother you and Jack. Emery might come too with the twins."

"I'd love to meet the twins," I tell her, probably sounding a little too excited about a pair of toddlers. "Jack told me all about Rory and Emery and their kiddos, but it's wonderful to meet everyone."

"You are such a sweet lass, *gràidh*. Cannae believe Jack wouldn't let anyone meet you until now." She touches Jack's arm. "But you had your reasons, didn't you? You're a sweet laddie, *mo luran*. You and Autumn are good for each other, I knew it the moment I saw you together."

I just met Mrs. Brody, but already I adore her.

She toddles off to dust the office while I cook for Jack.

And I ask him what "*mo luran*" means.

"It means 'darling boy'," he says. "Mrs. Brody is the only human being on earth besides Emery who would dare to call Rory a silly pet name. She's always called him *mo luran*, though."

Over dinner, we laugh and talk about where we want to go next. The more time I spend with Jack, the more comfortable and natural it feels. Maybe we aren't wild and crazy like in Vegas, but we're both opening up and relaxing more than we have in a long time. I'd bet a million dollars Jack hasn't been this at ease and happy since the night we got married. I can risk a million bucks on that bet because I know Jack, all of him, not only the parts he lets everyone else see.

"Tomorrow, we should go to Skye," he says over dessert.

Mrs. Brody made the blueberry tray cake we're eating, and it's delicious.

"Skye?" I say. "You mean the island?"

"No, I mean we should fly up into the heavens using our invisible fairy wings."

"Ha-ha." I devour another mouthful of cake, then point my fork at him. "You've gotten a lot more playfully sarcastic this week."

"Because I'm feeling more playful. And randy. And…happy." He looks faintly surprised by his own statement. "I haven't felt this way since…"

"Las Vegas."

"Aye." He leans back in his chair, smiling with deep satisfaction. "The Isle of Skye is a beautiful, magical place. Kirsty, Isla, and Elspeth like to tell everyone they go there on the summer and winter solstices to do Wiccan rituals in the nude. None of us has ever seen them do that, so I think they're having us on."

"But you think the island is magical."

"Not literally. But there is something special about Skye." He pushes his chair back and pats his thigh. "Come here, *mo chridhe*. My lap is getting cold."

Jack wants me to sit on his lap. I don't think he's ever asked me to do that before.

He crooks a finger at me.

I climb onto his lap and loop my arms around his neck, and he loops his around my hips.

"Let's spend the night on Skye tomorrow," he says. "Rory and Emery own a house there. It's very old, but it's been restored to its original glory."

"I'd love to sleep there."

He smirks. "I'd love to fuck you there."

"We can do both, you know." I nuzzle his cheek. "Will you show me the magical Isle of Skye? You're the best tour guide in the world."

"How many tour guides have you met?"

"Just you." I kiss his cheek. "But I still know you're the best. At everything."

"I've been to Rory and Emery's house on Skye, but I've never taken a woman there." He pulls me snug against him, our faces inches apart. "I've never wanted to take anyone there, but I cannae wait to show you the island. It's renowned for its dark skies that make for excellent stargazing."

"We could combine stargazing and sex."

"I love the way you think."

We feed each other the rest of the dessert, but we go to sleep instead of having sex that night. In the morning, Jack calls Rory to ask if we can stay at the Skye house. He says yes, of course. All the MacTaggarts will do anything to make sure Jack and I stay together and live happily ever after like the rest of Jack's married relatives.

But we're not married. Jack suggested it when I first arrived, but only because he was panicking about me showing up pregnant. That's all it was, right? If he asked me to marry him, for real and not while panicking, I would say yes.

We gather snacks and bottled water and juices from the kitchen to take with us on our road trip to Skye. Mrs. Brody helps us with the food, picking out the perfect snacks for our journey. She also handwrites a list of the best things to do and see on Skye since Jack doesn't know the island well and I've never been there. That woman is a treasure.

After carrying our booty out to the car, we go back inside so I can use the bathroom. Pregnancy is making me need to pee so often that I'm seriously considering adult diapers as a solution. When I emerge from the ground-floor bathroom, Jack is leaning against the wall beside the door.

"Ready?" he asks.

"Yep. Though maybe we should grab another bag of potato chips. I've been having a major craving for those lately."

"Can't let your cravings go unsatisfied, can I?"

Jack takes my hand as we head for the kitchen which is located in the guest wing. That means we go through the dining room to get there. Just as we push through the swinging door into the kitchen, we both come to a screeching halt. Well, not literally. We do stop very quickly, so fast that I stumble into Jack and he almost crashes into the door.

Emery is sitting on the island with her legs hanging off the edge, her thighs spread so her husband can fit between them. Her dress is hiked up to her waist. His pants are in a fabric puddle at his feet.

And yeah, they froze in the middle of having sex.

Wow, Rory has a great ass.

Jack raises his brows. "I hope Mrs. Brody cleans the counter with bleach after you two have been in the house."

Rory rolls his eyes. "We thought you and Autumn had left."

"We did, but she needed to—ah, to get more potato crisps."

Nice save, Jack. I'm sure he almost blurted out that I needed to pee, which I suppose could have led to Rory and Emery suspecting I'm pregnant. I think Emery figured that out the other day, but I doubt she would've said anything to her husband. Jack and I haven't decided when to share the news.

Emery leans back, stretching out one arm to grab a bag of chips off the counter. She tosses it to Jack, then wraps both arms around her hubby again.

"Thank you," Jack says, trying so hard not to look at Rory and Emery's lower bodies.

We hustle out of the house and get on the road.

Jack insists on driving the whole way so I can enjoy everything there is to see. Our journey takes us north of Ballachulish and Loch Fairbairn, through more jaw-droppingly beautiful scenery. Eventually, we cross over a cute little bridge that Jack tells me is a swing bridge which means the center portion pivots on an axis to swing sideways and let boat traffic go through. I've never seen a bridge like this before, but I imagine there are probably a few in America. I'd gone on solo road trips, but I haven't seen all of the US, not even close.

I've got all of Scotland to experience now.

As we leave the bridge, Jack peers into the rearview mirror and squints like he's trying to see something.

I twist around to see out the back window. "What are you looking at?"

"Nothing, I guess. But I'd swear that same black car has been behind us ever since we left Loch Fairbairn."

"This is a main road, right? Lots of people drive down it every day."

"Aye." He shakes his head, returning his attention to the road. "I'm imagining things."

We both brush off his moment of paranoia, and our journey continues. We pass by so many lochs that I stop trying to keep track of them, though Jack tells me the name of every single one. He makes sure I notice every point of interest along the way, and we stop often so I can relieve my annoyingly frequent needs. He doesn't care. In fact, he seems happier the closer we get to our destination. Our trip takes us through various villages, some tiny, some larger, some in-between. I'm enraptured by the landscape, the buildings, the people walking down the streets, everything.

My tour guide insists we stop in the village of Dornie to get gas—petrol, as Jack calls it—and so I can see the Eilean Donan Castle. It occupies a little island slightly offshore, but there's a walking bridge that accesses it. After that, we're on the road again. Jack says we're almost to the island when we pass through an adorable village called Kyle of Lochalsh.

Before I know it, we're on the Skye Bridge, crossing over open water and then an island, followed by more open water. At last, we touch down on the Isle of Skye.

"We're here!" I announce, probably a little louder than necessary. I can't help it. For the entirety of our marriage, I'd longed to see the Highlands, really see them. But all Jack would show me was Inverness, and not much of that.

"It's another fifteen minutes to Rory and Emery's house." He throws me a sidelong glance. "At least we know we won't run into the pair of them shagging in the kitchen this time."

My gaze veers to the window and the view outside.

I'm on the Isle of Skye. With Jack. And we're going to have sex under the stars.

Life is pretty damn amazing these days.

Chapter Thirty-Four

Jack

I love watching Autumn take in the scenery and the sights. No one else I've ever known has gotten so excited about a wee castle on an island or sheep in a pasture. During our whole journey across the Skye Bridge, she grinned like a giddy lassie who's on her first school field trip. I love her more every day, and I wish I'd never refused to show her the Highlands or let her meet my family.

Christ, I was an eejit back then. And during our blind date. And during the first few days after she turned up on my doorstep.

I have all the time in the world to make up for those mistakes. Ever since I confessed to Autumn that I'd been humiliatingly devastated when she left me, I feel lighter and freer. I have no more secrets from her, but I still have questions I need her to answer.

The second we pull into the semicircular drive in front of Rory and Emery's house, Autumn flings her door open and leaps out. I get out of the car the normal way, but I can't help smiling at how excited and jubilant she is just to be on Skye. She spreads her arms wide, gazing at the two-story house like it's the Great Pyramid of Giza.

Since I know she'll want to hear everything about the house, I come up beside her and say, "This is a manse, which means it was originally the home of a clergyman."

As we walk into the house, I explain how the decor and furnishings are historically accurate. Autumn loves that. She thinks the antique drinks cabinet is "so pretty," then she laments the fact she can't drink right now.

"I've never been a boozehound," she says, "but I do miss having the occasional glass of wine. Taking care of our baby is priority number one, though, and I'll do anything to make sure our son or daughter is born healthy."

"Our bairn will be." I pull out a bottle and show it to her. "But you might be interested to know Talisker whisky is made on Skye. My cousin Lachlan swears by it, but most of us prefer Ben Nevis. It's made in Fort William."

"You Scots are really into whisky, aren't you?"

"It's like blood to us. We can't live without it."

I haul our bags into the bedroom downstairs while Autumn stretches out on the sofa for a wee nap. Being in the car all day has left her knackered. When I walk into the living room, she's asleep, so I head to the kitchen to make our dinner. Rory said he and Emery left the kitchen stocked with dry goods and frozen foods. I have plenty of raw materials for making Autumn a hearty meal that will restore her vigor.

Just as I'm putting the food on two plates, she ambles into the kitchen. Lifting her chin, she sniffs the air. "Mm, that smells yummy."

"Have a good lie-down?"

"Yep. Now I'm all refreshed and ready for dinner, followed by stargazing."

"It isn't dark enough yet for that."

"We'll eat slow, then."

And we do exactly that. Talking during dinner slows our meal down quite a bit, but it's good to have more time to chat to her. I feel like I haven't really known Autumn until this week, but now we're learning everything about each other. When she's eaten her last bite of food, I ask the question I've been thinking about all day.

"Why have you jumped from job to job instead of settling down?"

She shrugs. "Like I told you before, nothing ever fit. I always intended to keep one job, but none of them worked out that way."

"Why do you think that is?"

"Therapist Jack has woken from his slumber," she says with a smile, but it fades quickly. "I don't know. I spent most of my childhood trying to be whatever my mom and dad wanted me to be. I played soccer, even though I hated it. I got into advanced classes for math and science, but I hated that too. By the time I was a senior in high school, I knew I couldn't be a soldier or a doctor like my parents. But I had no clue what I did want."

"Because you'd always done what your parents wanted."

"Yeah, I guess."

I rest my arms on the table and gaze at her across its width. "Hasn't there been even one thing that made you happy? One activity?"

She hunches her shoulders, biting down on the corner of her lip. "Not that I can think of. My parents and my sister knew before they graduated from high school what they wanted to be. They had their paths mapped out. Me? I'm pathless, like a baby deer lost in the woods."

"You are not lost, Autumn. You just haven't found your path yet, but there's nothing wrong with searching." I focus on the top of her head until she finally raises her face to look at me. "Maybe the problem is that you subconsciously gave up on finding your place in the world because you couldn't satisfy your parents' expectations. You lot need to have a real, honest conversation about all of this."

"Talk to my parents?" She winces, then sighs. "Yeah, I know you're right. Avoidance is so much easier, though. I'm a coward, after all."

"Bollocks. You are a brave woman. You can do it, and I'll be right by your side when you see them."

She stares at me like she's just realized I'm a nutter. "How can you say I'm brave?"

"You moved to another country on the other side of an ocean to be with me. And you're never afraid to meet new people or share your feelings." I smile, remembering our time in Las Vegas. "I also know you're not afraid to have sex in a casino."

"That was hot. But sometimes it feels like another lifetime."

"Well, then we must've been reincarnated this week. I've never felt more alive than I do now, with you."

She smiles, and it's sweet but almost shy too. "I love you, Jack, an awful lot."

"I know. I'm very lovable." I wink at her. "When I'm not holding my ex-wife hostage, that is."

"Yeah, that was weird." She grins. "But kind of hot too. Especially the part where you crawled into my bed in the dark."

"Maybe I'll do that again sometime." I absolutely will, but it should be a surprise for her. "Let's go outside and wait for dark so we can watch the stars. I don't know the constellations, but it will be a sight to see anyway."

"Let's go."

The house sits on a hill, and the backyard has a lovely view of the island and the sky, so we spread a blanket out on the grass and lie down. Since it can be a bit chilly after sunset, we brought two extra blankets, one for each of us. While we lie here waiting for full dark to arrive, I tell her more stories about barmy things my family members have done over the past two years.

When the last glow of the setting sun has finally extinguished, the stars fire up their glittering flames. The sky is so dark on this island, free of virtually all light pollution, that I swear I can see into the heart of the universe. Or I might be turning poetic because I have Autumn beside me, snuggled up with her head on my chest.

"It's so beautiful," she murmurs. "I've never seen this many stars before."

"Aye, it's bonnie." I raise a hand to point at the sky. "Look at that. It's the famous Haggis Major constellation."

She laughs. "Sheep intestines in the sky? Ew."

"Haggis is made with a sheep's stomach, not the intestines."

"Right. That's way less icky."

I point at a different spot in the sky. "That's the Flying Kilt constellation. If you look closely, you can see the bloke's cock underneath there."

A laugh snorts out of her. "Never knew stargazing could be R-rated."

"The ancient people who first named these stars were a randy lot, you know." I take her hand, closing my fingers over hers until only her index finger is straight. Then I use it to trace a line in the sky. "Here's the shape of another constellation. It's called *Slat* Major Penetrating *Brillean* Minor."

"Translation, please."

"Big cock penetrating wee vagina."

She bursts out laughing and doesn't stop until her eyes are watering and she's started to hiccup. Once the hiccuping has subsided, she wipes her eyes and taps a finger on my chest. "Hate to shatter your illusions, but my vagina is bigger than your dick. Has to be, or you'd never fit inside me."

"It was a joke, *gràidh*. Don't take it so personally." I slap her erse. "You need to develop a thicker skin. And I happen to think your *brillean* is just the right size for fucking you."

"Give it up, Jack. You can't sweet-talk your way out of the worst sex metaphor of the century."

"No more metaphors." I roll over to cover her body with mine. "Time for the real thing. Are you ready to shag under the stars on the Isle of Skye?"

"Yes, yes, yes."

"Cannae wait to sink my *acainn cungaidh* into your *cìrean coilich* and rub my *bagais* against your *bodach beag a' bhàta*."

She wriggles under me, spreading her thighs. "I need another translation, Jack."

"Any translation of Gaelic sex slang won't be literal." I rub my erection into her, though our clothes keep me from doing what I'm about to say. "I said I cannae wait to sink my healing tool into your rooster's comb and rub my testicles against your little old man of the ship, which means I want my cock inside your body and my balls rubbing on your clitoris."

"Wow, you Scots have the most bizarre sex slang. But oddly, it makes me even hotter for you. My little old man of the ship is aching for your…whatever the hell you just said."

"No more talking. Time for a hands-on translation."

Aye, we shag under the stars. It's bloody brilliant, and she comes twice before I'm done—because, she claims, the way I whisper dirty Gaelic to her while we're fucking makes her "hotter than the surface of the sun."

We're both in need of a good night's sleep after that so we can rest up for the journey home tomorrow. I tell Autumn we can stay another night, but she wants to go home. Aye, she calls it "home." I've heard her say that before in reference to my house, but this time feels different. We are a couple, not two exes trying to make peace with each other for the sake of our bairn. No, we're together now in the romantic sense and in every other way that matters.

And I want to marry her. Again.

But I should wait awhile. It's only been a week since she arrived in Scotland. How long can I wait to ask her to marry me? Not long, that's for certain.

In the morning, we begin our journey home. Autumn wants to drive today, so I let her.

"Remember to drive on the left side of the road," I tell her.

"Yes, Jack, I know. I lived in Scotland before." She gives me a sly smile. "Or maybe you've blocked out that time in your life."

"No, I could never forget you, *mo chridhe.*"

"Aw, you're so cute when you're sucking up." She turns the key in the ignition, starting up the engine. "I loved visiting Skye and having sex under the dark-dark heavens, but I can't wait to get home and get started on our new life together."

Should I ask her to marry me now? Maybe I shouldn't interpret her statement as concrete proof that she wants us to live together as man and wife.

While Autumn pulls the car out onto the street and follows it through town, I give her instructions on how to get to the Skye Bridge. As we cross onto the bridge, my mobile chimes with a new text message. I dig the mobile out of my trouser pocket and bring up the text. It's from…Hamish Clacher? Why is he texting me? It's inappropriate since he's no longer my client.

I need you, the text says.

Talk to Dr. Murray, I reply. He's your therapist now.

He's a numpty. I need you, please.

Ring Dr. Murray.

I start to put the mobile back in my pocket, but it chimes again.

Another text from Hamish. Then another. And another. They all say similar things about how he needs me, no one else will do, please can't I meet him, how could I have left him. I feel bad for Hamish—he's clearly having a problem—but he needs to talk to *his* therapist. Dr. Murray knows more about Hamish's condition than I do since I haven't seen or spoken to him for ages.

I send Roy Murray a text and stuff my mobile back into my pocket.

"What was that all about?" Autumn asks.

"A former client is having problems again. I told him to talk to his therapist because I can't be involved anymore." I relax into my seat. "You'll need more instructions once we get to Kyle of Lochalsh."

She salutes. "Yes, sir. Ready to receive my orders."

By the time we reach Fort William, it's almost lunchtime. Autumn wants to eat when we get home, and I agree. Holidays are nice, but home is the best place to be. As we enter Fort William, I swear I see a black car following a short distance behind us, and I swear it's the same car as yesterday. No, I'm being paranoid. It's a similar car, not the same one.

We stop for petrol, and the black car continues down the road.

Aye, it was paranoia for sure.

Chapter Thirty-Five

Autumn

Jack drives the last leg of our journey home, and the second he pulls into the driveway and shuts off the engine, I leap out of the car. Stretching my arms above my head, I sigh with contentment, closing my eyes. Loch Fairbairn feels like home to me, more than Inverness ever had and more even than Nevada where I grew up. Maybe Inverness would've felt like home too if Jack hadn't decided I should meet no one. I've forgiven him for that. The past doesn't matter anymore, and the future is all I care about.

I tip my head back, open my eyes, and smile up at the sky.

A mottled white blob hangs up there, surrounded by blue sky and a smattering of wispy clouds.

That can't be the moon, can it? No, it's daytime. Well, duh, sometimes the moon is visible during the day. The longer I stare at the moon, the prettier it seems, and I smile again.

Jack comes up beside me. "What's got your attention, *gràidh*?"

"The moon. Isn't it beautiful in the daytime?"

"Aye. Looks full or almost full too. Maybe that's a good omen."

"Of what?"

He slides an arm around my waist. "Things to come."

I turn my face to him just as he looks at me. Our lips almost brush. "A cryptic prophecy? Hmm, and you say you don't believe in magic."

"Not the sort Kirsty and her sisters believe in, but there are other kinds of magic." He pulls me closer until I'm snugly molded to his body. "Shagging under the stars was magical, for sure."

"Can't disagree with that." My body decides it's time for my bladder to wake up and start screaming. "Ooh, sorry, I need to rush inside for a pee break."

"I'll get our bags while you deal with your…needs." He digs his keys out of his pocket and hands them to me. "The bronze one is for the door."

"Thanks."

Giving him a quick kiss, I rush to the door and manage to get it unlocked without any problems, then I trot through the living room and down to the bathroom. Once I've taken care of things, I go into the living room to peek out the windows. Jack is talking to the elderly woman I've seen tending to her flowering bushes at the house next door. Scots seem like a very chatty bunch, so he might be out there for a while. They're both smiling, clearly having a fun conversation.

I head into the kitchen to start lunch. When Jack comes inside, maybe I can have our meal ready and waiting. He's been taking care of me so much lately that it'll be nice to do something for him—other than sex.

Halfway to the island, I freeze.

The back door is open.

An intruder? Here in Loch Fairbairn? This doesn't seem like the kind of town where break-ins happen, but I suppose they can happen anywhere. Or maybe Jack's brother or one of his cousins has a key and came inside to…do something. Yeah, sure, and they left the back door wide open.

I spin around, planning to run outside to get Jack.

But I don't get the chance.

The second I whirl toward the doorway, I'm confronted by a strange man who blocks the way. Behind him, I glimpse the living room and the front door, but Jack must still be outside. My pulse revs up, and I stop breathing for long enough that my ears start to ring. Forcing myself to breathe normally, I try for a casual approach to bumping into an intruder.

"Hi, can I help you?" I ask. Sure, it sounds dumb, but I can't think of anything else to say or do. This is my first experience with a home invasion.

The man gapes at me, his longish red hair curling wildly around his face. I decide he looks thirtyish, not that his age matters right now. He's not tall, but not short either, and his skinny body doesn't seem all that threatening. The wild look in his eyes does.

"Where's Jack?" he asks, and now I know for sure he's Scottish.

A local boy? This guy seems to know Jack, and I can't help wondering if he's a client.

"Jack isn't here," I say. "Why don't I call him and find out when he'll be home?"

"I know he's here. I saw you come home with him a few minutes ago." The man scratches his head, screwing up his face. "But then I had to use the bog, and after that, you came inside and I had to hide in a closet."

He'd been in the house when I was relieving myself in the bathroom? The one he'd just used, probably seconds before I did?

I feel queasy, but I don't think it's pregnancy hormones this time.

"Let me call Jack," I say, sidling toward the landline phone on the counter.

"Stop!" the man shouts, his wild eyes getting even wilder. "I need Jack. Now."

"And I'll tell him that. If you'll just let me pick up the phone and dial his cell number."

"Cell?" The intruder stares at me like I'm insane. "Ahmno going to jail. No, no, I cannae do that again."

Oops. I forgot most Scots say "mobile" not "cell."

"I meant his mobile number," I say, then I dare to inch my arm out toward the landline phone.

The intruder rushes at me.

He seizes my wrist and yanks it behind my back. His hot breaths bluster against my cheek when he hisses, "Ye willnae keep me from him. Ah know yer game, ye bloody *sassenach*."

I know the term *sassenach* refers to an English person, but I'm American. Guess this guy can't tell the difference.

"Take it easy," I say. "Let's both go outside so you can talk to Jack."

"No, ye rang his cell. He's getting ready to lock me up, and ahm dead certain it's only because yer wanting him to do it." The intruder seizes my other wrist, pinning both behind me using one hand. He's surprisingly strong for a skinny guy. "Where can I find a rope or tape?"

Yeah, those are exactly the words a girl wants to hear when she's being held captive by a crazed intruder. I have no idea why he thinks I care about whether Jack locks him up in a jail cell or a padded room. I don't even know this man's name. But if he ties me up and does who-knows-what to me, I will personally toss his ass into the worst prison on earth where he can stay for the rest of eternity.

But if he hurts Jack, I'll kill him.

The man yanks my wrists, shooting pains through my shoulders. "Rope and tape. Where are they?"

Jeez, I've only lived here for a week. I have no clue where Jack keeps stuff like that. Somewhere in the kitchen, I'd guess. There aren't many places to store those things in this house.

"Try the pantry," I say, nodding toward the large cabinet-like closet that has bifold doors. "I think it's in there."

My captor drags me with him as he scuffles over to the pantry and flings the doors open.

Oh thank God. I see two rolls of duct tape.

Why am I grateful for that? It's way too early for Stockholm syndrome, and besides, I can't see myself ever developing sympathetic feelings for this guy.

He drags me over to the kitchen table. Grabbing one of the chairs, he pushes its backside up against the table, then thrusts me onto the seat. While he struggles with the duct tape, I glance around in hopes of finding something I can use as a weapon. If I could hit him over the head, and at least stun him, maybe I could make it to the front door and outside. Jack would see me, and the jig would be up for this frantic nutball.

I don't see any useful objects other than a whisk. *Damn.*

The intruder finally manages to tear off a length of tape.

Panic grips me, and I try to leap out of the chair.

My captor shoves me back down onto the seat. "Donnae be doing that again. Ahmno wanting to hurt ye, but ah cannae have ye getting in the way."

This nutball doesn't want to hurt me. Am I supposed to thank him for that?

He slaps the strip of duct tape over my mouth, but it sticks to only one corner. The rest hangs loose, flapping every time I exhale through my nose. My captor doesn't seem to notice, though. He proceeds to bind my wrists together behind the chair with more tape. He does a better job of securing that, but still, I feel some leeway here like maybe I could get out of my makeshift bindings if I wriggle my hands just right.

The intruder reaches into his back pocket and pulls out a gun.

He aims it at the floor.

My heart skips a beat, maybe two or three. A hard shiver rattles through me, raising all the hairs on my body. I think even my nose hairs stand at attention. My mouth has gone dry too.

"You don't need that," I say, speaking around the flapping duct tape while trying to sound calm and reasonable. Jack is much better at that. "I won't run away, I promise. And I'm sure Jack wants to talk to you, so you don't need to, um, point anything at either of us."

I hear the front door open and shut.

Why didn't I scream for help? That never even occurred to me.

Jack marches into the kitchen and stops. He swerves his gaze toward me and arches his brows, then he shifts his attention to my new best friend. "Hamish? What are you doing here?"

"I need ye, Jack, please."

Jack glances at me, then takes a few steps toward my captor, who he called Hamish. "Aye, your messages said as much. Let's sit down and talk. Autumn doesn't need to be here, so let's have her wait in here while you and I go into my office."

"She'll call the police," he says, managing to snarl and whine simultaneously.

"All right. We'll talk here, then." Jack starts to move toward me but halts when Hamish aims his gun at my head. Jack holds up his hands. "It's fine, Hamish, I'll stay right here."

He's standing halfway between me and the island. Hamish is an arm's length from my chair, and he's bouncing back and forth on his heels while one finger taps the gun's barrel just above the trigger.

"Tell me what's wrong," Jack says. "Maybe I can help."

Wow, is he fabulous at sounding sympathetic yet professional.

Hamish waves his gun toward me. "Who is she? Why do you have a woman in your house? It's meant to be the two of us."

Jack scrunches his brows tightly, and his mouth slants down at one corner. Though he looks baffled and tense, he still sounds reasonable when he speaks. "Tell me what's going on with you. I'm listening."

Hamish staggers up to Jack. He grabs Jack's shirt and fists it in his hand, aiming his earnestly despondent expression at my ex-husband. "Donnae ye remember? How we got on, and how you looked at me. You're so kind, and you understand me better than those other therapists do. I should be with you, Jack."

Oh dear lord. The heartbroken look on Hamish's face, the tone of his voice, the way he's leaning toward Jack while holding onto his shirt...

Hamish is in love with Jack. And my ex-husband has no clue that's what's going on here.

Guess I better find a way to let him know before he says something that clues Hamish in to the fact Jack doesn't share his feelings.

Yeah, sure, piece of cake.

When Jack held me hostage, sort of, it had been strangely sexy. This is nothing like that. And I pray I can communicate to Jack what's going on here without setting Hamish off.

Chapter Thirty-Six

Jack

Why is Hamish clutching my shirt and leaning so close that I can smell his whisky-laden breath? Why is he looking at me like I'm a celestial being who descended from heaven to save him? It makes no sense. Aye, Hamish has obsessional tendencies, but he's never been dangerous. I can't understand why he's tied up Autumn or why he's brandishing a gun.

Behind Hamish, I see Autumn rubbing her cheek on her shoulder. Half of the strip of duct tape over her mouth has come loose, and she seems to be trying to pull the rest off.

I want to push Hamish away, but I don't think that's wise. He's agitated, almost frantic, and I need to figure out why.

"What's fashing you, Hamish?" I ask. Haven't I asked him fifty times already? I wish he'd just tell me so I can get a read on him.

"I need you," he says with a fervency that makes my skin crawl. "Please, donnae leave me again."

What is he on about?

"I didn't leave you," I say. "Things weren't working out, so I referred you to another therapist who I hoped would be more able to help you."

Movement draws my attention to Autumn, who stops waving her head around when I look at her. She's peeled the strip of duct tape off her mouth, though it dangles from her cheek.

She mouths what looks like "he loves to."

Who loves to what? I have no bloody clue.

Hamish releases my shirt and lays a hand on my cheek. "I know I'm difficult, and that's why it didn't work out for us. I can be better. With you, I know I can."

"Why don't you have a seat, Hamish? We'll both sit at the table and talk."

Autumn's head-waving catches my attention again. She mouths, "He loves to."

Maybe I would understand if she'd finish her sentence. All I can do is shake my head.

She rolls her eyes toward the ceiling, her mouth crimped.

Hamish caresses my cheek.

I step sideways, needing a wee bit of space from him. He's getting far too tactile for my comfort. "Let's sit, Hamish. At the table."

Autumn flaps her head wildly until I look at her. This time she mouths with exaggerated lip movements. "He loves you."

I stare at her. No, that can't be what she was trying to say. I misinterpreted her lip movements. Mouthing isn't an accurate way to communicate.

And for about five seconds, I believe that.

Then Hamish seizes my face in both hands and mashes his mouth to mine.

For a moment, I'm so stunned I can't move. Then I slap my palms on his chest and shove him away.

Hamish stumbles, teeters, then crumples to the floor. His gun flies out of his hand, skittering across the floor until it bumps into my foot.

I pick it up—and blow out a growling breath. "Plastic, Hamish? You held us hostage with a fucking child's toy?"

Am I shouting at him? Donnae care. This bastard tied up Autumn and pointed a gun at both of us—a fake one, though we hadn't known that.

Tossing the toy gun into the rubbish bin, I stalk up to Hamish who's still lying in a heap on the floor. "What the bloody hell are you playing at, Hamish? I should give you a right good skelping for this. I am not your therapist anymore, and I have no feelings for you."

Hamish starts to cry. "But I love you. I know you feel the same way. You wouldnae have been so nice and so understanding unless you love me."

Christ, it's true. Nice guys finish last. Or in this case, nice blokes get taken hostage by the poor sods they tried to help.

I crouch beside Hamish. "I'm sorry, but I don't love you. Deep down, I think you know that. You're not a bad person, but you need more help than I could ever give you. Dr. Murray will do everything he can for you, but I think you know what has to happen here."

Hamish nods, sniffling. "You need to ring the police."

"Aye."

He scrambles to get into a sitting position with his knees drawn up to his chest. Hugging his knees, he rests his head on them.

I free Autumn from the tape binding her wrists and pull her into my arms, kissing her forehead. Without letting go of her, I pull out my mobile and ring the Loch Fairbairn police station.

Within five minutes, two constables arrive and handcuff Hamish, then lead him out of the house. He keeps his head down, but I can tell he's crying. Maybe I feel a twinge of empathy for him—I hadn't been able to help him, after all—but I don't feel bad enough to forgive him. Not yet. He took Autumn hostage and threatened us both with a gun we had believed was real. Autumn and I will both need time to process what's happened.

Our neighbors on both sides of the street come out of their houses to see what the commotion is, and several walk over to ask if we need anything. Autumn would have enjoyed meeting more people under better circumstances, but right now, we need to be alone. No one is offended by that.

I ring my parents to let them know what happened, so they won't hear about it through the village grapevine. Ma wants to come over to take care of us, but I assure her we're fine and promise we'll visit soon. I also ask her to let the rest of the family know. That way, I can focus on taking care of Autumn. She'd started to tremble a touch a few minutes after the constables took Hamish away. I'm sure it's the crash after an adrenaline rush, nothing to worry about, but she needs to rest.

Once we're back inside the house, I pick her up and carry her across the living room, heading for the hallway. She wraps her arms around my neck and rests her head on my shoulder. The fact she's not complaining or teasing me about carrying her tells me how exhausted she is. Our trip to Skye had been wonderful, but it was tiring. Then we came home to a hostage situation.

I take Autumn into the guest room and set her down on her feet. Rubbing her arms, I ask, "How are you feeling, *gràidh?*"

"Okay. Could use a nap, though."

"Do you want to eat first?"

She shakes her head. "Nap now, eat later. If you're hungry, go ahead and have a piece." She smiles teasingly. "Like how I used a Scottish term?"

"I love it. You're becoming more Scottish every day."

Autumn sits down on the edge of the bed and lets out a long breath. "I learned something about myself today."

"Did you?" I kneel in front of her, laying my hands on her knees. "Tell me."

"I'm stronger than even I realized. Somebody took me hostage, and I stayed calm despite being terrified. I'm not a wimp or a loser or a bad mother. Maybe I haven't found the right career yet, but I found my true path." She trails her fingers over my cheek. "It's with you and our baby."

"Aye, it is." I turn my face into her hand to kiss the palm. "I've always known you're brave and clever, but I hadn't realized exactly how incredible you are until now. I'm proud of you, *mo chridhe*, and honored to have you in my life."

"I should get taken hostage more often. You positively gush afterward."

"Please don't ever scare me like that again."

"I'll do my best." She yawns and shakes her entire body. "Mind if I lie down?"

"Of course not."

She crawls across the bed and stretches out on her back with her head on the pillow. She hasn't bothered to pull the covers back or move the decorative pillows that cover the one she sleeps on at night. And she still has her shoes on.

I sit on the bed and take her shoes off for her.

"Mind staying with me?" she asks. "I know you must be hungry, but I'd love it if you could lie down with me until I fall asleep. If I fall asleep."

"Anything for you." I climb onto the bed and settle in beside her, drawing her against me with an arm around her shoulders. "Close your eyes, lass, and try to rest."

"Not as sleepy as I thought I was, but this feels good, cuddling up to you. Can't get enough Jack snuggle time."

I comb my fingers through her hair, inhaling the scent of it. Holding her eases the tension I hadn't realized was still tightening my entire body. It drains away little by little, and the memory of what happened less than an hour ago recedes, replaced by a sort of contentment I've never experienced with anyone else. Only Autumn makes me feel relaxed, at peace, and free.

Maybe I need a daily dose of Autumn snuggle time.

No, not maybe. It's a dead certainty.

"We should sleep in the same bed from now on," I say. "If that's what you want. I want it for sure."

"So do I. Which room, though?"

"This one. Mine is a place to sleep, but yours is a home."

"I like this room." She lifts her head to look at me. "I've been meaning to ask you. Why is your guest room decorated with girlie stuff? Do your female cousins visit you a lot?"

"No one visits me. You're the first person ever to sleep in this room."

She eyes me warily. "Um, did you make this room for…me?"

"Yes."

"When? Last week?"

I link my hands, tugging her closer. "I created this room a few days after I moved into the house. Until this week, I would never have admitted the reason for that. But it's because I always hoped—wished might be a better word—that one day you'd come back to me. This room was always meant for you."

"Oh, Jack." Her lips tremble a little, and she blinks her eyes several times quickly. "That's the sweetest thing you've ever done."

"Don't cry, please. I might start crying too."

"You? No."

I raise my brows. "But I told you how I cried when you left me."

"That was a horrible moment. This is a beautiful one."

Aye, it is a beautiful moment. I wouldn't have thought a home invasion could lead to a moment like this, but I don't care if the fact it did makes me a nutter. I feel closer to Autumn than ever before, and suddenly, I need to ask her a question.

I roll us both over so she's under me and I'm lying half on top of her, braced on my elbows. "This week, I learned something very important. I love you, and I need you with me forever. I have my own family now with you, me, and our child. It's time to make it official."

Her eyes widen a touch, and her lips curl into a bonnie little smile.

The melodic chime of the mantel clock in the living room reaches us in here, striking the hour—six o'clock.

"Autumn, I need to ask you something." I push my arms up straight and gaze down at the woman I adore. "Will you marry me?"

"Yes, Jack, I will. And this time, it's for keeps."

"Aye, you'll be stuck with me for the rest of your life and forever after that. There's no escaping this time."

She grabs my shirt and pulls until I lie down on top of her. "Don't want to get away from you."

I kiss her slowly, imbuing it with all the passion she inspires in me and all the love I have in my heart. And with her, that's enough to last until the universe disintegrates. When we peel our lips apart, she gazes at me with more love than I ever imagined I'd see in any woman's eyes. But she's not any woman. She's my...soul mate.

"Fuck," I groan, sounding miserable because I bloody am. All my married cousins, who I had called barmy for believing in rot like soul mates, will love this if they ever find out I thought the words, much less spoke them aloud.

"What's wrong?" Autumn asks.

"My cousins have been right all along. It's galling."

"Right about what?"

I slide partway off her, just to be sure I don't crush the mother of my child. "You are my soul mate, *mo chridhe*. They told me things like that are real, and I rolled my eyes at them."

"Well, I've known you're my soul mate since the night we met. But I get why you, a rational and pragmatic psychologist, needed years to figure that out."

"Let's not tell my cousins about it. And especially not my brother."

"My lips are sealed." Her face goes blank for a moment, then her eyes widen and her mouth falls open. "Jack, you'll never believe it. Kirsty was right."

"About what?"

"She told me you'd say four words that would change everything, and you have. Will you marry me, that's what you said. It's four words, Jack. *Four words.*"

I huff. "Any four words could fulfill a vague prophecy like that one. What if I'd said 'take out the rubbish'? That's four words."

She gives me a light punch in the gut. "That's not the whole prediction. Kirsty also told me it would happen when the moon is high."

"And?"

"When we got out of the car, I saw the moon. It was high." She points toward the ceiling. "Up there. In the sky."

"That's where the moon generally is."

"But it was high. And then you said those four words." She sits up, her mouth open, her lips curving up at the corners. "And I heard the living-room clock strike six. Kirsty said when the moon is high and the clock strikes six, four words will change everything. She was right."

"Well, I—That's rubbish."

Isn't it? There's no such thing as ESP or "witchy" powers, as Logan's sisters like to call it. If Autumn wants to believe in that nonsense, it's her prerogative. I will never believe it. Never. Does that sound like a desperate attempt to deny the truth? I did tell Autumn she's my soul mate. So maybe...

No, it's bollocks.

Autumn kisses my cheek. "You can think about that for a while. Take as long as you need. Not sure I believe it one hundred percent, but I can't deny her prediction came true."

I can't think of a thing to say to that.

She stretches and exhales a satisfied sigh. "I'm suddenly starving."

The woman I plan to marry, again, jumps off the bed and trots down the hallway. All I can do is stare at the bedspread.

A second later, her head pops into view. "Come on, Jack."

Later, I'll think about Kirsty's prophecy. Much later. Right now, I have more important things to do, like feeding my fiancée.

I leap off the bed and follow Autumn.

Aye, everything is different now. And I love it.

Chapter Thirty-Seven

Autumn

Jack might think Kirsty's prediction is "bollocks" and "rubbish," but he's softened his stance on meddling. We both know his cousins and his brother are trying to "help" us, but Jack doesn't get annoyed about it anymore. At least not nostril-flaring, foot-stamping annoyed. In the weeks after the hostage incident, members of his extended family keep stopping by our house to see if we're all right and whether they can do anything for us. Jack and I always invite them to come inside and chat for a while.

It goes something like this, every time.

"So, when will you and Autumn get married? We can suggest some very romantic places to visit on your road trips. You two are so sweet together. Have you thought about having children? Yours would be adorable. We're thinking of having a shinty match and/or another ceilidh and/or Highland games and/or anything else we can think of that sounds like an excuse for all of us to pester you two about your relationship in a pseudo-casual setting."

Okay, that's not exactly what they say. But it's not far off.

I love every last MacTaggart I've met, but their need to "help" us has turned into an obsession. When I visit Kirsty's store, she shows me a wooden bin full of pretty, polished rocks. I think she's just being a good hostess, but her real motivation becomes obvious when she picks up a dark-red stone and places it in my palm.

"This is garnet," she says. "It symbolizes devotion, passion, and love. It also promotes an open heart and protects you from negative energy. I want you to have this stone, as a gift."

"Oh, I couldn't do that. You're running a business, and I can afford to pay for this."

"No, no, it's a gift from a spiritual sister. We might not be blood relations, but I feel we're kindred spirits in many ways." She closes my fingers around the chunk of garnet. "Please accept this. Maybe it will open Jack's heart to you even more and eliminate any negative energy lingering between you two."

New Age meddling? That's a first for me. But Kirsty is such a sweet person that I can't refuse her thoughtful gift.

"Thank you, Kirsty," I say. "And I feel like we're kindred spirits too. I don't believe in everything you do, but I feel like I've known you for a lot longer than a couple weeks."

She folds her hands around mine. "I'm glad. We're going to be the best of friends, I'm sure."

"I'd like that." Something she said back when we'd first met resurfaces in my mind, and I have to ask her about it. "You told me once that you know what it's like to be with a man who's afraid to open up to you and who doesn't understand your ways. I got the feeling there's a story behind that. If you ever want to share it with me, I'm a good listener."

"Yes, you are," Kirsty says with a smile, but it fades quickly. "There was a lad I knew when I was a student at the University of Edinburgh. His name was Luke Turner, and I fell for him completely. He loved me too, or so he said. At the time, I wasn't as open about being a Wiccan, and I was afraid to tell Luke about that part of me. When I finally did, he called me a lunatic and broke off our relationship. He even transferred to a university in America, to get away from me, I think."

"That's awful. Kirsty, I'm so sorry that happened to you."

She shrugs. "It wasn't meant to be, I suppose. I can't help thinking about Luke sometimes, though, and wondering if…" She shrugs again, and I swear I see a hint of tears glistening in her eyes. "Doesn't matter. That time is long gone. Luke isn't as open-minded and forgiving as Jack."

We talk more about the stuff in Kirsty's shop, then I leave her so I can find Jack and give him a big hug. He has never called me a lunatic, and I'm incredibly grateful he's such an understanding person. I can't help feeling bad for Kirsty, the way she lost a man she seems to have loved deeply, all because he couldn't handle her witchy side.

But the meddling starts up again, and I don't have time to think about Kirsty anymore. Most of the meddling involves members of Jack's family "accidentally" bumping into us on the street, then shanghaiing us into a lunch or a dinner or a "wee gathering" at a restaurant or somebody's house. Maybe we should tell them we're engaged, and we've filed our twenty-nine-day notices, so they don't need to meddle anymore, but Jack wants to wait until we've had a chance to tell his parents. I wonder why he doesn't suggest informing my parents, but I'm too chicken to do it myself. I find out why he hasn't mentioned that when I'm washing the dishes after lunch one day.

The doorbell rings.

Jack is in his office with two clients, a married couple, so I hustle out there to open the door.

My parents are standing on the porch. Looking at me. Seeming confused.

I open my mouth, but it takes a few seconds before I can speak. "Mom? Dad? What are you doing here?"

My father hits me with his hard-as-steel soldier stare. "A Scottish man called us and suggested we should come see you. He claimed to be your ex-husband, but we had no idea you'd ever been married. What is going on here, Autumn?"

Mom lifts her brows at me. "Yes, Autumn, what is going on?"

Oh shit. One of Jack's relatives must have called my parents.

"Uh, why don't you come inside?" I say, stepping out of the way and gesturing for them to go into the living room. "We can talk about all of this."

Mom and Dad stride into the house and sit down on the sofa.

I take the chair Jack usually sits in and fidget, because I cannot get comfortable anytime soon. There might not actually be a bunch of pins sticking out of the cushion to prick my bottom, but it feels that way.

How do I start? I haven't told my parents anything about my life for years. We have the occasional polite phone conversation, but I avoid talking about myself.

Dad sets his hands on his thighs and drums his fingers.

"Um, well…" Yeah, I'm off to a great start. "A lot has happened. I know we haven't talked much in…well, ever, I guess. I have stuff to explain."

My tummy is churning, and I feel itchy all over, but I know I need to come clean. So I take a deep breath and dive in. Fourteen minutes later, according to the mantel clock, I finish my story. Except for one last thing.

"Jack and I are having a baby."

Yeah, I kind of blurted that out with no preamble.

My parents stare at me blankly.

"That means you're going to be grandparents," I say. "Again, I mean. Michelle already gave you two grandkids, but now you'll have one who's half Scottish."

Could I have thought of a dumber thing to say?

Mom rouses from her catatonic state first. She blinks slowly, then shakes her head the tiniest bit. "This is quite a shock. You were married and divorced but told us nothing about it. You've jumped from job to job, lived in

Scotland for a while, and now you're getting married again to the same man who we have never met."

"That's the gist of it." I fiddle with my shirt hem. "Jack is a good man. You'll like him. Right now, he's in his office down the hall talking to clients, but he should be done any minute."

"Clients?" Dad says, finally snapping out of his catatonic state. "What does this Jack do for a living?"

"He's a psychologist. A great one."

"Oh."

I think my parents are both still in shock.

A door opens down the hall, and soft voices draw closer.

Turning around in my chair, I spot Jack and his clients coming toward us.

Jack puts a hand on the husband's shoulder and whispers something to the couple, then they hurry out the front door. Jack stands behind my chair, smiling politely at my mom and dad.

"You must be Autumn's parents," Jack says. He walks over to them and offers his hand to my dad. "I'm Jack MacTaggart. It's a pleasure to meet you."

"Dennis Flowerday," Dad says, shaking Jack's hand. "And this is my wife, Brenda."

Mom shakes Jack's hand too.

He perches on the edge of the coffee table, hands hanging down between his thighs. "I'm glad you both accepted my offer to visit us here in Scotland. It's about time we got acquainted."

Dad aims his steely glare at Jack. "What are you doing with my daughter?"

"Marrying her," Jack says, seeming completely unfazed by my father's attempt to intimidate him. "I love Autumn, and I will do anything to make sure she's happy. I understand this is a shock to you, but nothing you can do or say will make me leave your daughter. We've both made mistakes in the past. That's over, and we are going to have a family of our own now. Autumn and I would love for you to be a part of our life, but I won't stand for either of you making her feel unworthy. I will toss you out the door on your erses if you hurt her."

I want to throw my arms around Jack and kiss him. He is such a wonderful man.

My dad glares at Jack for a few more seconds, then he smiles. "All right. I've decided I like you, MacTaggart. I've never seen my daughter so happy, and I have to thank you for that. And for the record, we have never thought Autumn was unworthy. I know we let our disappointment show too much and too often when she didn't want to join the army or become a doctor, but we've always known she's a smart, capable woman. Just wish she'd realized it sooner."

"Yes," Mom chimes in. "But Autumn underestimates herself, and I'm sure that's why she drifts from job to job. Autumn, if we made you feel unworthy, we're both so sorry. It wasn't our intention. We were never disappointed in you, only ourselves, for not knowing how to help you reach your full potential and be happy. You're so different from us, and from your sister. It was hard to know how to be there for you."

Dad nods in agreement. "Honestly, we thought you were disappointed with us for being such rigid parents."

For a moment, I can't speak. I gape at my parents, suddenly feeling like I've misunderstood so many things. We all have. My parents thought I was disappointed with them while I assumed they thought I was unworthy of their love. Maybe they showed they cared in a different way. I couldn't see it until now because I am not at all like my parents or my sister. I'm a free spirit, and they're rule followers. They have to be in their jobs.

Jack invites my parents to stay until the wedding, which will be in two weeks. We spend that time getting to know each other. Better late than never, right? Michelle and her family will join us when it gets closer to the big day.

A few days later, we go to the home of Jack's parents so my mom and dad can meet them, and so we can break the baby news to everyone. Greer and Alistair don't know about the wedding yet either. Jack and I have been too wrapped up in nurturing our renewed relationship to think about anything else.

When we get to Greer and Alistair's house, Callum is there, which is perfect. We want him to hear the news too. The rest of the family will have to wait a little longer, until I've reached week twelve of my pregnancy. That's the goal we set, and it's when all the pregnancy books say it's a good time to make the announcement. I introduce my parents, and Greer drags my mom into a bear hug while babbling in Gaelic.

Jack's mom has made us a delicious meal. Once everyone has finished eating, Jack and I exchange glances, and we don't need to say a word to each other. He knows what I want and vice versa. We agreed ahead of time that he should be the one to tell his family.

He clears his throat and dives in. "We have some news."

Greer, Alistair, and Callum all look at Jack.

"Autumn and I are having a bairn," he says. "She's ten weeks pregnant. We wanted you to hear about it first."

Greer starts crying and laughing at the same time. She holds a hand over her mouth, then moves it down to her chest. "Oh, *mo luran*, this is wonderful news."

"We're also getting married," Jack says. "We filed our notices already, and we'd like to get married in two weeks. Can you and Brenda plan a wedding that quickly?"

Greer springs out of her chair and races around the table to hug us both, one arm around Jack and the other around me. She kisses our cheeks too. "Donnae worry. The MacTaggarts know how to throw together a big do in a short time. I should call Sorcha and Aileen. Oh, and Glenna and Mary too."

I think she's talking about the mothers of the other MacTaggarts of Jack's generation. I've met them, but sometimes I have trouble keeping all these Scots straight.

Greer rushes over to hug my mom, who's still sitting in her chair. "You're a MacTaggart now, ye know. That means every mother in the family will lend a hand with the wedding. But you and I will be in charge. Aye?"

Mom looks a touch confused, but she smiles and nods. "Yes. Looking forward to it."

Jack sighs heavily. "Ma, remember ye cannae tell anyone about the pregnancy yet. We're waiting until the twelfth week."

His mother makes a face that expresses motherly exasperation so well and with such affection that I can't help smiling. She slaps Jack's arm. "How many books did you read that told you that? There's no magic milestone for when to announce baby news. Ten weeks is good enough." She looks at me. "But if you'd be more comfortable waiting…"

"Greer is right," my mom says. "You don't need to wait. It's close enough."

"I guess that's all right," I say. "We did read books and stick to the advice in them like it's the law of the land. Let's tell everyone right away, huh, Jack?"

He glances at his mother, then at me, smiling just enough to let me know he's not annoyed the women in his life are ganging up on him. "All right. Let's share it far and wide."

Callum grins. "I'll be an uncle soon. Glad you're giving Ma some bairns because I'm never doing that."

"Not yet," Greer says.

Jack leans forward, aiming his narrowed gaze straight at Callum. "I'll have a right good laugh when you walk down the aisle, mate."

Callum scoffs.

And Greer hurries to find a phone and spread the news, all of it, not just the wedding part.

Before we know it, I'm twelve weeks pregnant and the ceremony is in two days.

Chapter Thirty-Eight

Jack

What does a bloke do when every woman in his life, even the ones who aren't his fiancée, have banded together to turn a wedding into an extravaganza? I expect that sort of thing from Alex, but this is my wedding, not his. Autumn has joined the cult too. She's spent two weeks conspiring with my mother, her mother, and the matriarchs of every other branch of the MacTaggart clan to plan our wedding without any input from me.

I might be feeling a wee bit excluded. Which is childish. I can't help it, though. I've barely seen Autumn since the day we told my parents about the wedding and the bairn, and I've only shagged her twice since then.

Twice in two weeks? No wonder I'm losing my mind.

Yesterday, Autumn declared we will not sleep in the same room on the night before the ceremony, much less have sex. She also insists that I sleep at home while she stays the night at Dùndubhan.

"It'll be romantic," she claimed.

Bod an Donais. How am I meant to survive until the wedding night? I know the wait will be over tomorrow, but my cock thinks it's going to shrivel up if I don't make love to her soon.

Autumn rings me at midnight on the eve of the big day.

"Want to have phone sex?" she asks, her voice a sultry purr.

"Is that allowed? You said no sex before the wedding."

"This is virtual sex, honey. We say dirty things to each other while masturbating."

"Yes, I know what phone sex is." I can't believe the words that tumble out of me next. "But I'd rather wait until we can have the real thing."

"You're such a romantic in disguise, Jack."

"I wouldn't mind having a blether with you, though. Havenae seen or spoken to you since this morning. I miss you."

"Aw, you are so sweet. I miss you too."

We talk for a while, though mostly I listen to her sharing stories about the crazy things that happen when an entire clan of Scotswomen rope two American women into planning a wedding with them.

Alex had wanted me to have a stag party, but I vetoed the idea. If I can't be with Autumn tonight, I'd rather be alone. Since Alex didn't have a stag party, I have no idea why he thought I should. Maybe he planned to trick me into doing something embarrassing, like the spectacle he made of his nuptials.

The next day, Autumn and I get married.

Everything is set up on the green at Dùndubhan, the venue Autumn and I had chosen. We shared a wonderful night here during that first week after our reunion, so it seemed like the right place for our wedding.

I watch her walking up the aisle toward me with her father, and my throat goes thick. She's so beautiful, so sweet and kind and clever and brave. That woman is mine—and I'm hers. We gaze into each other's eyes during the entire ceremony, but I barely register the words the minister speaks or the vows we recite to each other. Once we've exchanged rings, I rouse from my trance-like state just as the minister tells me I can kiss my bride.

Throwing an arm around her, I haul Autumn into me and crush my mouth to hers. She relaxes against me, moaning softly.

Cheers break out. Several people whistle.

I sweep my bride up into my arms and carry her back down the aisle. I don't put her down until we've reached the outdoor party area set up not far from where the wedding took place. It's a garden party, with potted plants and flowers since the green at Dùndubhan has only grass. The actual garden isn't big enough to accommodate all the guests.

My in-laws are having a blether with my parents, and my sister-in-law is talking to the American Wives Club. Everyone's getting on well these days.

After setting my wife down on a chair at one of the tables, I take a seat on the one beside her.

She grins. "We're hitched. That really happened, right? I didn't dream it."

"It's real." I drag my chair closer to hers and clasp one of her hands. "And this time, it'll stick."

"Wow, that's a romantic way to phrase it."

"You know what I mean." I kiss her hand. "There's no getting away from me this time. I'll hunt you to the ends of the earth if I have to."

"Oddly, that is kind of romantic." She leans over to kiss my cheek. "I love you, Johnathon Alistair MacTaggart."

"I love you too, Autumn Cynthia Flowerday MacTaggart."

"Just Autumn MacTaggart will do."

"You can keep your name if you like. I won't be offended."

She leans back against her chair and splays a hand over her belly. "I'm taking your name because I want to, Jack. And I want our baby to have it too. We're a family—you, me, and the kiddo."

Six more months to go. Then we'll be parents. Sometimes, it does feel like a dream—but only in the best way.

"I want to get a job eventually," she says, "but not until after the baby's born. Is that okay?"

"You can do whatever you want, *mo chridhe*. Take your time finding a job that makes you happy. Wait six months or six years, however long you need."

She looks down at her belly, which is slightly rounder than it used to be. "I want to spend as much time as possible with you and the baby. Might not get around to finding a career until way after the kid's born."

"My income is more than enough to support the three of us for as long as you need, if that's what you're worried about." I bend toward her to touch my lips to hers. "There's no rush."

Kirsty comes over to sit at our table and chat to us. She and Autumn have become good mates, but my bride is also friends with lots of other people, including some who aren't related to me. I'm glad she's settling into our new life so well. I feel like I've finally settled into my life after decades of fumbling to get it right. Autumn is responsible for that, and I'm more grateful than anyone can know that she came back to me.

"Come by the shop anytime," Kirsty tells Autumn. "I'll be happy to teach you about Wicca."

What had Autumn asked Kirsty? Something about wanting to learn more about that mystical bollocks Kirsty and her sisters like to dabble in. I hope my wife isn't thinking about becoming a witch. She doesn't need spells to make me want to shag her.

"Thanks," Autumn says. "That's so sweet of you, Kirsty."

My cousin smiles, but then her attention swerves to something behind me, and her mouth falls open. Her eyes go wide too. She works her jaw like she's struggling to remember how to speak.

"Hey there, Kirsty," a male voice says from behind me.

Kirsty leaps up so quickly her chair topples over backward. "Luke? What are you doing here?"

I turn in my chair to see who's behind me.

A man wearing a posh suit but no tie stands there, his gaze locked on my wee cousin. He hooks a thumb in his waistband, cocking one hip. "Nice to see you too, Kirsty. What, no hello kiss?"

He's American. I've never seen this bloke before, but Kirsty obviously knows him.

My cousin shakes her head, her mouth still gaping. "You cannae be here. Crashing a wedding is…rude."

"Crashing?" the man says with a chuckle. "One of your pals invited me. He called yesterday. His British accent confused me for a minute, but then he said he's married to one of your cousins, and it suddenly made sense. Kind of."

"But I—You—" She stumbles backward a few steps. "You hate me. Why would ye want to be at my cousin's wedding?"

"Alex Thorne said you're in trouble and you need me. I should come right away, he said." The man walks over to Kirsty, halting an arm's length from her. "I might think you're insane, but I never turn my back on a woman in need. So, what's the problem?"

"Whuh—" Kirsty blinks several times, so fast her lashes almost become a blur. "You flew here all the way from America because a stranger told you to?"

"Nah." The bloke shrugs. "I've been living in the UK for three years. Joined a private research institute down in England."

Logan stalks over to our table and stops beside his sister. He levels his deadly calm glare at the stranger. "Who the bloody hell are you and what have you done to upset my sister?"

"I'm so sorry," the man says. "I've been disrespectful, haven't I?"

"Aye, and you're one second away from being dead on the grass."

The stranger chuckles again. "I guess that's a Scottish saying? Well, anyway, I'm Luke Turner. Kirsty's ex-boyfriend."

Alex Thorne ambles over to us. "What's going on over here? Looks like quite the rammy."

Kirsty slowly rotates her gaze toward Alex, her face impassive. "You did this, didn't you?"

"What if I did? You lot meddled in my life, so I'm returning the favor. You'll thank me later."

Luke Turner glances at the crowd of Scots gathering around us, then he looks at Kirsty. "Could we go somewhere more private to talk?"

"Aye."

She seizes his arm and drags him through the doorway into the garden, out of sight.

I'd known the wedding might turn into a wild affair, but I could never have predicted this. Kirsty must not have foreseen it either.

While Logan argues with Alex about whether he's a bleeding ersehole, I take the opportunity to spirit my wife away from the crowd. We stop near the garden door, but I don't intend for us to go in there. I have other plans for my bride.

I finger the neckline of her wedding gown. "Do you have something on under this dress?"

"A slip, yeah. A bra and panties too."

"Good. Take the dress off."

"What? You mean right here?"

"Yes." I shed my jacket and shirt, now wearing only my kilt, socks, and boots. "Get rid of the dress, *mo chridhe.*"

She turns away, peeking at me over her shoulder. "Unzip me, please."

I do that, and she shimmies out of the dress, leaving it in a pool on the grass.

"What now?" she asks.

"Run."

"Excuse me?"

"I said run, Autumn. I'm going to chase you."

She grins and races away, toward the corner of the castle wall.

And I chase her.

My wife keeps glancing back at me, grinning and laughing. I shout wordlessly like a true Scots barbarian.

"She's legging it already?" Alex calls out. "Better lock her in the dungeon when you catch her, mate."

"There's no dungeon at Dùndubhan," Rory says. "How many times do I need to tell you people that?"

Alex and Rory keep shouting things, and more voices join in, but Autumn and I have rounded the corner of the wall. I catch her around the waist, hauling her over to the wall, and push her up against it. My body pins her there, so she won't be legging it anytime soon. She doesn't want to, I know that.

We're both breathing hard.

"You caught me," she says. "What now?"

"Ahm going to fuck ye, wife. Right here, right now, and everyone will probably hear it when ye come for me."

She wraps both arms around my neck and one leg around my thigh. "Go for it, wild man."

Aye, she is the perfect woman for me. And this is our happy ending, in every way imaginable.

**Want more of Kirsty and Luke? Experience
their story in *Spellbound in a Kilt*.**

Love the

Hot Scots

series?

Visit
AnnaDurand.com

to subscribe to her newsletter
for updates on forthcoming books in the series
&
to receive free gifts for signing up!

Anna Durand is a bestselling, multi-award-winning author of contemporary and paranormal romance. Her books have earned bestseller status on every major retailer and wonderful reviews from readers around the world. But that's the boring spiel. Here are the really cool things you want to know about Anna!

Born on Lackland Air Force Base in Texas, Anna grew up moving here, there, and everywhere thanks to her dad's job as an instructor pilot. She's lived in Texas (twice), Mississippi, California (twice), Michigan (twice), and Alaska—and now Ohio.

As for her writing, Anna has always made up stories in her head, but she didn't write them down until her teen years. Those first awful books went into the trash can a few years later, though she learned a lot from those stories. Eventually, she would pen her first romance novel, the paranormal romance *Willpower*, and she's never looked back since.

Want even more details about Anna? Get access to her extended bio when you subscribe to her newsletter and download the free bonus ebook, *Hot Scots Confidential*. You'll also get hot deleted scenes, character interviews, fun facts, and more! Plus you'll receive the short story *Tempted by a Kiss* and bonus chapters for in ebook and audiobook formats.

Visit AnnaDurand.com to sign up.